JULIAN GRA

CLAUDE HOUGHTON OLDFI
and was educated at Dulw
ant and worked in the Adr
for active service because
West End actress, Dulcie Be......, ...
Chiltern Hills. To a writers' directory, Houghton gave his hobbies
as reading in bed, riding, visiting Devon and abroad, and talking to
people different from himself. He added: "I like dawn, and the dead
of night, in great cities." He disliked fuss, noise, crowds, rows, and
being misquoted, or being told how much he owed "to some writer
I've never read."

Houghton's earliest writing was poetry and drama before turning to prose fiction with his first novel, *Neighbours*, in 1926. In the
1930s, Houghton published several well-received novels that met
with solid sales and respectable reviews, including *I Am Jonathan
Scrivener* (1930), easily his most popular and best-known work, *Chaos
Is Come Again* (1932), *Julian Grant Loses His Way* (1933), *This Was Ivor
Trent* (1935), *Strangers* (1938), and *Hudson Rejoins the Herd* (1939).
Although he published nearly a dozen more novels throughout the
1940s and 1950s, most critics feel his later works are less significant
than his novels of the '30s.

Houghton was a prolific correspondent, generous in devoting his
time to answering letters and signing copies for readers who enjoyed
his books. One of these was novelist Henry Miller, who never met
Houghton but began an impassioned epistolary exchange with
him after being profoundly moved by his works. Houghton's other
admirers included his contemporaries P. G. Wodehouse, Clemence
Dane, and Hugh Walpole. Houghton died in 1961.

By Claude Houghton

The Kingdoms of the Spirit (1924)
Neighbours (1926)★
The Riddle of Helena (1927)
Crisis (1929)
I Am Jonathan Scrivener (1930)★
A Hair Divides (1930)★
Chaos Is Come Again (1932)★
Julian Grant Loses His Way (1933)★
Three Fantastic Tales (1934)
This Was Ivor Trent (1935)★
The Beast (1936)
Christina (1936)
Strangers (1938)
Hudson Rejoins the Herd (1939)
All Change, Humanity! (1942)
The Man Who Could Still Laugh (1943)
Six Lives and a Book (1943)
Passport to Paradise (1944)
Transformation Scene (1946)
The Quarrel (1948)
Birthmark (1950)
The Enigma of Conrad Stone (1952)
At the End of a Road (1953)
The Clock Ticks (1954)
More Lives Than One (1957)

★ Available or forthcoming from Valancourt Books

JULIAN GRANT LOSES HIS WAY

CLAUDE HOUGHTON

VALANCOURT BOOKS

Julian Grant Loses His Way by Claude Houghton
First published London: Heinemann, 1933
First Valancourt Books edition 2015

Copyright © 1933 by Claude Houghton Oldfield

Published by Valancourt Books, Richmond, Virginia
http://www.valancourtbooks.com

ISBN 978-1-941147-46-7 (trade paperback)

All Valancourt Books publications are printed on acid free paper
that meets all ANSI standards for archival quality paper.

Set in Dante MT 10/12

CONTENTS

PART I

ADVENTURE IN PICCADILLY

A

He stopped and turned sharply, as if someone had called him, then looked round in order to discover his whereabouts.

Tremulous sunshine shed a glamour over Knightsbridge. He decided that he must have left home soon after dawn, for the shops were asleep and the streets deserted, yet he had no recollection of leaving the house and no sense of destination. He stood motionless, half-surrendering to the illusion that the town would awake, not to the frenzy of mechanized traffic, but to the rhythmical beat of horses' hoofs. Some magic in the virginal atmosphere made the past more actual than the present. Perhaps the houses and the hidden squares were dreaming and he was sharing that dream.

He walked on slowly. . . .

Although he realized that it was ridiculous, he felt that he had just parted from two strangers. The more his logical faculty rebelled against this impression the more it claimed him. Gradually he became convinced. He did not know whether they were men or women; where he had encountered them; or what they had said to him. But of two things he was certain: a unique quality had distinguished them and the decision to leave them had been his.

As he walked on he seemed to remember a sudden rapture which had possessed him on finding himself with these strangers. He had had no presentiment of their approach, no clue to their identity, yet, directly he had become aware of their presence, those problems which had perplexed him for years dwindled to insignificance. Thought had become clairvoyant. While he had remained with them he had been the centre of an ever-widening serenity.

Yet, inexplicably, he had become conscious of a desire to leave them. Their presence had ceased to create a sense of fulfilment and had become a challenge. Something deep in him had rebelled against them, denied them, clamorously protesting that to remain in their company was to jeopardize everything which gave life value. He had attempted to devise an excuse for leaving them when, suddenly, he had found himself alone, walking through Knightsbridge in the early morning sunshine. . . .

He dismissed the whole subject with an irritable movement of his shoulders. Recently he had been far too speculative and it was evident that this indulgence had resulted in a temporary inability to distinguish between facts and fictions. It was grotesque to imagine that he had just parted from two strangers! He was alone, walking through Knightsbridge on his way to an appointment. Everything was entirely normal. It was true that, at the minute, he could not recall his actual destination, but this lapse had no particular significance. It was unusual to be out so early, consequently the unfamiliar aspect of the commonplace had distracted him. Nevertheless, this failure of memory was intriguing, for it was obvious that only exceptional circumstances could have occasioned his leaving the house soon after dawn.

A few minutes later he paused outside a tobacconist's. The shop was shut but, near the entrance, was a large mirror with white lettering at top and bottom which announced that there was a barber's saloon on the first floor. He crossed to this mirror, stood in front of it, and studied his reflection.

He saw a tall clean-shaven man with a broad powerful head; eyes in which the flame of a once intense curiosity still flickered; a full firm mouth; and a resolute chin. Individuality characterized an attractive figure and gave distinction to the clothes which seemed a projection of their owner's personality. The image reflected in the mirror was a dominating arresting one. He took a step nearer it, removed his black, soft felt hat – thereby revealing thick auburn hair – and studied the almost imperceptible lines which concealed, as in a hieroglyph, the history of his interior life.

"Forty-five," he whispered to himself.

This recognition of his age quickened no regrets – it was a fact and interesting as such – but it caused him to contrast the reflection confronting him with his memory of the one his mirror had presented when he was twenty. He decided that the only link between the two images was his name.

"Julian Valentine Grant."

He pronounced each word deliberately in a clear resonant voice, then turned abruptly and continued his walk in the direction of Piccadilly.

Julian *Valentine* Grant. It was odd that he had used his second name a moment ago, for it did not belong to him now – it belonged to his youth, from which he seemed to be separated by several lives. Even to remember it was a creative act. He had almost forgotten that Valentine formed part of his name. He was Julian Grant. There was something hard and purposeful in the sound of the words, something entirely practical – a weapon-like quality. It was the name of a man in this world, wholly concerned with it, adequate to its demands. Julian Grant! For twenty-five years he had been known only by that name. It represented him: it epitomized his personality; it symbolized an achievement of which only he was aware. He had demanded and received recognition because he was Julian Grant, not by reason of a renown which made him influential. He had no recognized title to eminence. He had created a synthesis to which no label could be attached other than that of his name.

But the interposition of the word Valentine destroyed this correspondence. It introduced a strange disturbing element. Valentine! It was the name of a Christian martyr in the reign of the Emperor Claudius. What link had Julian Grant with a fanatic of the third century? It was this world which claimed him, not the chaotic realm of spiritual exaltation.

Somewhat amused by his irritation he walked on rapidly till he reached Hyde Park Corner, then, after a moment's irresolution, he entered the Park and wandered about aimlessly till eventually he sat down near the Daisy Walk.

Overhead a bird was singing; two or three rabbits were scampering over the rich green turf beyond the little lake to his right. No one was visible. Every now and again he heard the hoot of a motor in the distance. A vague dreaminess possessed him; then, with a swift sense of discovery, he knew that autumn had come. There were no material signs of its advent, but the atmosphere was dominated by that pause which heralds the slow decline of the year. Soon wraiths of mist would blur the contours of the trees; leaves would become traitors; the russet days would steal softly by.

Reverie captured him, that reverie in which shadows are more real than thoughts. It seemed that he was looking down on his life from a great height and so was unable to detect its familiar settings. He was not conscious of time till the movement of people near him and the sullen drone of the traffic forced him to recognize that the world was awake and about its affairs.

He rose hastily, suddenly apprehensive that he was neglecting urgent matters, and walked quickly till he reached Piccadilly. As he made his way towards the Ritz the curious theory occurred to him that he had spent over twenty-four hours in the Park, and consequently had emerged into the sunlight of another day. He was ridiculing this nonsense when his attention was diverted by a remarkable figure approaching him.

It was a beggar, walking in the gutter, clad in the most fantastic costume imaginable. On his head was a battered cardboard crown, crudely daubed with gold paint; clutched in his right hand was a clumsy imitation of a sceptre; and flowing from his narrow shoulders hung a tawdry purple robe which aped regality in a highly ludicrous fashion. The man was unshaven, dirty, with great gaping rents in his boots through which his naked feet were visible.

But what amazed Grant was that this unfortunate was striving to assume an air of immense dignity. He held his head high, distributed bows of gracious condescension first to one side, then to the other, and generally tried to behave like a monarch on a ceremonial occasion of the first magnitude. Yet, although his attitudes no less than his appearance rendered him remarkably conspicuous, the passers-by ignored him. Grant pondered this mystery, eventually deciding that the man's costume and antics were an advertising device; nevertheless it seemed peculiar that everyone was so familiar with it that it no longer excited attention.

But when this buffoon was only a few yards distant Grant became indignant. Why should this man's necessity be exploited in such a humiliating manner? Only poverty could have forced him to accept this degradation. Grant glanced at the passers-by and his anger increased.

"It's infamous!" he shouted. "Infamous!"

Amazed by this outburst, of which normally he would have been quite incapable, he hurried past the Ritz, then turned down St. James's Street, seeing and hearing nothing.

A sense of futility oppressed him. Why had he made such a fool of himself? That clown in the gutter was no more absurd than the people on the pavement – they were all travesties, mountebanks, or counterfeits. What was ridiculous was his own indignation – nothing else.

He turned into Pall Mall and continued to walk quickly till he reached Waterloo Place. Then he hesitated. Should he look into his club, or go to a café in Piccadilly Circus? Better go to a café and have a cocktail.

B

Now as Julian Grant turned from Pall Mall into Waterloo Place it seemed to him that two events happened simultaneously – the sound of the traffic ceased and the sunlight faded. Silence and darkness encompassed him. London vanished like a scene on which a curtain had fallen.

He stood motionless, experiencing a strange interior excitement. This dramatic disappearance of the familiar kindled his sense of wonder. Would the outline of a new creation be revealed when the rays of the sun penetrated the darkness? Or would the street lights suddenly flash out and blatantly re-establish the normal?

But as the minutes passed Grant became uneasy. It was extraordinary that no one moved or spoke. The streets had been thronged, consequently there must be a number of men and women quite near him, yet the silence was so absolute that he might have been alone in the middle of a vast plain. Also, the profundity of the darkness disturbed him. It was impossible to see even the shape of his own body. He was beginning to be definitely alarmed when a sound reached him – a sibilant sound which advanced and receded with rhythmic regularity – but the attempt to imagine its origin was interrupted by the further dis-

covery that there was a glow in the sky as if great furnace doors
were being slowly opened.

He stood like a waxwork, incapable of sensation, but as the
light grew more intense a scene slowly emerged from the shadows. He saw a miniature bay, dappled with the hues of sunset,
held in a crescent of cliffs. White crested waves rode proudly
towards the beach, while a solitary seagull overhead kept utter-
ing its plaintive cry. Serenity hovered like a presence over the
scene.

He recognized it instantly. It was a bay in Cornwall. He had
visited it twenty-five years ago, and it was inalienably associated
with a woman long since dead – and long forgotten before she
had died. What spell had conjured it from the darkness? It represented an episode, not an epoch, and therefore it was only inci-
dental to the theme of his destiny. Yet now that he saw it again
it was difficult to remember his life during the intervening years.
By imperceptible degrees this scene from the past captured him,
circumscribed him within its own emotional limits, thereby
reducing all experiences outside its frontiers to the impalpable
or the unreal.

Dorothy!

The name emerged in the centre of his thoughts and her
image rose before him like a vision. Her beauty was remarkable
by reason of that which it awakened, rather than by its fidelity to
accepted standards. It was the beauty of a child – and its appeal
therefore was to wisdom, not knowledge.

Dorothy! He had met her here twenty-five years ago. On
their last evening together they had stood by the sea, watching
the sunset. The next day he had to go to London, but their plans
had been made and, directly it was possible, he would return.
She would wait for him here. And he had never returned, never
seen her again, and his indifference had risen like a mountain
range between them. Then, when she had ceased to be even a
memory, he had heard she was dead.

But at this point Grant's reminiscences ended abruptly. Two
figures had appeared on the beach – a man and a woman. They
were standing motionless, twenty yards in front of him, and
it was evident that to have reached their present position they
must have passed within a few feet of him. It was remarkable

that he had not heard them. But the satisfaction he derived from their presence soon dispelled all speculation as to the manner of it. He felt that he had been isolated from humanity for hours and that now, at last, he would be able to discuss the extraordinary events of the last few minutes. Never had the prospect of conversation been so exciting. He hurried towards them, eager to hear their adventures and to compare them with his.

A cry broke from him and he began to gesticulate wildly. The woman was Dorothy and the man was himself. They stood, looking out to sea, just as they had done on their last evening together – twenty-five years ago.

Fear invaded his being like a subtly stealing poison. Fantastic thoughts swept through the dark emptiness of his mind like bats flitting in and out of a ruin. Which was the real, which the illusion – the Julian Grant of forty-five, or the Julian Grant of twenty? Which was the actual, which the imaginary – this sunset-hooded bay, or the darkness from which it had appeared? His reason spun like a leaf in a whirlwind of conjectures, fears, memories, till, finally, he realised nothing but the necessity for flight.

He turned and began to run. And, as he ran, a vibrating mechanical roar grew louder and louder. Then he heard someone shouting quite near him, the sunshine flashed out like a limelight, and he found himself on the threshold of Piccadilly Circus.

C

The air quivered with the rattle of pneumatic drills, operated by a squad of workmen in the middle of the Circus; a youth shouted the latest racing information; policemen disciplined the desires of the insatiable traffic. Crowds of nondescript people thronged the pavements, stared at the shop windows, swarmed round the 'buses, hurried, loitered, or risked all in an attempt to cross the Circus. Mellow sunlight flooded the scene.

He felt like a sleepwalker suddenly awakened. Consequently, although he recognized Piccadilly Circus, the incongruity between his state and his environment was such that, emotionally, he remained in a dream, while, mentally, he was aware of the actual.

Gradually, however, the familiarity of his surroundings restored him to normality and he began to assess the events of the last few minutes in less fantastic terms. What had happened? An episode had materialized – that was all. It had risen from the night of the past with such seeming reality that it had induced the belief that it was actual. If this had happened in a dream it would not have seemed in the least extraordinary. To be afraid, or excited, was ridiculous. He had had a psychic experience of a definite and well-recognized type. Years ago, when such things had interested him, he had read of many similar cases.

But even if this were not the true explanation it was useless to try to discover it in the uproar of Piccadilly Circus. He began to walk slowly towards the subway when, suddenly, he noticed a man slouching across the street in his direction. He was looking down, his hat was pulled over his eyes, but nevertheless Grant recognised him. The dejection of his attitude, his shabbiness, and his entire disregard of the dangers of the traffic, were too characteristic to leave any doubt. It was Clarence Harlowe. Directly Grant saw him, he turned and began to walk rapidly in the opposite direction, knowing that overwhelming reasons existed why a meeting must be avoided, although unable to remember any of them. Yet, paradoxically, he was now aware that his having left home soon after dawn had been occasioned by the necessity for keeping some appointment which was directly and mysteriously connected with Harlowe.

He continued to walk quickly down Jermyn Street, then turned to the right and soon afterwards reached Piccadilly. The possibility of encountering Harlowe being no longer a menace, all routes were open to him, but this recovery of freedom only produced indecision, till he remembered that his original intention had been to go to a café and have a cocktail. He began to stroll towards the Circus, half amused and half disturbed by the reflection that not more than ten minutes could have elapsed since he had stood at the corner of Pall Mall and Waterloo Place and decided that a café was preferable to his club.

Before he had covered a hundred yards, however, all lesser problems were banished by the discovery that his sight was abnormal. Twice, in rapid succession, his surroundings dwindled to obscurity and it was only as a result of intense concentration that they regained their usual perspective. Conversely, for a few seconds, he saw everything with extraordinary clarity – to such a degree that even the buildings became unsubstantial – while he experienced a conviction of power so absolute that the world seemed only a thought in his brain, and one which he could hold or dismiss at will.

He hurried across the Circus – eager to reach comparative seclusion – but just as he was about to enter the Metropolitan Café, the swing doors opened and a man appeared carrying a portfolio. He looked at Grant, then laughed.

"It's just the same in there as it is everywhere else. You can't stay long anywhere."

"Possibly," Grant replied. "All the same, I'm going in."

"I know how you feel," the stranger went on, after glancing at him again, "but it doesn't work."

"What doesn't work?" Grant demanded irritably.

"The attempt to deceive yourself, of course! Why are you going into this café? Because you want to escape from the un-reality of the crowded pavements. And in half an hour you'll long to get back to the life of the streets. I do just the same, although I know it's useless."

He put down the portfolio, undid his overcoat, and began to look for something in his pockets. Grant was about to speak when he noticed the eccentricity of the man's clothes. His coat looked as if it had been borrowed from a short stout man, his waistcoat from a tall thin one, and his trousers from a giant. It was difficult, however, to decide whether his suit was actually an anthology, or whether its scarecrow effect was the result of its owner's extreme emaciation. But although he was desperately thin, the vitality of the eyes was remarkable, and Grant sustained a shock when his companion turned towards him and he encountered their direct glance for the first time.

"Ah! Here it is!"

He held up a diminutive key for Grant's inspection.

"Is that the key of your portfolio?"

"Yes. I thought I had lost it. I want to show you something."

"Hadn't we better go in and have a drink?" Grant suggested.

"No – thank – you!" the stranger replied with peculiar emphasis. "I find it's essential to know when to move on. I'm like

Cinderella – I have to enjoy myself with one eye on the clock. Otherwise, midnight strikes – and I'm done for."

He laughed mirthlessly, picked up the portfolio and unlocked it.

"I'm only showing you this," he went on, "because you were once interested in art."

"How do you know that I've ceased to be interested?"

"Everything is in a man's face," his companion replied, in the tone of one stating the obvious. Then he extracted a large drawing and handed it to Grant.

"Tell me what you think of that."

It depicted a scene in a café – so extravagant in design and execution that imagination was necessary to detect any resemblance to the Metropolitan. It satirised the latter by contrasting it with the artist's conception of the desirable. The treatment was dominated by a love and knowledge of perversity which extended to every detail. But the artist had not only created a café of decadent splendour in mockery of the Metropolitan, he had transformed its patrons, for the men and women revealed at the numerous tables bore little resemblance to everyday humanity. They were studies in mental and emotional corruption, delineated so subtly that the degree of recognition would vary with each observer.

"I see why you believe that everything is written in the face," Grant said at last, still studying the drawing.

"Perhaps you also understand what I meant by the remark that it's essential to know when to move on. Still, I'll give you an example. I went into the Metropolitan about a couple of hours ago. Everything was normal. That suited me admirably. I don't know why, but for the last day or two I've had a passionate desire for the normal. Anyway, I sat down and looked round. Then, gradually, I began to see the café – not as it is – but as I've shown it in the drawing. So I knew it was time to move on in pursuit of the commonplace."

He laughed abruptly, but Grant did not respond. He had made a discovery in the drawing, and one which interested him.

"I was so absorbed by your men and women," he began, "that I've only just noticed the infernal brood hovering about their heads."

"What on earth are you talking about?"

"Those phantoms, imps, devils – or whatever you choose to call them – flitting above the tables, like materializations of the thoughts and desires of the men and women below them. I suppose your idea was to indicate the psychic states of those degenerates?"

The artist seized the drawing and gazed at it apprehensively.

"There's nothing of the kind!" he shouted.

"But of course there is——"

"I tell you there isn't!"

Grant shrugged his shoulders and pointed to the top of the drawing.

"I suppose you'll tell me that there isn't a spectre, just below the ceiling, controlling the phantoms, and – through them – the men and women at the tables."

"*That?* That's the chandelier!"

Grant gave a short laugh.

"Sorry! I thought it was a symbol representing the spirit of the café."

The artist took the drawing, thrust it into his portfolio, which he locked, then said slowly:

"I'm glad it amuses you to discover things which don't exist – and I hope it will continue to amuse you."

He turned abruptly and walked away, disappearing almost immediately in the crowd.

Grant hesitated for a moment, then went through the swing doors into the café. He had known the Metropolitan for years and had therefore witnessed its gradual decline in popularity. It had been rebuilt recently – a restaurant had been added – but this grandiose transformation had not attracted new customers and apparently had offended the old ones. Actually, there was something pathetic about this pseudo-magnificence, which was so obviously a concession to an age which demanded the huge and the vulgar. The ghost of the old building still dominated the new one, mutely invoking the return of former serenities.

He looked round: the place was nearly deserted and the avenues of empty tables depressed him. Several waiters stood motionless, with the patience of their tribe, scanning distant horizons. A man at a table near the entrance was crouched over a crossword puzzle. A few yards away, an old man and a young woman were having an intricate argument as to the precise time at which they had arranged to meet. Only a niggard daylight could penetrate the badly-placed windows, with the result that it was not dark enough to switch on the lights and not really light enough to dispense with them.

Grant wavered, then decided to stay. He chose a table near the middle of the café, sat down, and tried to remember what had occurred just before his conversation with the artist. Instantly, however, he found that he was visualizing Knightsbridge as he had seen it in the early morning sunshine. It was curious how he had had the impression that two companions had just left him. But before he could evolve any explanation he seemed to see himself in the autumn stillness of the Daisy Walk. Then – swiftly, vividly – the image of the buffoon he had seen in Piccadilly rose before him. He was still in the gutter, but now the artist was by his side – and they were laughing at him.

Grant leapt to his feet. Why hadn't a waiter appeared? The damned place was empty, yet no one came to take his order! How typical of an age which chattered endlessly about efficiency! He'd go somewhere else! He'd send for the manager! He'd——

He noticed that there was a cocktail on an unoccupied table a few yards distant. Probably it was waiting for a regular patron who would appear at any moment to claim it. Grant decided to take it. That would be a hint to the management to attend to a customer who was present before it anticipated the wants of one who had not arrived.

He crossed to the table, picked up the cocktail, then returned to his seat.

Two men came in, talking loudly, and sat down near him. One produced a cigarette case and said to his friend: "Try one of these and tell me what you think of it. They're a new brand."

. . . Dorothy! It was extraordinary how clear those two figures had been on the beach of that bay in Cornwall. What a strange element would enter life if – suddenly and without warning – scenes emerged from the past so triumphantly actual that they obliterated the present! And yet, now that he was able to review the experience logically, perhaps its most remarkable feature had been his inability to remember his life during the intervening years. Supposing that scenes from the past rose before him now, and he witnessed each in turn, revealed with that clarity which had made that forgotten episode in Cornwall seem so real. If now, at this minute——

He looked round the café, at first listlessly, then with startled interest. It had become surface without solidity – a ghostly travesty of itself. But soon darkness descended – and from the depths of that darkness he heard his father's voice.

And it seemed to Julian Grant that he saw the house in which he had been born. The sun was shining and birds were singing.

PART II

I

THE HERMITAGE

The house was old, half hidden by trees, and stood far back from a narrow Kentish lane with high hedges. Sometimes a farmer's cart would rattle lazily by, but usually the silence belonged only to the birds. A close scrutiny of the crumbling pillars at the entrance to the drive revealed the name – The Hermitage.

There is something in the aspect of certain houses which immediately quickens speculation as to their occupants. Instinctively, it is felt that the people living in them must be exceptional. The Hermitage was of this class. Whether it wakened curiosity by reason of its extreme isolation, or by the beauty of its setting, or because of the dream aura which enveloped it like a mist, would be difficult to decide. It may have been all or none of these, but it is certain that anyone in the least imaginative passing down the lane and half-glimpsing the old house – tranquil amid tranquillity – would have paused to wonder concerning the lives of those it sheltered.

Julian had lived in The Hermitage till he was nineteen and, after leaving it, had returned only once for a few tragic weeks. Every memory of it was associated with his father – Nathan Grant – for The Hermitage bore the impress of his personality as intimately as a long-worn garment. To think of it was to see Nathan Grant: a spare elusive figure, with scholarly features and eyes which suggested the inspired vehemence of an Old Testament prophet. To see him was to recognize that he lived from a different centre from that which animates most men. He bore the signature of thoughts and emotions different in kind from theirs. Everything about him proclaimed that he belonged to that visitant order of beings whose presence on this earth seems an accident, and whose activities necessarily appear eccentric to residents.

The house was always silent. Everything was subordinated to the demands of that activity which throbbed like a pulse in Nathan Grant's study on the ground floor. In one sense, the whole house was little more than an extension of this study, for not only had its library invaded every room and landing, but the intensity of its atmosphere had also penetrated everywhere. To cross the threshold was to enter the world in which Nathan Grant had his being – the world of the saints and the mystics.

Since he came down from Oxford he had given his life to the study of metaphysics. He belonged to that diminutive group of men and women – produced by each generation – to whom the interior life is the one reality. The life of the senses, which is so self-evidently real to most men, was to Nathan Grant only the activity of a waking dream. To him, an absolute value was essential. Inevitably, therefore, he was attracted to those in all ages who had had a genius for God. These were they who had awakened from the mesmeric dream of sense, who had divined life's inmost secret, seen the vision, and known the glory. And – to Nathan Grant – all activities other than theirs were illusory.

Circumstances conspired to allow him to live the life of a student. Soon after he came down from Oxford, his father died – leaving him sufficient means to live in The Hermitage, where he had been born. His brother, who was his only surviving relative, bought a business in the north of England which proved progressively successful. He was a bachelor, and, although he saw little of Nathan, he had a respect for him which verged on veneration. Financially, therefore, Nathan Grant was independent, and in consequence he was outside that arena into which most men leap and from which nearly all are carried. Hence, for a man of his temperament, the only menace to his studies lurked in the possibility of an unsuccessful marriage.

It did not materialize, for – at the age of thirty – Nathan Grant married a woman so essentially his counterpart that she might have been created to serve him. Muriel's horizon was his interests. To her, his eminence was as obvious as the sun. She sacrificed all the pleasures and duties of the average woman to foster this genius whom she regarded as little less than a god. Domestic affairs were delegated to a housekeeper in order that she might be free to undertake the duties of a secretary, thereby relieving him of all mechanical labour in regard to his studies. She was vigilant to shield him from every commonplace demand, with the result that his isolation from the everyday world became complete.

Nathan Grant was forty when Julian was born and Muriel was thirty-eight, but although Julian's arrival necessarily affected changes in their relations, it did not involve a transfer of Muriel's allegiance. The claims of her husband remained paramount. A first-class nurse was engaged, and the work in the silent study continued as before, week after week, month after month. . . .

Till the age of ten Julian had been very delicate, therefore early impressions lacked that definition which usually characterizes them. Events had seemed remote at the time of their occurrence, consequently his memories of them were pervaded by a dream-like quality.

Probably the dominant emotion of his childhood had been an intense curiosity concerning the lives of other children. When he was well, and the weather was fine, he would spend whole days in the garden playing with imaginary companions, for whom he invented names and histories till he became so convinced of their actuality that he believed they were living quite near him and that one day they would meet. When he was ill, or woke in the night, he would try to visualize the homes and parents of these imaginary friends – contrasting their circumstances with his, and wondering whether their houses were as silent as The Hermitage. For, intuitively, he knew that his environment was unique, although he did not realize till years later that the chief cause of his isolation was his father.

Nathan Grant had no friends in the vicinity. The social life of the neighbourhood was ruled by the Vicar, but as the latter regarded those who believed that religion had any relation to life as fanatics, his visits to The Hermitage ended abruptly, and were never resumed. Gradually it became established that Nathan Grant was an eccentric, and – in the Vicar's most intimate circle – it was confidently asserted that he was an atheist.

Julian's childhood was therefore solitary. He was considered too delicate to be sent to school, consequently his early education was entrusted to a governess. Later, she was superseded by a resident tutor, but his presence in the house so disturbed that seclusion which was considered essential, that after a few months his engagement was terminated and Julian's father became responsible for his education.

The effect of this decision was that Julian passed wholly under his father's influence. Nathan Grant had a genius for instruction – he quickened Julian's intelligence, inspired his imagination, captured his curiosity. Study became an adventure. Julian ceased to dream of the life beyond his horizon. He became a reflection of his father. In a short time he was far beyond his contemporaries mentally, but he knew nothing of everyday life. Much later he believed that his father had willed this ignorance but, at the time, his devotion to him was absolute.

At the age of twelve Julian's health was perfect, but there was a conspiracy to pretend that he was still too delicate to be sent to school. Nathan Grant feared any contact with the outside world, and this was the reason Julian was kept at home. But he did not care – then. To become like his father was his only ambition. So he remained with him, and the only people he ever met were Nathan Grant's queer friends who came to stay periodically – people whose interests were identical with his, people who were lost in this world, appalled by it, afraid of it, and who were therefore striving to believe in another. They regarded Nathan Grant as a master. They read his books, wrote to him, consulted him about their souls. All their conversation related to mysticism and the mystics. St. John of the Cross, Ruysbroek, Dionysius the Areopagite, Böhme, Meister Eckhart, and so on. Naturally these names conveyed nothing to Julian as a child, but the very sound of them seemed to create different coloured lights in his mind.

One by one the years passed, and Julian continued his studies in the monastic silence of The Hermitage.

But at last he woke from the spell of his father's hypnotism. Nathan Grant's brother came to stay when Julian was about eighteen. He had visited The Hermitage at long intervals, but this time he talked to his nephew. He told him about his business in the north, explained current affairs, asked about his future – till

Julian realized that outside The Hermitage was a world of which he knew nothing. A fever of curiosity possessed him. Nathan Grant saw the light of it in his eyes and knew that it heralded that of which he was most afraid – Change. He tried to delay their separation. He refused to let Julian go into his brother's business because he resented his interference. The knowledge that Julian was about to go into the world was agony to Nathan Grant. Julian would be a link between it and him.

But now Julian's will was stronger than his and at last he agreed that he should be articled to his brother-in-law – Mandell. And so, when Julian was nineteen, he escaped. He left The Hermitage and did not return for three years.

II

THE YEARS IN MANDELL'S OFFICE

A

Mandell's offices were situated in a stuccoed house at the end of a cul-de-sac near Lincoln's Inn Fields. The exterior was dingy, the interior so dark that the uninitiated had difficulty in finding the narrow stone stairs. Nevertheless, an air of self-satisfaction predominated – subtly suggesting the respectability of the dreary. A churchyard chill haunted the entrance, even on the warmest day, and a cumulative silence made any movement seem sacrilegious. Everything was as musty as the folios of an ancient ledger.

Mandell's offices were on the first floor and had been there for sixty years. To enter them was to receive the impression that their contents had been hidden for ages in an underground vault till, eventually, they had attained the maturity which qualified them for use. Everything seemed old: the clients, the clerks, the furniture, and the methods. . . .

Albert Mandell was a curious figure, a cumbrous barrel-shaped man, heavily bearded, wearing a rusty frock-coat. His movements denoted great deliberation. A certain pomposity indicated that Mr. Albert Mandell was aware of an intimate relationship between himself and Destiny. He stared at the world,

rather than looked at it, and the rigidity of his body was in perfect correspondence with that of his opinions.

When it was suggested that Julian Grant should enter his
office as an articled clerk, Mandell had been profoundly disturbed. He wrote several ponderous letters to his sister, Muriel,
clearly defining his objections, but – to his intense irritation –
she ignored these in her replies, which continued to repeat her
original request with progressive emphasis. The correspondence
might have continued indefinitely but, finally, Muriel – using her
intimate knowledge of her brother's character – appealed to his
sense of duty. This approach caused Mandell to experience that
hatred which only a relative is capable of arousing. But he was
beaten and knew it. For years the word Duty had figured as a rod
in his vocabulary. It was his turn to kiss it. He surrendered, and
Julian Grant joined the firm – to the amazement of the stuccoed
house, the clerks, and the furniture.

Julian never forgot the first interview with Mandell. He
entered the bleak private office with its massive table, littered
with documents, at which Mandell sat each day from ten till six
with the immobility of an idol. Rows of black deed-boxes covered the walls from floor to ceiling, with the exception of the
space over the mantelpiece in which a yellowing portrait of
Mandell's father looked sternly down. When he was ushered
into this crypt, which was the holy of holies to the clerks in the
outer office, Mandell was studying the draft of a will, and continued to study it for several minutes – leaving the youthful Julian
to contemplate the glories of a successful legal career.

Eventually he looked up, surveyed his visitor lugubriously,
then began a long oration in a hollow monotonous voice. It consisted of a series of warnings, delivered in such a manner that
the effect was the reverse of the intention. Mandell succeeded in
investing virtue with gloom, and vice with glamour. Julian heard
little of it. The sweep and stir of this tumultuous London, which
he had glimpsed for the first time, seethed and surged through
his being like a mighty music which had just ceased. Now he
was listening to an old man in an airless silent room. He was
saying something about life and its perils: he was warning him:
he kept repeating the word, youth, in a tone which implied that
it was some dread disease. But soon Julian ceased to listen to

this voice, the very sound of which chilled the rapture pulsing through him. Subconsciously, he recognized that this old man hated everything unlike himself. He loved this office on the first floor of the stuccoed house in the cul-de-sac: he loved its silence, its respectability, its gloom. It had become life to him, and he feared all that denied it. Therefore he hated youth – for youth rebels, destroys, creates.

It is probable that Mandell partially realized his failure, for he ended the interview abruptly, summoned his head clerk, and consigned Julian to his care.

As the weeks passed it became evident that Mandell had evolved a simple method to negative the effect of Julian's presence – he ignored him. Although no definite instructions were given to the head clerk, he divined his employer's wishes with the insight of a sycophant. Twenty years' sedulous study had made him clairvoyant concerning Mandell. Soon a tacit conspiracy existed between them, which had no other aim than the preservation of the ancient routine from the contaminating influences of youth. In practice this meant that Mandell must encounter Julian as seldom as possible and – to insure this immunity – the head clerk obtained a small room on the floor above to which the interloper was duly banished.

The clerks in the outer office experienced a crescendo of sensations during this period: first, at the entry of an articled clerk – for which no precedent existed; next, at his confinement on the second floor; thirdly, at the head clerk's attitude towards him. But the culminating sensation was occasioned by Julian himself.

On every level he was a stranger to their experience. Not only was he separated from them physically – as he resembled a youthful god – but, mentally, he was equally remote. The discovery that he could read in several languages, and was familiar with subjects of whose existence they were ignorant, caused them to regard him with pitying scorn – which was mitigated to some extent by the further discovery that he knew nothing whatever about everyday life. But although they would have liked to patronize him by parading their worldly knowledge, the desire to ingratiate themselves with Mandell and the head clerk remained paramount, hence they feigned indifference in regard to Julian while inwardly obsessed by curiosity concerning him.

There was one exception – Rawlings. He was about fifty and was rendered somewhat conspicuous by a dome-shaped very bald head, small twinkling eyes, and a blotchy complexion. He was attracted by Julian but, as his life outside the office was definitely dissolute, he had better reasons than his colleagues for subservience to his superiors. It was essential for Rawlings to remain unnoticed. Consequently any advances to Julian were reserved for very favourable occasions, and even then they were liable to misinterpretation owing to the uneasiness of his manner.

But Julian cared nothing for Mandell or his clerks. To him they were waxworks – wholly unresponsive to the miracles surrounding them – whereas he was intoxicated by the life of this unknown London, which obliterated everything less clamorous than itself. It deafened and dazzled him: silencing the voices of memory with its insistent uproar; destroying old loyalties by the fervour of its demands. The Hermitage with its books and abstract speculations dwindled to unreality. The world which his father had rejected now confronted him, and something in the depths of his nature yielded an instant allegiance. A curiosity as great as his ignorance flamed up in him. A thousand voices rose to him from the surging streets, but he did not understand the purport of one of them.

It follows that he welcomed his isolation in Mandell's office. It gave him what he had never possessed and what he passionately desired – liberty. It is true that he had to go to the stuccoed house in the cul-de-sac each day, but he soon discovered that his banishment to the second floor relieved him of the restrictions of supervision. No one cared whether he was in or out. It was vaguely assumed that he was studying and that if he wanted any advice he would ask for it. As to Mandell, the success of his policy caused him to regard Julian with a deepening dislike, for he felt that the latter's acceptance of it proceeded from contempt. Also, but more interiorly, Mandell was disturbed by the knowledge that he was treating his nephew unfairly, and – as he could not endure the smallest menace to his self-satisfaction – he eventually decided to do his duty. Consequently he wrote to his sister, informing her that he feared that Julian lacked the qualities essential to the legal calling. Then, with royal condescension, he asked Julian to dine at his house in Stoke Newington.

Muriel sent a trivial reply and Julian refused the invitation. Mandell had done his duty – and could now abandon himself to a whole-hearted hatred of his relatives, which he did, and from which he derived the usual satisfaction.

Soon Julian ceased to do anything at the office. More and more frequently he left it for two or three hours to wander about the streets, trying to familiarize himself with this incredible London which had flashed into his consciousness with the fantastic reality of a dream. Each day he explored it with impatient curiosity, as if fearful that it might vanish as dramatically as it had appeared, and almost every hour he became more perplexed by the discovery of his ignorance.

As a result of his father's influence, and the monastic seclusion of life in The Hermitage, he knew nothing of the mechanism of everyday existence. The simplest human contacts – the purchase of some article in a shop, a casual conversation with a stranger – were intricate problems to Julian. To him, others were foreigners, although he spoke their language, consequently he remained an onlooker at a spectacle in which he passionately desired to play a part. This isolation, however, was not only psychological. Nathan Grant's determination to keep Julian unspotted from the world had been reflected in the arrangements made for him in London. Rooms were obtained near Mandell's office in the house of an old servant. All meals were provided for him there and the monthly account was rendered to the father, not the son. This arrangement not only restricted Julian's physical liberty, it also placed him under the observation of an informer. In addition, his allowance was reduced to a minimum, for even Nathan Grant knew enough about city life to realize that lack of money eliminates many possibilities.

Nevertheless, owing to the effect of sudden transition from The Hermitage to London, it was some months before Julian recognized the nature of the restrictions by which he was tethered. When he did he experienced bitter resentment, for – in this final attempt to isolate him – he detected the spirit of that policy which had always motivated his father. Julian's memories only confirmed this discovery. His father had willed that he should live just such a life as his own. In every instance he had found an excuse to deprive him of normal associations. He had hypnotized him: elevated his own ideal before him till he had desired nothing else, till he had ceased to believe in the existence of anything else. He had been mesmerized and robbed! And now, although he had escaped to London – as the result of rebellion – he was still held prisoner by the tentacles of his father's will.

His letters to The Hermitage became less frequent and contained only trivialities. A passion for experience possessed him. It was no longer enough to wander about the streets, gaping at the life surrounding him. He wanted to go to these restaurants, visit these theatres and music halls, find his own friends, read books which represented or interpreted this human drama at which he could only stare with ignorant eyes. But in everything he was thwarted by lack of money. He would gladly have sacrificed meals if this abstinence had provided the price of a book or a seat at the theatre, but – owing to his father's foresight – the student's prerogative of pawning his appetite was denied him. He had only one asset – the books he had brought from The Hermitage – but his ignorance was such that it was many months before he realized its cash potentiality. Directly he did, he sold every volume, spending the proceeds on theatres and music halls. But the money was soon exhausted and the return of penury produced a dejection hitherto unknown. He was becoming desperate when one night, wandering through the back streets of Soho, he ran into Rawlings.

The latter had just emerged from a public-house. His hat was on the back of his head and he was humming a popular song in praise of life in the army. But he stopped abruptly on seeing Julian and an expression of consternation flashed into his small eyes, then – with an effort towards dignity – he waved his hand and was about to walk away when Julian seized his arm.

"Wait a minute! I want to talk to you."

"Talk? What about?"

"All sorts of things."

Rawlings surveyed him doubtfully.

"You won't let on?" he inquired at last.

"Let on?" Julian repeated, mystified.

"Yes, you know – to old Mandell."

"Of course not. Where shall we go?"

As they were standing outside a public-house, Rawlings

regarded this question as superfluous. He turned on his heel and
Julian followed him down a narrow passage into the private bar.
The place was crowded, but Rawlings – neatly outwitting a com-
petitor for the solitary table in a recess – was soon seated and was
about to ask Julian what he would drink, when he noticed that
the latter was looking round with great curiosity.

"First time you've been in a pub?" he asked.

"Yes."

"Ah!" said Rawlings, reminiscently. Then, after a pause:

"Well, what's it going to be?"

"I don't want to drink."

"Thought you said you wanted to talk?"

"So I do – but what's that got to do with it?"

"Everything – as a rule."

Rawlings ordered a double whisky for himself and a dry
ginger ale for Julian. Then he continued:

"Well, fire away. But don't forget all this is between you and
me. There are *two* Rawlings – you're looking at one of them,
and you'll see the other at the office to-morrow. Mind you don't
confuse them."

Then, without any preliminaries, Julian began to tell Rawlings everything about himself. Rapidly, almost breathlessly, he
described his father, The Hermitage, his education, the life he
had lived till he was nineteen, his rebellion, and his arrival in
London. Words poured from him in a torrent. He forgot time,
place, and audience in the exaltation of expressing thoughts and
emotions accumulated during months of solitude. He explained
the arrangements which had been made for him in London, how
he was fettered by them, and emphasized his determination to
escape. He raced on and on: describing his contempt for Mandell, his hatred of the office, his curiosity concerning all activities
of which he was ignorant, and his absolute decision to explore
and understand everything which had been denied him. When
at last he stopped it was only because it was physically impossible to continue.

"'Strewth!" said Rawlings, after a long silence.

"I had to tell someone everything. It's a good thing I ran
into you – and not one of the others. I know you won't say anything."

"Not me! Well, I've heard some histories in pubs but nothing like this. D'you mean to say they don't give you any money?"

"Practically none."

Rawlings took a pull at his drink, then scratched his head.

"I'll tell you the queerest thing of the lot, if you like," he announced at last.

"What's that?"

"You – in old Mandell's office! Talk about a firework display in a churchyard! I'm a pretty good misfit in that office, but I'm nothing to you. Still, you won't stay – and I shall."

"How do you know I won't stay?" Julian demanded.

"You'll get what you want – because you want it badly enough. You're that sort. I'm not. I wanted things once, in a weak sort of way, then started drinking so as to forget that I hadn't got them – and never should have them."

"What sort of things?"

Rawlings looked at him inscrutably.

"Things you read about in books. When I was your age, I thought all sorts of things would happen to me. And what *has* happened? Old Mandell – and whisky – and a woman now and again."

He lit a cheap cigar, then began to question Julian on certain parts of his narrative which he had found obscure. In ten minutes he had assimilated the essentials and his astonishment increased.

"Seems to me that you're like a monk who's just been shot out of his monastery. Your father must be a bit crazy, if you ask me. I can understand his thinking that this world is hell, but he ought to have let you find that out for yourself. You've got imagination, and you expect a lot, so it wouldn't have taken you long. But the point is that *then* you'd have known as the result of experience – not hearsay."

"But *is* it hell?"

"Course it is! Go an inch under the surface and you'll soon discover that. But it was your right to make your own discoveries. Why, God bless my soul, a man can't imagine his own heaven till he's found his own hell."

They talked on till closing time, then wandered about the streets discussing one subject after another. At last Rawlings came to a standstill.

"Better go home now. We might have another night together soon."

"The sooner the better."

"And not a word to old Mandell! They know nothing about me at the office. They still think I'm a respectable married man."

"Well, aren't you?"

"Good Lord, no! My wife and I separated years ago. She was all right in her way, but she made life seem like an endless wet Sunday. I've a room in Kennington – you might come over one night."

This was their first real meeting and it formed the foundation of a curious friendship. Rawlings was a ruin, but he still retained traces of a genuine originality. His faculties had atrophied, as a result of weakness and environment, but contact with Julian's vitality revivified them. Forgotten horizons began to glimmer on the frontier of his mind. For years he had regarded his early beliefs and aspirations intolerantly – he had even ascribed his failure to them – but now he was glad to remember them. He no longer cared whether they were illusions or not. Life had been real when he possessed them, and with their disappearance it had become a monotony – rendered endurable only by false stimulation. So the effect of his association with Julian was to quicken all that had died in him. Rawlings suddenly discovered that he was surrounded by ghosts.

For Julian this friendship proved an initiation. As Rawlings had had to earn his living since he was fifteen, he was familiar with the battlefield of normal existence. It follows that what was mysterious to Julian was commonplace to him. But Rawlings, being imaginative, recognized the relativity of his knowledge. It represented facts on a certain level, and to this extent had value, but it was limited and unrelated to wisdom. To him the sordid was the actual – not the real. The real was somewhere just out of sight, round the corner, a glory which some had beheld but which he had failed to glimpse. Nevertheless, he was destined to believe in it. Finally, when the squalors of a wretched marriage were succeeded by loneliness, and when his solitary confinement in Mandell's office was recognized as permanent, he began to drink in order to forget what he dared not deny. His complexion became blotchy, but – this apart – he managed to conceal the outcast under a genteel exterior.

They spent thrilling nights together. When Rawlings made some extra money by a lucky bet, he would take Julian to a restaurant, or a theatre, or to some obscure music hall in the East End. Or they would go to a concert, or a fight, or the gallery at the opera; it did not matter what or where, for Julian's hunger for experience was insatiable. He swept Rawlings out of his old haunts so tempestuously that on several occasions the latter forgot to get drunk.

Often Julian would say to him:

"You always pay for everything; it's impossible!"

To which Rawlings invariably replied:

"Take what you can while you can get it. The day will come when you won't want it. I'll pay now – you can pay later."

When Rawlings had no money to spare they would spend long nights in his room at Kennington, examining his books and discussing every imaginable subject. The mental contrast between them was as absolute as that on the physical plane but, as each possessed in abundance what the other lacked, their friendship was mutually stimulating.

Several months passed. Their intimacy was never suspected at the office as neither gave any indication of it. Then, as a result of an impulse of Rawlings', a new element entered Julian's life.

B

For the second time Rawlings counted the five-pound notes spread out on the table in front of him, evidently unable to believe there were twelve, then he said to Julian:

"Good thing you're here, or I should think this was the start of D.T. Well, there it is – sixty pounds. Mind you, if an accurate account were prepared, showing all the doubles I've backed on one side, and sixty pounds on the other, I don't say that the balance would look pretty. But the fact remains that I've got home on a double at last."

He crossed to the window and pushed it up to its maximum extent. It was a hot summer night, and Rawlings' room, being an attic, had attained almost tropical intensity. The sentimental lament of a barrel-organ and the shouts of children rose from the airless street. Somewhere in the distance the puffs of a railway engine sounded like the gasps of an expiring monster. The inert atmosphere was almost tangible.

Rawlings removed his coat and waistcoat, yawned, then – as Julian remained motionless on the couch in silent prostration – he looked round the room despondently. He glanced in turn at the ugly gas-bracket, the derelict bedstead with its hideous counterpane, the worn linoleum, the peeling wallpaper, and asked himself for the hundredth time why he stayed in such a hovel. Then, as always, he remembered the books. There were too many to move and he was too lazy to go through them and sell those he no longer wanted. Also the place was cheap – and the landlady recognized that a man must get drunk sometimes. Of course he would go one day – that was certain. The possibility of living here when he was old, really old, was terrifying. But, of course, that would never happen. He would sell most of his books and move into a small flat. He might stay for a few months but, eventually he would leave, that was certain.

"How long have you been here?"

Rawlings winced as if Julian's question were an accusation.

"Well, as a matter of fact, I suppose it's some years now. Yes, it must be. But I'm moving next spring. I'm going to take a small flat somewhere."

Julian did not reply. Rawlings began to wander about the room, then, finding the silence oppressive, he paused near Julian and asked:

"What are you doing about holidays? Going home?"

"No, my people are going to my uncle in the north. He's not been well lately. I don't know what I shall do – stay here, I suppose. Where are you going?"

"Richmond Park. Never get further afield than that nowadays. Do you know that I've only been to real country once in my life?"

"You don't mean that?"

"Don't I. And it was thirty years ago – just about. Wait a minute. I'll show you something."

He crossed the room and tried to open the top drawer of a cheap piece of furniture near the washstand, but, as ever, it yielded neither to force nor to persuasion. Rawlings turned despairingly to Julian.

"My God! Would you believe that I've studied this damned drawer for years, trying to learn its secret? If I'd spent as much time on a violin, I'd be a second Kubelik."

He seized the two china handles resolutely:

"Now! Come out – will you!"

He gave a sudden tug. The drawer flew out, hit him on the chest, and fell to the floor with a crash.

"It's all very well for you to laugh," he protested ruefully. "It does that about every six months – suddenly behaves as if it were the product of perfect workmanship. To hell with it, anyway!"

He rummaged among its contents till he discovered five or six drawings, which he handed to Julian.

"This is the place I went to. I got these drawings from an artist I ran into down there. Have a look at that one."

It depicted a miniature bay, held in a crescent of cliffs.

Julian studied it intently for some moments, then asked:

"Where's this place?"

"Cornwall."

"It looks marvellous."

"Go there for your holiday."

Julian stared at him, but Rawlings continued:

"Take some of the notes on that table – and go."

"But – but – what about you?"

"Me! No, thank you! I don't want to go there again. Besides, in a way, I *couldn't* go. It wouldn't exist for me nowadays."

"Don't understand."

"Well, it's like this. I went to that place on twenty pounds, which was what I got when my father died. I was about your age and I stayed there nearly a month. I don't know what I didn't believe – then. Anyway, I'm not going back. Let sleeping dreams lie – that's my motto. But *you* go. Take the money – and don't argue. And don't tell your people you're going. Write to them on arrival. And let them guess how you got the money."

Julian protested and a long discussion followed. But, a week later, he left for Cornwall.

C

Dorothy was about his age and lived with her sister in a cottage near a tiny bay in Cornwall. He met her two days after his arrival. They greeted each other as if they had long been friends – and each day of his visit they spent together. When he left, they were secretly engaged. . . .

At the time of his visit, the division in Julian's life was absolute. On one side was The Hermitage: on the other – London. Any relation between them seemed as remote from probability as a friendship between Nathan Grant and Rawlings. In fact, the disparity between these men revealed the extent of Julian's rebellion. Nevertheless, there were moments in which he realized that if his father feared the arena of normal existence, it was equally true that ordinary people were afraid of solitude. Nathan Grant had dared to confront the universe within him. He had explored the spectral. To ignore him – to regard him as negligible – was to repudiate those greater than he. He was not only Nathan Grant – he was also a symbol.

Without realizing it consciously, Julian was seeking a reconciliation between the demands of The Hermitage and those of London. In Dorothy's presence this problem was projected in the terms of a new perspective, which transformed it and promised a solution.

The effect of Dorothy was to create a state of consciousness in which he was aware of a great potentiality. He felt that something had been born in him – something which he must guard and treasure, without seeking to understand. In its own time, and in accordance with its own mysterious laws, it would reveal all that was necessary for him to know. In the meantime he must wait, knowing that no sign – intelligible to ignorance – would be given.

In her presence, a new spirit possessed him. It unified his experience, and it revealed the irrelevance of many problems formerly regarded as urgent. The conception of a great synthesis stirred in him. His life attained the intensity of a prophecy. All things became possible.

D

One night, some months after his return from Cornwall, Julian was in Rawlings' room in Kennington. Neither had spoken for some minutes. Julian was lying on a broken couch by the fire, reading, while Rawlings inspected the contents of his wardrobe in the attitude of one facing a crisis.

"I'm below the Mandell standard," he muttered to himself, "there's not the slightest doubt about that."

He went to the table and studied the whisky bottle despondently. If he had a drink now he would not be able to have one later. That was evident. Also, he had only one cigar. Rawlings wavered. Then, remembering that in these matters anticipation is more potent than memory, he dismissed temptation. With him the last drink and the last smoke just before going to bed constituted a rite rather than an indulgence. He glanced at his watch. Two hours to wait.

A succession of dreary thoughts began to lumber across his mind like a train of camels crossing a desert. Several of his creditors were becoming unpleasant: the allowance to his wife was in arrear: the head clerk was looking him up and down more and more frequently: a new suit was essential: his bookmaker had threatened to call at the office.

He began to pace the room, but the need for diversion soon became a necessity. He paused and turned to Julian:

"Are you going home for Christmas?"

Julian did not reply. Rawlings glanced at him, at first casually, then with interest. It might have been the grace of his attitude, or an effect of the firelight, which caused Rawlings suddenly to appreciate his physical distinction. He stared at him as if he were seeing him for the first time. He seemed remote from the ugliness of his surroundings – a splendid anachronism – and Rawlings realized in an intuitive flash that their friendship was an incident, not an institution, and that eventually he would be lonelier because of it.

"Sorry! What did you say just now?"

"Only asked if you were going home for Christmas."

"No, I'm not – for several reasons. One is that my father

hasn't been too well lately. And there's another reason, but it's not easy to make clear."

"Well – try. I'm sick of my own thoughts. I keep seeing my future – and that's not my idea of amusement."

He sat down near Julian and gazed into the fire.

"First of all, you'll have to understand this," Julian began after a pause, "my father loathes any external change. That's why he kept me at home, and that's why he tried to stop me going into Mandell's office. Well – for the same reason – he probably doesn't want me at The Hermitage nowadays."

"Don't follow you," Rawlings announced abruptly.

"It's like this, as I see it. He's used to my not being at home. He's established a new routine – one which assumes my permanent absence. If I turned up, I should upset that routine. You've got to understand that he lives in the centre of a circle, and ignores everything outside its circumference. That's the position."

"You're not as bitter about him as you used to be."

"I understand him better – that's why."

After a silence Rawlings asked:

"Did you tell me some days ago that you were going to ask for a bigger allowance?"

"Yes – and I did. I wrote stating that I needed twice as much. Also, that I owed money. Then I pointed out that I wanted to move to new rooms. I didn't give any reasons. I heard from him the day before yesterday. He agreed to everything and enclosed a cheque – which, by the way, I'm giving to you. There it is. I have endorsed it."

Rawlings glanced at it. Instantly his mental scenery became transformed. The miasma of depression was dissipated: vistas of delight opened invitingly. Creditors, the head clerk, his bookmaker – who, a few minutes ago, had seemed the instruments of malevolent destiny – became no more menacing than scarecrows in a sunlit landscape.

He stretched luxuriously. It was pleasant to feel like a patron in regard to his creditors – and it was joy to keep reminding himself that he would change his bookmaker immediately.

He glanced again at the cheque.

"I say, Julian, do you think I ought to have all this?"

"Why not? I must owe you more – really."

Rawlings said nothing, then – suddenly – he remembered the cigar and the whisky. Abstinence was no longer necessary. He leapt to his feet, lit the cigar and mixed himself a drink.

"Shan't be a minute."

He left the room and descended rapidly to the basement where he discovered his landlady.

"I want a bottle of whisky and some cigars," he announced authoritatively.

"I daresay. *I* want my rent."

"Damn your rent! You shall have it to-morrow. Look here!"

He produced the cheque, which she regarded without enthusiasm.

" 'Tain't like the last one, I hope."

This comment wakened bitter memories and Rawlings began to remonstrate angrily.

"Oh, all right, all right!" she interrupted. "Suppose you can wait five minutes, till the girl gets back, can't you? She's gone over the way to get a jar of pickles for the second floor front."

Two minutes later Rawlings was seated opposite Julian – a perpendicular line of smoke rising from his cigar and the drink within reach of his hand. A little loose talk about women would have provided additional stimulation, but – remembering Julian's aversion to this form of excitement – he remained silent. Julian's values concerning women were a mystery to Rawlings. More than once, when money had been plentiful, he had offered to buy him the caresses of a street-walker, but on each occasion Julian had refused. As Rawlings saw it, only one of two explanations was possible: either the influence of The Hermitage was still potent in this respect, or Julian had standards and satisfactions which he refused to reveal.

It was necessary, therefore, to find another subject. Rawlings discovered one without much difficulty.

"What – exactly – made you write to your father about your allowance? You say you didn't give any reasons – well, why didn't you write months ago?"

"It's difficult to explain," Julian replied slowly, "especially as I'm not certain that I know myself. I suddenly felt that it was best to write and say what I wanted without giving any explanations. I felt it would be better to do that than to bombard him with reasons. You see, since I came to London, I've discovered him – so to speak. When I was with him, I couldn't see him – he was too near me."

"All the same I'd like to know what he thought of your letter. I bet it made him sit up."

"I don't believe it worried him a bit. It was probably a relief. It told him finally that I'd gone my own way – and he's accepted the fact. He's not human, you know, as the word's used. He's an artist in his way."

"Damned if I understand that, but one thing's certain: *you've* altered."

"Think so?"

"I'm certain of it. You've a better grip on things. You're not nearly so excited as you used to be. You not only know what you want – you're beginning to learn how to get it. God! I wish I were in your shoes."

"Why?"

There was a knock on the door. Rawlings rose. The whisky and the cigars had arrived. He mixed another drink, then began to pace up and down the room.

"Why?" Julian repeated.

"Because you're going to have a great life – that's why."

"In Mandell's office?"

"Damn Mandell – and his office! You won't stay there. You'll get where you belong one of these days."

"And where's that?"

"How the devil do I know! I only know where it isn't. It isn't The Hermitage – and it isn't the office – and it isn't here. But you'll find it all right. Why, you could do anything with your looks and your brains. If I'd half your assets I'd turn myself into a syndicate. You can laugh. I'll bet the day will come when you won't be able to believe that you used to come here and waste your time with me."

"I'm certain you're wrong there."

"You'll see. And when that day comes, you take my tip and don't be sentimental and imagine that you ought to keep up with people you've outgrown. Your job is to find your own crowd. Other people are only travelling companions. I wish I'd known that twenty years ago. I had my chance – in my small way. But I was a mug. I did what other people wanted me to do. See what I mean? Thought I'd be able to help 'em if I did. Well, *look* at me. No damned good to anyone, self included."

Neither spoke for some minutes. Rawlings returned to his chair and gazed at the fire as if seeking the solution of some mystery. At last he slapped his knee triumphantly. "I've got it!"

"What's that?"

"I've been trying to remember when I first noticed that you'd altered. It was soon after you came back from Cornwall."

Julian gave an evasive reply. He had not told Rawlings anything about Dorothy. It seemed to him that silence had kinship with sanctity. Their love was a hidden talisman, ruling their secret destiny.

He changed the conversation skilfully and succeeded in interesting Rawlings in another subject. Half an hour later he left him. . . .

As the months passed Julian became convinced that the theory concerning his father which he had outlined to Rawlings represented the facts. No invitation came from The Hermitage. It was true that his mother's letters frequently referred to a visit, as if it were inevitable, but these references were invariably followed by explanations as to the necessity for postponement. His father was ill, or was occupied with the proofs of a new book, or had had so many visitors lately that absolute seclusion was necessary. Naturally, Julian was not deceived. These excuses were a smoke-screen which failed to conceal a new phase of his father's tactics.

Nathan Grant had accepted his defeat – represented by Julian's departure from The Hermitage – and was now only concerned with the maintenance of that isolation which was the indispensable background to his activities. In all things he was absolute. Julian had chosen London and, by so doing, had become an inhabitant of that world which Nathan Grant was determined to deny. The fact that Julian was his son did not affect the issue. Julian had become a potential disturber of the new routine necessitated by his absence. As its rhythmical functioning was essential, he was not wanted at The Hermitage.

This banishment did not disturb Julian. It was their separation, not their intimacy, which had revealed his father – and this new understanding tended to focus his admiration rather than diminish it. His detachment enabled him to realize Nathan Grant's qualities. Perspective emphasized what was great in him. Even his defects – like his shadow – bore witness to his stature.

This new understanding of his father was one effect of his love for Dorothy, which had transformed Julian's insight into vision. The fact that London no longer intoxicated him was another. His curiosity concerning the life surrounding him had not diminished, but he ceased to regard it with the hysteria of a child at its first pantomime. Once it had dominated him – now he was studying it. And, as a result, he could appreciate imaginatively his father's values concerning it.

Soon, however, an event occurred which disturbed the tranquil exterior of Nathan Grant's life. His brother died suddenly. This necessitated not only a visit to the north but a protracted one, for Nathan was the sole executor under his brother's will. The affairs of the estate were somewhat complicated, and it was several months before he returned to The Hermitage.

The results of this contact with the everyday world were remarkable. His desire for solitude became a passion. He saw no one, refused to write letters, and never mentioned Julian's name. As his eccentricity increased, Muriel became frightened. She rushed to London to see Julian, but her emotions rendered her so incoherent that only one fragment of their conversation remained in his memory.

"He only wants to be alone. But that's not all. He tells me nothing – nothing! He resents any questions. I feel that my presence is a burden to him. He never works – he never reads. He just sits alone in the study, staring in front of him. It's dreadful – dreadful!"

The weeks passed but the news from The Hermitage remained the same. Julian stayed in London. He would have gone to Cornwall, but as Dorothy and her sister had had to go abroad for an indefinite period, he wrote to her several times each week, elaborating plans for a long holiday on her return.

Late one night he returned to his rooms to find a letter from his mother. The address was written so illegibly that the delivery of the letter surprised him. He opened it and deciphered the scrawled lines with difficulty. They told him that his father was dead. He had died in his sleep.

Julian did not go to bed that night. Early the next morning he left for The Hermitage. He was numbed mentally and emotionally. The familiarity of the normal had vanished. Every object existed in stark isolation, wholly divorced from its usual associations. Nevertheless, he understood that he had not realized his father's death. He only knew of it. Realization would come later – and then the universe of memory would claim him. . . .

Muriel's surrender to despair was absolute. She remained motionless, as if she were drugged. She ignored all conventional duties, refused to go to the funeral, and left her letters unopened.

The days passed but her condition did not alter. At last the doctor whom Julian had consulted became alarmed.

"Something will have to be done," he announced after a series of unproductive visits. "There's no mistaking the signs. She's no will to live. That's obvious – and it's serious."

"I don't think she ought to stay here," Julian replied. "She finds him everywhere."

"That's perfectly true, but do you think you could get her to go away?"

"There's only one chance. I've been talking to Maud – that's the servant – and she reminded me that mother has an old school friend in Italy. They've written to each other for years. As I could see that things couldn't go on like this, I wrote to her yesterday and asked her to come here. I thought perhaps, later, mother would go back to Italy with her for a time."

"It's the only thing to be done. I won't be responsible for her if she stays here."

Several weeks later Muriel left for Italy with her friend. Julian returned to London, where a number of business affairs awaited him. Nathan Grant had left forty thousand pounds, for he had inherited the whole of his brother's fortune. Under Nathan's will, Muriel was given a life interest in the estate and, on her death, the capital passed to Julian.

The months went slowly by. Each week Julian wrote to his mother, but her replies were infrequent, brief, lifeless. It was from her friend that he learned the facts. Muriel was gradually slipping away from life as she had no link with it. She had lived wholly through her husband and, lacking him, the world was a wilderness. Different surroundings, association with strangers, failed to create new interests. She had only one desire – and that was to die.

Julian went to Italy for a month, but his visit was a failure. Muriel had decided that he was responsible for her husband's death. If he had remained at The Hermitage Nathan would not have died. This was her theme – and she repeated it endlessly with innumerable variations. He returned to London. Three months later she was dead. . . .

So, at the age of twenty-two, Julian inherited forty thousand pounds.

III

STELLA

A

A day in early spring.

Julian strode across the park, striving to silence the rhapsody of thought and emotion which exhilarated and disturbed him. Although some months had passed since he had inherited a fortune, it was only during certain moments that he realized the amazing change in his circumstances. Such a moment now possessed him – obliterating old boundaries and illuminating new frontiers.

He walked on quickly, careless of direction but aware of a necessity for speed. An interior excitement throbbed in him like a beaten drum. All things were possible! *All things.* He was free, he could choose. Freedom meant choice. This platitude swept him with the impetus of a discovery. All his life he had been tethered – consequently whole regions of experience had been closed to curiosity – but now he was free. Three deaths had given him freedom.

Suddenly – and for the first time – a question presented itself: did he regret those deaths? Each had contributed to his wealth or independence – did he regret all, or any, of them?

The question became a challenge, but he still hesitated to answer it. Then, recognizing that hesitation itself was an answer, he decided that the question was too embarrassing to be analysed. He dismissed it, and began to review his relations with others during the last few months, his first choice being Mandell. . . .

The discovery that his nephew had ceased to be Julian Grant and had become forty thousand pounds gave Mandell a psychological stroke from which he never fully recovered. When he first heard the news, he could only repeat the words – forty thousand pounds – in a tone of such deep religious awe that the head clerk had the greatest difficulty not to murmur Amen. After which they stared at each other in silence for nearly a minute – blank calling to blank – till at last Mandell asked incredulously:

"Forty *thousand* pounds, Mr. Minchin?"

"Forty thousand pounds, sir."

"My – God!" said Mandell, slowly, reverently, and truthfully.

But this ecstasy of adoration did not last long. Soon regrets and misgivings began to darken the golden landscape of Mandell's mind. His treatment of Julian had been a mistake. Yes, it had been a mistake. He had failed to foresee possibilities. Not to realize this was to perpetuate an error. To remind himself that he had done his duty by his nephew was irrelevant. The boy had become a bank. Obviously, therefore, it was necessary for his conception of duty to soar to a celestial plane. He must protect Julian from those who would adapt their tactics to the change in his circumstances. And the best means of accomplishing this would be for Julian to leave the administration of his affairs to him. Probably the boy would recognize that duty – no less than self-interest – rendered this action obligatory. The most elementary conception of justice demanded it. It was scandalous that his father, Nathan Grant, had employed another solicitor. The least that Julian could do was to make amends. Surely he would realize that relationship involved duties as well as pleasures. After all, blood was thicker than water.

But Mandell discovered that it was easier to formulate the desirable in the privacy of his own mind than to behave as if it were the inevitable when confronted by Julian. His nephew's manner disconcerted him. Not only did he remain obstinately silent, he also watched Mandell's efforts to acquire a new manner

as if the latter were attempting the feats of a professional con-
tortionist. This reception of his advances disturbed Mandell to
such a degree that he was reminded of the only other crisis of
his career. Ten years ago one of his daughters had become a
Catholic. But this Julian question was not a spiritual issue. It was
serious.

A secondary cause of perplexity was the discovery that his
clerks no longer regarded him as a superman. They were still
subservient – they still spied on one another and brought him
the fruits of their labours – but it was evident that Julian dominated their imaginations. He was young, single, handsome, and
need never work again. All their frustrated desires, all the ghosts
of their ambitions, thronged like beggars in the shadow of his
opulence. What was Mandell compared with this romantic
splendour? His life was over and, in one sense, it had not been
very different from theirs. He had lived on the treadmill which
had claimed them, and he would die on it. At the best, his position was that of a warder, and a warder spends most of his time
in prison. But – Julian!

To each clerk Julian represented a different type of deliverance. To Robinson, he was Security – and so an end to those fears
symbolized by the words The Future. To Baker, he was Fishing
– a mossy bank by a stream, a sunny sky with lazy clouds, the
song of a bird overhead, and an inn at the end of the day. To Fish-
enden, he was a Harem – in which incredible beauties plotted or
sought for his favour. To Jenkins, he was All Those Things His
Wife Wanted – which he had not been able to give her. To Mud-
bury, he was Divorce. To Sinclair – Children. And to the head
clerk, Mr. Minchin, he was Setting Up in Practice for Himself
– with a few of Mandell's clients for a nucleus. And so on. With
their imaginations functioning so luxuriantly, it was inevitable
that the clerks should regard their employer from a new angle.
Mandell dwindled to life-size proportions.

In a few weeks, however, this comedy achieved a staccato
ending – and one which became a recurring *motif* in Mandell's
dreams.

It was nearly four o'clock. Mandell was alone in his private
office, confident that he would not be disturbed, when the door
opened and Julian appeared. Now no one had entered Mandell's

office without knocking for a quarter of a century. The non-observance of this ritual was peculiarly embarrassing on this occasion, for Mandell was so absorbed in speculation concerning his nephew's intentions that Julian's sudden appearance caused him to start guiltily. He soon recovered his normal manner, but for some moments he felt like a man who had dressed hastily before a visitor.

Nevertheless, he attempted to produce the smile he had studied for his nephew's benefit. It perished in the chrysalis stage of its evolution, however, for Julian announced casually:

"I've come to say good-bye."

"Good-bye!"

"Yes."

"You mean – I take it – that you've decided to have a holiday."

"No; I'm going."

Mandell felt that he had been transported to a strange region in which conventional standards of conduct were unknown. He stared at Julian with his mouth open, but – as the latter was looking round the room with the expression of one regarding a horror for the last time – Mandell feared that if he remained silent any longer Julian would depart without further explanation.

"I'm afraid I don't understand."

"I've come to say good-bye; I'm going," Julian repeated.

"You don't mean that you're leaving this office?"

"Of course. Did you imagine that I should stay in it?"

"But – but – your career – the law?"

"If I'd ever cared tuppence about the law, I should have left here long ago."

Mandell's mind reeled. Till now he had believed that every man's ambition, secret or professed, was to be a lawyer: yet here was his own nephew telling him that he had never cared tuppence about the law, and that, if he had, he would have left his office!

"The law is a great calling," Mandell said mechanically. It was his favourite remark at home, so the words formed themselves automatically. "It's a great calling."

"Possibly."

Mandell began to fidget with the buttons of his waistcoat. He was making a fool of himself! What did it matter to him whether Julian stayed in the office or left it? He wanted him as a client, not a partner. It must have been the manner in which Julian had announced his departure that had surprised him and made him talk nonsense. Certainly no one had ever addressed him in such a tone. He only hoped the clerks in the outer office had not heard. Julian's voice was rather resonant. But there was no good in thinking about that now. Somehow he must retrieve the position. Probably that man-of-the-world manner, which he sometimes adopted with his clients, would be the most efficacious.

He leaned back in his chair and became expansive.

"You must excuse me, Julian. Fact is, I was thinking about a client's affairs when you came in and so I understood you imperfectly. You're entirely right, of course. With your fortune, you wouldn't stay here – naturally. You want to spread your wings. Very right and proper. And I don't suppose you will want to be burdened with business affairs——"

"I've arranged all that."

"I see . . . I *see*. Well, don't imagine that I am questioning the wisdom of those arrangements. Far from it. How could I, when the details are unknown to me?"

A long inviting pause, then recklessly:

"But this I will say, for *this* it is my duty to say: everyone is not as frank and as open as you are. I wish they were – but they're not."

"You mean: it's difficult to find a decent lawyer?"

Mandell hesitated. He did not mean that – he did not mean anything. He had one objective: to prolong the interview by talking about something. But Julian's question had to be answered and at last a couple of clichés darted into Mandell's mind.

"There are black sheep in every fold, Julian. But do remember this, my dear boy – blood is thicker than water. Naturally, you need professional advice, and I should be most happy – most happy——"

"Yes, I understand that – perfectly. I've given Minchin the key of my room upstairs. I don't think there's anything else, so I'd better go."

"But surely we shall be seeing you again?"

"I doubt it. Not for some time at any rate. Good-bye."

The door closed behind him. Mandell sat staring at nothing with his mouth open.

* * * * * *

Julian paused and looked round. He had reached Hyde Park Corner. His memories of the Mandell comedy had made him forget his surroundings. He glanced at his watch – one o'clock. After some hesitation he decided to go on to Piccadilly Circus, lunch at some restaurant, and possibly go to a matinée afterwards. He walked on slowly.

Piccadilly looked very gay in the sunlight. The breeze was a fragrant prophecy of spring. Suddenly the curious knowledge possessed him that he was destined to remember this day – that it would emerge from a host of forgotten days like the face of a friend in a crowd. Instantly the most trivial detail became arresting. A pretty woman glanced at him as she passed, and he knew that this stranger would be immortal in his memory – part of the sparkle and animation of this spring day with its sudden sunlight and glossy fleeting clouds. It was rapture to be young, rich, free! To respond with the whole of one's being to the drama of life! Yet only a few months ago he had been a prisoner in that stuccoed house in the cul-de-sac, with little likelihood of any companionship except that of Rawlings.

Rawlings! . . . They had not met for over three months, and no meeting was in prospect, but Julian repudiated all responsibility for the change in their relations. Rawlings had become an enigma. From the day on which he heard that Julian had inherited a fortune he avoided him. When Julian suggested that they should dine together he invented unconvincing excuses, and it was only the former's importunity that eventually secured a meeting one evening in Rawlings' room. It was not a success, however. Rawlings spoke little, drank a lot, and generally invested the proceedings with a valedictory atmosphere which depressed and irritated Julian.

"I've something for you," Julian had announced after a long silence, "and you've got to take it."

"Eh? What's that? Something for me?"

"Yes, and you've got to take it," Julian repeated. "Here it is."

It was a cheque for two hundred and fifty pounds.

Rawlings studied it at arm's length for nearly a minute.

"Why are you giving me this?"

"Because you've spent so much on me, and because——"

"The last cheque you gave me squared all that."

"Well, I – I want you to have it."

"I see . . . All right . . . Thanks."

Rawlings put the cheque on the mantelpiece, then helped himself to another drink.

Julian began to talk quickly, introducing one topic after another, striving to counterfeit the enthusiasm of former meetings. But, eventually, he realized that physical proximity is not necessarily intimacy. They were in the same room, but not in the same world. The man opposite him – huddled in a broken arm-chair, drinking whisky after whisky, and giving monosyllabic replies to questions – was a stranger whose name he happened to know.

Finally Julian's social technique failed and the conversation flickered out. When the silence had become menacing Julian consulted his watch with an emphatic gesture and announced:

"It's getting late. I'd better go."

Then several things happened so rapidly that – in retrospect – they seemed to have occurred simultaneously. Rawlings sprang to his feet, stood swaying heavily, then said in a voice which Julian had not heard before:

"Let's make this the end."

"I don't understand. Why?"

"Because it *is* the end."

"But *why?*"

"Because the world's the world, and you are you, and I am I. That's why. It doesn't matter much if you don't recognize the beginning of something, but you've got to recognize the end. I don't know much, but I do know that. Come on, let's shake hands and have done with it."

"You don't mean that we're not going to have any more nights together?"

"We've had our nights! We've had them, I tell you! For God's sake don't let's spoil 'em by pretending. Everything depends on its background – and the background's changed."

"I don't see why, just because I've come into money——"

"You *do* see why. You'd be a fool if you didn't. Will you stay in the same rooms, will you go to the same tailor, eat in the same restaurants, stick in Mandell's office? Not likely!"

"But a friend's different."

"Don't you believe it. And you don't – underneath. Are you going to travel third class for the rest of your life because you've a friend who can't afford to go first? Sentimentality never got anyone anywhere. You can't live to-day as if it were yesterday. Let's shake hands and have done with it."

They shook hands. For a second Rawlings' eyes blazed into his, then he groped his way down the dark stairs and out into the night. . . .

Julian looked round and discovered that he had reached the Ritz. It was a relief to become aware of his surroundings again, for the memories of that last meeting with Rawlings made him uncomfortable. This was not the first time they had claimed him and, on each occasion, he had been disturbed by the fact that Rawlings had foreseen that their friendship was doomed. Previously, however, Julian had evaded the issue by electing to believe that they would meet before long. But, to-day, after a separation of several months, the knowledge that their rupture was final defied casuistry. It had to be admitted, with several of its implications, greatly to the disturbance of his self-satisfaction.

Soon, however, he banished the subject by remembering that Dorothy was affected more intimately by the change in his fortunes than either Mandell or Rawlings. The discovery of this new theme was so opportune that he overlooked any significance in the fact that Dorothy occupied the third place in his review, not the first.

The news of Julian's fortune had not affected her in any way. She remained what she had always been, thereby differing conspicuously from Mandell and Rawlings. This continuity created a reaction in Julian in which pleasure and irritation were fairly evenly represented. Her fidelity to her own stature gave him pleasure: her lack of excitement irritated him, for it seemed to minimize his importance. But, with the passing of the weeks, irritation began to predominate, possibly as a result of Dorothy's assumption that he would join her in Cornwall almost immediately. It was difficult to make her understand that his business affairs were numerous; that more spacious horizons demanded a new mental orientation; and that the choice of a flat in the West End was an issue of first-class importance. But, as he had just written to say that he would arrive in Cornwall in less than a week, he decided that everything relating to Dorothy could be dismissed now as it would be discussed then.

He paused outside a bookshop and gazed at the throng hurrying past. The traffic seethed and surged round him like an incoming tide. He felt that the river of his life was about to encounter the roaring adventure of the open sea. A sense of liberation thrilled him. A consciousness of power throbbed in him like a new mysterious pulse.

He glanced at the books in the window and saw a volume which attracted him. He hesitated, not wanting to be burdened with a book for the whole of the afternoon, then, remembering his affluence, and the sense of authority it gave him over others, he decided to order the book and tell the man to send it to his rooms.

As he entered the shop a woman turned and looked at him – at first idly, then with vital interest. He stopped short and they gazed at each other. She was the only customer; the solitary attendant had disappeared. Her beauty and a subtle aura of elegance held him captive. A gleam of amusement flashed in her eyes, then she smiled. Julian stared at her, feeling inadequate, and not a little embarrassed. Then, just as footsteps at the back of the shop heralded the return of the attendant, she came towards him with outstretched hand.

"It's delightful to see you again."

He took her hand, but incredulity made any response impossible. His ineptitude intensified her amusement.

"Delightful!" she repeated. "I knew I should run into you somewhere."

An obsequious attendant appeared and proffered a volume for her inspection.

"I think this is the book you described."

"Yes, that's the one. Send it with the others, will you?"

"Certainly . . . certainly." The voice was almost a purr. "They shall be sent to Upper Brook Street immediately."

She turned to Julian.

"Having found you again, I'm not going to let you escape. Which way are you going?"

The attendant opened the door and they left the shop together.

B

When they had walked a few yards towards Piccadilly Circus, she paused:

"Better have luncheon somewhere, don't you think?"

"But – you – I – there's some mistake," Julian stammered, then added explosively: "I don't know you."

"That's why it's exciting."

"But why did you speak to me?"

"You're so obviously a unique person. Where do you think we'd better go? Some restaurant in Soho? Explanations in the street are so uncomfortable."

They crossed the Circus.

The encounter had happened so quickly that Julian felt a spectator, not a participant. But, even in his bewilderment, he recognized the dexterity with which she had created a situation and provided it with a sequel. He glanced at her diffidently. Not only was she disturbingly beautiful, it was evident that she also possessed an assurance equally remarkable. It inspired the least of her movements and individualized her fashionable clothes. It gave her a masculine background, and, as a result, her beauty acquired an enigmatic – almost paradoxical – quality. Julian's brief scrutiny convinced him that she was outside the boundaries of his experience.

She stopped at "The Fragonard" and looked up at him.

"What do you think?"

He indicated his ignorance with a gesture.

"I think it will do," she went on, "but we'll go to the little room at the back."

He followed her through the restaurant, aware that their appearance attracted attention, and was relieved to discover that the back room only contained six small tables, five of which were unoccupied. His sense of seclusion was deepened by the fact that, as the solitary window was more ornamental than practical, each table was softly illuminated.

She indicated one in a corner.

"Here?"

They sat down and almost immediately a waiter appeared with a menu.

"I'll order, shall I?" she asked. "You still seem rather bewildered."

"I wish you would," he replied gratefully.

While she made a selection, he studied her with candid curiosity. She was tall, she had dark curly hair, and her figure was one of Nature's inspirations. But it was the cameo beauty of the face which held Julian. It quickened many diverse emotions simultaneously. It tantalized his imagination while etching itself in his memory. He half forgot that she was a woman and gazed at her with the enthusiasm of an art student suddenly confronted by a masterpiece.

Consequently he experienced a shock on discovering that she had raised her eyes and that their glance was meeting his. Intense amusement flickered in their dark depths greatly to his discomfiture. He looked away awkwardly, feeling like an impertinent schoolboy.

"Well? And my age?"

"Your – *age!*"

"Surely it was an item in your inventory?"

"I never thought of it."

"I'm thirty-three."

"I can't believe you."

"And you are——" she broke off and glanced at him. "Twenty-one?"

"No – twenty-three."

"So that's settled. I suppose names come next as we must call each other something. But Christian names will do – much more exciting. Won't you tell me yours?"

"Julian."

"Mine's Stella."

"Stella!" he repeated. Then, after a silence: "Tell me this——" But she checked him with a quick movement of her hand. Just as the waiter reached the table, she asked:

"Have you been here before?"

"No, never." He hesitated, then added: "I rather like it, but I can't believe that the sun's shining outside; I feel that we're dining."

"Perhaps we will dine here one night."

They continued to talk generalities till the waiter disappeared, then Stella asked:

"What were you going to say just now?"

"I want to know why you spoke to me."

"I've told you. You're so obviously a unique person."

"But do you speak to everyone who looks like a unique person?"

"Invariably!"

She laughed at his bewilderment, then went on:

"Do tell me something about yourself."

"But I want to talk about you."

In spite of this assertion, however, his replies to her questions soon developed into a monologue which revealed the three main phases of his history. He told her of his life at The Hermitage; gave an account of the years he had spent in Mandell's office; and explained the circumstances in which he had inherited a fortune. But although he exerted himself to make this narrative interesting, one region of his consciousness was occupied exclusively with the beauty of this stranger who was listening to him with her eyes.

"Of course, coming into this money has rather bowled me over," Julian concluded. "So many things have become possible so suddenly that it's difficult to know what to do first. I don't believe I've realized it yet, but, all the same, I'm awfully excited, underneath. Still, I've made up my mind about one thing. I'm going to take a flat in the West End and then——"

"You're going to listen to me, Julian."

The note in her voice surprised him and he looked at her quickly.

"And the first thing you're going to promise me," she went on, "is that you won't tell every woman who speaks to you in the street that you've just inherited forty thousand pounds."

"But – but I'd tell you anything."

"Listen to me, you ridiculous child. What do you know about

me? Nothing – not even my full name. I speak to you in a shop, because the exceptional attracts me and I have a flair for discovering it; I suggest that we have luncheon together, and inside ten minutes you tell me everything about yourself, simply because you're attracted by my appearance. You haven't the remotest idea of the world you're in."

Julian flushed and began to protest, but she interrupted:

"Still, it's providential that I did speak to you. *I've* a remarkably clear idea of this planet – as you will discover. In the meantime, promise me that you won't talk to strangers – especially attractive ones – and tell them that you've just inherited a fortune."

"All right. I promise. But I'm glad I told you, all the same. You're going to let me see you again, aren't you?"

"Often!"

"Soon?"

She laughed at his impetuosity.

"Here's the waiter, and you've eaten nothing."

"How could I eat anything?" he demanded almost irritably.

She said nothing while the waiter attended to them, but amused herself by contrasting the compliments to which she was accustomed with those unconsciously proffered by Julian. She alone existed for him. Everything proclaimed it, though, possibly, his inability even to eat was the most gratifying testimony.

"Tell me about this flat you're thinking of taking."

Julian began to describe its situation and advantages with graphic enthusiasm, explaining that, although he had decided to take it, he did not propose actually to sign the agreement just yet. He added that he might be going away for a few days but that, on his return, he would settle everything finally as quickly as possible.

"I wish I could show it to you," he concluded, "because I know I'm ignorant about this sort of thing."

"I shouldn't be in a hurry, if I were you. I think you could get something with much more individuality."

They discussed possibilities at some length, then – inevitably, as it seemed to Julian – the conversation branched to his plans for the future. Time stole away unheeded, till Stella looked at her watch and announced:

"I must go."

"Don't go yet."

"I must. It's nearly three." She lowered her voice. "Even the gentleman in the corner opposite has had to stop eating and is becoming curious."

"But when am I going to see you again?"

She thought intently before she replied:

"I'm going away to-morrow, but only for a day or so. Shall we say Friday week, here? I'll meet you at this table at one-thirty."

She rose and he followed her through the restaurant. When she reached the pavement, she stopped and turned to him.

"Remember: you're not going to talk to strangers."

"I shan't talk to anyone till I see you again."

"Perhaps we'd better have full names now. What do you think?"

"Yes. Mine's Julian Grant."

"Just – Julian Grant?"

"Well, as a fact, it's Julian *Valentine* Grant."

"I see. Mine's Stella Farquharson."

There was a silence, then she added – half-mimicking the manner in which he had answered her question: "Well, as a fact, it's *Lady* Stella Farquharson."

"Then – are you married?"

"Certainly! Surely you noticed my ring? My husband is Sir James Farquharson."

"I've just heard of him."

"Everyone has just heard of him."

She held out her hand.

"What are you going to do now?"

"I haven't the remotest idea," Julian replied mournfully.

"You could fill in an hour by having something to eat."

A moment later she left him. . . .

Julian wandered aimlessly through the intricacies of Soho, seeing and hearing nothing. Exciting thoughts darted and flashed through his mind like dragon-flies. She was beautiful! He had attracted her! She had promised to meet him again! His imagination luxuriated in glowing possibilities. Then memory began to reproduce attitudes, gestures, sentences, till he found he was involved in an attempt to recapitulate their conversation.

In due course this process led to the discoveries that his

account of himself had contained no reference to Dorothy, and that, in view of his engagement with Stella for Friday week, he would have to postpone his visit to Cornwall.

C

During the ten days which separated him from his next meeting with Stella Julian experienced the successive stages of infatuation. For the first two days he seemed to see her everywhere, then, without warning, this visual memory abandoned him so absolutely that he was unable to remember one of her features, or even the line of her figure. At times her voice enriched every silence: at others, its music eluded him. Then – when he had despaired finally of ever recalling face, figure, voice, attitude, or gesture – a vision of her flashed from the darkness to mock his sluggard imagination.

When three days had passed it seemed to Julian that nothing had happened to him before their meeting. Life had begun in that bookshop in Piccadilly. Also he recapitulated their conversation so frequently – elaborated and analysed it so imaginatively – that soon he was unable to believe that they had spent little more than an hour together. To isolate that hour from the hopes, emotions, and excitements it had quickened proved impossible. It represented the end of everything he had known and the beginning of something new, mysterious, which fascinated and frightened him simultaneously.

When six days had passed, however, and the world surrounding him remained unaffected by the revolution which was transforming his universe, a doubt from the darkness stabbed him like an assassin's dagger. Perhaps all this was a dream – perhaps Stella did not exist!

To Julian's romanticism this possibility soon became the probable, thereby bringing the end of the world appreciably nearer. He began to consider ways of establishing her identity. The idea of consulting the police occurred to him, but he dismissed it impatiently. A policeman was too prosaic a person to be honoured by any such inquiry. Besides, it took very great courage to ask a policeman anything. No; it would be better to try that man in the bookshop. But at this point Julian remembered that the attendant had told Stella he would send her books to Upper Brook Street. That was enough for the moment. He would ascertain whether such a street existed. That would be evidence in its degree.

Having proved that Upper Brook Street was a fact – and having stared at the exterior of "The Fragonard" for half an hour, in order to convince himself of its actuality – Julian's terror diminished. Finally, having consulted the telephone directory, thereby establishing that Sir James Farquharson, Bt., M.P., lived in Upper Brook Street, Julian was satisfied that Stella did exist, but this satisfaction was qualified by the discovery that her husband was also a reality.

He had been so obsessed by Stella that he had forgotten she was married. Now he was forced to realize it. At first he felt that she had been guilty of disloyalty to him, but, recognizing eventually that such an indictment lacked a logical foundation, he began to speculate on the desirability of marriage as an institution. Having speedily arrived at the conclusion that, in the instance which interested him, marriage meant that Farquharson owned Stella, that they lived in the same house, and that consequently he saw her every day, Julian was soon in flaming revolt against the immorality of such a relationship. Humour and intelligence both abandoned him. His infatuation demanded romantic backgrounds, infinite freedom, thrilling possibilities. A husband represented the ordinary, the pedestrian, the world of fact. Stella belonged to the plane of poetry, glamour, imagination. It was monstrous that any man owned her!

There was only one hope. Possibly her husband was old, really old – over forty. But one thing was certain – marriage was a damnable institution.

When this fine frenzy of indignation passed, however, Julian suddenly remembered that *he* was engaged to be married. But this knowledge, as it related to that void in which he had existed before meeting Stella, seemed as unsubstantial as if it concerned a stranger. Nevertheless it served to remind him that he must tell Dorothy that it was impossible for him to join her in Cornwall. He considered writing, but, as a letter would necessitate explanations, he decided to wire, which he did, and instantly returned to the world of Stella.

His impatience to see her again made him irritable and irritation induced a more critical survey of their meeting. He remembered that she had been amused by his inability to eat and this,
in turn, reminded him that she had eaten with epicurean enjoy-
ment. In retrospect, this seemed somewhat gross. A beautiful
woman ought not to eat – anyhow in public – and certainly not
when she was listening to him. It lowered her ever so slightly in
his imagination. Romance demanded stature: a repudiation of
the material. Imagine Juliet eating a sandwich on that balcony!
But that was not all. How alert she had been! *He* had forgotten
the waiter's existence, but, on each occasion, she had been aware
of his approach. She had even noticed the man in the opposite
corner. She had mentioned his concentration on his food and
how, finally, when he had had to cease eating, he had become
curious concerning them. All these details only deepened the
first impression she had created, but nevertheless they irritated
him. He wished she had been as unconscious of her surroundings as he had. He wanted desperately to believe that their meeting had meant as much to her as it had to him. For, to Julian,
being infatuated, and so in a state of emotional chaos, only the
impossible seemed the desirable. Limits, rules, institutions were
regarded as insults hurled at him by a jealous world.

One result of this critical survey of their meeting was a determination to cross-examine Stella at the next. With this in view
Julian memorized a series of questions, decided not to discuss
himself, and elaborated a stratagem for discovering Farquharson's age.

Despite these logical preparations, however, when the Friday
arrived, he reached "The Fragonard" at eleven-thirty, immacu-
lately dressed, then wandered about Soho while his imagination
stretched him first on one rack then another. Thus, no sooner
had he vanquished the fear that Stella would not keep the appointment, than he was tortured by the doubt that possibly he
was out in his reckoning and that to-day was Saturday. He endured for a quarter of an hour before he remembered that a
newspaper would provide proof as to the day's identity. Finally,
having had his shoes cleaned twice, with an interval of half an
hour between the two operations, and having bought a button-
hole at twelve-thirty and thrown it away at a quarter to one, he

entered "The Fragonard" at one o'clock, sat down at the corner table, wholly and desperately convinced that, whether or not Stella existed, she would certainly not appear.

She arrived precisely at one-thirty. Also, at one-thirty, Julian's carefully prepared programme collapsed.

She greeted him with the information that she had found a flat which she thought might attract him, adding that they could go and inspect it the next morning if he had nothing better to do. After which she consulted the menu, made a discriminating choice, then asked Julian what he had been doing with himself since their last meeting. She smiled at his incoherent reply; insisted that on this occasion he must eat something; reminded him that others were present and that, even if they had been alone, it would be a little embarrassing to be stared at as if she were a monstrosity of some kind. But these hints were conveyed so graciously, with such delightful little gestures of the hand, that their chief effect was to establish a deeper intimacy.

But what amazed and excited Julian was the manner in which she conveyed the most glorious information in a parenthesis and in a tone which implied that it was totally unimportant. Thus, when he asked her whether it was really true that she would show him the flat to-morrow, she replied:

"Yes. I want you to see it. We'll go round about twelve. I shall be free during the next fortnight. But you mustn't pretend to like the flat if you don't."

She would be free during the next fortnight. Did that mean – could it mean – that she would meet him frequently? The question glowed in his eyes, and he believed that her smile was an affirmative answer.

Then something happened, something which welled from an unknown depth, which he was as powerless to control as he would have been to create. He lowered his head and heard himself say:

"You know – of course – that you're – beautiful."

When the words were spoken, stillness possessed him. He sat motionless, awaiting a cataclysm.

"I'm glad you admire me, Julian."

There was a different note in her voice. It conveyed sincerity, pleasure, pathos.

She began to talk rapidly, giving him instructions in the manner of one discussing trivialities. She explained that if they were to meet frequently they would inevitably run into people she knew. Then, in a few sentences, she told him the name and address of the people at whose house they had met, briefly described them, and indicated that she was relying on him to collaborate with her effectively in this fiction.

"There mustn't be any mistakes, Julian."

"I shan't make any mistakes."

"I wish I were as certain. You might be word-perfect, but your expression might be wrong. It won't do for you to stare at me."

"I shan't stare at you."

"You're staring at me now."

"Oh, well; there's no one here you know."

"Are you certain?"

"You'd have spotted them."

"But you mustn't count on me! You're hopeless. I shall have to hide you until I've civilized you."

"I don't care what you do so long as I see you."

"Finish your coffee. We must go."

"Go!"

"Yes. I'm taking you to a matinée." . . .

That night Julian's exaltation banished sleep. The day had so triumphed over his expectations, the future promised so much more than yesterday's hopes, that he abandoned himself to an ecstasy which surged through him like a flood tide.

He had asked none of the questions he had prepared; he still knew nothing of Stella's life; he had no conception of her plans or her motives; he only knew that she was beautiful – that he had told her she was beautiful – and that they were to meet frequently. She had become the map of his life: everything outside her was non-existent. Books, thoughts, projects, which had formerly excited him, were as remote as nursery toys. His old life had ended. Dorothy, Mandell, Rawlings had dwindled to ghosts. Something new, something which he did not understand, had leapt to life in him like an armed man, clamouring for conquest. He surrendered to this strange force, half fearfully, half exultingly. All the frontiers of his being had extended. It would be necessary to explore in order to discover these new boundaries.

Of his former self only his name remained. He had become the instrument of a mysterious power which exalted and subdued him, revealing and concealing itself simultaneously. A power which captured the whole of his imagination but refused it the satisfaction of a single definite image. The fact that now it was denying him sleep seemed to symbolize its tyrannical disregard of everything formerly accepted as normal. It was at the command of this new power that he had told Stella she was beautiful. And now – even now as he paced restlessly up and down the room – a secret knowledge whispered that the demands of this dark power would become articulate, no matter how stern his resolutions might be, and despite the obstacles created by his inexperience.

He paused before a long mirror and gazed at his reflection. He was young, handsome. The poise of the head and every line of the body denoted vitality.

He felt that he was seeing himself for the first time, and he had the curious sensation that he was naked.

D

The flat which Stella had found looked down on one of those rather broad passages which run from Piccadilly to Jermyn Street. It was at the top of a two-storeyed house. A hosier's shop accounted for the ground floor, a lady sold antiques and bric-à-brac on the first, the floor above being the flat. It was reached by a narrow staircase and consisted of two rooms and a bathroom. It owed its individuality partly to the fact that it was a surprise to discover that the second floor was designed for private residence. A stranger climbing to the upper storey, having passed two shops on his journey, would expect to find storerooms. Instead of which, he would enter a bright, if somewhat diminutive, flat with attractively-shaped rooms, unaccountably quiet considering their proximity to the Piccadilly traffic.

Julian had only to see the flat in order to decide to take it, much to Stella's amusement. She had some difficulty in preventing him from going immediately to the agents to sign a twenty-one years' lease.

"But you must think it over, Julian."

"Why?"

"Well, how will you arrange your things?"

"Haven't got any things. We'll buy some to fit the rooms."

"But it may be too hot in summer, and too cold in winter. It is at the top – you realize that?"

"The rooms I've lived in for years are at the top. I'm not particular. I like this awfully. I shall take it. Let's go and buy the furniture."

"Now? The flat will have to be decorated first."

"All right. Let's go to a decorator."

"But you don't even know what the rent is."

"I don't care what it is. I'm going to take it. I've a good many books – and I expect to buy hundreds – so the sitting-room will look like a library. You'll help me – won't you? – about the decorations, and the furniture, and all the rest of it?"

"I'll help you. You are certain you really like it?"

"Certain! Only you could have found it. Dine with me my first night here."

"If it's possible."

"I shan't move in till it is possible."

During the next few weeks Julian was occupied wholly with details concerning the flat. It seemed to him at the time that it was he who made the necessary decisions regarding the more important arrangements, only realizing in retrospect that Stella had been responsible for every one of them. The question of service was an example.

"Naturally, the servant will have to sleep out," Julian remarked, when the flat was ready for occupation.

"You'll only have one in the morning, I suppose?"

"But I shan't always want to dine out."

"You can have dinner sent in. You'll get a much better one. Don't you think it would get on your nerves to have a servant here all day?"

"Perhaps you're right. Anyway, I'm moving in on Saturday. You'll dine here, won't you?"

Stella thought intently.

"It will have to be Monday, Julian. Better come here for coffee after dinner. Much simpler."

"All right. Then – remember – I want to ask you all sorts of questions. We've met often enough lately, but they've been business meetings. You must tell me about yourself."

"Very well. We'd better dine early – absurdly early. Shall we say seven o'clock?"

"Yes, and come straight on here afterwards."

They reached the flat soon after eight on the Monday evening. The weather was boisterous. Every now and again heavy drops of rain lashed the window-panes.

He took her cloak and she stood in front of the fire, stretching her hands towards the blaze. It was the first time Julian had seen her in evening clothes. He watched her in silence for nearly a minute.

"Well?" She turned to him with a smile.

"I've made one discovery about you – only one."

"Only one? In all these weeks? What is it?"

"You're not to laugh if it's wrong. It's this. Nearly always you create an impression of complete assurance. You know what I mean? You look as if you're capable of taking on the world single-handed. Then, very rarely, suddenly, you look as if you had lost your weapons."

"That's very penetrating."

"You're laughing."

"I'm not." Then, after a pause: "Aren't you going to sit down?"

"Yes – you sit there. This is marvellous. I can't believe it."

"I can't – sometimes." Then suddenly: "Tell me, Julian, what would you be doing now if we hadn't become friends?"

"I don't know really. Probably I should be in Cornwall."

"Why Cornwall?"

"I may tell you some time. To-night we're going to talk about you. Who are you, Stella? What are you? I don't know the least thing about you."

"Smoke a cigarette, and I'll tell you. I didn't tell you before because there might have been no point in it."

"I don't understand."

"We might have been bored with each other after a few meetings."

"Bored!"

"You never know. Where shall I begin? I'm rather a lonely person. Do you know that?"

"But you know hundreds of people."

"Which isn't a bad definition of loneliness. I've no brothers, no sisters, no relatives – or, rather, I've not seen any of them for years and would much rather not. My mother died when I was eighteen. I had just returned from a very grand boarding school. She was a darling. My father said she was so supernormal that she seemed exceptional. So, at eighteen, he and I found ourselves alone together."

"What was he like?" Julian asked impetuously.

"He was the most remarkable person I've ever known – the only one who has influenced me."

"What was his name?"

"Oliver Prescott."

"Well, what happened?"

"Mother's death removed the only restraint Oliver had ever known. He was an adventurer – not in the bad sense, till much later. He was in the army originally and won the V.C. in some frontier trouble, but he sent in his papers a few years after he married. When I knew him, so to speak, he had been everywhere, done all sorts of things and made nothing of any of them. How shall I describe him to you? He had the temperament of an artist – with none of an artist's talent. He was interested in everything – and never held long by anything. He had not been faithful to my mother physically, but she was the only stability he had ever known. When she died, he discovered me."

"How old was he then?"

"Forty-one. He married absurdly young."

"And you were eighteen?"

"Yes."

"Go on."

Stella laughed. "You really want to hear all this?"

"Every word of it."

"Very well, but tell me when you get bored. Oliver discovered me with enthusiasm. I should tell you that, on the few occasions when he was at home during my holidays, the life I experienced was very different from that at the boarding school. We were educated on the assumption that we should all lead lives of luxurious leisure – and that everything else was nonsense."

"Was your father rich?"

"He had what he earned, which was usually nothing. My mother had the money – and left it to him."

"Where did you live, Stella?"

"In Chelsea. It seems odd to be telling you all this."

But Julian was insistent.

"What did you mean when you said just now that your father *discovered* you?"

"He did discover me. He hadn't taken much notice of me before, but now he talked to me with the utmost frankness on every conceivable subject. Finally, he announced that my intelligence had survived education. An achievement, he added, which was extremely rare in the long history of England."

"So it is – almost unknown."

"He was a queer man. Not easy to describe. He had a passion for the exceptional. If he hadn't, I might not have spoken to you in that bookshop. I told you he's the only person who has influenced me."

"You love him, Stella?"

"I did – and I do."

"He's dead then?"

"Of course he is."

"Sorry! How stupid of me!"

Julian threw his cigarette away. There was a long silence broken only by the rain beating on the window-panes.

"Do go on," he said at last.

"What? Oh yes, of course! My mother's death meant that Oliver had money and so could indulge every whim. He sold the house in Chelsea, and then we roved all over Europe together."

"You were with him all the time?"

"Yes. They were incredible years. They don't seem like the past, they seem like a former world. He hid nothing from me. He had a mania for odd friends. I met them all – and most of his mistresses. As his taste was excellent, I never encountered a stupid man or an ugly woman."

"God! How marvellous!"

"I've had to get used to both. But that comes later. You want to ask something. What is it?"

"It's only this," Julian began, then hesitated. "Well, what I mean is, didn't he think his type of life might affect you?"

"He'd worked all that out. He said to me once: 'You've will, character. You demand quality. You won't make a fool of yourself. Or, if you do, you'll know you're doing it – so it won't matter.' I don't know whether he was right or wrong, but that's what he said."

"He'd plenty of money all this time?"

"Oh dear, no! He was far too generous. We were often very hard up. And, once a year, Oliver got drunk – and remained drunk for a month."

"What did you do, Stella?"

"Waited."

"How oddly you said that! What else happened?"

"All sorts of things. Sometimes he'd get a kind of religious mania. He'd suddenly begin to study some strange creed. This activity usually preceded one of his drinking bouts. He said that drink was a substitute for God."

"For – *God!*"

"Yes. Does that surprise you? He said that everything was a substitute for God: drink, art, travel, women – everything."

"Do you think that, Stella?"

"I think one world at a time is enough."

Julian said nothing. Suddenly Stella exclaimed:

"Julian! We've forgotten the coffee!"

"Good Lord, yes! I'll make it."

But Stella doubted his proficiency, so he followed her into the tiny kitchen. As he watched her prepare the coffee – in a manner which convinced him of the amateur nature of his own method – it seemed unbelievable that they were here together alone. He glanced at her bare shoulders, the line of her neck, the dark curly hair. She was beautiful, and she was here with him – alone. He watched her delightful hands, marvelling at their distinction and the dexterity of their movements. But although she was so near him, she seemed remote – separated from him by her knowledge and experience no less than her beauty. She was more a stranger now than when he had known nothing about her.

In a few minutes they returned to the sitting-room. "Who taught you to make coffee, Stella?"

"Oliver."

"It's odd how you call him by his Christian name."

"I always used to. He liked it."

"How long were you abroad with him?"

"Seven or eight years. We came to London fairly often – naturally. On one visit, some time before we came back for good, we met James Farquharson. I was about twenty-four then. He was thirty-six. He went quite mad about me. We really went abroad again to escape."

"You weren't in love with him then?"

"Neither then nor now. A year later we had to return. Funds were exhausted. Also, the craziest idea possessed Oliver, and he plunged into the only folly he had not committed. He suddenly imagined he was a financier."

"But you say he had no money?"

"My dear Julian, financiers operate with other people's money. Oliver had great charm, he was very eloquent. You felt it an honour to be robbed by him. He capitalized those gifts and became a company promoter. He floated several companies. One, unfortunately, was successful. Oliver saw himself as a Napoleon of finance. He became reckless. Finally, he committed a fraud."

"A *fraud!*"

"I never understood the precise nature of this 'irregularity,' as he called it. I remember that he explained it to me as 'the sort of thing which, if you do in war, you get a V.C. and if you do the same sort of thing in finance you get a broad arrow. Two different types of decoration.' Anyhow, it was imperative to get ten thousand pounds inside twenty-four hours."

"Hadn't he any friends?"

"He had cost his friends quite a lot when he had reached this stage. He committed the 'irregularity' because he couldn't raise another sixpence, despite superman efforts. So, one way and another, the shape of Wormwood Scrubbs prison was becoming pretty clearly defined."

"But what did he *say*, Stella?"

"He said: 'I'll get five years' certain – perhaps seven. That doesn't bother me a damn. Give me quiet in which to think – never had any yet. It's you, Stella. What the devil will you do? Not a bob, and a name with a broad arrow on it.' That's what he said."

"And what did you do?"

"That night I went to Farquharson."

She rose slowly, then stood leaning against the chimney-piece, staring down into the fire.

"I went to Farquharson," she repeated. "I explained everything. He said he'd save Oliver if I would marry him. I told him I would marry him provided he realized that I did not love him – and that I was not to be cross-examined regarding my actions or my friends. On the other hand, I promised that there should never be a scandal. He agreed to everything with pathetic enthusiasm. Oliver was saved. I was married within a month. A year later, Oliver caught a chill and died. He cried like a child on his deathbed because he said he'd let me down."

She swung round quickly, making a gesture as if to repulse her memories. Julian rose instinctively and stood facing her. Her eyes were filled with tears, but the leash of her will still held her emotions in check.

The next instant Julian's arms were round her.

"I love you! I love you! You can do what you like – I don't care – you know now. Even if you never see me again, I'm glad I've told you. I never knew that anyone could be so lovely as you are. I can't forget you for an hour – day or night. I'll never forget you – never!"

The courage of extremity possessed him. His grasp tightened and he kissed her lips. Then he left her, flung himself into a chair, and buried his face in his hands.

Gradually a new silence filled the room – a silence which wove mysterious bonds between them. The inevitable had happened, but to each it seemed unexpected, strange, miraculous. The future was conspiring with the present. Issues were being determined – which they might discuss, deny, or question – but these issues were in the keeping of a will which belonged to neither, as it was born of both.

A coal fell from the grate. Stella moved slightly and her dress rustled. The rain pattered against the window.

She went and sat on the arm of his chair. He remained motionless, apparently unaware of her proximity. He was not thinking of what had happened, of her, or of anything. It seemed to him that at any moment something which he did not understand would be made clear. It would not be explained – it would be shown.

She began to caress his hair with her hand. She was not looking at him. She was gazing at the point of her shoe, deliberately considering whether her green shoes were more effective than those she was wearing. It was a device to elude thought. This silence was dear to her; it was more subtle than any caress, more persuasive than any speech. It symbolized her surrender. All subsequent surrenders would be less than it, though derived from it.

She slipped down and sat at his feet, leaning her head against his knees. A minute passed, then she looked up at him.

"Stella!"

"Poor darling!"

"I was terribly afraid you'd be angry."

"How could I be angry?"

"Well, it was frightful nerve. Can't imagine how I had the pluck."

The schoolboy phrases amused her and she laughed.

"We shall have to be serious, Julian."

"I *am* serious. Never more serious in my life. I'm done for. I depend on you hopelessly. I'll be like a madman when you go. For God's sake lean back so that I can see you."

"There!"

"But you must be uncomfortable."

"No – it's rather a favourite attitude. I want to ask you something, Julian. Have you ever had a lover?"

"No."

"Why not? The Hermitage upbringing?"

"Partly, I suppose. I knew nothing when I came to London. Rawlings enlightened me. He used to go with street-walkers. I couldn't do that. I don't know why – but I couldn't . . . *Stella?*"

"I love you, my dear."

He took her hands and raised her as he rose.

"You mean you'll——"

"Yes, but wait! You've got to listen to me, Julian. You must listen. You——"

"You darling!"

"Julian!"

"By God, you're adorable!"

"You *shall* listen, or I'll go and never come here again."

"I'll listen."

"Go and sit over there – and smoke while I think."

Julian lit a cigarette and watched her wander about the room, moving first one thing then another, finally replacing them in their original positions.

And he knew that whatever she said he would only half understand, for the knowledge that she loved him was music which became more rapturous every minute.

"I can't think clearly," Stella said at last. "I never thought all this would happen yet. I suppose I'm terribly in the wrong – I don't know. Still, something like this would have happened to you sooner or later. You might have a more disastrous beginning. But one thing's certain, Julian. Everything will have to wait."

"Wait!"

"Yes. Do listen! You've met no one, been nowhere. I shall save myself suffering if this doesn't happen. It can only end one way."

"You must be mad!"

"I should be if I deceived myself. But all that doesn't matter. I shall be going away soon."

"What for?"

"My dear Julian, one doesn't stay in town all the summer."

"But where are you going?"

"Scotland in due course. We always do exactly the same things, each year, at exactly the same time, with exactly the same people, to whom we always say exactly the same things. Surely you realize that I'm on the social treadmill?"

"I only realize that I want to see you every day."

"But you can't – and I should become as commonplace as breakfast if you did. No, you go away, too – and see what happens. And then we'll meet in the autumn."

"It's going to be absolute hell, Stella. Where the devil shall I go?"

"Spain. The women are glorious."

"You can laugh, if you like, but it's no joke for me. I'm not going anywhere. I shall stay here and wait till you come back."

"Do as you like, but I think that would be stupid."

"Can I write to you?"

"No, never! You understand? *Never.* I can't be too emphatic about that. You must promise me that you will never write."

"All right, I promise. You're awfully serious."

"I've reason to be. And don't tell anyone about me, Julian, will you? I'm sorry to be tiresome like this, but you're inexperienced, darling, and I cannot make one mistake – not one. You do understand, don't you?"

"I understand. Simply tell me what I'm to do – or what I'm not to do – and I'll obey you blindly. But there's one thing I shan't do – and that is change. I shall be here, waiting for you, when you come back. There's no doubt about that – none!"

After a pause he went on:

"There's more I want to know——"

"Oh, Julian, my angel, not to-night!"

"Are you tired?"

"Exhausted. So exhausted that I want you to let me go soon. It's different for you. I have to wear a mask – and masks have to fit. I hope you will never discover that fact. Let's sit down till I go, and we won't talk."

"All right. Lie on the couch and let me sit by your side."

"Is that wise?"

"I only want to look at you – honestly, that's all. Just to look at you – and try to believe that it's all true. There! You're marvellous. You don't know what you've done to me, Stella. I can't recognize anything. Can you understand that? I've lost everything I ever possessed – even my memories . . . I know I promised not to talk."

"It's all right, my dear."

"Swear that you won't change your mind."

"I promise you."

"And you do love me?"

"I do love you."

E

Their subsequent meetings, prior to Stella's departure, were few in number and brief in duration. Julian felt that this neglect represented a policy, although Stella attributed it to engagements which could neither be broken nor postponed. He resented it, feeling that he had rights over her, and not realizing that her recognition of those rights differed from his. His imagination was concerned wholly with himself: hers wholly with him. She was conscious of difficulties, dangers, potential sufferings which did not exist for Julian. He was narrowed to one end: how and when to take. She was concerned with one problem: how and when to give. She bore a double burden: a realization of his inexperience, and the knowledge of her responsibility. Julian saw only the sunlight: Stella was aware of every shadow.

It was only when she had gone – and then only during certain periods – that Julian was able to regard their relations in less emotional terms. He remained in London, for, in spite of Stella's advice, he decided that there was companionship in daily association with scenes reminiscent of her. They confirmed her reality when doubt invaded him. He peopled his world with memories and hopes, and so lived in a void, suspended between the immediate past and the immediate future.

During certain periods, however – frequently separated by several days – a mental clarity suddenly illumined a number of facts; or revealed a relationship between incidents hitherto regarded as unconnected.

On one occasion he was astounded to discover that, whereas his infatuation for Stella had deprived him of any feeling concerning Dorothy or Rawlings, memories of The Hermitage began to emerge more and more insistently. Possibly the contrast between his present ecstasies and the ideals of Nathan Grant were responsible. For Julian realized that his father would have seen in these ecstasies merely the delirium of sexual imaginings. That was the fact, and to Julian it was fantastic. This rapture which possessed him was Life! It was Life, beating urgently on the very door of his being! He could no more disown it, deny it, or dominate it than he could quell the rhythm of his pulse. He had not invoked it. It had risen before him like a mountain, created in a night by an earthquake – offering the possibility of new altitudes, unimagined perspectives. What had he to do with those petty renunciations which cowards nicknamed courage? In his outlook, it dwarfed his father to imagine those who would range themselves with him and applaud his values. Mandell would be among them – Mandell, who had died to every emotional impulse, every generosity of heart or mind, years and years ago! And those queer, lost, unhappy people who used to visit The Hermitage and discuss their souls endlessly, they, too, would judge and condemn him! Why was it that his father – who had been an eagle compared with these nonentities and psychic invalids – would join with them in sentencing him? Nathan Grant, totally removed from them in every other particular, would have echoed their meaningless jargon concerning sexual morality! He would have talked about adultery. Adultery! What a word! It was more like a kick.

Well, he – Julian – had one answer to all of them. And that answer could be stated in one word – Stella!

Nevertheless, when this indignation abated, he recognized that – confronted by the memory of Nathan Grant – he had been stung to passionate eloquence in his own defence. No such necessity existed in regard to Dorothy and Rawlings. As to the former, she had written weeks ago to ask what had prevented his coming to Cornwall. He had not replied – and he knew that he would never reply. No heated mental controversy had preceded that decision. It had formed like an icicle, and hung like one in his brain. As to Rawlings, their rupture had been of his making. It was the extravagant whim of an eccentric man – and had to be accepted as such. At the time he had protested, without result, and he had given him a cheque for two hundred and fifty pounds. Possibly, as things had turned out, he did not regret Rawlings' decision. He had done nothing to inspire it and would certainly do nothing to reverse it.

Once, while thinking about Rawlings, it occurred to him that Stella was his successor. It was Rawlings who had initiated him to a degree into the intricacies of life as it is lived. Now he stood on the threshold of an infinitely deeper initiation represented by Stella's experience, position, and above all by her love. Julian recognized his ignorance. He knew that such knowledge of the world as he possessed originated either in Rawlings' underworld discoveries, or in books, and he realized therefore that it was derivative. Valid individual experience could only be acquired by entry into the arena. He was confident, impatient, and inactivity made him irritable.

But although he was obsessed by himself during this period,

and consequently indifferent to others, nevertheless he noticed that he attracted more attention than formerly. Many women glanced at him in the street – a fact which surprised him, for he did not realize that the emotional awakening he was experiencing enhanced his appearance and vitalized his whole personality. These tributes to his attraction did not interest him individually, but, collectively, they created a secret satisfaction, for they revealed that Stella's preference was less miraculous than he had imagined.

Always his thoughts returned to her, and it was as a result of endlessly analysing his memories that he became aware of a relationship between certain of her actions and statements which hitherto he had not detected. In retrospect, it became significant that – at their first meeting – she had half dissuaded him from taking the flat he had described to her; and – at their second – she had greeted him with the announcement that she had discovered a flat which she thought would attract him. Had she made a decision during their first visit to "The Fragonard"? Had she willed, or foreseen, the future?

The question excited him. His infatuation had obscured the significance of certain events at the time of their occurrence, but now, owing to her absence, it emerged with increasing clarity. He remembered how she had advised him to have a servant only in the mornings. Had she known – then – that they would dine together in the flat frequently; that she would visit him in the afternoon and sometimes at night, and that therefore privacy was essential? It was obvious that she had known, but none the less the knowledge intoxicated him. So her intentions regarding him were not born of a whim, they were based on a policy. The very situation of the flat was a tribute to her foresight. For her to be seen entering the building would require no explanation – she was on her way to Mrs. Peters' shop on the first floor. She had foreseen and calculated everything. God! To be so beautiful and to be so practical! It was genius!

One by one, he remembered the instructions she had given him: not to make himself conspicuous by staring at her in public; not to mention her to anyone; never to write to her – no matter what the circumstances might be. How emphatic she had been! She had covered the risk of encountering one or other of her friends when she was with him by contriving that fiction concerning their meeting. He remembered the way she had said: "There mustn't be any mistakes, Julian." Also, how intently she thought before replying when he suggested a date for their next meeting. All these details possessed an organic unity. It was not remarkable that – long ago, when reviewing their first visit to "The Fragonard" – he had been surprised by her awareness of every movement in the restaurant. He began to understand why she possessed such assurance, and why he had told her that, usually, she looked as if she could engage the world single-handed. She brought the imagination of an artist to the organization of the practical. Her desires did not blind her as his blinded him. Her father had recognized her qualities: he had told her that she had will, character. Julian's admiration began to soar on mightier pinions.

This flight was arrested, however, by a new speculation – and a dark one. Might not this skill, foresight, and diplomacy be the cumulative result of much experience with many lovers?

Certain questions have only to be asked for the least desirable of all possible answers to seem the only one. Jealousy darted into Julian's mind, corrupting his thoughts to spies. It ransacked his memories, chose witnesses with specious impartiality, prompted their evidence, till suspicion darkened into certainty. Only with the return of reason did he appreciate the omissions, the crudity of the deductions, the insistence on the basest interpretations. But, at its first onslaught, jealousy blinded its victim in order that he should have no alternative but to listen.

A frenzy possessed Julian. . . . All those years she had spent in Europe – she must have been besieged by men! Her father's type of life was itself a provocation. She had admitted that she had known only interesting men during that vagabondage – but she had given no indication of her relations with them. She had met her father's mistresses – it was inconceivable that she had not had lovers. And, after marriage – a marriage to a man she did not love, and to whom she had dictated terms safeguarding her freedom – was it to be believed that she had been faithful? It was grotesque to imagine it! She was an expert in deception. *That* was the explanation of her foresight. But why had she left him to guess? Or did she consider him so inexperienced, so unintelligent, that he would remain permanently blind to the obvious? One thing was certain: he would demand to know everything on her return.

But this ferocity tormented him only for a few days and with its cessation came a vision of Stella to humble and console him.

He was sitting in an arm-chair, unable to read, when he remembered the night she had sat at his feet looking up at him. He saw her again as she had been then. Her dark eyes gazed into his with an absolute sincerity. Her beauty, her distinction, the atmosphere of elegance which isolated her, all refuted the indictment of his jealousy. It was valid only in her absence. Present, she created her own standard and could be judged only by her peers.

In an instant Julian's imagination became her inspired advocate. What was the evidence against her? The years she had spent in Europe with her father? The type of life he had lived? The fact that she did not love her husband? And who had supplied all this evidence? Stella! Why, good God! she needn't have told him a word of it! She had voluntarily given him her confidence and he had used it to defame her. She had told the truth – all the truth – because it was her nature to reveal everything or nothing. She had honoured him, and he had insulted her. He would kiss her feet when she returned and beg forgiveness. There were no questions to ask. She had volunteered so much that her silences commanded respect. . . .

The days went by. Julian's inner intensity was such that they seemed to pass quickly. Although he was occupied exclusively with his own thoughts, in one sense he was incapable of thinking. His mind had become a stage on which desires dramatized themselves. He was the cast and the audience of his passion. He ached for Stella's return, and discovered an infinity of variety in the monotony of that longing. Hopes jostled memories in the wings of his mind. Curiosity, deep as his ignorance, issued challenge after challenge to his imagination. Fear, wonder, awe, egotism, worship held the centre of the stage in turn. Now the scene was set in shadowless sunshine; now it was a darkness haunted by voices calling to him in a language he did not understand.

Daily, hourly, her dominion over him widened and deepened. Her absence collaborated with his imagination to effect his complete surrender.

F

She had promised to come to him the first afternoon she was free after her return. As the autumn approached, Julian kept daily vigil in the flat from two o'clock onwards. He had dinner sent in and spent hour after hour listening for a step on the stairs. Not once since her departure had he attempted to imagine the consequences of the relationship soon to be established between them. His need for her was too absolute. A starving man does not worry greatly as to what he will do when hunger is satisfied.

Early in October, one afternoon just before five o'clock, a ring of the bell pealed through the flat. Julian leapt to his feet. It couldn't be! He had been listening so intently——

It was Stella. No sooner had he opened the door than she darted in and closed it behind her. Julian had scarcely realized her presence before both her hands seized his.

"Well?"

"Stella!"

"Glad?"

"Can't believe it – don't believe it."

Her laugh answered him.

"Come into the sitting-room. I can't see you in this accursed hall."

Still holding her hands, he backed into the sitting-room, drawing her after him.

"What's happened to you? You look like a girl."

"That might have been a shade more subtly expressed, don't you think?"

"Yes, but you know what I mean."

"Fortunately."

She smiled at him, withdrew her hands, then wandered about the room, looking at things, touching them, as if she demanded tangible proofs of her return.

Julian watched her in silence. She had altered – he had not been wrong. She was serene, withdrawn into herself. Happiness pervaded her like a perfume. Her lips, usually compressed, were parted as if anticipating an opportunity to smile. Her whole nature was *en fête*.

His desire to take her in his arms became more insurgent every minute, but an instinct warned him to respect her mood. She was so evidently luxuriating in all the implications of her return that it would be vandalism to destroy her soliloquy. His desire for her – his long solitude with only that longing for company – had refined his perceptions. He sat on the arm of a chair and studied the glory of her figure, which seemed to shine through her smart clothes.

She ran her hand through his hair, as she passed on her journey of re-discovery, but remained silent. She inspected the bedroom, studied everything minutely, then switched on the light in the hall – the better to inspect it – finally returning to the sitting-room.

"Tea?"

"Yes, of course. I'm so sorry. I'll get it."

He disappeared. She sank into an arm-chair, stretched luxuriously, then picked up the book Julian had been unable to read and turned over the pages without glancing at one of them.

In a few minutes Julian returned.

"If this tea isn't right, it ought to be. I've forgotten none of your instructions."

"Tell me about yourself – what you've been doing – everything!"

"I've done nothing."

"You didn't go away then?"

"No."

"I do think that was rather stupid."

Julian said nothing.

"You can't have just sat here," Stella added.

"It's exactly what I did do."

"I'm afraid you're going to make tremendous demands, Julian."

"I am – tremendous. . . . What's the tea like?"

"Delightful! You respond to training, however, which is fortunate."

"You didn't kiss me when you arrived."

"I shall before I go."

"I can't believe it."

"It's perfectly true."

A long silence followed, which Julian ended by announcing explosively:

"I've got a confession to make. I had a frightful fit of jealousy when you were away. I thought the most hideous things about you. You've got to forgive me."

"I forgive you. Then – later – when I become jealous of you, you'll forgive me."

"All that's nonsense."

"Oh, my dear, if you knew what heaven it is to be back!"

"Did you hate it, Stella? I can't help hoping you did, but did you?"

"Desperately! Nothing but bores and rumours of bores. Don't speak of it! Oliver was right. He did let me down. It wasn't his fault, but he did, nevertheless. Those years in Europe made conventional life impossible. If you're to live in England, you must never leave it for long."

"I've just thought of something, Stella. Why shouldn't we elope?"

She had spoken seriously, just before Julian made this original suggestion, consequently its effect surprised him. Stella laughed helplessly.

"Oh, Julian, my dear! I wasn't wrong – you *are* a unique person."

"But I'm perfectly serious," he protested indignantly. "I'd run away with you to-morrow. Why not? I've money."

"Of all the hundred reasons, I will tell you only one – I made a bargain. Come and sit on the arm of my chair. I want you to listen to me."

"You haven't changed your mind?"

"No. It won't irritate you – will it? – to be told that you're rather inexperienced."

"I know I am."

"Then – just for a few months – will you do what I tell you? I'll always have a reason, though I may not always give it. Will you?"

"I'll do anything, Stella. So long as you come here, let me love you, and love me a little; I don't care about anything else."

He took her in his arms and kissed her again and again. He began to whisper the inevitable, the eternal, vocabulary of desire

– each word of which seemed a discovery to him. She surrendered to his embrace, and her surrender made him bold.

"When, Stella, when?"

"Soon, my dear. I promise you – soon."

"Yes, but *when?* All these weeks I've been alone, waiting. I – I can't go on any longer."

She rose slowly and stood by the fireplace.

"I'll tell you what I'll do," she said at last. "I'll come to breakfast on Saturday. Don't look so surprised. Tell your servant that you're going away for the week-end and so you won't want her. I'll not only come to breakfast – I'll get it."

"But can you cook?" Julian asked, so astonished by this statement that he forgot the urgency of his desires.

"Certainly! I had to cook for Oliver often enough. I shall have to go in ten minutes, but I'll come on Friday night, and we'll have coffee together. Please don't argue, Julian. Let us have ten minutes' peace. It's my last chance to-day."

"All right. But I want to give you something. I want you to have this."

It was a key to the flat.

"That's sweet of you, Julian."

A quarter of an hour later she left him. . . .

It was ten o'clock when she arrived on the following Friday. She entered the flat so silently that Julian did not know of her arrival till she appeared in the sitting-room.

"How late you are, Stella! It will be time for you to go before we know where we are."

"But I'm not going."

"You're not——"

"Going! Wait, I'll show you."

She vanished into the hall, returning immediately with a dressing-case.

"*Stella!*"

G

The early morning sunshine was slowly restoring contours and shapes in the bedroom. Julian was still asleep. His right arm was outstretched and his head rested upon it. Stella, half raised on her elbow, was watching him.

He breathed silently. Except that his right hand was clenched – as if to indicate that some memory had penetrated his dreams and quickened resolution – his attitude proclaimed a total surrender to sleep.

As she watched him, fragmentary thoughts drifted across her mind, leaving no more trace than summer clouds. The shape of her own bedroom rose before her – distinct, implacable, empty. All the details of her normal day filed through her memory. They seemed to relate to a woman she had ceased to know. Then she remembered how she had said to her husband: "I shall probably go away for the week-end as you are going to the Richmonds'." He had said nothing – and she knew he would not ask her where she had been. She half wished he would. A breach of one of the terms of their bargain, on his part, might indicate dissatisfaction with the whole of it. But she would not provoke him to action by humiliating him. This was one reason why she did not want Julian to write. Nevertheless, she would have welcomed a rebellion she had not incited. She was bound to him only by the agreement she had made with him. The position he had given her – the luxury with which he surrounded her – had not the binding power of a hair. Any happiness she had known had ended with her bargain: any she might obtain depended on exercising those rights she had reserved.

She was Julian's lover. Happiness had beckoned her, and she had obeyed, though she had no delusions as to what lurked in its shadow. . . .

How young he looked, sleeping there by her side! An aura of youth enveloped him. She smiled as she thought of their meeting in that bookshop in Piccadilly, only a few months ago. She loved his ardour, his impetuosity, his unconscious egotism. But, above all, she loved his inexperience. It would prolong their seclusion. It provided a valid reason for hiding him. For a few months she would be his world. Then, at the best, she would share him with the world. She would give everything and make only one demand – that he should not lie to her.

Julian stirred, then sighed. She smiled in anticipation of his surprise at finding her by his side. He opened his eyes dreamily like a child. Then they flashed with recognition.

"Stella . . . Stella!"

His arm crept round her and he laid his head on her breast.

"Why didn't you wake me? Sleep has robbed me of you. How long have you been awake?"

"Nearly an hour, I suppose."

"What have you been thinking about?"

"All sorts of things."

He raised his head and looked at her long and seriously.

"I wish you weren't so beautiful."

"Why?"

"I'd feel more sure of you. Kiss me – you must kiss me."

She took his head between her hands and kissed him.

"You're being very sweet, Julian."

"Why? What do you mean?"

"It doesn't matter – but you are. You owe The Hermitage more than you think."

"What on earth made you say that?"

"Because it occurred to me, and because it's true. I've a lot of questions to ask you about it some time. And a good many about that Mr. Rawlings you used to know."

"But why – *why?*"

"Because I want to know all I can about you."

"You're an angel, Stella."

"On the contrary, I've seduced you from virtue. I kidnapped you because I was lonely. But you are happy, Julian, aren't you?"

"Happy!"

His tone expressed contempt for the word's inadequacy. He lay back and drew her head on to his shoulder.

"We shan't get up to-day, Stella, shall we?"

"Oh, my dear, really, I think we'd better."

"But why?"

"Well, in the first place, it's usual. And, in the second, it's a delivery from temptation."

"But you'll sleep here so seldom."

"I shall be here to-night."

"Why didn't you tell me before?"

"Because I love surprises myself – and get so few – that I thought I'd give you one. Now, tell me something."

"Anything! What is it?"

"Are you hungry?"

"Yes."

"Then I shall get breakfast."

"You certainly will do nothing of the kind. I shall get it."

"No – really not. I'd rather, Julian. I'm fastidious. You remembered to get some food, I suppose?"

"Certainly!"

"What?"

"Sausages."

"How *male* – and how disgusting! Are there any eggs?"

H

Destiny fostered their love during the next few months. Unexpected circumstances, relating to her husband, enabled Stella to visit Julian more frequently than she had anticipated.

They met only in the flat. Julian did not protest, recognizing that the effect of this isolation was to secure an absolute privacy for each meeting. His sense of possession – of which he was beginning to be conscious – was deepened by this intimacy which permitted the gratification of every caprice.

Inevitably, each made discoveries in the other. Possibly the chief, for Julian, was Stella's abandonment of that weapon-like quality which had first impressed him. Its disappearance made it easy to imagine the companion her father had had during those Bohemian years abroad. This new Stella had a passionate impetuous nature, imperious in its demands, generous in its sympathies. She possessed an intelligence – impatient of traditional sanctions, but without arrogance – which yielded homage only to the exceptional and the courageous. Instead of a cliché morality, she adhered to a code – the cardinal article of which was not to lie to anyone who inspired the slightest respect. Her judgments proceeded from a collaboration between her intuition and her intelligence. Consequently, whatever values they lacked, they possessed that of revealing her. Recognizing this, she never committed herself in the presence of fools. She had that quality of will essential to the Bohemian condemned to play a part in conventional life.

Emotionally she was ruled by her mood. According to it, she gave or withheld. For her, passion was a surrender of her whole being: not an experiment in sensation. It was born in the heart, not the head.

"How does she live with a man she does not love?"

Julian asked himself this question more and more frequently without discovering an answer.

A minor incident occurred which seemed to indicate that Stella was conscious of the change which Julian had detected in her.

One night, which she had promised to spend with Julian, she entered the sitting-room soon after ten o'clock. She stood in the doorway and announced:

"Lady Farquharson."

"She is unknown to me," Julian replied.

"Do be patient. She will soon disappear. She will vanish with these clothes."

"And who will be revealed?"

"Stella Prescott . . ."

She granted the absurdities demanded by his infatuation with smiling acquiescence, and in such a manner that his veneration increased. Julian experienced all the delights, all the vicissitudes, of first and passionate love. She was not a woman to him, she was Woman. She was the answer to all his ignorance, all his imaginings. She was the words of that song the music of which had long troubled his heart. Worship blended with desire, transformed it, waking wonder, awe, mystery. The poet in his nature blossomed beneath the kindling rays of this love. He confused her with the emotions she wakened: identified her with the visions she inspired. He dowered her with all the wealth of his imagination till he was dazzled by her opulence.

But, to this frenzy of infatuation, the present hour only seemed substantial if he were assured of its successor. Hardly had she arrived, before he demanded to know when they would meet again.

"But I am here, Julian. Isn't it enough?"

"No – it's not enough. You're here now, but you'll go in a few hours. I must know when I shall see you again."

"You make it impossible for me to forget that I am ten years older than you."

He stared at her, too astonished to reply.

"You make it impossible," she went on, "by showing me that – for you – the present is less than the future. For me, now, this hour, this minute – is all that exists. I am here, with you. For me, that is everything."

"But can't you understand – don't you understand – that, not knowing when I shall see you next——"

"And do *you* understand," she interrupted, "that for me to come here to-night has involved thought, patience, ingenuity?"

His repentance was so absolute that she forgave him instantly. She sat down, then held out her arms.

"Come to me, Julian."

He knelt at her feet, and rested his head on her knees.

"Listen, my darling. I give you all I can: my freedom, my love – everything. Perhaps I even risk for you what many women would value. Suppose that – each hour I was with you – I was thinking about the life to which I had to return. I might as well stay away. There is only Now, Julian – there is only *Now*."

"I was mad, Stella. I ruin everything."

"It's your curiosity. It makes you indifferent to what you possess. Don't think about the future. If I had given it a thought, we should not be lovers – and so to-night would not be ours."

These lightning flashes of antagonism illumined for Julian, not merely temperamental differences, but a knowledge in Stella which only emotional intensity revealed. Its discovery gave him much the same sensation as that experienced by a swimmer who, believing himself to be in his depth, finds he is out of it. Inevitably, therefore, his interest in her increased, with the result that he became more curious concerning those aspects of her life of which he was ignorant.

One evening when she had managed to spend a couple of hours with him before dinner, he suddenly remarked:

"You've not told me much about your husband, have you?"

"You've never asked."

"Well, I suppose——" He broke off awkwardly.

"You suppose you were too busy loving me."

"No, that's not fair, Stella. It's because I love you more every day that I want to know everything about you."

"Nothing before it's necessary isn't a bad rule. You'll meet my husband one day, then you'll see for yourself."

"I shall meet him?"

"Of course. You don't suppose – do you? – that I shall be able to hide you like this indefinitely. Once I have trained you a little, you will meet my husband and some of his friends – and some of mine. I shall launch you into the world, Julian."

She rose and stood staring down into the fire.

"What do you mean by training me?"

"You're not a social being, my dear; how could you be? You've been nowhere – met no one. You show every emotion – express every thought. You'd reveal our secret in five seconds."

"I'd never let you down, Stella."

She turned and faced him, unable to hide a smile.

"Not if you dined at my house?"

"Of course not."

"Remember: I'd be Lady Farquharson and you'd be Mr. Grant."

Julian's expression denoted such astonishment that Stella laughed helplessly.

"Oh, Julian! And you said you wouldn't let me down."

"I begin to see what you mean," he said slowly, evidently greatly perplexed. Then, after a pause: "Lady Farquharson – Mr. Grant! Good God, what a damned farce!"

"That's why you need training – and rehearsals. There might be enemies in the audience. Which is also worth remembering."

"I believe your life's hell."

"I know it is."

He made her lie on the couch and covered her with caresses. But, eventually, his curiosity re-emerged and he began to ask a number of questions.

"Do you really want to know about it?" she asked wearily. "Well, I'll tell you a little – the rest you must discover for yourself. I don't want to prejudice you."

"First, tell me about your husband."

"I shan't be fair to him."

"Why not? You're always fair."

"It's impossible to be fair to anyone who bores you. You've never been bored by anyone, have you?"

The idea was a new one to Julian, and it was some moments before he replied:

"No, I suppose not – only by circumstances."

"That's entirely different," Stella announced decisively. "You can change them in all probability – with a little luck. But if a man bores you, and you're bound to him, you're helpless. And, incidentally, so is he."

"I don't see that."

"What can he do? Every time he comes near you he makes you shrink. He can't beg your forgiveness – as he could if he'd ill-treated you. There's nothing he can do. And if he loves you, his nervousness makes him worse than ever."

"But does he love you?"

"Of course. Otherwise there'd be no problem. He's not difficult to describe. He's forty-five – heavy, solid, sound – a perfect representative of the tradition to which he belongs. He's the third baronet, and rich. His father lived and died in the hunting-field. James, however, was born in a top hat and a morning coat, and did all those things that top hats and morning coats invariably *do* do. That's a statement of fact – not a criticism. Inevitably he went to a public school and Cambridge, just as his father had done – the same school, the same college. He never questioned the dogmas of his class. He accepted them with enthusiasm – even when he was twenty-one. At least, so I was told by the only friend he has who ever criticises him. James puts up with it because the friend in question is the son of a lord. . . . Why are you laughing?"

"You're so amusing, Stella. You've an enormous sense of comedy."

"I need it, I assure you. Now, I say nothing against being a Tory, but I do say that to be one – with enthusiasm – at twenty-one is indecent. When one gets older, it's understandable to regard Property as the sole reality. But not at twenty-one. However, James had a passion for Vested Interests, the Established, and the Orthodox even in his cradle – and he still has. He entered politics when he was well on the right side of thirty – to the amazement of his brothers, who are inseparable from horses, and who therefore live in the stables. . . . I do think you might be serious, Julian. All this is no joke for me."

"Poor darling! I won't laugh again."

"I can tell you little about his political activities. When I agreed to marry him, I made it clear that I was not going to rush round his constituency, having suddenly discovered a convenient passion for the working-classes just at election time. This I can tell you, however. He gives large sums to the party funds – and many quite gifted members of the party are afraid of him."

"Good Lord! Why?"

"He is sincere and he is stupid. In England, those qualities carry a man further than brilliance or originality. For one thing, they are immediately recognized. The stupidity is called common sense – but that is a detail. If I were not his wife, James would probably become a national figure. You know: the backbone of England. Incidentally, that's a significant phrase – it denies the supremacy of the head."

"Don't think I quite understand, Stella. Do you mean he ought to have married a wife who loved him?"

"Good Lord, no! Heaps of wives don't love their husbands. But he ought to have had a wife who looked the part. You know – dowdy, with a bazaar-opening expression. Well, I don't look the part. His crowd know that I don't belong to them."

"Of course you don't belong to them! I'm glad they've the intelligence to recognize it."

"They haven't. But they have an infallible instinct for that sort of thing. Fortunately, they attribute my peculiarities to those years I lived abroad. I even let them think I was educated in France."

She settled herself more comfortably, then took his hand.

"Don't let's talk about them any more, Julian. I haven't long to be with you to-day."

"Well, we won't after this – not for ages. But if you say I shall meet these people some time, I must know something about them. Besides, you're so amusing. You speak as if you weren't English."

"I'm not – and neither are you. To be English, you've got to be in the tradition. My years with Oliver put me outside it. You're outside it. You were brought up in The Hermitage – a kind of library in the Garden of Eden. Don't look so surprised. I'll prove to you I'm right. Do you give all your leisure and all your thoughts to sport?"

"I should think not!"

"Then you are not a young Englishman. Oliver said that he had an immense admiration for England, but, nevertheless, he could not live in it. He also said that there would never be a revolution here because it would interfere with cricket or football – or whatever it is they do. So *you'd* better let them think that you were educated abroad. You know several languages, so it will fit in all right. I'm perfectly serious, and I know what I'm talking about. A captive studies his gaolers."

Julian did not reply for some moments, then he turned to her impetuously.

"You're a complete mystery to me, Stella."

"Why, darling?"

"Why do you go on with it all? You – who have everything. Beauty, intelligence, everything! I can't understand it."

"Quite simple, really. If it had not been for James, Oliver would have gone to prison. Also, I made a bargain – and I shall keep it as long as he does. You *must* have a code in this world, Julian. Otherwise you're just a tiresome person who breaks all the rules and becomes a general nuisance. I've a code – and I stick to it. And I'm utterly indifferent as to what people would think of its terms if they knew them. And now kiss me – I shall have to go soon. Do let me become Stella Prescott for half an hour."

She closed her eyes and listened, half-smiling, to the passionate phrases which accompanied Julian's caresses. Each response he made to her beauty compensated her for the suffering sometimes inflicted by his egotism. On several occasions recently Julian had pressed her to remain, and had shown impatience while she had explained the necessity for departure. Also, more and more frequently, he had made demands – irrespective of her mood – and although her will always triumphed over his, the necessity for asserting it destroyed the pleasure of her visit. Although she recognized the inevitability of these incidents, nevertheless she was driven to seek excuses for them. There was only one – Julian's youth – but to be obliged continually to remember it reminded her in turn of the years which separated them.

I

Stella's chief discovery during this period was Julian's passion for ideas.

It had been eclipsed, first by the excitements of wealth and freedom, then by infatuation, but now it often dominated him – greatly to Stella's perplexity.

Not only had Julian been educated by Nathan Grant, he had idolized his father during the process, with the result that ideas represented a reality for him and one to which eventually he always returned. His rupture with The Hermitage, his subsequent friendship with Rawlings, had changed the level of his thoughts, but had not diminished their intensity. Temporarily, his passion for Stella had lulled his mental enthusiasms, but – with gratification – they became more ardent.

He began to tell her of the books he had read, those he intended to read, his talks with Rawlings, and his ideas and theories concerning a remarkable diversity of subjects. It seemed to Stella that, as his interest deepened in his theme, he forgot everyone and everything unrelated to it. When he discussed books she had read – and they were not a few – she was amazed by the extent of his knowledge and the insight of his criticism. But – and this was more frequently the case – when he was concerned with those speculations which had interested his father, and attempted to establish a synthesis between them and those which now interested him, Stella could only listen – understanding nothing, but convinced that her inability was caused by her own ignorance, not by a lack of lucidity in Julian's exposition.

What chiefly astonished her, however, was Julian's obsession with those subjects. More than once the suspicion occurred to her that if she were to glide noiselessly out of the flat, a considerable period would elapse before he became aware of her absence. Her spirit of comedy, which she sedulously fostered, derived ironic satisfaction from the fact that she was married to a man without a single idea, and the mistress of one intoxicated by them. Nevertheless, occasionally she experienced a pathetically impotent type of jealousy, and one which made her supremely wretched. Any attempt to convince herself that she was exaggerating Julian's obsession was frustrated by the knowledge that, during those years with her father, she had mixed almost exclusively with intellectual nomads, and was therefore no stranger to those with a similar enthusiasm. Her father had always expressed his ideas to her with remarkable candour, and they had not been those of an unimaginative or orthodox man. These recollections only served to convince her that Julian was unique – the conclusion she had hoped to evade.

One result of Stella's discovery was that she, in her turn, became interested in those aspects of Julian's life concerning which she knew little. Consequently she began to cross-examine him minutely regarding his life at The Hermitage and his friendship with Rawlings. Previously she had been satisfied with the main outlines, but now she demanded details.

Julian supplied them eagerly, recognizing that description sometimes establishes a perspective unobtainable by private analyses. Stella soon discovered that it was unnecessary to prompt him by questions, for, in the course of an hour, Julian succeeded in outlining a remarkably accurate sketch of Nathan Grant – and one which astonished Stella.

"I never knew there were such people——"

She had reason to regret this comment, which Julian interrupted in order literally to deluge her with an account of the mystics – their histories, aspirations, achievements and ecstasies. Strange-sounding names flashed like rockets from the dark storm of his explanation. Theories, beliefs, speculations, dogmas – concerning the nature of the infinite, heaven, hell, sin, temptation, death, free-will, conscience, providence, the unitive life, and the supernatural – rolled like roaring breakers over the stunned Stella. When, at last, Julian made an impatient gesture and broke off to explain that it really was quite impossible to give even an inadequate idea of the subject without devoting considerable time to it, Stella – who had imagined that the subject was as exhausted as she was – hastened to assure him that she had a sufficiently clear idea of his meaning for the time being.

She then timidly inquired whether these things had interested Rawlings.

"*Rawlings!*" Julian exclaimed, highly indignant. "Of course not! Rawlings was an imaginative drunkard – a gambler – a dreamer – a failure. That's what Rawlings was. But he knew more than he could express – he'd read quite a bit – and he saw life with his own eyes."

"You were fond of him, Julian?"

"Yes – quite. You see, Stella, you must realize that when I went to Mandell's office, I knew nothing whatever about life as it's lived. Rawlings was my second education. The streets were our books. Even so, I was only a looker-on. That's why you find me so ignorant. I *am* ignorant. It explains why I wanted to know all about the kind of life you lived with your father – and your life with your husband. It's all new to me, unbelievable as that may seem to you."

Stella was silent for a minute, then she asked:

"Do you ever see Rawlings?"

Julian started. He thought they had abandoned the subject and had no wish to return to it.

"No, I haven't seen him for months."

"How's that?"

"It's a long story, Stella."

"All the same, I want to hear it."

Reluctantly he related certain of the details of their last meeting, but Stella, by persistent questioning, eventually succeeded in obtaining a full account.

"So, you see," Julian concluded, "the rupture was his decision. Perhaps it was for the best, all things considered."

A long silence ensued, during which Julian glanced at her more than once. Attitude and expression both denoted an interest in the scene he had just described which surprised and irritated him. He had a suspicion that her interpretation of it differed from his, and was not reassured when she said:

"Your friend was not a fool, Julian. And he was not wrong in believing that everything depends on its background. I think I should like him. Perhaps we shall meet one day. Was he really the only person you were intimate with during those three years?"

Then, urged by some obscure impulse, he told her about Dorothy.

To his amazement, he discovered that her story required only a few sentences. Stated in words, their history was utterly commonplace. He had forgotten her for months, but he had not forgotten that mysterious rapture she had quickened in him. Yet – now – as he listened to his account of their relations, it was indistinguishable from some tediously sentimental romance. He became ashamed and ended abruptly. Stella was not in the least interested.

Later, Julian remembered that he had not mentioned their engagement.

He began to discuss books again till the time for Stella's departure had nearly arrived.

"I must go in five minutes, Julian."

"What a nuisance!" he replied abstractedly.

She glanced up at him. She was lying on the couch and Julian was standing by the fireplace. She saw that his expression of annoyance had been wholly mechanical. He was not thinking of her.

A determination to attract his attention possessed her. She altered her position, with deliberate awkwardness, in such a manner that her legs were revealed. Then she closed her eyes and lay motionless.

Directly she felt his arms round her, a hatred for him – the result of contempt for herself – so dominated her that she repulsed him roughly.

A few minutes later she left the flat.

J

A week passed before Julian saw her again.

On arriving, she ignored his protests, refused to give any explanation of her neglect, and stayed only long enough to communicate a decision.

Julian learned that his seclusion was to end.

"I want you to meet one of my friends, then – later – you must come to the house. It's time you met someone."

"Who is this friend – a man or a woman?"

"A man – Frank Derwent. If he likes you, it's probable you'll meet people through him. Two words of warning: Derwent isn't a fool, though he sometimes pretends to be; and – remember – I'm Lady Farquharson. You've met me, quite recently, at the

Irwins'. You haven't forgotten what I told you about them, have you?"

"No. When shall we meet and where?"

"We're lunching to-morrow at one-thirty at 'The Fragonard.'"

Julian smiled.

"The corner table?"

"No, the one opposite. I shall expect you then."

When he was alone again, Julian discovered that the prospect of emerging from seclusion excited him. The significance of this fact, and its implications, did not occur to him. He was most concerned to remember that he *must* call Stella – Lady Farquharson. . . .

Julian was the first to reach "The Fragonard," but five minutes later Stella arrived with Derwent. The latter was about forty, very tall and big-framed: his most conspicuous feature being his gay courageous eyes.

He greeted Julian with almost boyish good humour and generally evinced a desire to obtain the maximum pleasure from their meeting.

"Stella takes pity on me when I'm in town," Derwent explained to Julian, when the lunch had been ordered. "Shows me her latest discoveries, don't you know? If they like me, she drops 'em quick – realizing that she's picked a loser. Thought I'd better warn you."

Julian could not think of an appropriate comment on these remarks, but Stella rescued him.

"It still amuses you to under-estimate yourself, Frank?"

"My dear girl," he began, with an emphatic diagonal movement of his hand, "I assure you that I know myself to the bone. I haven't an illusion left. I know a little about fishing and nothing about anything else. I muddle myself with reading occasionally – I admit – but that's only to create a habit for those dreary years when old age has me half crippled in front of a fire all day."

Stella turned to Julian.

"You'll discover, Mr. Grant, that my friend's originality extends to not recognizing itself."

"Don't believe a word of it!" Derwent exclaimed, with genuine apprehension.

"You can't insist that you're commonplace without explaining why Lady Farquharson remains your friend," Julian managed to say, delighted to have made a remark, and to have cleared the Farquharson hurdle.

"I've told you – sheer pity. Also, I get about a bit, and she likes travellers' yarns. Reminds her of old times."

Conversation proceeded easily, but, during its progression, Julian's inner attention became centred in Stella. Her attitude towards him was so exactly that demanded by her part that the danger of using her Christian name receded. Soon, Julian believed that they had met only recently and, eventually, this conviction triumphed even over his memories. Stella – by gesture, look, inflection – recognized an intimacy with Derwent from which Julian was excluded. The former was the friend: the latter the acquaintance. Her manner to each subtly indicated the distinction.

Before half an hour had passed, Julian was so hypnotized by Stella's attitude that, if Derwent had left them, he would have continued to call her Lady Farquharson. Underneath he was wretched. He felt he had lost her: that the past represented a caprice of which she had wearied. She had reverted to the woman of their first meeting, and he wanted to sit and stare at her as he had done then. Admiration, jealousy, humility contended within him. It became increasingly difficult to make any contribution to the conversation. He felt like a schoolboy in love with an elegant, fashionable woman who was unaware of his existence.

More than once, however, by a question or a glance, Stella reminded him of his social responsibilities. He forced himself to simulate interest in the topic they were discussing and even managed to introduce a new one. All belief in his power over Stella, of which recently he had become confident, dwindled and died. He was afraid of the consequences of failing to please her. In the space of an hour he had become a supplicant for her smallest favour.

When the coffee was brought, Stella announced:

"You will have to smoke your cigarettes without me, I am afraid. I have to hurry away, but that's no reason why you should."

Five minutes later she left him. Julian remembered disconsolately that he did not know when they would meet again.

Derwent, however, had enjoyed himself, and consequently was talkative. When they had finished their cigarettes, he suggested they should go for a stroll in the Park.

"Pity to miss a fine afternoon. Also, I'd like a walk because lunch isn't my meal normally."

They talked generalities till they reached the Park, then Derwent asked:

"You've only met our friend recently, haven't you?"

"Yes, very recently," Julian replied – the red flag of danger fluttering in his mind.

"And what about Sir James? Met him?"

"No – not yet."

"Oh, my dear fellow, you certainly must meet Sir James. Be a power in the land one of these fine days."

"What's he like?"

Derwent's laugh was famous – not undeservedly – and Julian was startled by hearing it for the first time.

"Like!" Derwent echoed. "He's like the leading article in a popular newspaper come to life. Mind you, I've the highest respect for Sir James. You've noticed, I daresay, that one reserves that phrase for high-principled people who bore one until death seems the only friend. Still, this I must say for him, he has courage. And a courage which, in one instance, reached heroism."

"That's a pretty useful tribute. What was the feat of valour, or is it indiscreet to——"

"Why, marrying Stella, of course."

"Don't understand, I'm afraid," Julian replied, thinking the comment a safe one.

Derwent stopped and looked at him in astonishment. One of his eccentricities was the belief that everyone knew his opinion on certain subjects without ever having heard it.

"Any man who marries a beautiful woman is a hero."

Having made this categorical statement, in a tone of melancholy conviction, Derwent walked on – gazing at the sky with a speculative expression.

"That's an interesting theory," Julian said encouragingly. "I wish you'd explain it."

"Doesn't need much explanation, my dear fellow. It's a self-evident proposition. Take Stella. Fancy being married to her, and in love with her. Sheer hell, I assure you. Well, that's poor dear James's position."

Julian hesitated, longing to ask a question, but aware of the necessity for caution. After a pause, Derwent continued:

"I can talk like this about Stella because she's heard it all and only laughs. God alone knows why she married Farquharson. There's a story there – but I don't know it, and I doubt if anyone does. Anyway, it would be hell for any man to have married her."

"I do wish you'd explain why."

"Well, let's put it this way. I'm not married. Guilty of every other folly – but not that. If I *did* marry, however, I'd choose one of those pudden-faced ones. You know the type? Directly you see 'em, you think of a nursery. But a good-looker like Stella – with brains! Not a second's peace this side of the tomb – not one, I assure you!"

Julian exploded with laughter, greatly to Derwent's surprise. He had spoken with grim emphasis and quite seriously.

"All very well for you to laugh," he went on. "I've seen that wretched James look at her like the damned in hell look at a cup of water they can't reach. Then I glanced at *her*. Looking like a vision, proud, cool, self-assured, aware of her power, playing the part of hostess to the manner born! And I thought to myself: 'It's a thousand to eighty she's thinking of her lover.'"

They had reached the Serpentine. Derwent produced a piece of bread from his pocket, which he broke and threw to the ducks.

"Always bring these damned brutes some bread. God knows why, because they're as fat as aldermen."

Julian welcomed this diversion. Derwent's remark about Stella and her lover had frightened him. He remembered her warning that Derwent was not a fool – and decided to be doubly vigilant.

Nevertheless, when they walked on, curiosity forced him to ask:

"Have you known Lady Farquharson long?"

"Oh yes, ever since her marriage. By the way, it's a mercy they've had no children. One of Farquharson's brothers is a pal of mine. We go fishing together. I liked Stella immensely directly I saw her. Fact, I'm devoted to her. All I say is – thank God I'm not married to her. Wish I'd met her father. Proper wrong 'un,

I believe, but devilish interesting. Played hell just before he died, I'm told, and I'll bet she had the devil's own time with him when they were knocking about Europe."

"I can see why you're surprised she married the type you say her husband is," Julian remarked, trembling at his audacity. But, as his infatuation for Stella had now attained its original intensity, the desire to continue to discuss her made him reckless.

"My surprise turned to pity long ago. So will yours when you meet James. Ah! Now – that's a damned good example!" Derwent exclaimed, brandishing his walking-stick energetically. "Stella asks you to the house one fine day, and you meet James. Pretty, isn't it?"

"Don't understand – sorry!"

Derwent came to a standstill.

"You're too modest, my dear fellow. All the same, you must know that you're a good-looker yourself. Well, Stella introduces you as someone she's met at one of her odd friends'. James takes a quick glance – and probably sinks on to the rack to be tortured. You've everything that he never had, or has lost – youth, looks, imagination, vitality. And there's Stella standing by you."

Derwent looked at Julian with the expression of one awaiting a comment which the context had rendered inevitable. A sudden fear of this man's insight chilled Julian, but he knew that he must reply – and immediately.

"He must be used to that. You say she has odd friends. I know so little about her that I'd no idea she had friends apart from his. Surely he knows the Irwins?"

Derwent dismissed the question with a growl, then walked on.

"Of course she's her own friends," he said impatiently. "There's no woman living could stand James neat."

They entered Kensington Gardens and strolled about for half an hour, Julian giving an edited account of his history – Derwent having first provided a sketch of himself which had required only a few sentences. He had a thousand a year and had never worked in his life. He spent half of his time fishing and the remainder wandering about the world, looking at things, and praying he'd run into interesting people who wouldn't be bored by him.

Each having outlined a background, the conversation became

less personal. Julian discovered that his companion possessed curious odds and ends of knowledge on many out-of-the-way subjects which he revealed casually, in the manner of one discussing the weather.

"Half-past four," Derwent announced. "Wouldn't care to have a cup of tea at my place, I suppose? I've a bit of a flat near the Brompton Road. So it's not very far away."

"I'd like to very much."

Twenty minutes later they reached the flat.

"Nothing elaborate, you see – though this is a big room. There are only two and a bathroom. It's a service flat, and I can always let it furnished when I go away – which is a comfort for the poor and oppressed. Sit down, and I'll see about some tea."

Julian wandered round the spacious sitting-room, which was severely masculine in atmosphere. It contained only a few pieces of furniture – all large, however – arranged in a manner which represented the triumph of the obvious. The walls were covered with book-shelves, housing a miscellaneous collection of volumes in which no semblance of order was discernible.

Julian inspected this library, which seemed to mirror the mentality of its owner. Travel books predominated, but among them Julian discovered massive volumes dealing with psychical research, ancient civilizations, Eastern religions, and the occult. He had half completed his investigation when the name "Nathan Grant" leapt at him.

He took the book down and opened it. It was an anthology of mysticism, and was the only one of Nathan Grant's books known outside a circle of students. Julian turned over the pages, reading extracts haphazard.

"Ah! having a look at old Nathan Grant, are you?"

Julian started. He had forgotten Derwent.

"Name-sake of yours, incidentally. No relation, I suppose? Departed this life two or three years ago, I was told. Daresay he wasn't sorry. Ah! here's the tea – let's see what we can make of this."

A maid entered and placed a tray on a table near the fire. When she had gone, Julian asked:

"Is this the only book of Nathan Grant's you have read?"

"There's another up there somewhere," Derwent replied,

waving vaguely at the shelves. "Study of Eckhart – or one of those lads. Quite beyond me. After a page or two, it fell to the floor with a thud. Try one of these scones. They're not too bad if only the louts would cram on a bit more butter."

Julian did not reply immediately. The incongruity of Derwent's interests suddenly seemed extremely ludicrous. It was a full minute before Julian was able to say:

"Seems odd to me that this sort of thing interests you." He pointed to Nathan Grant's book. "I'm only judging by appearances, I admit, but I should have imagined – just seeing you – that you would never have given it a thought."

Derwent sighed deeply as he put his cup down with one hand and took a scone with the other.

"It's living alone, I suppose. If you spend a lot of time by yourself, you get a bit queer at times. Doesn't last, because you hurry off shooting or fishing – and so become merged in the general illusion."

"I want to know exactly what you mean by 'a bit queer.'"

"Ah, now, I can tell you that," Derwent replied impressively. "I thought that out once . . . Good God! I believe it's gone! Yes, it's gone! My brain's like a dustbin – it's emptied daily."

"Well, wait a minute," Julian suggested. "Perhaps you'll remember."

"Probably shall if I wake in the night. I often get a lucid interval just as I turn over to plunge again into the abyss of slumber."

A moment later Derwent slapped his knee triumphantly.

"I've got it! You get a bit queer when you're forced to face the facts of human existence. I remember hammering that out, years ago, in a squalid boarding-house in Sydney."

"Meaning – *exactly?*"

Derwent looked at him, wide-eyed and open-mouthed.

"Why, my dear fellow, surely to God that's clear enough. Here you are, on this planet – surrounded by mysteries and understanding nothing – for a very few years and then you're whisked off. Those are the facts and, if you think about 'em, you get a bit queer. So you hurry off and mix with those who never give them a thought – which is the most staggering fact of the lot."

"I agree with every word of that."

"Don't tell me *you* ever think like that?"

"Nathan Grant was my father."

"Good God! Not really?"

"Not only that," Julian went on, "he educated me. I know every book he has written – and most of the works of the writers who interested him."

"You don't mean to say you've read that book on Eckhart?"

"Yes, all of them. He wanted me to live as he did, and to carry on his work, but I rebelled and came to London. Later, I was left enough money to make me independent. Now, I've filled in the gaps in what I told you in the Park. But – and this is important – I don't want you to tell anyone else."

"You can count on me. I know every chatterbox always says that, but I mean it. Still – when anyone asks me to keep something secret – I always like to know who else knows. Does Stella?"

"Yes, but it didn't convey much to her. She'll forget it – if she hasn't already. These sort of things don't interest her."

"That's true enough," Derwent agreed, stretching himself. "A woman who's as good-looking as Stella doesn't bother about the facts of existence. Why should she? She's beautiful, and beauty is one of the facts – thank God!"

Julian stayed half an hour longer, most of which was spent in answering Derwent's questions concerning Nathan Grant.

When he left, Derwent went to the top of the stairs with him.

"Been a devilish interesting afternoon," Derwent pronounced as he shook Julian's hand. "Now, look here, I'm going away for about ten days, but do come round after that when you feel like it. Course I may run into you at Upper Brook Street when you go to see poor dear James."

Julian began to descend the stairs.

"Mind you," Derwent called after him, "I've the highest respect for the baronet."

His great laugh echoed through the building. A moment later his front door banged.

K

Julian had found Derwent stimulating. It was not till he reached home, therefore, that he remembered his fears regarding Stella. Then they returned – with reinforcements – and he surrendered to them abjectly.

The more he reviewed the evidence, the more convinced he became that she had tired of him. In retrospect, three facts attained grim significance: she had repulsed him brusquely, that evening when she had been lying on the couch; she had not come to see him for a week; and her last visit had been merely to communicate a decision.

It was obvious that she had decided to break with him, but, as she did not want to abandon him, she had arranged that meeting with Derwent. She had detected that they had interests in common. She foresaw that eventually he would meet some of Derwent's friends, and so would be delivered from loneliness. It was logical, skilful, damnable!

He paced up and down the room, raging inwardly. But the woman whose image was torturing him was not the one who loved him, and had given herself to him. It was the woman he had to address as Lady Farquharson – the woman of their first meeting. She was so removed, so impregnable! The knowledge that she must inevitably excite the admiration of others was a whip to his pride. Not only had he lost her, but the very memories which asserted his former possession became unreal. And he could not go to her, he could not write. He could not send her a message through Derwent, as he was going away for ten days. He could only wait. And it was impossible to wait.

If she had been coming to-night, this would have been the most interesting day of his life! Derwent had intrigued him: their conversation had excited him. And now he was in hell because of Stella.

An odd thought occurred to him. If she *had* been coming to-night, the pleasure he would have derived from seeing her would have had no link with that he had experienced with Derwent. Of this he was certain. Could it be that there was an absolute division between his mental and emotional lives?

The question was swept away by an onrush of new fears, every one of which confirmed his darkest imaginings. Over an hour passed, but he still continued to pace the room.

At last the postman's knock made time and place actual. He went slowly into the hall, realizing that Stella would not have written, but grateful for any distraction.

There was only one letter. He took it into the sitting-room and slit open the envelope without looking at it.

The letter was brief, and informed him that Dorothy was seriously ill, and was leaving for Switzerland immediately. Then followed the Swiss address and a signature.

The first reading conveyed nothing to Julian. Dorothy? Switzerland? What was it all about? He was concerned only with Stella. Probably the letter was not meant for him. The postman had made a mistake; he——

Then he read it a second time. Yes, of course! It was written by Dorothy's sister. But how did she know his address?

The envelope had fallen to the floor. He picked it up and saw that it had been re-addressed from his old rooms.

Irritability blazed through him. Why the devil had she written? The letter contained no request. What did they imagine he could do? Rush to Switzerland? Surely nothing could have been more final than his silence?

He raged up and down the room, one thought tumbling over another. Presumably, in a day or two, Rawlings would write – despite all those fine words of his at their last interview. Well, the man they were thinking about was dead. That was the fact. He died when he met Stella.

Julian continued to fume in this manner till he convinced himself he was being victimized. Then, very deliberately, he screwed up the letter and threw it into the fire. While he watched it burn, he remembered that it contained Dorothy's address in Switzerland. . . .

Three days passed. At about ten o'clock, on the night of the third, when Julian had finally renounced all hope of Stella, the door opened and she appeared. He was lying on the couch and did not see her, till, hearing a movement, he turned his head.

He crossed the room and took her in his arms, unable to speak. For nearly a minute they stood motionless, clinging to each other.

"Glad?"

"I thought you were never coming again, Stella. I was *certain* you weren't."

She did not reply. A moment later, Julian exclaimed indignantly:

"You're laughing!"

"I can't help it, darling. You're so clever – and so stupid."

"Stupid?"

"Gloriously – sometimes. Let me go now. I'm tired – utterly exhausted. I want to lie down, smoke a cigarette, and hear how you got on with Frank."

"Tell me this, first – are you staying to-night?"

"Yes – but – I'm a friend you're putting up for the night. Understand?"

"As long as you stay, that's all that matters."

He made her comfortable on the couch and gave her a cigarette. A long silence followed, which Stella ended by asking:

"Well, aren't you going to tell me about Frank?"

"Oh, damn Frank! – as you call him."

"Why? Didn't you like him?"

"Yes, I did – but that's not the point. I don't know where I am with you, Stella. . . . And I absolutely forbid you to laugh."

"Sorry!"

"I don't know where I am," Julian repeated mournfully.

"Don't quite see what we can do to define our relations more clearly."

But Julian was determined to be serious.

"In the first place, Derwent says you have odd friends."

"Half a dozen, perhaps."

"Well, how the devil do I know that you'll be faithful to me?"

Stella's attempt not to laugh was a failure.

"Surely, angel, you're the last person to complain of my lack of fidelity. You're not James. Besides, in six months you won't care twopence."

"If you think that——"

"I know it," Stella interrupted. "No – listen! You've met Frank. He doesn't know a lot of people, but he knows one or two in all sorts of different circles. You'll meet them and – through them – you'll enter the worlds to which they belong. You'll be popular

– and you've a tremendous curiosity. Any need to go on?"

Julian turned to her angrily.

"All that applies much more to you."

"I haven't your freedom – or your curiosity."

"You mean that——"

"I couldn't have an affair unless I was in love – and you could."

"Stella!"

His voice was vibrant with indignation.

She rose wearily, crossed to the fireplace, then stood with her back to him, looking down into the flames.

"Shall I tell you something, Julian? Shall I tell you why I didn't come here for a week, why I arranged you should meet Frank, and why I've left you alone these last three days?"

"Well, I think you might. But you've just said something pretty awful, you know."

"Wait! You remember that afternoon you talked for hours about things I didn't understand? I was utterly wretched. I had a dreadful dinner-party that night and I was longing to forget it. But you'd forgotten my existence. Then – just before I had to go – then——"

She broke off, but continued almost immediately.

"Then I *bought* your attention."

She turned to him swiftly.

"You remember? You understand?"

"Yes. I understand," Julian said slowly, not looking at her.

"I left a few minutes later. I knew we'd reached the end of an act. The curtain was down, and I had time to think."

She returned to the couch and sat by his side. Nevertheless, she was unaware of him. She seemed to be watching her thoughts. Her intensity imposed silence. It was some time before she went on.

"Soon, I saw clearly that I'd have to share you. I'd known it from the beginning, but all the same, it seemed like a discovery. So, it comes to this: if, in a month or so, you still want me, I shall be a preference – not a habit. I only ask one thing of you, Julian. Don't lie to me – ever."

"I *can't* understand you, Stella. You were so happy when you came."

"I was amused because all my tricks had worked. But they

wouldn't have continued to work. It is better to deal with the facts."

He was about to begin a long tirade, but Stella checked him.

"No, Julian. You may as well believe me without argument. A few months, at the most, will show. Now, tell me about Frank."

Julian hesitated, then obeyed. He gave an account of his afternoon with Derwent, but, actually, his thoughts were concerned with Stella's confession. For it was a confession. Ten minutes ago he had been certain that she had ceased to care for him: now, he not only knew that she still loved him, but that she was willing to share him with others.

This knowledge made him a stranger to himself. It made him accept her valuation of his possibilities. That he had the power to retain her love, without any surrender of his own freedom, transfigured Julian in his own eyes. How convinced she must be of his power to grant such a concession before any had been demanded! To placate is the policy of fear. She was afraid of losing him and – unlike Othello – was eager to keep a corner in the thing she loved.

These were the thoughts which thrilled him while he was telling her about Derwent. He glanced at her more than once. She was listening to him with head slightly bent, one hand held out towards the fire. The pale beauty of her forehead, outlined by the dark hair; the cameo loveliness of the face; the rhythmic joy of her figure – held him, hypnotized him, and seemed to mock the flatteries of his private thoughts.

Lacking proof, it was impossible to believe in her confession. . . .

"So you told Frank that Nathan Grant was your father?"

"Yes, but I asked him not to tell people."

"Why?"

"I don't know."

"And did you tell him how much money you have?"

"No, Stella. I just said I was independent."

"I think you were wise. Never tell people more than is necessary."

"You're glorious, Stella. You do exactly what you want to do, and you never take an unnecessary risk. In fact, so far as I can make out, there's only one risk you *do* take."

"And which is that?"

"Your trip up the flight of stairs from Mrs. Peters's shop on the floor below. You run no risk going up to the first floor – because you're on your way to Mrs. Peters. But you do run a risk on the second flight – because there's no explanation but the true one. Mrs. Peters *must* have seen you either coming or going. After all, she lives in those back rooms."

"She knows all about it, my dear."

"She *knows!*"

"Certainly! She was a friend of Oliver's. He started that business for her when she became a widow, and I send her most of her customers. But, apart from all that, she is the loyalist creature living. I heard about this flat from her and, soon afterwards, I told her everything."

"You never make any mistakes, Stella."

"Not in little things. Oh, Julian! I'm so tired."

"Well, listen, darling. Smoke another cigarette while I put some odds and ends away in the other room. It's devilish untidy, I'm afraid. You see, I'd no idea I should be putting up a friend for the night."

"Very well, but do hurry. I can't keep my eyes open much longer. I ache with exhaustion. It's been an awful day. Push the couch nearer the fire, will you?"

"There! I shan't be more than a minute or two."

When he returned she was nearly asleep. He watched her for some moments, then the light of an idea leapt into his eyes.

He took her hands and helped her to rise, then held her in his arms.

"Are you only a friend I'm putting up for the night?" he whispered.

It was so long before she made any response that he thought she had not heard. At last she shook her head.

His arms tightened round her, but she remained motionless. Suddenly her body quivered convulsively.

Surprised, he held her at arm's length and looked at her. There were tears on her cheeks.

"Stella! You're crying!"

"I can't help it. I . . . I do sometimes."

IV

ENTER JULIAN GRANT

A

During the weeks following Stella's confession, Julian entered two worlds simultaneously – the Bohemian and the orthodox. At the end of three months he had many acquaintances in the former and several in the latter.

His entry into the Bohemian world was effected so swiftly that no sooner was he aware of its existence than he found himself an inhabitant. It was only necessary to be accepted by two or three of Derwent's friends in order to become a member of that polyglot society which, in those days, lived precariously in attics or basements, and frequented cafés or underground night-clubs from six in the evening till any hour the following morning.

Eligibility for membership depended on the possession of one qualification in a liberal list. For a man, vitality on some level was perhaps the chief, but physical attraction, impudence, eccentricity, and talent were also passports. For a girl or a woman, contempt for respectability was essential: and an ability to listen highly desirable. Wit, or beauty, instantly achieved a precarious eminence. But money alone only secured its owner the privilege of paying for everything from which, psychologically, he was excluded.

What first amazed Julian was the rapidity with which acquaintances multiplied. Often he would go to a café to keep an appointment with one of Derwent's friends; whom he usually found at a table with half-a-dozen men and women. Soon, these people were talking to Julian as if they had known him for months. His inexperience, the readiness with which he expressed each thought and betrayed every emotion, occasioned no comment in a society where only restraint was unknown. Usually, towards midnight, someone would remember that there was a party somewhere. Half an hour later Julian found himself in a studio, full of strangers, separated from his original companions, but, nevertheless, when he left, he had collected a dozen new acquaintances and nearly as many invitations to forthcoming festivities.

This sudden contact with a number of bizarre personalities fascinated him. The intellectual and moral freedom interested and amused him. But, almost from the outset, what secretly delighted him was the knowledge that there was no necessity to become involved emotionally. He had no desire for a repetition of the Rawlings episode. He determined to reserve all the privileges of a spectator – and he was quick to detect that deserters from Bohemia excited little more comment than recruits.

Derwent, who seldom penetrated into this half-world and only when loneliness had reached a crisis, had had misgivings as to its effect on Julian. He left London soon after the latter's initiation, but on his return, two months later, was eager to hear an account of his experiences. They dined together the second night after his arrival, but the subject was scarcely mentioned till they reached Derwent's flat soon after nine o'clock.

"Well, how are you getting on with the geniuses? Met Brewster to-day and he told me you were in everything up to the neck."

"I'm studying two worlds simultaneously," Julian replied, "and finding it great fun. I can tell you what I think of the Bohemian easily enough. Only a fool could be deceived by it. Which explains why practically all the old men in it *are* fools. It is interesting that the arts have the least intelligent camp-followers of any profession."

"It's easy to let your hair grow," Derwent said meditatively.

"Exactly! I'm sceptical about the originality which advertises itself in externals. Such people delude themselves with theories about unrecognized genius. Incidentally, there have been precious few geniuses who received no recognition of any kind during their lives. Three-quarters of these people have formed a conspiracy to deceive themselves by trying to deceive others. That's why they herd together. Good God! an artist – a real artist – is nine times out of ten as tortured a being as a saint in the making."

"All the same, you find them interesting?"

"Frightfully! – for the time being. Besides there's a handful of genuine outcasts and real students – and perhaps twenty people with talent. Do you know what amuses me? To listen. The conversation throws little light on its subject – but a lot on the contributors. People's values interest me – and it's amusing how they reveal them without knowing it."

Derwent glanced at him. He had expected enthusiasm, or disappointment – not an analysis.

"This tells you a lot," Julian went on. "Several of them would like me to pretend that I'm an artist. Incidentally, those who have produced nothing have the greatest reputations. But I've no use for psychic drugs. I'm not a creative artist – and I know it – and I tell them so. For me, Bohemia is an episode. Remember: I'd met no one. Now, I have crowds of acquaintances. And I could walk right out and be forgotten in a week. That suits me – and that's what I shall do one of these days."

Derwent filled a pipe slowly, humming a tuneless song during the operation. People revealed themselves to him more clearly by their way of speaking than by their actual statements. Julian's tone surprised him, but he gave no indication of this fact when he asked:

"So you haven't fallen in love with one of those little models?"

"Good God, no! They amused me at first, but I soon got bored. There are three clearly-defined types. There's the type who is determined to be fiercely natural – and takes her clothes off at parties to prove it. There's the type who believes that some artist will immortalize her – and so tries to cultivate a Mona Lisa smile. And there's the type who is determined to be original. You know what I mean? Won't shake hands when she's introduced, won't pass anything at supper, doesn't answer if anyone makes an everyday remark, and so on. A negative kind of originality – based on what she won't do and isn't. I've only met two models worth a damn. And they were just affectionate children."

Derwent said nothing. After a long silence, Julian added:

"Oddest thing of the lot is that it's all so familiar to me that I feel I've done it before – often."

"Ah, my dear fellow, I know that feeling a damned sight too well. It's all right so long as you only experience it in regard to one or two of your activities. But if you feel it about all of them, you're done for."

"What do you mean?" Julian asked quickly.

Derwent put his pipe down and sighed profoundly.

"Better give you an example," he said at last. "I was sitting here one night about three months ago in front of a dying fire, and suddenly I felt with extraordinary intensity that life was rushing past me – and that I was missing everything. I saw myself with amazing detachment. A man sitting alone – missing everything. Well – would you believe it? – I puzzled my brains for half an hour and – by God! – the only thing I could think of was to hurry off and find a harlot."

Derwent's laugh shook the room.

"Well, up I got, put on hat and coat, then suddenly I almost heard an inner voice say: 'You've done this thousands of times in thousands of lives.' So I took off hat and coat, went back to my chair, and watched the fire die."

"You've a lot of the mystic in you, Derwent."

"No, not a lot – just enough to make things a bit unreal at times. But *you're* going to have a hell of a time. You know that, of course?"

"Why? What the devil makes you think that?"

"Sheer feeling, really. Still, take what you've just said about the crowd you've been mixing with. It ought to have taken you at least three years to see them as you do. If you're ever going to have any happiness, you must surrender to one illusion after another. You don't. Your opinion of those models is one example. All wrong at your age, my dear fellow. You ought to have found them amusing. Much better to get a jolly memory out of them than a psychological analysis. Of course, I'm only talking now in terms of ordinary human happiness. But it's a mistake to underrate it – as you'll discover when the chance of ever experiencing it vanishes finally."

"Doesn't all that come to this – the fools get the best of it?"

"Well, perhaps you're right. Anyway, let's have some drinks. Must drink a bit, you know. To my horror, I've found lately that I keep forgetting that I want one. What shall it be – whisky-and-soda?"

"Yes – all right – anything."

Julian had risen and was pacing the room restlessly. The interruption irritated him. Derwent had no mental consistency. Once a subject had been abandoned, he seldom returned to it. He never knew what he was going to say, and rarely remembered anything he had said.

Derwent handed Julian a drink.

"Tell me if that's not right. Oh, by the way, I rang Stella up to-day. Seen anything of her?"

"Yes – quite a bit really. I've been to Upper Brook Street and met her husband. I shan't tell you about that though. You'd accuse me of making another analysis. But what you said just now interested me a lot."

"Probably valueless. If I listen to myself when I'm talking, I blush to hear such nonsense."

"Your prophecy that I'll have a bad time," Julian went on, as if Derwent had not spoken, "and all that about those models interest me. Incidentally, I'm more human than you think – I've slept with two of them."

"But the point is – that comes last in your memories."

"I don't pretend it meant much to me, or that I ever think of it. Anyway, one thing's certain: I'm going my road, and I'm going to the end of it. There's something I want to discover and I'm going the quickest way about the job. Most lives are ruined by sentimentality. I'm going to explore everything that wakes my curiosity."

"You've certainly moved along the last few months. Dare say Stella's noticed it."

Julian glanced at him. Derwent was staring into the fire with an expression of wide-eyed innocence. Nevertheless, the knowledge that this man knew of his relations with Stella suddenly possessed Julian. Also, he realized that Derwent loved her in a queer way of his own.

"Stella understands," Julian replied, using her Christian name for the first time in Derwent's presence – greatly to his secret amusement. "And what is more, she can adjust herself. Naturally she's noticed that I've altered. I tell her everything."

"Did you tell her about those two models?"

"Of course!"

"Ah!"

Derwent picked his pipe and stretched himself. Some moments elapsed before he said:

"Remember I told you once – in the Park – that I wouldn't be married to a good-looker like Stella for anything in the world?"

"Yes, I remember."

"I doubt whether it was altogether true. I'd probably run off with her to-morrow – although I know it would be sheer hell."

"Good God! Why?"

Derwent swung round to him almost fiercely.

"Why! Because she's a thoroughbred. And when you've met as many mongrels as I have, you'll know just what that means – and just how rare it is. And one sign of a thoroughbred is that it doesn't show when it's being hurt."

"Yes, by God, you're right! She's unique."

The ensuing silence became embarrassing. A frontier had been reached. Either Stella must cease to be their theme, or Derwent must be relieved of the restrictions imposed by a fictitious ignorance. There is a limit to a discussion in which the truth is only implied – and they had reached it.

"You only realize her quality when you compare her with others," Julian said at last. "I'll give you a case in point. Do you know Clytie Lessing? – the famous blonde with the white skin?"

"Yes, I've met her. Always think she's got a kind of cold-storage atmosphere."

"So she has. Her husband will die of frostbite. I can't stand her. She's so damned proud of her virtue – flaunts her fidelity to that rich old husband till you feel it would be a promotion for her to become a prostitute. She tried to patronize me once – but it didn't come off."

"No? Not really? *Do* tell me, my dear fellow. Always hoped she'd take a toss. What happened?"

"Nothing very much. She was being virtuous and giving me chaste advice, so I told her the story of the saintly woman on pilgrimage to the Holy Land."

"Never heard it," Derwent cut in. "I'm brutally ignorant. What was it?"

"Well, this woman, being a saint, had no money. She walked hundreds of miles on her way to the Holy Land, till she reached a river which it was essential to cross. At last she found a ferry-man, but he refused to take her over without payment. She told him she had no money. He replied that he'd ferry her over if she gave herself to him. She considered the sacrifice of chastity a trifle compared with the jeopardizing of her high enterprise. Also – that it was super-sensuality to rate virginity too highly. She gave herself – and so reached the Holy Land."

"And you told that story to Clytie Lessing?"

"I did."

Derwent hugged himself, rolled about, and roared till the glasses rattled.

"Given the world to have seen her face!" he managed to exclaim at last. "What did she say? What did she do?"

"She said nothing. She rose – a study in wounded dignity – and left me. When we meet now, she looks like a polar spectre. I'm not certain that I've finished with her though. We shall see."

When Julian left, an hour later, Derwent said casually:

"Oh, by the way, Stella is lunching with me to-morrow. Wouldn't care to come along, I suppose? Wish you would, if you're free, because I'll have to leave her directly after lunch. We're meeting at the Café Royal at one-thirty."

"I'd like to come very much. I haven't seen Stella for nearly three weeks."

B

Julian's first few visits to Upper Brook Street were a series of ordeals. If he had foreseen the dangers and difficulties which awaited him, he would have deferred his entry into Farquharson's world till he was more experienced. But Julian was ignorant of his ignorance. Also, Stella's confession – and his success in Bohemia – had created the belief that he was adequate to any social demands.

This illusion was soon dissipated. To enter Farquharson's house was to realize a number of facts so dramatically that each attained the dimensions of a discovery. First, and above all, the necessity of becoming as good an actor as Stella was an actress instantly emerged, for he had to collaborate with her performance. He shared the limelight which beat down upon her: the eyes of her audience were watching him. He must hide his desires, mask his motives, feign indifference – while remembering that the effect of over-emphasis is to destroy the illusion it seeks to create. In one word, Julian discovered that to be the secret lover of a married woman transforms every social occasion at which she is present into a tight-wire act – which must not be recognizable as such, and which therefore must be performed with an arm-chair confidence.

It was fortunate for Julian that the limelight only illuminated him intermittently. In order to deceive people, it is necessary to understand them to some degree. Julian had no knowledge of his audience. He knew literally nothing of the standards, outlook, and traditions of the class to which Farquharson belonged. It was inevitable, therefore, that mistakes were numerous, but – owing to Stella's foresight – the fiction that he had been educated abroad had become current, and was regarded as an explanation of all minor peculiarities.

Eventually Julian discovered that most of Farquharson's friends had private incomes, and that nearly all of them were self-satisfied, overfed, and convinced of their national importance. Property, Food, and Bridge constituted their trinity. Sport, investments, servants, and ailments were perennial topics of conversation. The existence of God received a nominal recognition, but actual devotion was reserved for the aristocracy. In every sphere – politic, economic, and social – they were the adversaries of Change: unless it were demonstrably certain that the proposed innovation would benefit their interests. Where this was the case, change was hailed as Progress.

To Julian, it was an obvious, definite, materialistic world – the inhabitants of which were as convinced of their sincerity as they were unaware of their motives. Ethically, they had no problems – whatever they did was justified by the fact that they did it. Criticism revealed the "outsider." Financial operations – in which the speculative element was removed owing to the possession of inside information – were legitimate, desirable, inevitable. To serve as a director on the boards of numerous companies; to draw the fees for doing nothing; to be wholly ignorant of the nature of the business in every instance – was to render public service. "What's wanted is men of character." No inconsistencies were recognized. A man could continue to kill or maim hundreds of birds, hunt foxes or stags, patronize coursing, and remain an ardent supporter of the Society for the Prevention of Cruelty to Animals.

Everything was departmentalized in terms of tradition, custom, and self-interest. Independent thought did not exist. Contempt for the higher faculties – the imaginative and the meditative – was absolute. England was theirs, for they were England.

It follows that the Union Jack always fluttered gallantly in their minds. They were not only patriotic – they were the only patriots. Patriotism was their property – and they exhibited it at each Parliamentary election in order to prove possession. Of that patriotism which alone has any reality – reverence for the great and generous spirits of one's race – they were ignorant. Mentally and emotionally, they were capable only of clichés. To listen to them was to be half hypnotized into the belief that, apart from their set, the world was uninhabited.

Right or wrong, these conclusions represented Julian's final estimate of Farquharson and his more intimate friends. A considerable time elapsed, however, before self-confidence gave the detachment necessary for psychological investigation. At the outset, everyone and everything were unfamiliar: Stella, her husband, guests, conversation, and manners. Also, although Julian was rich, he had never experienced luxurious surroundings. Inevitably, therefore, he was impressed by the atmosphere of wealth which pervaded the house like a faint perfume; the frictionless functioning of everything; the mask-like servants, who performed prodigies, without anyone being aware of their existence.

Fortunately for Julian, he eventually received noteworthy attention from a very eminent person. Lady Sarah Spooner was eccentric, but as she was very wealthy, and extremely well-connected, her peculiarities were regarded as the flourishes of an aristocratic spirit. She was over sixty, white-haired, somewhat bent, and always carried an ebony cane. Her hands were claw-like, her countenance nut-crackery, but she had fine eyes, and the rare virtue of saying what she thought, in an impulsive and staccato manner which – on occasions – definitely disturbed the parrot-house. She was invariably late, always left something behind her, and addressed people in a tone which suggested that they only existed in order to answer her questions. She was the widow of a distinguished general, and never ceased to lament destiny's error in making her a woman.

The first time Julian saw her, she made a characteristic entrance. She arrived just as luncheon was over, demanded an omelette, then sat opposite Julian – who welcomed any diversion gratefully. The last half-hour had been difficult. The men had discussed sport or investments in terms which were meaningless jargon to Julian: the women had chattered about their friends, their clothes, their servants.

"No one's to wait for me," Lady Sarah announced. "You've all finished – you'd better go."

"Most certainly not," Farquharson began, but she interrupted:

"Don't want any of you, James." She swept the table with a hawk-like glance. "Ah! that young man can stay and keep me company." She indicated Julian with a stab of her right forefinger. "Don't know him, but I like strangers. Most friends are as monotonous as a snoring man. Will you stay and keep an old woman company?"

"I will stay with the greatest pleasure."

Sincerity transformed the commonplace words. Julian had been wretched and this was deliverance.

A few minutes later they were alone.

"You're a very handsome person. What's your name?"

"Grant – Julian Grant."

"Hah!"

She looked at him so searchingly that Julian's glance wavered.

"You're an art student – evidently."

She ignored his denial. Her scrutiny of his features had convinced her that he was a student, and his appearance suggested that he was interested in the arts. Lady Sarah elected, therefore, to regard him as an art student – subsequently informing everybody that he was one – with the result that Julian became labelled. It was useless for him to tell Farquharson's friends that he was not an embryonic artist. Lady Sarah had told them that he was, and it was obvious that so wealthy and highly-connected a personage would be more likely to know the nature of Mr. Grant's activities than the young man himself.

"Talk to me while I eat this omelette. And don't tell me any lies."

"Why should I tell you lies?"

"Most people do," Lady Sarah replied, attacking the omelette vindictively. "Explain why you're here."

"Surely that's simple enough. I'm a friend of the Farquharsons."

"Rubbish!"

"But – but – I *am*," Julian expostulated weakly.

"Rubbish! I've known James Farquharson twenty years. I've known you five minutes. You've nothing in common. I suppose you're in love with Stella."

Julian started, flushed, then looked apprehensively over his shoulder. Lady Sarah's voice was terrifyingly penetrating. She glanced at him, detected his distress, and instantly tried to re-assure him.

"No one will overhear. And if they do, it doesn't matter. No one takes any notice of what I say because I always speak the truth. You've good taste. If I were a man – which I ought to have been – I should have fallen in love with her myself. I'm glad you can still blush. Why don't you smoke? It's very evident that you want to."

Julian lit a cigarette. He liked this odd crotchety woman, who ignored convention, and rapped out remarks like revolver shots. After a minute's deliberation, he decided to take a risk.

"May I come to see you, Lady Sarah?"

"Certainly! Why do you want to?"

"Because I like you – and because you could help me."

"How can I help you? Three-quarters of me is in the grave. I suppose you mean you're a fish out of water here and want a tip or two."

"That's it – precisely."

"You listen to me, young man. I shall tell these people that you are coming to luncheon with me. That will settle your troubles. Most of the people here are fools. Have you met Clytie Lessing?"

"I've met her – but she doesn't like me."

"She's the biggest fool of the lot – and the greatest humbug. That was a *very* good omelette."

A moment later Stella came into the room.

"Ah, my dear, how charming you look. And how delightful of you to leave those horrid people to come and talk to a mouldering old woman."

She took Stella's hand and pressed it to her cheek.

"Has Mr. Grant been amusing you?" Stella inquired.

"Mr. Grant – as you are careful to call him – is a very handsome young man, who is nevertheless not a fool. He is lunching with me to-morrow. You're a magnificent person, my dear, and a clever one. You realize that audacity resembles innocence."

"I choose not to understand you," Stella replied. "If you weren't a darling, you'd be a danger. May I come to luncheon with Julian to-morrow?"

Her use of his Christian name delighted Lady Sarah. She shook with soundless laughter, till Julian feared she would fall to pieces.

"You're the only sensible woman I know," she managed to say at last. "You're frank – when frankness is possible – and you defeat fools with their own weapons. Of course you can come to-morrow. And now I'd better go and talk to some of those stupid people. You stay with Mr. Grant – who is too young to know how fortunate he is."

She tottered off, leaning heavily on her cane. Directly she had disappeared, Julian turned to Stella.

"Well! That beats everything! You made no attempt to deceive her."

"It would have been useless, my dear. She's in a different class from the rest. Besides, now she's an ally. If anyone ever suspects anything, she'll simply say 'Rubbish!' – and that will be the end of it. She rules the lot of them, because they're all snobs. You liked her?"

"Immensely! But she's a frightening old bird: suddenly said to me: 'I suppose you're in love with Stella!' My God! I nearly slid under the table."

"Listen, Julian. I'll have to go back in a minute. James is going away to-morrow for a week. When can I see you?"

Julian thought intently before he suggested:

"What about Friday? No! wait a minute – Saturday. Come for the night on Saturday."

"Very well. I'll come to dinner. What are you going to do now?"

"I'm going to walk to Chelsea. I'm asked to tea at Sinclair's studio. He's got a crowd coming. Anyhow, I'll see you at Lady Sarah's to-morrow."

"You'd better wait till she goes. She won't stay long. Leave with her and see her to her carriage. By the way, don't mention cars – she hates them. She thinks they're just a craze which will soon die out. I *must* go. Good-bye, darling."

"Good-bye, bless you." . . .

Lady Sarah's prophecy that her championship of Julian would solve his social difficulties was soon confirmed. His next visit to Upper Brook Street was a revelation. Even Mrs. Fromings spoke to him! Now, this was a notable triumph, for Mrs. Fromings only recognized the eminent – and even demanded solid qualifications in those she discussed. For instance, if, say, the Dentons were mentioned in her presence, she would instantly exclaim: "The *Dentons!* do you mean the Dentons of Denver Park?" And if the Dentons referred to were *not* of Denver Park, Mrs. Fromings retired into polar isolation – only thawing into humanity again when a name, surrounded by an estate, relegated the Dentons to their native obscurity.

When Mrs. Fromings next met Julian, however, she not only inquired how he was, but also expressed pleasure on hearing that he was well. These gracious attentions were not overlooked by Mrs. Ramage, who asked him to luncheon, having first assured him of her passionate interest in the arts. Julian was still pondering the significance of these favours when Colonel Dibbs, the author of the standard work on Pig-sticking, said "How do?" – a conversational achievement without precedent so far as Julian was concerned.

Julian was stunned, but new triumphs awaited him. Clytie Lessing's customary and almost imperceptible nod was transformed into a smiling bow, and even Farquharson managed to exchange a few remarks instead of instantly finding an excuse for leaving him – which was his usual procedure.

It was the change in Farquharson which especially interested Julian. It intrigued his perversity to talk with him, while inwardly contrasting their relations with Stella. Hitherto he had lacked the necessary assurance, but – as his confidence increased – he began to seek Farquharson's company more and more frequently.

Observation, even from a distance, however, had provided Julian with a fairly accurate estimate of Farquharson. In every respect, except one, the appearance was the man. He was heavily built, slow in movement, pompous in manner. Superficially, he was impressive. He corresponded admirably to the popular conception of a public figure. His clothes were irreproachably formal, he always wore a buttonhole, and invariably regarded the world with a "Rule, Britannia!" expression. Above all, he had the gift of making the commonplace seem the profound. His political speeches consisted wholly of clichés – but clichés enunciated with such solid self-satisfaction, and with so genuine a belief in their originality, that those who heard him were delighted. It flattered them to recognize their own mental prejudices strutting about in evening-dress. It relieved them of any necessity for thought by creating the illusion that they were thinkers. It follows that Farquharson was an immense favourite with the popular Press.

Julian easily detected the reason for his growing political importance. He reduced every problem to a slogan – and one which epitomized insularity, bombast, ignorance. On one joyous occasion – during a period in which he kept repeating "Keep The Foreigner Out," with parrot-like monotony, in public and private – he urged the electors of a South London constituency to vote for Blumenthal. Why not? God had chosen the Jews, and Farquharson had chosen Blumenthal, rather than "one of those damned Socialists" – of pure English descent.

To Farquharson, criticism and envy were synonymous. He was blind to his own inconsistencies, but had the eye of a hawk for those of others. He ignored the arguments of his adversaries; he repeated in order to prove; and he became immensely patriotic whenever anyone was ill-bred enough to question his motives. Also – and more important – he possessed the aggressive sincerity of the self-deceiver. He was genuinely surprised that everyone did not agree with him. He stood for common-sense, the obvious, and – above all – morality. He was vastly sentimental. He won one election through a photograph appearing in the Press which depicted him comforting a little girl who had lost her doll. He patronized his social inferiors, was dignified with his equals, and a flunkey to his superiors. Clever people might laugh at him – party-leaders might find him embarrassing – but Farquharson depended on neither. Stupidity was his ally. His friends confidently prophesied that he would end up as Home Secretary.

But this was the public figure, not the private man. It was

the latter who interested Julian. He knew his secret, and consequently was not deceived by externals. Farquharson had a thousand interests, but only one passion – his love for Stella. It throbbed beneath the solid-seeming foundation of his life like an underground river. She was the one beautiful fact in his existence – the palm tree in his desert. His love for her was as dumb, as uncritical, as constant as that of a dog. He knew that she did not love him, but, normally, this knowledge lacked power to wound, for his humility was too great – and his imagination too small – to conceive the paradise her love would create. It was enough that she lived with him, that he saw her every day, heard her voice, or her step on the stairs. Sometimes, when she was out, he would go to her room and gaze at the feminine proofs of her existence which it contained. They seemed to confirm the miracle of their daily life together.

No one knew of this passion. Stella herself was ignorant of its depth and intensity. It was hidden behind Farquharson's conventional exterior like a masterpiece in a drab-looking house.

There was no mental or emotional liaison between the public and the private Farquharson. The former was convinced that woman was an inferior being: the latter regarded Stella with the eyes of a slave. To retain the least of her favours, he would have granted the most extravagant of her demands. There is no jealousy where there is no claim to possession, and – in the supreme instance of Stella – Farquharson had no sense of ownership. Church and State had sealed her his, but nevertheless this staunch upholder of the sacred rights of property felt a trespasser in her presence.

He refused to realize that she was unfaithful. He knew it, as men know that one day they will die, but – like them – he thrust realization from him. Often he was hunted by the fear that she would tell him of her infidelity. While she remained silent, he could half persuade himself that knowledge was only suspicion. He was spared the pangs of knowing her lover's name. A confession would compel realization. Her infidelity would cease to be anonymous.

Frequently, during the last year, her candour had made him tremble. Once she came into his study and announced:

"I'm going away for the week-end."

The tone of her voice, the expression in her eyes, were a challenge. In the silence which followed the bare statement, he felt her will goading him to question her.

"Yes, I see. Very well," he heard himself say. "I – I hope you enjoy yourself."

The fatuity of the last sentence made him writhe. He attempted to obliterate it by talking rapidly, scarcely knowing what he was saying till, greatly confused, he ended abruptly.

She waited till the silence became almost unendurable, then said half contemptuously:

"I shall be going away for several week-ends. And for odd nights fairly frequently."

"I understand, Stella."

"You understand?"

"I mean: I want you to be free. Your happiness is everything to me – everything!"

He was not looking at her and so did not see that her expression softened. A moment later she made a despairing gesture with her hand and left him. . . .

When Stella was away, Farquharson invariably drugged himself with work in order to deaden his emotions. Whether he remained in town, or whether he went to his country house in Norfolk, one of his secretaries was on duty all day, and – after a solitary dinner – Farquharson continued to work till long after midnight. But no drug could deliver him – when he woke in the night – from thoughts which flickered like lightning across his mind, illuminating his situation with pitiless clarity.

He did not know where she was. . . . This fact rose like a spectre from the pit. Everything he possessed – wealth, security, ambition – seemed to crumble like a castle of sand fretted by an incoming tide. He experienced all the terrors of an unimaginative man stretched on the rack of imagination. Finally, one certainty emerged – she was in the arms of her lover. And, in his humility, Farquharson prayed that this lover would cherish her – that she would never suffer through him as he was suffering through her.

Stella's friendship with Julian did not seem particularly significant to Farquharson. She had always had her own friends, and Julian was her latest discovery. It was true that he was young and handsome, but as several of her men friends also possessed those qualities, they did not confer a unique distinction. It was possible that he was her lover, but the likelihood was not greater in his case than in those of two or three others.

Nevertheless, Julian's personality disturbed and perplexed Farquharson. He felt embarrassed when they were alone together and therefore avoided him, but, as it was clearly impossible to ignore anyone who was a favourite of Lady Sarah Spooner's, he sacrificed feelings to ambition and began to seek Julian's company.

Julian welcomed his attentions, although he despised the motive which prompted them. He knew there were two Farquharsons, and he was fascinated by the secret drama enacted behind the pompous exterior of the public one.

Soon, close-range observation almost convinced him that Farquharson's love for Stella was greater than she imagined. In order to reach certainty, he began to discuss her with ever-increasing intimacy. He praised her beauty, her intelligence, her wit, and her clothes – while Farquharson fidgeted, flushed, and began sentences which he failed to finish. But if these conversations racked him, they also convinced him of the innocence of Julian's friendship with Stella. They created a very different certainty in Julian. He became confident that Farquharson would submit to any humiliation rather than risk a rupture with Stella. . . .

One night Julian and Derwent dined with Stella at Upper Brook Street. Farquharson was guest of honour at a public dinner and was not expected home till about eleven. Derwent left soon after ten-thirty, but – somewhat to Stella's surprise – Julian stayed on.

"You'd better go, my dear. He may come in any minute."

"I'm going to wait till he does. You're coming to the flat to-night, Stella."

"You must be mad!"

"Not a bit of it. I've made a lot of discoveries lately – and the chief one is that all your precautions are unnecessary. It wouldn't matter tuppence if you told him the truth. Anyhow, you're lovelier than ever to-night – and you've got to come back with me."

"But I tell you it's impossible, Julian."

"Get your things, and leave the rest to me. I'll talk to him. I'll tell him Lady Sarah wants his advice about something. Incidentally, that's true – I asked her to consult him. He'll purr with delight. Then I'll tell him that some friends of the Irwins are giving an impromptu dance and want you to come. The friends in question are going to put you up as it will be a very late affair."

"But do listen, Julian——"

"Not to a word! You're coming. I want you. I've a lot to tell you. You *must* come."

Stella did not reply. It was over a month since she had spent a night at the flat.

"It's our only chance," Julian went on. "I'm going away soon."

"You're going away!"

"Yes, that's one thing I want to talk about. Get your things. I'll arrange everything."

Stella surrendered.

"Very well. I'll go now. I'm not anxious to be here when you tell him."

A few minutes later Farquharson arrived. He accepted the situation with even greater docility than Julian had anticipated.

Just after eleven, they left in a taxi. Farquharson stood on the pavement and watched it drive away.

C

Directly the taxi started Julian took Stella in his arms.

"Wait! do wait, Julian!"

"Not another second. I'm not bothering about him any more. It wouldn't matter if he were sitting opposite. Now I'd better give the driver the real address."

"Not till we're round the corner."

"Good Lord! what's it matter?"

He gave the necessary instructions, then took her in his arms again. Five minutes later they reached the flat.

"Now, while I get into a dressing-gown, take off some of your things and make yourself comfortable. Then we'll have a cigarette and talk. Hope you're not tired."

"I'm not tired, Julian."

"Good. Shan't be two minutes."

When he returned she was lying half-dressed on the couch.

"Stella Prescott at home," he announced. "And ten minutes ago we were with James. I've discovered the fascination of these sudden transitions."

"Since when?"

"Oh, only recently. I suppose it's one result of seeing you in the Farquharson setting. You seem so remote, so impregnable. I've watched you often – imagining you as you are when you're here. And I determined that you should go from one to the other in a flash. And to-night you've done it."

"That's perversity, Julian."

"Perhaps. Do you remember you once said that Rawlings was right in believing that everything depended on its background? Well, why shouldn't desire depend on its background just as much as anything else?"

She did not reply, and after a pause he went on:

"I wonder how many other people we know have a secret passion like James. It would be interesting to investigate."

"Have you a victim in mind?"

"More or less, but that's not the point. Let's stick to James for a minute. No more ridiculous precautions, Stella. I know we've got to deceive others, but we needn't bother about him. He's your slave."

"Why hurt anyone unnecessarily, Julian? God knows I must hurt him often enough. I've begun to be sorry for him lately."

"You'll tell me in a minute that you wish you were in love with him."

"I do – you need have no doubt about that."

"Stella!"

"It would solve everything."

"And what about me?"

"You'd be all right, Julian. I've discovered that I belong to the little people who want happiness. You don't. You only demand that life shall be interesting."

"You're talking nonsense――"

"I'm *not* talking nonsense! I'm a weak fool to have come here to-night. You don't want me."

"That's not true. It's――"

"It was only your perversity made you bring me here. Loving

you puts me in your power. But there's a limit in me, Julian, and if you drive me to it, I'll never see you again – however much it may hurt. You're becoming half a stranger – and yet I go on loving you. My God! it's funny really. I suppose I shall suffer through you as James has suffered through me."

"You're all wrong. I tell you there's no one like you."

He took her in his arms and kissed her.

"I shall always need you, Stella. I get impatient if I have to wait for you. I know there mustn't be a scandal. Dignified respectability is James's chief asset. A scandal would ruin him. People would suddenly realize that he'd always been ridiculous. I know all that. All I mean is that we need not make unnecessary sacrifices. I'm not a stranger. Other women make me want you more. It isn't just your beauty. There's something unique in you."

"But are you happy, Julian?"

"I don't think in terms of happiness. I won't lie to you. I *do* demand that life should be interesting. Once life falls below a certain level, it's time to die. You said just now that you'd suffer through me. Well, it's true. Everyone suffers in his own way to the limit of his endurance. The greatest are those capable of the greatest suffering. We all get kicked into varying degrees of self-knowledge. I'll admit the perversity too, if you like. Can't you see that I'm discovering myself? But I know that I'll always need you in some way or other."

She pressed her cheek to his and he discovered that she had been crying.

"I can feel your heart beating against mine, Stella."

"I can feel yours too. . . . I wish we could die now."

"No – not yet."

"Yes – *now!*"

He laughed at her intensity.

"Listen, Stella. You remember you asked me never to lie to you?"

"Yes – promise you never will."

"All right, but it's a risk. One day I might want to tell you something but, if I did, you might hate me."

"Why?"

"There's a madness in me. Sometimes I'm afraid of myself."

"I don't care what you are or what you do. I love you. I lied just now. I'd rather suffer through you than be happy with anyone else."

"That's the voice of Stella Prescott! Now, be an angel, and make some coffee. Then I'll tell you something I want you to do for me – and why I'm going away."

When he was alone Julian began to pace up and down the room. The statement that sometimes he was afraid of himself was not an exaggeration. He realized that his present activities were undermining his deepest loyalties, but this knowledge only goaded him to seek new excitements in subtler experiences. Perversity urged him to experiment. It suggested projects which reason ridiculed, but which, nevertheless, continued to intrigue his imagination. One in particular was beginning so to dominate him that he was leaving London in order to render its execution impossible.

Julian paused near the window and stood motionless. He had told Stella that he wanted to tell her everything about himself. Should he give the real reason for his departure? Or – to take a more personal instance – should he admit that he would rather talk to her half the night than take her in his arms? She had said he was half a stranger – did she understand that he had become unfamiliar to himself? Did she realize that strange thoughts, new desires, occupied the territory of his life like an invading army, transforming the ordinary into the fantastic?

"Here's the coffee, Julian. Let's sit near the fire and smoke a cigarette. Oh, and there's something I want to give you. Here it is."

It was her key to the flat.

"I don't want that."

"No point in my keeping it, darling. You know too many people nowadays. I shouldn't dare to use it – so I may as well return it. I meant to give it to you long ago."

"You keep it. Oddly enough, it's one thing I want to discuss with you. I'm going to take a house. I want you to find me one, somewhere near Knightsbridge. You know, in one of those little squares. I can't entertain here, and I may as well spend some money on something. You won't let me buy you presents, so I'll take a house."

"When did you think of this?"

"I didn't, really. Old Lady Sarah told me I'd have to do something of the kind. She's been here once – and Derwent has been several times. Otherwise, only you."

"Do you mean to say you haven't had any of your Bohemian friends here?"

"No – I entertain them in cafés. Anyway, Stella, I'm tired of that crowd. Which is one reason why I'm going away. So find a house for me – and stick to your key. I shall keep this flat."

"You'll keep it! Whatever for?"

"I shall stay here when I want people to think I'm out of town. An instinct warns me I shall need a retreat. I shall probably buy a cottage in the country as well. I've no end of plans, but they'd take too long to explain. Still I can tell you this: I'm giving up Bohemia, and I don't suppose I shall come to Upper Brook Street as much in the future. We'll meet here, just as we used to do. I shall keep up with old Lady Sarah, because I like her, and because I meet people at her house whom I shouldn't run into anywhere else."

"Very well. I'll keep the key."

"Are you glad?"

"Yes, I'm glad. I've some questions to ask though."

"Well, let's have them."

"You've met heaps of people in Bohemia, haven't you?"

"Yes, heaps."

"How many do you want to go on meeting?"

"Well, Derwent doesn't count – I met him through you. There are only two: Brewster, the writer; and Sinclair, the artist. Why?"

"And at Upper Brook Street?"

"Only you. Why?"

"It's a little uncanny, that's all."

"Because I tire of people quickly? I'm only interested in people's possibilities. Most of them have so few that they soon become damnably monotonous. Life's too short for repetitions. Directly you've a pretty good idea what a meeting with someone will produce, it's time to find someone else. That's not arrogant, because I don't care if people drop me."

"And the nights I spend with you? Aren't they repetitions?"

"Only superficially."

"I don't understand that, Julian."

"You're not a slave. There's a frontier in you at which you would break with me. You said so yourself just now. There's something else too, though I'd probably be a fool to say what it is. Still, you say that your only demand is that I shall not lie to you."

"That's true – so you can go on."

"All right. Suppose a day came when I ceased to want you physically, would you still come here?"

"I will come as long as you want me for any reason. And the day you don't, say so – quite brutally – and that will be the end."

"And if I didn't see you for months, and then wrote – would you come?"

"Yes, my dear. I'm destined to love you – and you are destined never to love anyone. Better drink your coffee before it's cold. Then tell me why you're going away. Incidentally, I know some-one who will miss you."

"Who's that?"

"Clytie Lessing."

"What, in God's name, made you mention her?"

"Because she'll miss you."

"Only because I'm a friend of Lady Sarah's – and Clytie is a snob."

"I wonder. First, you snubbed her; then you ignored her. The novelty of such treatment may have intrigued her. A lot of men are mad about her – that's very obvious."

"I can't stand her! She's the only person I ever met whom I hated on sight. Auctioned herself to the highest bidder, got that old wreck of a husband, and now flaunts her fidelity like a banner! And all those idiots who admire her blonde hair and white skin accept her at her own valuation! Lady Sarah's told me a lot about Clytie. Don't talk about her!"

"Sorry! Tell me where you're going."

"Spain – Italy – and I'm meeting Derwent in Vienna at the end of next month. I don't know how long I shall be away – but I'm not expecting any wild excitements."

"Then why are you going?"

"Lots of reasons, Stella. One is that I want to collect myself – if you can understand that. I've only known extremes. First, The

Hermitage; then Mandell's office; then sudden wealth; then those marvellous months with only you; then frenzied social activity for I don't know how long. Once, I was Julian Grant. Now, there are a dozen Julian Grants."

"So you're going to study the twelve Julians in order to find out which is to play the lead?"

"Perhaps. Anyway, you've twelve lovers."

"That's not true. I don't exist for several of those Julians."

"Well, one of them is going to write to you – James or no James. And while I'm away you'll find that house for me and arrange everything?"

"I will . . . I wonder what you'd be doing now if I hadn't spoken to you in that bookshop?"

"We couldn't have missed, Stella. I wish to God those months had never ended when there was nothing in my world but your beauty. It was the pulse of my being. No woman can ever be to me what you were then. Why did you decide to share me with others?"

"Simply to accustom myself – by anticipation – to the loneliness waiting for me where our roads forked. Besides, my dear, I had lost you before I surrendered you. . . . Oh, Julian, how young you were! And what a darling! And – and you got sausages for our first breakfast!"

"I believe you're crying."

"You couldn't eat, that first time at 'The Fragonard' – you did nothing but stare at me. And you wanted me to run away with you. And you were jealous because you thought I had other lovers. But it's madness to talk of those days – it's like visiting a grave. Let's discuss the Knightsbridge house. There're some things I must know."

They talked for an hour, covering a number of subjects. Finally, Julian asked:

"Are you hungry?"

"Yes, I believe I am."

"Then I tell you what we'll do. I know an underground café in Soho. I go there sometimes – it's open practically all night. It's pretty rough – you know what I mean? – but that doesn't matter. Let's go there for an hour. We can have some more coffee and a sandwich."

"It's too late, Julian."

"It's only one. Come on, let's go. You won't wear evening clothes, naturally, but you've others in the next room. You'll see odd people there – impossible to imagine what they are or what they do. So different from James. Be a darling, and come."

"Do you want to very much?"

"Yes. I'm restless, Stella. It's safe enough. You won't run into anyone you know. That's very certain. It's a hell of a hole, but let's go."

"All right. It's a pity Oliver isn't alive. The sordid attracted him too."

D

Julian remained abroad for eight months, then an incident occurred, wholly trivial in itself, which nevertheless occasioned his return. . . .

One evening, in a café in Paris, he happened to glance at an English illustrated weekly. He turned the pages over mechanically, scarcely looking at them, till the discovery of a photograph focused his attention. He studied it for some minutes, then threw the periodical aside, rose abruptly and left the café. He had decided to return to England. Twenty-four hours later he was in London.

Two days after his arrival he called at Upper Brook Street and learned that Farquharson was in town, but that Stella was still in Norfolk. He left the house and walked slowly down Park Lane, reviewing possibilities till, finally, he discovered that the only person in London he wanted to see was Lady Sarah. Nevertheless, as he made his way to Berkeley Square, his thoughts were not concerned with his destination. They were occupied wholly with the project which had prompted his return to England. Eventually, he decided to evolve no plans regarding its execution. It would be more exciting to see whether destiny would collaborate with him.

Lady Sarah was at home. As Julian passed through the hall and up the staircase he was surprised to discover everything in confusion: maids were running about; men in green baize aprons were moving furniture; and a platform was being erected in the drawing-room, the door of which was open.

Lady Sarah received him in a small room which had been transformed into an office. He found her seated at a writing desk, littered with letters, her secretary by her side, notebook in hand. She looked like a witch dictating her memoirs.

"Take this letter, Blake. Telephone the man and tell him that one of us is a fool – and that I most certainly am not. What's the use of being old if you can't have your own way? You'd better go now. I'm going to waste ten minutes with Mr. Julian Grant."

"I am delighted to see you again, Lady Sarah."

"Rubbish! Come here – I want to have a good look at you."

Julian obeyed and submitted to a searching scrutiny.

"Hah! Been making a fool of yourself?"

"No – but I'm thinking of doing so."

"Is that why you've come to see me?"

"Certainly not. I've come to see you because I like you very much."

"Rubbish! What have you been doing?"

"I wandered about Italy and Spain. I spent a month in Vienna with Frank Derwent. I wanted to look at things, and I looked at them. I found an odd atmosphere everywhere. Derwent says war is inevitable. He thought so in 1900, when he went down the Danube, but now he's certain."

"Of course war is inevitable. Doesn't interest me personally, as I shall be in the next world. I propose to leave this one very shortly. Don't talk nonsense, but listen to me. Stella showed me the house she found for you in Knightsbridge. I hope you're grateful."

"I am – very. It's exactly what I want. Furniture, arrangements – everything. I even like the servants she's engaged to look after me. A young married couple – did she tell you? Stella is a genius."

"Stella is a fool. She's in love with you. Do you know that?"

"Yes."

"Don't dare to say 'yes.'"

Lady Sarah gave him a vigorous prod with her ebony cane.

"What else can I say? You wouldn't like me to lie to you."

"Stella is a fool. What's the good of being in love with an artist?"

"I'm *not* an artist, Lady Sarah! I wish to God I were!"

"You don't know what you are."

"That's absolutely true – unfortunately."

"You'll write to that little fool Stella to-day. D'you hear?"

"I will write to-day."

"And you will not say that I told you to."

"I shall not say that you told me to."

"Are you laughing at me, young man?"

"Certainly not. I'm much too frightened of you. I'm certain you're a reincarnation of Queen Elizabeth."

"Rubbish!"

Julian laughed, then indicated the document-littered desk and asked:

"Do you mind telling me exactly what you're doing?"

"Making a fool of myself. Turning the house topsy-turvy in aid of a charity – I forget which one. One or two stage people will perform, and preposterous prices will be charged. Also, there will be other forms of fraud. You'll come, of course. I'll send you a card."

"It's exceedingly kind of you. And the date?"

"Last day of the month. Only rich people wanted – preferably fools and snobs."

"As I said just now, it's exceedingly kind of you to ask me."

"Nonsense! I wanted to pay the stage people who are performing, but they are insulted by the suggestion. There's idiots for you! I'm being pestered by all sorts of impossible people who want to be asked. Not that I care who comes."

She glanced at a list in front of her, then turned to Julian.

"You can do something for me."

"Anything! What is it?"

"See James and find out which of his set ought to have cards. I'll give you some cards to distribute. Pick the richest. I was to have lunched at Upper Brook Street to-morrow, but have just discovered that the Lessings will be there. Tell James I'm too busy – and you go instead."

Julian laughed.

"Very well. That's more amusing than you know. I'll let you have a list of the people to whom I give cards. Perhaps I'd better go. You're very busy. Any message for James?"

"None!"

"Any for Lessing?"

"Tell him he's a fool – and his wife's a humbug."

"Certainly! They'll be delighted to learn that you think of them sometimes. Good-bye, Lady Sarah."

"Find Blake on your way out, and tell her to come here immediately." . . .

An hour later Julian telephoned Farquharson, explained the commission which Lady Sarah had given him, and instantly received an enthusiastic invitation to luncheon. Farquharson then expressed regret that Stella was away, as he knew she would be sorry to have missed him.

On arriving at Upper Brook Street, Julian learned that the Lessings were to be the only other guests. Also that they had been invited, as Farquharson and Lessing had business affairs to discuss.

"So it's a good thing you came, Grant, because – if you will – you could entertain Mrs. Lessing while her husband and I have a chat in my study."

"I shall be delighted, of course."

"Most kind of you. I think I hear them. It *is* pleasant to see you again. I hope Lady Sarah Spooner is well. A remarkable woman, most remarkable. She's got the brains of a man."

For Julian, luncheon possessed all the elements of high comedy. He explained in detail the nature of the commission Lady Sarah had entrusted to him, with the result that Clytie began to behave as if they were alone. She addressed every remark to Julian, snubbed her husband remorselessly, interrupted him repeatedly, and even patronized Farquharson. This was her way of showing that she belonged to Julian's sphere, not theirs. To meet him again had excited her: to discover that an invitation to Lady Sarah Spooner's depended on him fanned this excitement to frenzy.

Her methods were so ruthless that eventually the others allowed her to monopolize Julian. Her husband soon surrendered, but Farquharson fell fighting. Indignation urged him to battle. Once Clytie had regarded him as the summit of her social ambitions. Finally, however, he capitulated in order to retain a remnant of dignity.

Julian watched this comedy, but did not listen to it. He was studying Clytie. The famous hair, the white skin, the triumphant figure were emphasized by ravishing clothes; nevertheless, against his will, Julian was forced to recognize the commonplace personality which possessed these glories. It was evident that she despised her husband – a worried-looking stick of a man, thirty years her senior – and it seemed certain, therefore, that her vaunted fidelity could be no more than a pose. Julian decided, for the hundredth time, that it would be interesting to discover the extent to which she deceived herself.

He had anticipated that the comedy would achieve its climax with the departure of the men, and was not disappointed. Directly they were alone Clytie became seductive. This emotional barrage continued for a quarter of an hour, then she advanced resolutely towards her objective.

"I hear you've taken a house in Knightsbridge. I hope I shall see it one of these days."

"I hope you will."

"Did Lady Sarah Spooner suggest you should take it?"

"Yes."

"She's a great friend of yours, isn't she?"

"Yes."

A silence – during which Clytie nerved herself to storm the position, and Julian determined to ascertain whether she was prepared to compromise herself in order to obtain a card for Lady Sarah's.

"You *must* be a great friend of hers if she trusts you to invite her guests."

A rich rounded pause – then Clytie went on nervously:

"I hope you'll remember me when you make your list."

"I'd better be frank," Julian replied. "This is how I'm placed. I've only just returned to London, and there are still many details to arrange in regard to the house. So I had enough to do before Lady Sarah gave me this job. I shall spend to-morrow evening going into things."

"In your new house?"

"Yes."

"Shall I come and help you?"

Julian laughed.

"I should love you to, of course – but I shall be entirely alone, as the servants are going out. I can't begin the job till about nine-thirty, as I haven't a free minute till then."

Voices in the hall announced the approach of the others. Clytie turned to him impulsively and said in a whisper:

"I'll come at nine-thirty. Don't say anything."

"Of course not. Here's the address."

He gave her a card. The next moment Farquharson and Lessing joined them. Ten minutes later Julian left.

Destiny had collaborated with him. . . .

During breakfast the next morning, Julian said to his servant:

"You've had a lot to do lately, so I've got seats at the theatre for you and your wife. You'd better take them."

"I'm sure we're very much obliged to you, sir."

"Don't hurry back. I'm not sleeping here to-night."

"Will you be dining at home, sir?"

"No. I shall dine at the club. So you can go whenever you like."

"Thank you very much, sir."

Julian spent most of the day arranging his books. He dined early at the club and returned home at about nine o'clock.

It was a perfect autumn night. Everything was extraordinarily still. He stood on the steps, looking down into the square, unable to believe that he was in London. The memory of an autumn evening at The Hermitage held him for a moment – the scent and the silence of the half-wild garden enfolded him – then the present reasserted itself and he entered the house.

He wandered through the rooms, then descended into the basement. It was his first visit, and every detail interested him. He glanced into the servants' bedroom, looked into the kitchen and pantry, experiencing to a mild degree the sensations of a burglar. Everything existed to minister to his comfort – everything belonged to him – nevertheless, he felt an intruder. A sense of organic relationship was lacking. He was glad to remember that, to-night, he would sleep at the flat. . . .

He would receive Clytie in the study. It was on the first floor and faced the square. He entered it, closed the folding doors which communicated with the bedroom, then stood motionless studying the book-shelves which lined the walls.

Nearly nine-thirty. She would come in a taxi, not her car. He would stand near the window and wait. The discovery that he was only curious, not impatient, amused him.

The sound of a motor penetrated the silence. He parted the curtains and watched a taxi approach and draw up outside. He went downstairs slowly, feeling that he was watching himself.

"You're very punctual. Do you mind coming to the study? The other rooms aren't really ready yet."

Clytie smiled assent, but it was evident that she was very excited. They did not speak as they passed up the stairs.

"Here we are!"

"What a delightful room!"

"I'm glad you like it. Let me take your cloak."

Her evening clothes generously revealed her attractions. Julian glanced at her, then added:

"I saw your photograph in one of the weeklies a few days ago. Surely you were wearing this dress?"

"I was. Do you like it?"

"Immensely. Now, here's your card for Lady Sarah's."

Clytie took it mechanically. She had imagined that, at the best, he would have given it to her at the end of her visit.

"Is this really for me?"

"Yes. Are you surprised?"

"A little. I didn't think you'd give me one."

"Why not?"

"I've always thought that you despised me."

"And why do you think I let you come here to-night?"

"Well, I thought it might amuse you to give me the trouble – just to humiliate me – and then refuse to let me have a card."

Julian laughed.

"I see. Well, you have the card now – so you must have been wrong."

"All the same, you do despise me, don't you?"

"Yes – but that's of no interest to you. What's my opinion matter?"

"But I want to know why."

"Well, sit down, then I'll tell you. You can go at any minute, if my explanation annoys you. You've got the card – which was your reason for coming."

She laughed nervously, then sat in a chair which Julian had moved nearer to the fire.

"I've wanted to know your opinion of me for a long time."

"Why?"

"Well, I – I have. That's all. I don't know why."

"All right. I'll tell you. I think you deceive yourself with your own pose. You pretend to be a different woman from the one you really are. You're afraid of yourself. So you pretend to be someone else."

"And why has no one else made this great discovery?"

"Because they've taken you at your own valuation. That's why. All the men who admire you are afraid of you. They imagine you're the icicle you pretend to be."

"Perhaps it's fortunate, then, that you do not admire me."

"Why fortunate?"

"I don't know."

"But I do admire you – physically. You're extremely attractive."

"So you admire me and despise me?"

"Exactly! If I'm wrong in my analysis, I've insulted you – and you ought to go. If I'm right, it would be policy to go. Then I might think I was wrong."

She remained motionless, staring into the fire.

"You despise me for marrying a man for his money," she said at last.

"Nothing of the kind! You were yourself when you did that. You've not had the courage to be so since – or you would have taken lovers, instead of flaunting a fictitious fidelity."

"It is not fictitious!"

"It is – it's only of the flesh."

She rose slowly. Julian picked up her cloak. As he was putting it round her, his hands rested on her shoulders. She turned and looked at him.

The cloak fell to the floor. He took her in his arms and pressed her to him so fiercely that she was powerless.

"Julian! . . . *Julian!* . . . Let me go!"

"You don't want to go."

She hesitated, then threw her arms round him.

"I love you," she whispered.

"You do not love me – any more than I love you. What do we know about love?"

"Julian!"

"So your fidelity was only fear?"

"I was mad to come here to-night."

"You'll come here whenever I want you to. You understand?"

"I'd have come long ago – if you'd asked me. Where are you going?"

Julian opened the folding doors and switched on the lights.

E

He left the house just before midnight, walked till he found a taxi, then drove to the flat.

It was his first visit since his return, though he had sent Mrs. Peters a card on arrival asking her to tell the servant that he would turn up in a day or two.

He opened the door and entered the hall. Instantly memories of Stella surrounded him. He stood motionless for nearly a minute, then went into the sitting-room.

There was a letter on the table. He slit open the envelope, extracted a single sheet of notepaper, and glanced at the date. It had been written ten days ago.

It bore a Swiss address, and it told him that Dorothy was dead.

It was some minutes before he could remember who she was.

F

Julian discovered that the results of perversity reveal its nature. Nevertheless, even in retrospect, certain phases of its activity remained obscure.

At no stage in their relations had he willed to make Clytie his mistress. Of this he was certain. In the early days of their acquaintance he had formed a theory concerning her – he had been certain that she deceived herself with her own pose – but it had not interested him greatly at the time. Then, gradually and imperceptibly, curiosity had suggested that it would be interesting to test this theory. Reason rebelled against the stupidity of this suggestion, but Julian discovered that something deeper than reason was involved – something obscure, to which the stupidity of the proposed experiment was a potent attraction.

Again and again he sought to dismiss this project by enumerating arguments which revealed its fatuity. It offended his pride to be forced to think of Clytie Lessing. The fact that she could invade his imagination was intolerable. It reduced him to her level. His contempt for her was so absolute that it blunted his appreciation of her physical attractions. It was incredible that men could admire her. She was a shape, not a woman.

But neither reason nor pride prevailed against the insinuations of a perversity subtler than either. Finally, the desire to humiliate Clytie by stripping her of her pretensions became an obsession.

He had left England in order to render an experiment impossible, and before many weeks had passed he ceased to think of it. Nevertheless, eight months later, the chance discovery of Clytie's photograph was sufficient to make him alter his plans and return to London.

But his mood had changed. It seemed to him that he had become a detached speculator in possibilities. He would go to London just to see what would happen. The whole project tantalized his imagination. He had no standard as to what would constitute success or failure in his dealings with Clytie. He would test his theory, if an opportunity occurred. If not, he would probably forget all about it.

Now – she was his mistress.

This result seemed so disproportionate to his motives that Julian viewed it with the stupefaction of a child who, playing with a box of matches, suddenly discovers that the house is on fire. He had never been conscious of the slightest desire for Clytie. He had never visualized results; he had been interested only in possibilities. He was certain of this. His refusal to anticipate the consequences of his experiment had sharpened its excitement. Now, she was his mistress.

In retrospect, however, Julian was compelled to recognize that he had hated Clytie from their first meeting, and that everything which had happened since had resulted from a determination to humiliate her. Perversity had dominated him so subtly that he had remained unaware of this master motive.

But this perversity did not end with the discovery of it. It only entered a new phase. The physical contrast between Stella and Clytie had an attraction: the psychological contrast between his relations with them was intriguing. New possibilities enticed him. With Stella, desire had been a culmination: with Clytie, it was isolated. His affair with her became a descent into the underworld of sensation. He exploited her passion for him to the uttermost limit, experiencing excesses unknown and undesired with Stella. Stella was a world: Clytie – a madness.

During the next few months Julian's demands on Clytie became more and more imperious. It piqued his perversity to test her infatuation by multiplying their meetings till detection seemed inevitable. But he discovered that there were no limits to her recklessness. She told her husband the flimsiest lies with amazing audacity, and countered Julian's demands with suggestions so outrageous in their disregard of danger that he was forced to negative them. Her abandonment, on every level, astonished him. Finally, he became convinced that her pose of virtue had been a form of self-protection: a sub-conscious recognition of the perils involved in a surrender to her emotions. But this discovery did not interest him. He was concerned wholly with himself.

Stella had returned to London a few days after Clytie's first visit to Knightsbridge. She met Julian frequently, but although she went to the flat on several occasions, he did not suggest that she should spend a night there. To do so without telling her of his relations with Clytie was impossible: to explain those relations before they had ended was useless.

Three months later the end came. Julian had experienced the successive stages in an inevitable progression: – excess produced satiety: satiety – weariness: weariness – disgust: disgust – hatred. He entered the darkness of that degradation which shadows loveless desire. Lust was no longer a word. It was a dungeon in which he was a prisoner.

The realization of his state soon created a determination to escape. All the student in his nature awoke, demanding freedom. Pride – disassociating itself from his degradation by viewing it from above – saw Clytie as the cause of it. He began to regard her as a gaoler, not a fellow-prisoner, till, finally, his hatred of her became absolute.

One night, just as she was about to leave her house to visit him, he rang her up and severed their relations with curt brutality.

The next day he left for the country.

G

Julian's first action on his return, three weeks later, was to telephone Stella and ask her to spend the night at the flat.

She arrived at ten o'clock, gave him both her hands, then studied him intently – her eyes shining with amusement.

"What's the joke, Stella? James's reception of the news that his wife would not be sleeping at home to-night?"

"No – not that. He was rather surprised – and very naturally. It's nearly a year since his wife made one of her mysterious disappearances."

"It can't be a year."

"Very nearly. We went to that Soho café – you remember? – just before you went away."

"My God, it seems a century!"

"Still, the fact that you've asked me at last proves that I'm a preference, not a habit. I remember using that phrase ages ago. I've survived competition – and that's a very satisfactory sensation, don't you think?"

"You're adorable. Give me your cloak. Now, lie on the couch. I want to look at you for hours."

"Why?"

"Because your beauty isn't an accident. It isn't just the shape of your body. It's your soul made visible. I've never possessed you. No man will ever possess you. You cannot give yourself – you can only lend."

"Oh, my dear, all that only comes to this: I was your first lover and so you confuse me with your first illusions. But never mind about me. The point is that you're looking extraordinarily well – for the first time for months."

Julian did not reply. To-night, presumably, he would have to tell her about Clytie, and this knowledge irritated him. He did not want to talk: he only wanted to look at her. Her very presence was a caress. A cool fragrance seemed to surround her. He felt like a man who had wakened from a nightmare to find himself in a garden at dawn. But it was necessary to say something.

"Yes, I'm better, but I thought James looked very worried when I last saw him. What's wrong?"

"He's a little alarming nowadays."

"Why? What about?"

"War. He talks of nothing else. I think he's heard something from the inside this time."

"What makes you think so?"

"Because he isn't jubilant. You know how he's always revelled in the German menace? Well, now, he's very subdued. He keeps telling me in a whisper that war is certain – and soon."

"He's right – for once. Derwent said the same thing when I was with him in Vienna. What do they all expect? Europe's been preparing for war for a century. The mere fact that they had that conference at The Hague proved that they were all getting frightened of the inevitable. Any other news?"

"Only Clytie Lessing."

"*Clytie Lessing?*"

"Yes, didn't you know? Oh, of course, you've been in the country. She's been terribly ill – brain-storms, hysterics, and all sorts of horrors. Her husband's nearly demented. And the doctors can't discover the cause. It's a complete mystery. She's a bit better now, but she still lies in bed staring at something. She won't speak and she won't eat. I'm terribly sorry for her. I've been to see her several times."

"*You've* been to see her?"

"Yes."

"Why?"

"Well, after all, Julian, I know her pretty well. Also, her husband suggested that I should go, and as Clytie didn't refuse to see me – which she's done with nearly everyone else – I went. What else could I do?"

Julian did not reply. He rose to get a cigarette, then stood with his back to Stella, staring at the fire.

After a silence, she added:

"You don't seem very interested."

"I'm not."

He swung round irritably.

"I suppose I'll have to tell you about it, but it's a damned nuisance. I did want——"

"Tell me about what?"

"Why, Clytie Lessing, of course."

"What do you know about her?"

"Everything."

Her astonishment intensified his irritability.

"Everything," he repeated. "But for God's sake let's make this short, and then we'll talk about something else. I had an affair with Clytie – if you must know."

"You're joking, Julian."

"I'm not joking."

"But you always told me that you hated her."

"I did – and I do. It will be simpler if you do not try to understand. Just accept the facts: we had an affair – it ended three weeks ago – and she's evidently upset."

"Upset! She's been like a mad woman."

"Well, you say she's better now."

"I can't believe you said that – in that tone."

She crossed to the window, then stood motionless. The ticking of the clock seemed to become louder every moment.

"Is it true that you always hated her, Julian?"

"Yes."

"I don't want it to be true. I want it to be a lie – a lie you told thinking it would please me."

"It isn't a lie."

"Then how could you——"

"Oh, for God's sake, Stella, let's stop all this! You'd never understand if I talked for a month. I never imagined for a single second that things would go the way they did. I simply wanted to show her that her ridiculous pretensions did not deceive me. The whole thing was lunacy from beginning to end."

"And how did it end?"

"I rang her up and told her it was finished."

She turned quickly and looked at him as if unable to believe that he was serious.

"You – *rang her up?*"

"Yes. What was the point of having a scene?"

"There have been plenty of scenes since."

"Well, I don't suppose there will be many more. Hysteria soon burns itself out. She's not capable of tragedy."

"You'll have to go to her, Julian – and you'll have to go to-morrow."

"You're not serious, of course?"

"I'm perfectly serious."

"You can scarcely believe that it would do any good for me to see her. Do you want her to become hysterical again?"

"You must go for your own sake, Julian, not hers."

"I'm sorry, but that seems to me to be nonsense."

"So you won't go?"

"No."

"Very well."

Stella went to the couch, picked up her cloak, and put it round her.

"What are you doing?"

"I can't stay, Julian."

"You must be insane! I never knew you were so devoted to Clytie Lessing."

"I'm not, but she's a human being."

"She's a fool, I tell you!"

"Fools can suffer, Julian – though you'll never believe that."

"You can't go, Stella. I need you."

"You need no one. If you ever have a real need for me, I'll come to you."

She turned and went slowly out of the room. A moment later he heard the front door close. . . .

The next day he left England.

When he returned to London, the world was at war.

V

SNAPSHOTS OF JULIAN GRANT

I

The eleventh day of the eleventh month, 1918. . . .

The streets seethed with a shouting, cheering, delirious mob. Windows were thronged with people waving handkerchiefs, blowing whistles, beating trays, or yelling the latest patriotic song. Cars and taxis, hooting hilariously and festooned with humanity, moved inch by inch through the surging streets. Bells pealed jubilantly from every steeple. Flags fluttered triumphantly. The Armistice had been signed. . . .

Julian stood by the open window in the sitting-room of his flat, gazing at the endless host flocking down Piccadilly. His expression denoted complete detachment from the hysterical enthusiasm below. For some moments he continued to watch the spectacle with the eyes of a sober man at an orgy, then, with a half-amused, half-irritable gesture, he shut the window, lit a cigarette, and began to pace slowly up and down the room.

He was waiting for Frank Derwent. Their last meeting had been in Vienna some months before the war. It interested Julian to discover how much had to be forgotten in order to remember that meeting.

A few minutes later, Derwent arrived.

Superficially he looked younger, being weather-beaten and obviously in perfect physical health, but the eyes had a fixed expression and any attempt at gaiety seemed a plagiarism of his old manner.

They greeted each other as if they had met yesterday, then crossed to the window and stood looking down at the surging crowds.

"When did you get back, Frank?"

"Only three days ago. Devilish glad you phoned. This isn't a day to spend alone."

"We'd better drink and try to forget those idiots down there. Do you realize that I haven't seen any of our crowd for years? I scarcely know what you did in the war – or why you did anything. Get comfortable, then tell me."

Derwent stretched himself full length on the couch.

"I perpetrated the incredible folly of driving a lorry in France, my dear fellow. You can imagine the devastating effect of work after a lifetime of leisure. I assure you that I was about to don a dressing-gown, sink into an armchair, and do a little crochet for the rest of my mortal existence, when those bloody fools started fighting and – by God! – I found myself perched on a dud lorry, rattling over shell-scarred roads, scarcely knowing which was the accelerator and which the brake. No life for an old gentleman, I can tell you."

Julian handed him a whisky-and-soda.

"Underneath, you're a patriot, Frank. I envy you."

"But you went, my dear fellow."

"I joined at the end of 1915. Note the date – it's significant. I went because I was at the end of things – and for no other reason. I was in the line a month, and then I was wounded. That wasn't serious, but I had pneumonia badly afterwards."

"I hadn't heard that."

"Oh yes, I nearly went out. Eventually I was sent back to England. Then they discovered that I knew several languages, so I was given a job in the Intelligence Department. I've been in it ever since. And I propose to remain in it just as long as possible."

"Good Lord! Why?"

"Why? Because it delivers me from the horrors of freedom. If you've imagination – and are not an artist – you're done. Most people reel through life stunned by their daily toil. They're happy because they're half dead. Well, I've tasted the joys of the treadmill, and I'm not in a hurry to leave it."

"You're not serious, of course?"

Julian turned to him irritably.

"Never more serious in my life. If you want happiness, be a slave. Only a saint, or an artist, can endure freedom. If you're neither – and are too imaginative to be able to dope yourself with sport, or petty vices – life's impossible."

Derwent emptied half his glass, then asked:

"Had you discovered that in 1915?"

"Yes. I had a curiosity about life such as you cannot imagine. You were not educated by Nathan Grant. When I left The Hermitage I knew nothing. Soon, I was determined to know everything. I wanted to discover what this world – of which my father was so afraid – had to offer. Everything had an exaggerated value for me – especially Possibilities. Soon, the normal ceased to interest me. That's inevitable, if a man has the courage of his own curiosity."

Julian gave a short laugh, then added:

"That's a confession in the abstract. You probably know enough to translate it into the concrete. Anyway, I wish to God I was one of those fools outside, waving a flag, and yelling because the war is over. Do you imagine that one of those idiots knows that a subtler and more deadly war has begun – the end of which will not be flag-wagging and cheers? I don't claim to have been far behind the scenes during the last two or three years, but I've seen enough to guess the rest. But they can all go to hell their own way."

Derwent filled his pipe slowly.

"I understand a good deal of all that, but there's one thing I don't understand."

"What's that?"

"Stella."

"So she's told you?"

"She told me just before the war. You and she had had a quarrel. She didn't say what about, but she told me that you'd been her lover for years. I'd half guessed long before, of course. But you're never certain till you're told."

"Well?"

"I don't understand – that's all."

"You don't understand how a man, possessing a woman like Stella, could bother about anyone else?"

"No, I don't. If I'd been in your shoes, Julian, I'd have had only one problem – to believe in my luck."

"And you can't imagine a curiosity – a perversity, if you like – so insatiable that it had to explore hell as well as heaven?"

"No, I'm damned if I can."

"You would – if you'd been born and bred in a monastery.

And The Hermitage *was* a monastery. But you've lived alone a lot, so you must have explored that interior universe, hidden in each of us, of which most people take very good care to know nothing. You must have discovered that Frank Derwent didn't exist – that there were half a dozen Frank Derwents. And that, on occasions, a mad Frank Derwent pushed the others aside and announced that he was *the* Frank Derwent."

"Possibly! But you weren't alone – you had Stella."

"I'm not going to argue. Where is she, anyway?"

"Still in Paris. You know, of course, that they found James a sinecure job there early in the war?"

"Yes, I knew that. As James was a public figure – and over military age – his patriotism was peculiarly virulent. Have you seen them?"

"Yes, a few months ago. Haven't you seen Stella – or written – since you quarrelled?"

"No."

"That's pretty grim."

"Is she as beautiful as ever?"

"Yes, my dear fellow, she is. She always will be with those features and that figure. More beautiful, I think. Her beauty's deepened – if you know what I mean. She's had a hell of a time."

"And James?"

Derwent hesitated, put his pipe down, then said slowly:

"Well, I don't know. He gave me rather an odd feeling. Looks just the same, but there's something wrong with him. I'm sorry for the poor brute because he really is desperately in love with Stella. His life must be sheer hell. She makes gallant efforts, but the fact remains that her eyes go glassy with boredom directly his heavy step is heard."

Julian said nothing. A wilderness separated him from the world in which he had known Stella. It seemed impossible that it was only necessary to go to Paris in order to see her.

"Let's go to the club, Frank," he said at last. "There are a thousand things I want to discuss. It will be quieter there. I can't stand this din in the streets another minute. I'll go into the next room and change. I got up late and flung these things on. I shan't be very long."

He went into the bedroom, leaving the door open.

Derwent rose and studied the book-shelves. Eventually he took a volume down at random and glanced at the title-page.

"Good Lord!" he exclaimed involuntarily, then called to Julian: "Just found a book that poor old Lady Sarah gave you."

"I still miss her," Julian replied. "But she'd made up her mind to die long before she did."

Derwent replaced the book, then said slowly:

"I knew her when I was a kid. Always gave me a quid whenever I saw her. She'd the spirit of ten men. Grand old woman!"

Then, after a long pause, he went on:

"I'm clearing out of this damned town, Julian."

"Why?"

"Too full of ghosts. Twenty men I used to go shooting or fishing with have gone. I'm clearing out."

He began to pace up and down the room, muttering to himself, then he stopped abruptly and laughed.

"I knew there was something I meant to tell you, Julian. I met an old friend of yours yesterday."

"Who was that?"

"Mrs. Fromings."

"Just the same, I've no doubt."

"Just the same, my dear fellow. It will be many incarnations before a ray of light penetrates Mrs. Fromings. She insisted on telling me all the details of Clytie Lessing's divorce. I suppose you read about it in the papers?"

"I saw something about it some months ago."

"Well, the encyclopædic Mrs. Fromings told me a lot I hadn't heard. She said that right from the beginning of the war Clytie began to play hell. Had lover after lover till everyone in London knew about it, with the single exception of old Lessing. But he discovered eventually – and kicked her out of the house. Would you believe that old stick could have been so vindictive? Anyway, he divorced her. The co-respondent was a wretched lieutenant – who was killed a few days after Lessing got his decree *nisi*. Now, according to Mrs. Fromings, Clytie is a Lady with a Flat – somewhere near Clarges Street."

Julian returned to the sitting-room, buttoning up his coat.

"No, I hadn't heard all that. Come on, let's go. This infernal din in the streets is driving me mad."

II

A Cottage in Kent.
1924.

STELLA,

I have spent the whole of the night writing to you. These first two pages are a postscript.

Our last real meeting was the night of our quarrel, just before the war. If you had not left me that night, I should have forgotten you long ago. I know what it cost you to break with me, for you were in love with your idea of me, but your will triumphed. It is why I am unable to forget you.

Our meetings after your return from Paris in 1919 were meaningless. I was still in the service, I was living in Knightsbridge, and it amused me to entertain a good deal. We met often enough socially, but never alone. There was a contest of wills between us: I wanted you to come to the flat unasked; and you were determined that I should admit my need of you.

Then – was it two years later? I cannot remember – James had a nervous collapse and you had to go away. Did you know that, a week after you left London, I let my house and went abroad? I would have followed you, but my pride would not permit such a surrender. I did not return to England for over a year, then – learning that James was no better, and that you were with him in Norfolk – I went to New York and stayed there for several months.

All this time I did not write to you. I wanted my neglect to hurt you. You know, of course, that I have tried again and again to destroy that quality in you which compels admiration.

When I returned to London I learned that James was seriously ill again and that you had taken him to Vienna to consult a specialist. I was tired of travelling: to remain in London was impossible. I came to this cottage, which I had bought years ago, and I have been here ever since.

I have written what follows for two reasons. The first is to beg you to see me when I return to London: the second is to reveal myself to you – so far as that is possible. It would be truer to say "to reveal myselves."

If after reading these "extracts from an unwritten diary," you are willing to meet me, send a line to my club. I am leaving here almost immediately and I do not know exactly when I shall get to London. But your letter would be forwarded.

There is no perversity in you, Stella. It is the reason why we quarrelled about Clytie Lessing. So I want you to know, from the outset, that the incident with Clytie was *not* an isolated one. There have been many since – each more degrading, more stupid, more meaningless than the last. Probably it will be so to the end.

In an instant, and without warning, all my interests lose substance, and I enter a depression that is indescribable. Life is reduced to the monotony of an endless arid plain. Once this state has captured me, only the unreality of the monstrous has any attraction. I tell you that there is no limit to the follies suggested by an imagination that is functioning negatively.

Few people know anything about perversity. All social reformers – all painstaking creators of rationalistic Utopias – ignore it. They tell you that education, environment, will settle everything – that men have only to recognize where their self-interest lies in order to become "reasonable." Dreamers! Every great action, and every vicious one, is a repudiation of the claims of self-interest.

When I emerge from this state, and regard retrospectively the actions committed under its dominion, I feel that I am watching the activities of a madman. Later, the certainty deepens in me that all this is over and done with for ever, that I have experienced degradation for the last time. It is then, and then only, that I understand the meaning of the word "humility." Also I realize what the Spanish mystic meant when he wrote: *How many right feelings spring from the madness to which we are urged by the beast.* But – and this is the whole point – when that indescribable depression claims me again, the memories of the horror of degradation are impotent to deliver me. They are extraordinarily vivid, but they are impotent, nevertheless. And so, once more, I experience what Böhme calls "the qualification of the abyss." . . .

I would give ten years of life to be a creative artist. Once you said to me that your father, Oliver, had the temperament of an artist with none of an artist's talent. His predicament is mine. I,

too, possess psychic energy – with no medium for its manifesta-
tion. "Standing water breeds pestilence." Most men are whipped
by necessity to some activity. The need for money is the whip.
But it would be impossible for me arbitrarily to enter some profession. It would be impossible, and it would be cowardice. Also,
God knows there is no shortage of mediocrities.

Of course, there are a number of things I might do. I might
write books about books; or join one of those groups of earnest
people who are going to regenerate Europe with a theory; or
become super-artistic – and go to parties where everyone leans
on something and discusses Vitality. Or I might collect old prints,
or first editions, or take up hand-weaving. Or make a little niche
for myself as an eccentric. Or join the "end-of-the-world set,"
which is beginning to emerge, and which is destined to grow. Or
I might become an English Communist. After all, I have a private
income. Or I might save The Drama. I might back plays, produced by little societies, in which all the characters are definitely
"symbolic." During the intervals a lady plays Hebridean airs on
a harp. Or I might become a vegetarian, and preach the glad tid-
ings that man can live by whole-meal bread alone.

There are a number of things I might do.

I might go in for "good works." It's readily assumed that, if
you've money, you can do good. Pure materialism! The time
has come for the poor to do a bit of slumming. They ought to
be made to visit the Merely Rich. That would teach them what
suffering there is in the world – what emotional poverty, what
spiritual privation. But, if they learned that, revolution would be
inevitable, for that knowledge would destroy the most cherished
illusion of the poor – which is, that Leisure and Luxury are the
kingdom of God.

"What will redeem the poor from their poverty will redeem,
at the same time, the rich from their riches."

I know all the compromises, subterfuges, and evasions of
those in my predicament. But, unfortunately, I also know this: it
does not matter what you do, if it is real to you; and if it is not
real, and you are only pretending that it is, then you are trying to
turn the stones into bread. It is a temptation known only to those
who, in their degree, have been driven into the wilderness. . . .

It is clear to me, at last, why my father lived like a monk in

The Hermitage. He was a man to whom the spiritual world was more real than this one, but its reality depended on solitude. Everything in the everyday world seemed to deny his vision. In solitude, it had substance: in society, it became spectral. This was the reason why he feared and hated life as it is lived. His vision had not so penetrated him that he could look unmoved on all that denied it. Lesser lovers than he have sought solitude that their rapture might be real.

*   *   *   *   *   *

It's essential that you understand this, Stella: when I met you, the normal was the unknown. Everything that was commonplace to you was adventure to me. I had only gaped at life, like a rustic at a play, but – unlike him – I was sensitive, imaginative. Emotionally and mentally, I was aflame with curiosity. Everything that The Hermitage had denied was now offered. You, who have always lived in the world, cannot realize the intensity of my expectations, the fervour of my demands.

Inevitably, therefore, I raced from experience to experience, seeking in each a satisfaction which none had to offer. I had no fixed conceptions of the desirable, for I was not mesmerized by any tradition. Curiosity impelled me first to explore, then to experiment. I soon realized what the lives of others were, and I knew that I could not live as they did. I'll give you an example. In your set, I met the "successful." They were immensely self-satisfied; they patronized everything superior to themselves; and were so intoxicated with their own eminence that they regarded it as proof conclusive that all was for the best in the best of all possible worlds. But, emotionally, they were dead. Everything had been surrendered that the brain might possess a pathetic mastery in some activity or other. To sympathize was impossible. They were delighted with their deformity. They were cripples, proud of their crutches. . . .

Do you remember the night when I made you come from your house to the flat? James came with us to the taxi and saw us off. I had told him some lie about going to a dance. Later, you said that perversity had dictated my actions. You were right. Somehow I must explain, and it is not easy to explain.

You were my first lover. For months you were everything to me. But what I really valued was not you – the physical Stella. It was a quality in you which eluded possession. My imagination demanded so much from the flesh that disappointment was inevitable. But I rebelled against that disappointment. And that rebellion, too, was inevitable.

Sex represents the highest pinnacle of glamour in the human consciousness. I refused to admit that the actual was a travesty of my imaginings. But I had known only the normal. To sharpen satisfaction, I began to experiment. It intrigued me, that night, to take you abruptly from James to the flat. Swift, violent, or outrageous contrasts are the food of perversity. Shall I tell you why I had an affair with Clytie Lessing, whom I despised and hated? Because of the contrast it presented to my relations with you. Everything you gave me I dishonoured. Curiosity goaded me to perversity.

Do you imagine that I do not know the absurdity of all this? But I tell you, Stella, that our actions are only fantastic carica-tures of our experience in that inner universe, hidden in each of us, where we are concerned not with men and women, but with principalities and powers.

We know nothing whatever about ourselves so long as we are at home in the world. It is suffering which kicks us to self-knowledge. Suffering, by isolating us, initiates us into the mys-teries of interior life. We no longer live in terms of the visible and the tangible. We enter that inner realm where everything is conditioned by our mental or emotional states.

Once I believed that I was a man and that my name was Julian Grant. But, as I penetrated deeper and deeper into myself, I dis-covered that "I" do not exist. I am a series of personalities, a cycle of recurring states – each of which in turn calls itself Julian Grant. This very letter is an example. It is the product of a state – a mood – which, to-morrow, will have ceased to exist. If you were to return this letter to me, a few months hence, it would seem wholly fantastic. But, to-night, it is the truth. It calls itself Julian Grant.

Do not be deceived, Stella, for I assure you that I am not. It is the sane Julian who is writing this. (You will have noticed that what I call the *sane* Julian is an egotist to the pitch of madness. But let that pass. Let us assume that words have meaning.) Yes, it is the sane Julian. All the other Julians stand motionless, watching. They are waxworks, each awaiting the return of that state which will quicken it to life. Then, it will become Julian Grant. It will capture the imagination, dominate the will, and so control the understanding. And if it writes a letter, it will be very different from this one – and it will not be written to you. For the next Julian may hate you, Stella. It may derive its deepest satisfaction from attempting to destroy everything in you which the sane Julian admires. On the other hand, the next Julian may be unaware of your existence, or indifferent to it.

It all sounds a little tragic, doesn't it? And that, too, is false. Possibly I shall know ecstasy to-morrow.

This cottage is very isolated. It is in one of the loveliest parts of Kent and, incidentally, it is only ten miles distant from The Hermitage. Well, perhaps to-morrow I shall wander across meadows, or through winding lanes, wholly in harmony with myself and the loveliness surrounding me. I may experience that state in which everything I have known since I was nineteen is rolled up like a scroll, and I become again the student I then was. The beauty of the world will be but a dim reflection of a loveliness beyond apprehension; books will be stairways to the stars; and imagination a mirror in which the shadow of God is glimpsed.

Or, in a day or two, I may become the Julian who wants to live in his Knightsbridge house, entertain, and fill his life so full of social activities that thought becomes a memory. This Julian has emerged before, and will again. He has money: civilization caters for him regally. Everything is organized to divert him. With a stride he can enter that world the inhabitants of which stupefy themselves with the narcotic of pleasure.

At any moment I may become any one of a dozen men, each of whom calls himself Julian Grant. . . .

For the next few weeks, however, my actions are determined. I am leaving for Paris almost immediately. The reason is far from a pleasant one, but it exists.

If this letter seems long, Stella, you may be amused to know that I have destroyed three sheets for every one that remains. I have spent hour after hour writing to you. Now, it is nearly dawn. I have eluded the nightmare thoughts which threatened me. Soon, the external world will be real again.

I beg of you to come to the flat directly you return to London.

JULIAN.

*   *   *   *   *   *

Julian gathered the sheets of his letter together, then read them slowly. When he had finished, he crossed to the window, parted the curtains, and gazed into the darkness.

For five minutes he remained motionless, then he returned to the table, picked up the letter, and threw it into the fire.

Later, he wrote a three-line note asking Stella to come to the flat when she returned to London.

III

The sitting-room in Julian's flat was in darkness. The curtains were drawn and, owing to a thick fall of snow, only muffled sounds rose from the world outside. It was five o'clock in the afternoon. Julian lay on the couch. He had been asleep for two hours and still slept heavily.

A few minutes later he woke with a convulsive movement which shook the whole of his body. The lights had been switched on and a woman stood motionless in the doorway. The sudden illumination dazzled him, consequently he did not recognize her, but he rose quickly, stumbled towards her with an arm raised as if to protect himself, then came to a standstill and laughed.

"Stella!"

She neither spoke nor moved. After a long pause, Julian went on:

"Well, can't you believe it? It is I – Julian! Move, speak, do something! Or I shall think you're a ghost."

She took a step towards him, then stopped.

"Are you ill, Julian?"

"Ill! Why the devil should I be ill? I haven't shaved, and I'm exhausted, that's why I look queer. God! This isn't a very affectionate reunion after all this time. How long is it?"

She made a fluttering gesture with her hand, then went to the couch and sat down. Suddenly she shivered.

"It's terribly cold in here, Julian."

"Is it? Yes, I suppose it is. I forgot to light the fire. Wait a minute. There! You'll soon be warm. Stand up, I want to look at you."

He took her hands and drew her up, then studied her features intently.

"You're still beautiful, Stella, still unique – still living from some mysterious centre of your own. All the same, something's happened to you. You're a little frightened. Perhaps I am, too – for a different reason. We've both reached middle age. That is, we're going to discover whether our enthusiasms will stay the course."

He laughed and released her hands. She gazed at him for a moment, then unfastened her coat and knelt by the fire.

Her attitude, and her evident determination to remain silent, irritated Julian.

"I suppose you're so hypnotized by the atmosphere of crime which surrounds me that you're speechless. Is that it?"

"I don't think so."

"And you're not going to cross-examine me?"

"No. I read about it in the papers, of course."

"I was far too sick of it all to read the English papers. What did you gather from them?"

"Just the facts. An Englishman, Julian Grant, had been fired at by a Frenchman, who then attempted to commit suicide. You were uninjured, but the man was seriously wounded. His wife had left him a week before, and he was certain that she was with you. He was wrong, but would not believe it. That was about all."

"Yes, that's about all, if one omits the fact that the case dragged on for a year and that I had to stay in Paris and be questioned and cross-questioned till I nearly destroyed myself to escape the boredom of it all. First the fellow had to get well enough to be tried; then he had to be examined as to his sanity! My God! It was awful! The man was raving, so eventually he was pronounced sane. His wife would have left him if I had never been born."

"It was extraordinary that the wife managed to keep out of it all."

"She'd left France and no one knew where she was. I suppose the English papers assumed that we had been lovers?"

"Yes, more or less."

"That's amusing. I was a fool ever to have gone to Paris. It was sheer sentimentality. After that lunatic fired at me, I tried to escape, but it was impossible. The café was crowded. It's a miracle he didn't hit someone else. So I was in it for over a year – and was deluged by letters, suggesting marriage, from every mad woman in Europe."

He lit a cigarette and began to pace up and down the room restlessly. Then an idea came to him. He stopped by Stella and put his hand on her shoulder.

"Shall I tell you the truth of that affair in Paris?"

"No, Julian."

"Why not?"

"You're all I've got."

"I see. I envy you."

"Why?"

"You've memories to sustain you. Perhaps it's a pity I've come back. It may make it more difficult for you. Still, I'll try to collaborate. In fact, I'll begin now. I'll shave and dress. It may help you if I look the part. I shall be about ten minutes. You might think this over while I'm in the next room: – if ever I ask you to spend a night here, it will be an insult. That should tell you everything."

Stella rose wearily.

"I'll make some tea, Julian, while you change."

"Very well. I'll be as quick as I can."

When he returned, ten minutes later, she was waiting for him. Directly he entered the room, she went to him quickly.

"At last I recognize you! When I first came, I thought you were someone else. That's odd, because you haven't altered much."

"You don't think so?"

"No, not much. You've some almost imperceptible lines that you used not to have, but one has to study your face to detect them. You still look very young. I don't care what you are, or what you've done, I love you – I shall always love you."

"Certain?"

"Certain! Kiss me."

He took her in his arms and kissed her.

"It's been so long, Julian – so terribly long! I can't believe we're here again, in this room. It's like two ghosts meeting."

"Then we'd better have tea. I'm certain that English ghosts always have tea when they meet. Sit here, and tell me everything."

"There's only one thing to tell you."

"James?"

"Yes. Oh, my dear, it's such hell!"

"He's no better then?"

"Better! God alone knows what's happening to him."

"I'll tell you what I know, Stella, then you can finish the story. About 1920 he had a nervous collapse, then he got better, but a year or so later he had another, which dragged on endlessly. You were with him in Norfolk for the deuce of a time. Then, about two years ago – just before I went to Paris – I heard he was much better and that you were in London. You remember I sent you a line from the cottage."

"All that was nothing, Julian. It's the last two years. They think he's threatened with paralysis. He's had to give up everything. Imagine what that means for both of us. I feel as if I were chained in a trap which is closing ever so slowly. I – I don't know how to explain."

"I understand."

"No, you don't – you *can't!* These wretched specialists, on whom we've spent a fortune, keep asking me if I know of anything that is worrying him. They say that some mental disturbance is undermining his health. What answer can I give them?"

"What answer *do* you give them?"

"Anything – nothing! It's just hell, Julian. He sits reading the paper, or staring out of the window, all day long. And I know – I feel – that he wants me to be with him, although we can't find one word to say to each other. You said earlier on that I was frightened of something. You were right. I am."

"Of what – exactly?"

"I can see what the end will be, and I'm afraid of it."

"You may as well tell me, Stella."

"We shall become poor, relatively speaking. And I shall be with him, alone, in some flat. Yes, I shall!" she exclaimed emphatically, just as Julian was about to interrupt. "You don't understand. He's still living mentally in the pre-war world."

"Surely he's sold that huge place in Norfolk?"

"I begged him to sell it years ago. He wouldn't – and now we couldn't give it away. Many of his investments pay much less, and some nothing. Most of his money is in things which used to be absurdly prosperous and are now failing. We ought to leave Upper Brook Street. We shall have to soon, whether he likes it or not."

"And you say the doctors have had a fortune out of you?"

"Yes, a fortune, Julian. And it looks as if they're going to have another. He's like a man in a dream, staring at a world that is crumbling before his eyes. He can't believe it, he won't believe it! He sits there repeating clichés till I know that I must go mad if it lasts much longer."

"And he wants you to be with him."

"Yes. He never says so, but that's what he wants."

"Mute appeal, and all that?"

"Yes. It's hell, Julian."

He rose and fetched a box of cigarettes which he handed to her, then took one for himself. For some minutes they smoked in silence, then Julian said:

"There's one fact in the situation which ought to comfort you. His illness can't be due to worry caused by your mysterious disappearances from home."

"Why not?"

"You've not spent a night here since we quarrelled about Clytie Lessing."

"Yes, I have – again and again."

"What, alone? When I've been away?"

"Yes, dozens of times. And I've come here, often, in the afternoon. I still had the key. I *had* to come. Didn't you notice, when you came back, that I'd had a gas fire fixed in this room? I did that because it made it easier to come here for an hour whenever I wanted to. Surely you noticed it?"

"No, I didn't."

"You wouldn't have noticed if I'd turned this room into the bedroom!"

"Probably not. So you've come here often, alone, Stella?"

"Yes, often. I didn't lie when I said that you were all I've got. I *do* live on memories. I've altered, Julian. Once, I asked you not to lie to me. Well, now, I want you to lie to me. I want to believe that you are what I once thought you were. That's why I didn't want to know the truth about Paris."

"James read about it in the papers, I suppose?"

"Yes. He thinks you went out of my life years ago."

"Tell me – do you pity him?"

"Yes, desperately – when I'm not with him. This is how it works. I'm haunted by him when I'm alone, and when I'm with him I have only one desire – to escape. I've had years of loneliness, Julian."

"I understand. There's something else I want to know: have you seen Derwent? I haven't, not for ages."

"I met him a year ago. He hates London. He gave up his flat – you knew that? – and is living in Ireland. Why did you ask?"

"I wondered what he thought about James. Did he meet him?"

"Yes. He didn't say much, but he looked at me in that odd way of his, then asked where you were and if I'd seen you."

There was a long silence which Stella ended dramatically.

"Julian?"

"Well?"

"You don't think *I'm* responsible for what is happening to James?"

"I shouldn't ask that question, if I were you. It's wiser to say to yourself that you are you, and James is James – and leave it at that."

"You mean I *am* responsible!"

"You're not responsible, Stella, but you are the cause. How did he take it when you've told him – since he's been ill – that you were going away for the night?"

"Just as he always did."

"Never asked where?"

"Never! I know it was cruel to leave him and come here, but suffering makes you cruel."

"That's perfectly true, Stella. It's true, at any rate, till one has suffered so much that one's will is broken. But that only happens to saints. Most of us are determined to get something out of life

– somehow. It gets more and more difficult, but we're very persistent. Anyway, you've kept your bargain with him. Incidentally, he's kept his with you."

"I shall end up alone with him in a flat, and without very much money. I wouldn't mind about the money, given other things. But, without those things, it's going to be unendurable."

"All the same, I'd get out of Upper Brook Street."

"You think things will get worse, Julian? Generally, I mean."

"Yes. I'd get into a flat just as soon as you can. Everyone will recognize soon that Western civilization has got to be underpinned. There's going to be another Flood, Stella. So get into a flat – as we don't know how to build an ark."

He broke off abruptly and laughed.

"Don't laugh like that, Julian!"

"Sorry! The neurotic popped up through the trap-door. Let's get back to James. This is interesting, don't you think? You gave me what would have created paradise for James. I took it, used it, and threw it away. You believe that you'd be happy if you could live with the man you imagine I am. And Frank Derwent would run off with you if you beckoned him with your little finger. This is the world of frustration, Stella."

She did not reply. Julian went to the window, opened it, and leaned out. Snow was falling heavily. For some minutes he watched the flakes whirl to oblivion through the white glare of Piccadilly. The scene fascinated him. He forgot Stella, consequently the discovery that she had joined him made him start.

"Do come in, Julian. I'll have to go before long, and I want to ask you something."

He shut the window reluctantly.

"Well, what is it?"

"Why didn't you come back to London directly after that dreadful business in Paris?"

"I did, for a few weeks. You were away. I lived in Knightsbridge, entertained, and became a social being. I found it intensely amusing."

"Why?"

"My dear Stella, do remember that crime and mystery were my background. I looked up old friends: I went to the club. I was received with reservations. The English are very good at that sort of thing. They had been forced to think about me, and they had made certain interesting discoveries."

"What *do* you mean, Julian?"

"They had discovered that they knew nothing whatever about me. They began to ask who I was. A bit late, you'll agree, but in the old days they had just accepted me. You had given me one background: Lady Sarah another. But, now, they began to ask questions. Who *was* Julian Grant? Who were his parents? Where had he been educated? Why hadn't he married? Why didn't he do anything? They couldn't answer those questions. But they knew that I had just been mixed up in a highly scandalous affair in Paris. They knew *that*. So I was received with reservations – subtly and beautifully graduated. A first-class comedy, Stella, and one I exploited to the full. Then boredom descended, swift as a flash of lightning, and I went to the cottage for months."

"What do you do with yourself down there alone, month after month?"

Nearly a minute elapsed before Julian replied.

"Sometimes I live as my father used to live. This world dwindles to a shadow. I enter the universe within me. Everything that is called life seems as unreal as a dream. Imagination is serenity. I am a personality no longer: I am an identity. I am nothing, and everything. And then – quite suddenly – I become Julian Grant again."

"You're ill, Julian! You must be ill."

"On the contrary, I'm normal again. I've re-entered the world of men and women. I accept as substantial just what they accept. This world has become real to me again. And I mean to get something out of it, just like everyone else. I assure you that I'm quite terribly sane. . . . But you want to ask me something. What is it?"

"It's only this. Although I'm half afraid of you, I still want to come here and be with you. Can I?"

"Of course. It may be as well to ignore me sometimes, but that will become easy. Incidentally, you're dining here to-night."

"I can't, Julian! It's impossible!"

"You'll ring James up and tell him that you're dining out. Then I'll arrange for dinner here. I don't want to be alone to-night, and I'm not going to be."

"But – Julian——"

"Oh, for God's sake, Stella, don't argue! You mean he'll suffer? He'll do that whether you go or stay. We all have our destiny, and that's his. You'll have long enough alone with him in that flat. Hours and hours, years and years!"

"You're brutal!"

"We'll soon settle this."

He went over to the telephone.

"Julian!"

"Wait!"

A minute later she heard him say:

"Is that Sir James Farquharson's house? I'm speaking for Lady Farquharson . . . Yes. . . . Will you tell Sir James that Lady Farquharson is dining out, but she expects to be home about ten o'clock? . . . Yes, that's the message. Thank you."

He hung up the receiver and went over to her.

"Well?"

"I know that if I don't go now – and never see you again – you'll destroy every memory I have of you."

"Does that mean you're going?"

"I can't, Julian, I – *can't!*"

IV

"Will you tell me the time, please?"

Julian emerged from his reverie and glanced at his watch.

"It's nearly three o'clock."

The little girl thanked him, then ran away shouting:

"Doris! Nearly three o'clock! We'll have to go!"

Julian looked round listlessly. An hour ago he had entered the gardens in Lincoln's Inn Fields, but had been too absorbed to notice his surroundings. Now, he recognized them, and recognition suggested an adventure.

A two-minute walk would bring him to Mandell's office. On the background of his present mood, this fact seemed a fable. The years he had spent in that stuccoed house in the cul-de-sac were more remote than those of his childhood. Everything relating to them had been forgotten long ago. . . . Mandell! Albert

Mandell! The name represented a world from which Julian was separated by several lives.

He lit a cigarette, but threw it away almost immediately. He might as well go and see if the building were still there. Probably it had been demolished years ago, but, if not, it might be amusing to see it again. After all, he had to get through the day somehow.

He began to walk towards Mandell's office, surprised to discover that the nearer he approached it the greater his curiosity became. Only one more street to cross, and a corner to turn, and he would know whether the stuccoed house still stood.

It was there, but it was doomed. A notice affixed to the iron gates at the entrance to the cul-de-sac announced that a block of modern offices would shortly be erected on this important site. Julian scarcely glanced at it. He stood motionless, unaware of the present, conscious only of memories, which darted from every nook and corner, and circled round him like a flock of invisible birds. Everything claimed him. Julian Grant had returned. Would the Julian Grant of twenty years ago recognize him?

Twenty years? Yes, nearly twenty years since that last interview with Mandell – the interview at which he had explained that he was leaving the office finally, and the old lawyer had made a pathetic effort to retain him as a client.

He walked slowly down the cul-de-sac, glanced up at the dingy exterior of the last house, then pushed open the swing doors and entered.

Nothing had changed: the same gloom, the same silence, the same narrow stone stairs! Julian felt that he had stepped into the nineteenth century.

After a moment's indecision, he climbed to the first floor.

MANDELL AND CO.,
SOLICITORS.

This legend, in black letters, on the door of the outer office, confronted him. He glanced up the second flight of stairs, remembering the room to which he had been banished, but had no curiosity concerning it. It was the door of the outer office which interested him. Perhaps, in a minute, it would open and

Rawlings would appear. It was improbable, but not impossible. Julian seemed to see the dome-shaped bald head, the twinkling eyes, and the blotchy complexion. It was extraordinary how vividly he remembered him. He had not thought of Rawlings for years and years.

Or, perhaps, Mandell would appear, but that was even less likely. No, Mandell would have died of respectability – and Rawlings of drink – ages ago. Who else? He could only remember Minchin, the head clerk, and he remembered him only because the name was unusual. He would go into the outer office and ask for Mr. Minchin.

He opened the door and instantly he became aware of Change. The office was lighter: the furniture modern: the office-boy almost decorative. Mandell was dead. That was certain.

"I want to see Mr. Minchin."

"I'm not certain whether he's in, sir. Does he expect you?"

"No."

"What name shall I say, sir?"

"Mr. Julian Grant. You say you're not certain whether he's in or not?"

"No, sir. His room is on the floor above. Will you take a seat, please?"

"No, I'll go to his room, if you'll show me which it is."

"Certainly. Come this way, please."

He followed the youth till the latter stopped outside the room which once had been Julian's.

"I'll go straight in."

Julian opened the door and entered the room. Minchin was seated at a table reading a newspaper.

He looked up just as Julian closed the door, then rose slowly. For some moments they stared at each other.

"Mr. – *Grant!*"

"So you remember me."

"I do indeed, sir. I'd have known you anywhere. I'm afraid you couldn't say the same about me."

"You've not altered much, Minchin."

Julian did not explain that Minchin, having attained the fixity of an undertaker at the age of forty, could not alter drastically thereafter. It was true that he was bent, rather yellow, and had heavy pouches under his eyes, but, nevertheless, the most dramatic change in him was the shabbiness of his clothes.

"You've not altered much," Julian repeated after a prolonged scrutiny.

"Glad to hear you say so." Minchin pointed lugubriously at the floor, then added in a whisper: "I wish things down there hadn't altered."

"But they have?"

"Ah!"

After a dismal silence, Minchin continued:

"I can't believe that you've come back after all these years. Twenty years, it must be – very near. You've certainly changed very little, sir – considering."

"The change which interests me most, Minchin, is to find you occupying my old room. Still, I don't think we'll stay here. Let's go out and have tea somewhere."

"Certainly, sir, certainly."

Minchin took his bowler from its peg and brushed it vigorously. Then he picked up a pair of grimy gloves and a gloomy umbrella.

"Now, sir, I'm at your service."

They passed down the stairs in silence. When they reached the street, Julian asked:

"Where shall we go?"

"Well, if I might suggest, there's a little place just here where I go to lunch. It's very ordinary, of course."

"It will do admirably."

Minchin led the way. The knowledge that he would be seen with Julian in his usual haunt evidently gave him a melancholy satisfaction.

They descended a spiral stairway into a basement.

"Very ordinary, as you see. Now, sir, where would you like to sit? Here?"

"Anywhere."

"I always sit at this table."

A waitress appeared and Julian gave an order, then asked casually:

"I suppose you'll be retiring soon, Minchin?"

"Retiring! Why, since Mr. Mandell died——"

"So he is dead?"

"I made sure you'd know that. He died six years ago, almost to the day."

"Who's the head of the firm then?"

"Mr. Rose, sir. He married one of Mr. Mandell's daughters. Very different from Mr. Mandell. Turned everything upside down. Brought in new men and new methods. Mr. Mandell would turn in his grave if he knew."

"I take it that Mr. Rose did not consult you, Minchin?"

"He did not, sir. I've been ignored. I'm not consulted and I'm given nothing to do. I'm head clerk only in name. I suppose I know something, don't I? I started as office-boy and Mr. Mandell gave me my articles. But that counts for nothing. My day's over."

"Is that why you're in that old room of mine on the second floor?"

"Yes, that's why. I've often thought about you since I was up there. Mr. Mandell didn't act rightly by you, but——"

"I'm surprised you ever gave me a thought."

"A thought! At one time you were the talk of the office."

"Why?"

The waitress appeared, somewhat to Minchin's relief. To answer Julian's question might prove embarrassing.

But when they were alone again, Julian asked:

"Why did the office take any interest in me?"

"Well – you see – if I may say so – it was like this——"

"Out with it, Minchin!"

"Well, sir, surely it was only natural – with the papers full of your name some years ago."

"Oh, I see! You mean that affair in Paris? I'd forgotten about that."

Minchin started. To have been fired at by a mad Frenchman in a café in Paris! To have been the centre of a sensational case! And to have *forgotten* about it! Well, *Mrs.* Minchin would not have forgotten. She'd be very excited when he got back to Thornton Heath to-night and told her that he had had tea with the notorious Julian Grant.

"What happened to the clerks who were there in my time, Minchin? I don't remember their names."

Minchin narrated the histories of several at tedious length.

Julian interrupted him frequently as the old clerk kept reverting to his own grievances, contrasting his present degradation with his former eminence.

"If only Mr. Mandell had lived, sir! But that wasn't to be. And if he had, these new-fangled modern ways would have killed him. Just look at the state the country's in, sir! Things in the City are at a standstill. We're on the verge of ruin. I can't sleep at night for worrying about what's going to happen. I don't get the salary I used to – not by a long way. Much as I can do to exist."

Julian lit a cigarette.

"You haven't mentioned Rawlings."

"There's my memory again! It *does* play me tricks lately. All the interesting things go clean out of my head. Fancy you remembering Rawlings! He was a mystery, if ever there were one."

"What happened to him?"

"He's dead, of course. You knew that?"

"No, I didn't know."

"Died just after the war. I had the job of going into his affairs – and a nice state they were in."

"Tell me the facts – simply the facts."

"Well, sir, just after the war I noticed he was looking queer. Soon after he stayed away from the office. Ten days passed, and still no sign of him. Then Mr. Mandell asked me to find out what had happened. So I went to his place."

"Where was he living?"

"Kennington."

"Well?"

Minchin leaned forward and spoke in a confidential whisper:

"*You* never saw such a room, sir. The dirt! And the bills! It fair disgusted me. He'd died suddenly a week before I turned up and had been buried at West Norwood. I hadn't been in the room an hour before two men came in wanting money, and there was the landlady clamouring for her rent. It seems he'd been a terrible drunkard for years, but somehow he managed to hide it at the office. I always thought him a bit sly. But – and this is the interesting thing, sir – he had a good friend."

"I shouldn't have guessed it."

"He had a good friend, sir – a real top-notcher, no end of a swell. Just let me pour out another cup of tea and I'll explain."

Minchin, having refilled his cup, and having exposed his right cuff – which was not frayed – and having hidden the left one – which was – drew his chair nearer to Julian, and continued in an impressive whisper.

"I had to go through his letters and papers – to try to find out how things stood. He hadn't a penny, and he owed over three hundred pounds. But this is the point, sir. I could only find three letters, but they were from someone most of us had heard of."

"And the name?"

"Lady Farquharson. You've heard of *her*, of course – wife of Sir James Farquharson. Haven't heard much of him for some years, by the way. Well, Rawlings knew *her*. You could have knocked me down with a feather. She'd been to that room of his. Went there in 1914. One of her letters referred to the way in which she'd just turned up one night. Evidently that was their first meeting. And her last letter said that if ever he wanted anything, he was to write to her."

"Apparently he never did write."

"No, he never wrote. Bit cracked, if you ask me. Why she ever went to that hole of a room to see a drunkard like Rawlings is a mystery to me, sir. How did she get his address – and what did she want with him?"

"What did you do – when you'd ascertained how things stood?"

"I wrote to Lady Farquharson, telling her that Rawlings was dead and had a lot of creditors. Thought I'd better let her know, as she was interested in him."

"Did she answer the letter?"

"Oh yes, sir, she answered it. Wrote and said that if I'd let her know the amount Rawlings owed, she'd settle. And settle she did. Mr. Mandell was amazed. He tried to get Lady Farquharson for a client, but it didn't come off."

Julian put his cigarette out, then lit another.

"It's an interesting story, Minchin, but I'm not clear about one thing."

"What's that, sir?"

"You say that Rawlings died penniless – and that he had been buried some days before you went to his room. Who paid for the funeral?"

"His wife. I had to see her, of course. She hadn't had a farthing from him for years."

"How did she live then?"

"Well, she told me that about four years before the war Rawlings gave her a cheque for two hundred and fifty pounds. She started a dressmaking business and had done pretty well. How Rawlings ever got two hundred and fifty pounds is a mystery to me. And why he gave it to his wife was a mystery to *her*. But he did – luckily."

"Did she say whether Rawlings gave her his own cheque, or passed on one which had been given to him?"

"She didn't say, sir, and I didn't ask."

"Naturally."

"So that was the end of Rawlings, sir."

"As you say, that was the end of Rawlings. I shall have to go, Minchin."

"Sorry to hear it. It's done me good having a chat about old times."

Julian rose and paid the bill. Two minutes later he said good-bye to Minchin, walked slowly back to the gardens in Lincoln's Inn Fields, and returned to the seat he had left just over an hour ago. . . .

So Stella had visited Rawlings in 1914. She must have gone to him soon after the Clytie Lessing quarrel, but she had known, long before then, that one day she would go. She had often half hinted that there was a link between them, and one night she had asked where Rawlings lived. Finally, her loneliness had sought his.

It was interesting to visualize the setting of that meeting. That room of Rawlings' with its musty atmosphere, and the shouts and cries rising from the street below! He saw again the ugly gas-bracket, the derelict bedstead with its hideous counterpane, the worn linoleum, the peeling wallpaper. This had been Rawlings' background, that night in 1914. Probably he had been in his shirt-sleeves, smoking a cheap cigar, with a bottle of whisky on that rickety table by his chair.

The door had opened and Stella had appeared.

Would she have told him the history of their relations from their meeting in that bookshop to the night of the quarrel? Probably. Stella would have told him everything, or stayed away. What had Rawlings' thoughts been as he listened to her? Or, perhaps, he had been unable to listen. Perhaps he had sat motionless, staring at her, contrasting her with street-walkers – the only women he had met for years. But, eventually, he would have understood why she had come to him. And, perhaps, as the conversation had developed, he might have discovered that although she was beautiful, rich, and the wife of a well-known man – she, too, was an outcast. Rawlings had imagination. Possibly he had recognized——

"Pleasant to get in here, away from the noise, isn't it?"

Julian started. He had been so absorbed that he had forgotten his surroundings and so had not noticed that a jovial-looking man had sat down on the other end of the seat on which he was sitting.

He muttered some reply, glanced at his watch, then rose and began to walk in the direction of Kingsway.

The interruption had broken his mood and he thought no more of Stella's visit to Rawlings. What was far more relevant was the probability that she was at the flat now, waiting for him. Should he join her? or should he go to his club for a couple of hours?

He was too indifferent to make a decision. He walked on slowly. . . .

Stella and he were strangers. He knew that, of course, but this talk with Minchin had made him realize it. Realization might have come any time during the last three years, but – although she had visited the flat regularly during most of that period – he had not thought about her. Emotionally, he had been numbed, and so had been incapable of experience.

He had not kissed her since the night of their reunion. That must have been three years ago. Yes, three years. It was curious, but that night was the last vital memory he had of her. Every sound had been muffled, owing to a thick fall of snow. He had made her stay to dinner. Since then, he had not imposed his will on her. He had ignored her. She had come to the flat because her life with Farquharson was intolerable, and he had let her come because she made no demands. More often than not, they had been silent; sometimes she had read to him; and sometimes he had slept on the couch during the whole of her visit.

Now – as a result of that talk with Minchin – he was thinking about her. If loneliness had made her visit Rawlings in 1914, she must suffer a much greater loneliness now. For some months Farquharson had been partially paralysed. The house in Norfolk was stripped and deserted. They had left Upper Brook Street eighteen months ago and taken a flat. More dividends had dwindled and many had vanished: more and more money went to the doctors: and Farquharson, unknown to Stella, had speculated on the Stock Exchange. The final financial result of all these misfortunes was that the thousands in Farquharson's income had shrunk to hundreds. Now, they had one small car, instead of three large ones, and Stella no longer had a maid. Julian had discovered the last fact only recently. He had asked why she brought sewing to the flat, and she had told him. . . .

It was extraordinary how little she had altered physically. The expression of the eyes had changed, and the lips were more tightly compressed than formerly, but the figure was still magnificent.

Stella! If only he could feel some emotion in regard to her! But that was not possible. Minchin's revelations had not moved him in the least. Stella . . . Rawlings . . . the Julian Grant of 1914 – figures emerging from a mist on the far side of an abyss!

Suddenly he remembered a fragment of a conversation he had had with Stella about a year ago. It had occurred a few days after they had heard of Frank Derwent's death. He had died after a short illness in Ireland. The intensity of Stella's grief had amazed him.

He remembered saying to her:

"You haven't seen him for years, so you won't miss him much."

"I wrote to him every week. . . . Someone once said that a moment comes when you know you are old. It has come to me. I am old."

"I don't see that you've altered much."

"My hair is grey, Julian. That is, it would be if it weren't attended to once a month."

Yes, he remembered that she had said that. It was odd that he had forgotten it entirely until now.

He paused and looked round. He must have crossed Kingsway and wandered through the back streets, for he did not recognize the locality.

A minute later a taxi appeared. He hailed it and gave the driver the name of his club.

V

Julian looked out of the carriage window, then glanced at his watch. Nearly five o'clock. The train would reach Charing Cross in a quarter of an hour. . . .

He began to review the reasons which had occasioned his return, only to discover that every one of them seemed inadequate. It was true that it would have been difficult to ignore Stella's letter; nevertheless, he realized that it alone would not have effected an alteration in his plans. The flat? Why had he ever given it a thought? And those letters from his lawyers, in which they had repeated with monotonous insistence that they hoped he would call as there were matters concerning which his decision was essential: why had he not written asking them for details? Probably they had nothing to do, and therefore were magnifying trifles in an attempt to justify additional fees.

Irritability swept him: the thought of London was repugnant. For over a year he had been alone in the cottage, and whatever defects that mode of existence might possess, its advantages towered above them. He had indulged in an orgy of reading, seeing no one, and writing no letters. He had slept by day and read by night in order to emphasize his isolation. He had haunted the world, not lived in it. No one had known where he was. Now, he was returning to London. He would become involved in the mechanism of normal life, and God alone knew. . . .

He'd better glance at that letter from Stella. He had sent a line telling her he would be in the flat at five-thirty, but, although her letter had arrived only a few days ago, he had forgotten its contents.

He began to fumble in his pockets. Surely he hadn't lost it! It was the only letter he had had from her for months. She had written once, soon after he had gone to the cottage, but he had not replied.

Here it was! Now, what – exactly – was it all about?

He skimmed the lines, reading one word in three, and gathered that Farquharson's condition was critical. He was threatened with total paralysis. The situation was so desperate that they were leaving for Germany almost immediately in the hope that a new treatment, only to be obtained there, might prove successful. Stella ended by begging him to come to London to see her before they left. They would be away for a year.

He tore the letter into shreds and threw them out of the window, then – seeking distraction – he picked up a newspaper which someone had left in the carriage. He had not looked at one for a month.

The front page informed him that a General Election was planned for the end of October; that the appeal to the country would be by the National Government, in whose interest the Conservative organization would be fully employed; also, that the Conservatives were overwhelmingly of the view that anything that savoured of seeking party advantage should be ruled out, and that Mr. MacDonald should retain the Premiership.

Julian also learned that the value of the pound was fluctuating dramatically as the result of England's removal from the gold standard, and that speculation on the Stock Exchange had been stopped by an announcement of the General Purposes Committee that all bargains must be for cash.

He was about to turn the page when a statement in the right-hand column arrested his interest. Evidently some woman had committed suicide a few days ago. The case must have created considerable interest, as the report of the inquest had invaded the front page.

Apparently the woman had been a member of a number of night-clubs, but Julian's interest had been captured by the statement that many of her friends knew her only by the name of Belle. Details followed as to how she had been found dead by her maid. Then came theories as to the means by which she had obtained the poison. And, finally, a dramatic epitome of her financial difficulties.

Julian skipped a paragraph, then read:

"The most sensational disclosure, however, was that 'Belle' was formerly Mrs. Clytie Lessing. Her divorce, many years ago, attracted considerable attention at the time. Mr. Arnold Lessing, who died shortly afterwards, left the whole of his fortune to charity."

After which, the reader was invited to see the picture on the back page, and to read an article entitled: – "Belle – by One Who Knew Her," which appeared on page three.

Julian threw the paper aside. Stella would have read all this and would probably want to discuss it. She would imagine that he would be interested, not realizing that he had seen Clytie only twice since 1914. He had passed her in the street in London, some time in 1915, and – some years later – they had come face to face as he was leaving a restaurant in Paris. On neither occasion had either of them given any sign of recognition.

He was about to thrust the newspaper under the seat, then altered his mind and decided to take it with him. He folded it carefully and put it by his side.

A few minutes later the train reached Charing Cross.

Julian beckoned a porter and asked him to get two taxis. His luggage was loaded on to the first and the driver told to take it to Julian's house in Knightsbridge. These instructions had to be repeated in order to make the man understand what was required. Everything collaborated to intensify Julian's irritability: the man's stupidity; the noise and clamour of the station yard; the moving inferno of the Strand; the reek of the petrol-laden air.

"The damned place in a nightmare," he muttered to himself as he got into the second taxi, having given the driver the address of the flat.

If only Stella were late! It was imperative to have a few minutes to himself. But this hope was short-lived, for, as he mounted the second flight of stairs she opened the front door.

He entered the flat, with scarcely a word or a glance, went into the sitting-room, and tossed the newspaper on to the table. Stella followed him into the room.

"Haven't you any luggage, Julian?"

"No."

"I thought you'd been abroad."

"I've been at the cottage."

"For over a year!"

"Yes. We'd better talk about James and your visit to Germany. When do you go?"

"On Tuesday."

He sat down. Stella remained standing, gazing at him in great bewilderment. Finally, she became convinced that he was unaware of her and his surroundings.

"Well – when?"

"I've just told you, Julian. We go next Tuesday."

"What's the matter with him?"

"But I told you in my letter——"

"I daresay you *did* tell me in your letter! That was days ago – and a day is an age. Can't you tell me again what's happened to him?"

His voice was taut with irritability.

After a long silence, she began to speak rapidly, first explaining Farquharson's condition in detail, then she described the conflicting opinions of the specialists they had consulted. She gave instances of the successful results obtained by the new German treatment, and explained how, in the end, they had decided to try it.

When she had finished, Julian said nothing. She glanced at him, but looked away almost immediately. The intensity of his features frightened her. It was evident that he had not listened to a word of her narrative.

When the silence had become unendurable, Stella said:

"Of course this Crisis has made him worse. Things were bad enough, but they're going to be desperate. We had to sell investments to get the money to go to Germany. It's been a difficult business – with all these restrictions about going abroad. He looks pretty awful, Julian. I don't believe you'd recognize him."

He rose swiftly and went over to her.

"So you didn't go to see Clytie Lessing – or did you? Are you going to pay her debts, now she's dead, in the same way as you paid Rawlings'?"

His attitude was so menacing that she retreated.

"How did you know about Rawlings?"

Her voice was a whisper.

"Because I went to Mandell's office about eighteen months ago and talked to an old clerk there. That's how I know. But it doesn't matter. Don't tell me. I don't want to hear anything about it. There's something I want to ask you. Wait a minute. I must think. . . . How long will you be in Germany?"

"We shall be there a year. . . . Are you ill, Julian?"

"You always think I'm ill! I'm *never* ill!"

He flung himself into a chair. He had not looked at her once since he had entered the room.

"Julian?"

"Well?"

"Are you going back to the cottage?"

"How do I know?"

"But you haven't brought any luggage."

"It's gone to Knightsbridge."

"So you're going to live there?"

He did not reply. After a silence, she repeated the question.

"What? Yes, for the time being. It's been let furnished for years, but you can't do that any longer. No one has any money. It's been empty for months, except for the servants. Why do you ask? It's of no interest."

"Will you stay here sometimes?"

"Here! Of course not! The lease has run out."

She stared at him incredulously.

"You mean, Julian, you're giving up this flat?"

"I tell you the *lease* has run out! Even a twenty-one years' lease doesn't last for ever. It ran out last June. They let me have it for another quarter, but I've got to get out in a few days. They're going to pull the building down, or something. Why *do* you ask these questions? What on earth does it matter?"

"So we shan't meet here again after to-day?"

"No."

"What are you going to do with the furniture and things?"

"What? Oh, I don't know! Sell the lot – just as it stands. I came up to arrange about it."

"There's no point in my keeping my latchkey then?"

"No – none."

She went to her bag, extracted the key and gave it to him.

"I don't want it. It's no use to anyone. I tell you again, the building is coming down."

He threw the key into the waste-paper basket.

"I'll have to go, Stella. Is there anything else?"

"No – nothing."

He glanced at her for the first time, then rose swiftly.

"I'm going to Knightsbridge. Shall I drop you anywhere?"

"No."

"If you write, send letters to the club. I don't know where I shall be, or what I shall do."

"You've terrible courage, Julian."

"I've had the courage to be a spectator," he answered, in a tone which implied that her statement was a commonplace one, arising out of the conversation. "Are you ready? We'd better go."

She left him and wandered through the bedroom and the hall, looking at things. At last she returned to the sitting-room.

"Are you looking for something?"

"No."

They went out of the front door together. Julian banged it behind them.

She seized his arm convulsively.

"*Julian!*"

"What is it?"

She stood motionless, staring at the closed door. "What *is* it?" he repeated angrily. "Have you left something behind?"

"No – no – nothing!"

She began to laugh hysterically.

He took her arm roughly and helped her down the stairs.

VI

A YEAR IN A LIFE

A

He could not remember whether she had been in the restaurant when he entered it soon after one o'clock. He had become aware of her half an hour ago, and since then she had claimed all his attention.

Presumably she visited this little restaurant in Charlotte Street regularly, for the waiter accurately anticipated her choice on handing her the menu; and the proprietor, an Italian with the bearing of an impresario, personally superintended the preparation of her coffee – a favour accorded only to regular patrons.

She was about thirty, rather powerfully built, with a low broad forehead, and flame-coloured hair – the beauty of which was fully revealed as she was not wearing a hat. During the last ten minutes she had made more than one attempt to write a letter, but finally had abandoned it, and now sat, cross-legged, watching the life of the street through the open door. A cigarette burned itself away, unheeded, in an ash-tray in front of her.

Julian continued to study her, as if she were a model and he an artist, but he was not interested primarily in her appearance. An emotional quality pervaded her, informing each attitude and gesture, and it was this which attracted him.

He glanced at his watch. It was nearly three o'clock. Should he speak to her? or should he return to the crowded pavements of the sunlit streets? He would have to decide now, for it was impossible to remain any longer. He had paid the bill half an hour ago.

He would go – and not give her another thought! To waste a couple of hours with this woman would be merely another evasion of a problem which must be solved. He dare not continue to spend day after day wandering about the streets. Also, it was tragically obvious that her world was not his.

To reach the door, however, it was necessary to pass her table, and – to his amazement – as he came level with her, he heard himself say:

"You haven't finished your letter, then?"

"No, and I don't think I ever shall. I've been trying to write it for a week."

The rich tone of her voice imposed a momentary silence, then Julian said:

"We don't seem too good with letters. You can't write yours, and I can't read mine. Look at those."

He took a small pile of unopened letters from his pocket and put them on the table for her inspection.

"How long have you been carrying those about?"

"Two or three days – most of them."

"Why?"

"If I'm to explain, you must let me sit down – and we'd better have another cup of coffee."

"Well, why not? The coffee's quite good."

He sat down, beckoned the waiter, and gave an order.

For some moments she continued to gaze at the pile of letters, but eventually she turned and faced him for the first time. Her eyes were large, extraordinarily blue, and seemed to regard everything in general rather than anything in particular. But the mouth was her most revealing feature: it was full, richly curved, and almost tremulous with indecision.

"Do you come here often?" she asked suddenly.

"No. This is my first visit."

She glanced at him quickly, then, realizing that he was serious, she exclaimed:

"But you were here yesterday!"

He turned to her irritably, but her conviction routed his assurance.

"You must have made a mistake," he muttered, "I——"

"Oh, you were here all right! You were alone and sat at that table over there."

Again she glanced at him – then put her hand on his impulsively.

"You've been ill, haven't you?"

"Well, perhaps. That is, no – not exactly. It's difficult to explain. I – I suffer from loss of memory occasionally. That's all."

"So that's it. I expect that's why you've carried those letters about. You ought to open them. Why not start with this?"

She picked up the top one, thereby revealing a picture postcard.

"Well, what about that?" she asked. "Surely you've read *that!* May I look at it?"

"Do. Read it, if you like. It's not very interesting, I'm afraid."

The card was from Stella. On it she had written simply her address, not one word of greeting, and Julian had realized that the omission signified that she would not write until she heard from him.

She looked only at the picture, then handed the card to him.

"And what about the others?"

"They can wait. Here's the coffee."

Then, when the waiter had gone, he added:

"Aren't you going to tell me your name?"

"It's Madge."

"Just——Madge?"

"Yes. What's yours?"

"Julian Grant."

"That's settled then."

She poured out the coffee, then offered him a cigarette.

He discovered that he need say little, for she began to talk freely, passing from one subject to another, as if she had known him for months.

He listened only to the sound of her voice, however, for his innermost thoughts were probing the possibility that Madge might be deliverance. He could not spend another day alone – that was definite. The discovery that he had forgotten where he had lunched yesterday had frightened him. It was a dramatic illumination of his state: a flash from the darkness, revealing his peril. The statement that he suffered from loss of memory had been intended for a lie, but was it one? What memories had he of the period which had elapsed since Stella's departure? The sole effect of her card had been a realization of the fact that it was ten days since she had left London. Ten days was the actual measurement of that Sahara of time which separated him from that final meeting with Stella! Still, it was fortunate that he had told Madge that he suffered from loss of memory. It would cover any eccentricity of speech or gesture. It would——

"But which film actress do *you* like best?"

The question exploded like a bomb in the middle of his private speculations. He gave a kind of shout, then began to laugh. At last he managed to say:

"You cannot expect me to give a casual opinion on what is – after all – the only really momentous question now confronting humanity. But I promise you this: I'll study all of them, on the express condition that you come with me."

His outburst had startled her, but its ultimate effect was to deepen her conviction that he was recovering from a serious illness. She glanced at him, then said quietly:

"Very well, we'll study them together. What are you going to do now? I'm going home."

"I've no plans."

"Come with me, if you like. One or two people may drop in. Would you mind that?"

"Why should I? Where do you live?"

"Fulham."

"That doesn't sound like you."

"No? And what sort of person do you think I am?"

Julian pretended to study her, then announced:

"I should think life's kicked you about like a football."

"That's pretty good. Come on. Let's go."

"Yes, let's go."

As he followed her out of the restaurant, he discovered that she was taller than he had imagined; also, that he had underestimated her physical attractions. Her clothes were unorthodox without being defiant – a unique achievement, so far as Julian's observation went.

They walked down the street for some distance, then, just as Julian was about to hail a taxi, Madge touched his arm.

"We can get a bus over there."

He did not reply, but crossed the street in the direction indicated. Later, when they had boarded a bus, Madge began to talk again, but Julian only gave her half his attention.

He must ascertain her circumstances. If she were free, perhaps he would stay in London for a few days, meet her frequently, take her to picture palaces, restaurants, and so on. Possibly she was destined to deliver him from his present predicament. She made no demands – and they would remain strangers. She lived wholly through her emotions, whereas he——

She asked some question and he began to talk. A few minutes later she rose.

"We get off here."

"Already?"

"Yes, it's not far. We've a bit of a walk though."

They traversed several dingy-looking streets till at last Madge exclaimed:

"Here we are!"

A large four-storeyed block of flats confronted them, remarkable chiefly for its dilapidated appearance. There were several entrances, all rather ramshackle, and littered with scraps of newspaper blown in from the street. They passed through one of these and began to climb steep stone stairs, flanked by a rusty railing. Noises of every kind greeted them: loud speakers, gramophones, tradesmen hammering vainly on doors, the shouts of a violent quarrel, the screams of a child.

"Is it always like this?" Julian asked.

"Like what? Oh, you mean the noise! Yes, it's usually pretty noisy."

Julian paused to read a notice pinned to a front door. It informed humanity that the occupier would return at eight o'clock, and that parcels were to be left with the porter.

"The porter!" Julian exclaimed. "*Is* there a porter?"

At this moment, somewhat dramatically, the door of the flat opposite opened and the porter appeared. He resembled an old-time music-hall comedian, for, although he was in his shirt-sleeves, he wore a military-looking hat – the only remaining item of his uniform. Also, his expression denoted deep and permanent bewilderment.

Julian watched him descend the stairs.

"I don't think much of your porter, Madge. He looks as if he'd had a shock."

"He has nothing else. It's like this. There's a yard at the back where the children play. They're always quarrelling, and of course the quarrel spreads to the parents. Then the porter's dragged into it. He listens to so many lies that he doesn't know where he is. We'd better go on. I'm on the third floor."

"They might paint the place, don't you think?" Julian asked as they continued their ascent.

"They haven't the money. They only get seventy pounds a year for a flat here nowadays. Several are empty, and a lot of the tenants don't pay – although there are two families in most of the flats, and a lodger in nearly all of them. Nobody's got a farthing. Here we are!"

The flat contained three rooms – one the size of a cupboard – a diminutive kitchen, and a dark bathroom. It was the type of flat in which loneliness was possible, but not solitude, for the slightest movement of the tenants above, below, and on either side was clearly audible.

They entered the sitting-room. This was large, but, as it faced the back, it reverberated with the shouts and cries of the children playing in the yard below. The furniture was incredibly dreary. It was huge, heavy, Victorian, and seemed mutely to invoke annihilation.

"Interesting room," Julian remarked, after a swift scrutiny. "It combines the horrors of two centuries. Good God! What are all those?"

Fastened to the walls with drawing-pins were a number of photographs of quite terrifyingly commonplace people. Several of them bore inscriptions, such as: "Amy – Ramsgate, 1920. What Ho!" One represented a group on the steps of a boarding-house in Clacton. Everyone was smiling – and everyone had an arm round somebody else. Another depicted a large motor coach, outside a public-house, each of the occupants of which held a glass heavenwards. Underneath someone had printed: "Full up."

Julian examined several of these minutely, then turned to Madge.

"Perhaps you'll now tell me, exactly, what you're doing in this place?"

"So you don't think it's mine?"

"I know it isn't."

"All right, I'll tell you. Till a few weeks ago I was living with a man called Duncan in a flat near the Tottenham Court Road. He died very suddenly – we had lived together for three years. Well, he left me a hundred pounds. This flat belongs to George, who was a friend of his. George married a barmaid ten years ago and has come down in the world."

"Well, what are you doing in George's flat?"

"I was just going to tell you. Duncan left George a few hundreds, which he decided to waste – as he thinks everything's up. So he's taken Gracie – that's his wife – away for a year. They couldn't let the flat, and they daren't leave it empty, so they gave me a job as caretaker. The result is that I've nearly a hundred pounds and am living rent-free – which isn't too bad, is it?"

Julian looked round the room again critically.

"You don't seem to think much of it," Madge went on. "Better have a look at the bedroom."

The bedroom was worse. There was a strip of colourless carpet each side of a large brass bedstead, otherwise the boards were bare. An enlarged photograph of an overblown woman occupied considerable space over the mantelpiece.

"*That's* Gracie," Madge said encouragingly.

"Yes, I half thought it might be."

He sat on the edge of the bed and tried to assess the quality of a man's life who had married Gracie ten years ago, whose fortunes had declined ever since, and who rediscovered the world each morning in this room.

He was about to rise when he noticed a child's cot in the corner.

"Have they a child?"

"No, but Gracie's determined to think there's going to be one – some day. That's why that's there."

"I see. I think we'll go back to the other room. It's not so bad as I thought."

As they crossed the passage, Julian saw that the front door was open. He indicated the fact to Madge.

"Yes, I know it is," she replied. "Someone will turn up, probably, and I can't keep going to open it. Shall I make some tea? Or is it too soon?"

"Just as you like. Might as well, perhaps. I'll go into the sitting-room."

He crossed to the open window and stood looking down into the asphalt yard. He just noticed that three boys were playing, then gazed at the backs of the houses opposite. When he looked again into the yard, two of the boys were facing each other in belligerent attitudes, while the third – the smallest – stood whimpering a few yards from them.

"You 'it 'im!"

"I never!"

"You '*it* 'im!"

"I tell you I never!"

"Liar!"

A blow – a pregnant silence – a yell. Instantly two windows were flung open and two women's heads appeared simultaneously. Threats, accusations, imprecations, commands volleyed and thundered. Two of the boys were now yelling lustily, while the third loudly protested his innocence. Just as the hubbub had reached its maximum, the porter appeared – and was immediately claimed by each of the contending parties as an eye-witness.

Julian closed the window and began to pace slowly up and down the room. . . .

Madge was independent, and evidently liked him well enough. He would stay in London for a few days and meet her frequently. He——

"If you're getting bored," Madge called from the kitchen, "there are some more photographs of Gracie in the hall."

"I should be sorry to miss any photograph of Gracie. Will you show them to me?"

He went into the hall and a moment later Madge joined him.

They examined a number of photographs, revealing Gracie in progressive stages of expansion, and were so engrossed instituting comparisons that they did not notice the approach of a visitor. He, too, was unaware of them, for he crossed the threshold without realizing their proximity. Then he started violently, and came to a standstill.

He was tall, lean, and extraordinarily shabby. He had not shaved for two days and his complexion was mud-coloured, but he had fine intelligent eyes, which gave some stability to a remarkably unbalanced face. It would have been difficult to decide whether he was forty or fifty.

Seeing that Madge was with a stranger, he began to mutter something about having come only to return a book.

"But you'll come in and have tea, Clarence?"

"No – no, thanks – really. Just came to bring the book. That's all. There it is. Thanks so much. Good-bye."

He turned and walked away quickly.

"Who on earth's that?" Julian asked.

"That? That's Clarence Harlowe."

"You don't mean the actor?"

"Yes, I do. At least, he was one once, but he's not had a job for years."

"He's an extremely good actor."

"Well, perhaps that's why. I may tell you about him some time. I can't now. The kettle's boiling."

B

Their first meeting proved the precursor of many. Before a month had elapsed Julian decided to remain in London indefinitely.

During this period he became familiar with the chief events of Madge's life, but, in one sense, this information added little to his knowledge. In the same way as a destination sometimes indicates the nature of a journey, so certain people have only to be seen for their histories to be known. In such cases, facts serve only to confirm – never to illuminate. And so it was with Madge.

Julian discovered that she was illegitimate; that her mother had been on the stage; and that she had died when Madge was nineteen. Her subsequent history had consisted of a series of vicissitudes, seemingly inevitable, given her temperament and circumstances. She had been incapable of organizing her life, and had had neither relatives nor resources. Julian was not surprised to learn, therefore, that she had drifted in and out of theatrical engagements; been an artist's model; lived with an artist for a year or two; done crowd work for the films; starved; become a model again; and finally had been the mistress of a business man, Duncan, and had lived with him for three years in a flat near the Tottenham Court Road.

She related these details with such detachment that Julian appreciated the extent to which she lived in the present. The past was as unsubstantial to her as the future. Nevertheless, Julian said:

"You tell your story as if it were someone else's."

"Well, so it is, in a way. Things happen – and you get along somehow."

"Is that how you see life?"

"Of course! You can plan for the future, or think about the past, if you like, but it all comes to this in the end – things just happen."

"You don't believe in the will, then?"

"I don't know what you mean by believe in it. I know I haven't any."

As the result of subtly concealed cross-examination, Julian

learned the whole of her history. He discovered that she did not know the name of her father, who had died when she was eighteen, without leaving a will. Till then, her mother had received a generous allowance from him and, in Madge's belief, her death had resulted from his. But the dominant impression created by her attitude to events was that the essential in her had survived the onslaughts of experience. An immaculate quality pervaded her, an inner inheritance, not derived from the world and independent of it.

They spent curious days together. To her, Julian was a remarkable being, evidently recovering from a serious illness, who was attracted to her in a queer way of his own. She accepted him without curiosity and without criticism. With the single exception of Duncan, she had always appealed to an odd type of man, consequently Julian's eccentricities did not surprise her. He knew more than anyone she had met, had travelled more extensively, and – on rare occasions – revealed worlds of whose existence she was ignorant. Only one element in him disconcerted her – a sudden discordant gaiety, the falsity of which she instinctively recognized.

To Julian, Madge represented a way of escape, a severance with the past, a contact with living reality. He strove to obliterate his personality by identifying himself with her. The intensity of her emotions attracted him as a fire attracts a freezing man. He did not want to listen to her: he wanted to be silent; to watch her; to feel the world as she felt it. And he deluded himself with the hope that her proximity would thaw all that had frozen in him.

To contrast her with others was to realize her unique quality. She was wholly instinctive in an age so highly conscious that it had analysed everything out of existence. She was neither hysterical nor sentimental: she had no theories – no substitutes for Being. She lived from her own roots.

What chiefly convinced Julian of the accuracy of this analysis was the negligible extent to which her experience had moulded her. Had it been different, she would have been essentially the same. With others, the reverse was the fact – and Stella was one notable example.

It was not possible to think of Stella without visualizing her experience. It had fashioned her, restricted her, emphasized certain characteristics, created the woman she was from the dozen women once potential in her. If she had not married Farquharson – if she had not spent those years abroad with her father – her whole personality would have been different. She was aware of this. She recognized the extent to which she was the creation of her experience. For her, the past was not a vanishing pageant. It was an ambush in which she was still trapped.

With Madge, it was otherwise. Her experience, judged by orthodox standards, had been more desperate than Stella's; nevertheless, Julian did not feel that it was inalienably hers. Events had swirled round and over her, tossing her hither and thither, without affecting her. She remained what she was. A pitcher can be no more than full, though all the waves of all the seas break over it.

The weeks passed, and they met almost daily. As Julian's one demand was her company, it follows that he was indifferent as to where they went or what they did. Consequently her mood became the determining factor and, according to it, they would go to the pictures, or a theatre, or spend a day wandering through Richmond Park or Kew Gardens. His indifference amused her, and the discovery that, frequently, he was unaware of the way in which they had spent the time, only made her the more certain that he had been seriously ill.

As the winter advanced they began to meet more frequently in the Fulham flat, with the result that Julian encountered a number of her friends – especially Clarence Harlowe.

C

All sorts of odd people visited Madge at any time from three o'clock till midnight, and stayed for hours – talking, reading, or even sleeping, according to mood. It was clear that she had met some of them only recently – in circumstances similar to those of her meeting with Julian – but what chiefly interested him was their diversity, for it revealed, finally, the range and power of her emotional magnetism.

That Clarence Harlowe was unique, even in this company,

was proved by the fact that he had only to be present in order to make the others seem normal. This result, remarkable in itself, was rendered the more so by Harlowe's ignorance of it. It was achieved in spite of his efforts to remain unnoticed. He spoke less than anyone, never discussed himself, and was visibly embarrassed by direct questions. He violently repudiated the least suggestion that he was in any way remarkable, and generally evinced that passion for the normal which is often the distinguishing characteristic of those born outside its frontiers.

Certain facts, however, were revealed by his appearance, the most notable being poverty, loneliness – and the havoc created by these in a sensitive organism. But these were effects, and they served only to intensify Julian's curiosity. He determined to cross-examine Madge, for it was obvious that she knew more about Harlowe than anyone else.

One afternoon Julian arrived at the flat earlier than usual and, finding the front door ajar, he entered noiselessly and went into the sitting-room.

Madge was asleep on a couch: a slender ray of sunlight illuminating the beauty of her hair. He studied her for some minutes, interested by the discovery that the attitude of sleep emphasized her essential quality. Had he been an artist, he would have painted her as he now saw her. There was great potentiality in Madge – and sleep was its perfect physical representative.

She stirred uneasily, then woke with a start. Seeing him standing at the foot of the couch, an expression of fear and bewilderment distorted her features.

"I was dreaming about you."

He did not reply and after a silence she asked:

"You are there, aren't you?"

"Yes, I'm here."

"I thought I was still dreaming as you didn't speak. What's the time?"

"About half-past two."

She rose, then crossed the room, pushing her hair back with her hands.

"I can't understand it," she said at last. "I never used to sleep in the afternoon, but I've been dreadfully tired lately. You're very early, aren't you?"

"I wanted to see you before anyone turns up. I haven't seen you alone for some time."

She took a cigarette from a box on the mantelpiece, then sat in an arm-chair. As he remained silent, she glanced at him.

"You're all right, aren't you?"

"Yes, I'm all right. I'm a little curious about someone. That's all."

"Who?"

"Harlowe."

"Oh, Clarence! I believe you frightened him when you first came. He didn't come for some days. That was queer, because he's nowhere else to go."

"Where does he live?"

"I don't know."

"You – don't know!"

"No. He's very poor – you knew that, of course – but I mean really poor. He lives on a pound a week which his mother left him. She died years ago. He must live in some hole somewhere, but he won't tell anyone where it is."

"Why doesn't he get a job? He was excellent in character parts – he usually played eccentric old men. He was quite famous, then he disappeared."

"I've told you before that there are no parts for him in modern plays. He'll probably never get another job. They only put on farces and spectacle shows nowadays. Anyhow, I doubt if he could act if he got the chance. He's broken up. I pity Clarence more than anyone else in the world."

"Yes, he's interesting. Incidentally, he never mentions the stage."

"He daren't – that's why. He has a hell of a life. I thank God I met him when I did. Otherwise——"

Her intensity jarred on Julian, and he asked curtly:

"Hasn't he any relatives?"

"Only a half-brother. He's a lot older than Clarence – and rich. But that's no help, because they had a violent quarrel a year or two ago. Why are you so interested in him?"

"Because he's an interesting person."

Madge turned to him impulsively.

"I know what you are!"

"And what is that?"

"An author."

"I wish to God you were right! It's true that I've been collecting material for a book for some years, but it's extremely improbable that I shall ever write it."

At this point a visitor appeared, and half an hour later Julian left.

On reaching the street, he stood motionless for some minutes. He knew he would return to Madge's flat after dinner, but, now, the problem of the intervening hours confronted him. Finally, he decided to go to Kensington Gardens. He walked on slowly in search of a taxi. . . .

It was amusing that Madge thought he was a writer. It proved that she knew nothing about him, and he wanted her to know nothing. Fortunately, she was not curious, and so it had been necessary to tell her little about himself. She did not know that he had a house in Knightsbridge. He had told her that he lived at his club, not the one he actually frequented, but an obscure affair he had joined long ago, which he had not entered for years. Also, he had indicated that he had a private income of a few pounds a week. He had lied to her – it seemed to him – only because her ignorance of everything relating to his life enhanced the peculiar attraction she had for him. He regretted having told her his real name – at the first meeting. Often, since, he had feared that she, or one of her friends, would associate it with a somewhat sensational trial in Paris many years ago. This had not occurred, but it remained a possibility. He wanted her to know nothing about him – nothing!

He had no desire for her – of that he was certain. And it was equally certain that she was not in the least in love with him. There were no tragic possibilities in their relationship. It might end in any one of a dozen ways, but disaster was excluded.

How long had he known her? Something had affected his time sense recently, and so calculations were necessary to answer his question. In a few days it would be Christmas. He must have known her, therefore, for about three months. But that was of no importance! What was interesting was the future – *her* future. Her money would not last very long – till October, at the best. Yes, he remembered! She had told him that George and Gracie would return to the flat in October, and that all her money would have gone by then. And, after October, what? He must find out, some time, if she had ever given the question one thought. Probably not, and yet surely even she must realize that her old Bohemian existence was impracticable in a bankrupt world.

His thoughts became chaotic. He walked on mechanically, unaware of direction. Several empty taxis passed him, but he had forgotten the decision to drive to Kensington Gardens. Eventually, however, he became conscious of his surroundings, and discovered that he had reached Hyde Park Corner.

He entered the Park and walked rapidly till he reached the Serpentine, then paused and looked round. A keen wind whistled through the barren trees: the frail sunlight was fading. A dripping dog barked a frenzied appeal to its master to pick up the stick just retrieved and throw it again into the water. Gulls wheeled or darted overhead, piercing the air with poignant cries. A model yacht rode proudly through the miniature waves.

Julian was about to go when a man appeared, gazed at the scene for a moment, then produced a piece of bread from his pocket and began to throw fragments to the clamorous ducks.

Although the incident was entirely commonplace, on this occasion it probed some obscure memory in Julian, thereby acquiring a special familiarity for him. Then he remembered, and a name leapt into his mind – Frank Derwent!

Yes, ages ago, he had stood here with Derwent and watched him feed the ducks.

It had happened during their first meeting. They had lunched with Stella at "The Fragonard." Afterwards, Derwent and he had spent the afternoon together. They had had tea in his flat near the Brompton Road. Now, Derwent was dead. He had died years ago in Ireland.

Instantly, however, these memories became unreal. They seemed to exist in static isolation in a spectral landscape. He did not feel them, he saw them. They were familiar, yet fantastic – like waxworks of living people.

He turned and began to walk quickly towards Hyde Park Corner. He had been a fool to leave the flat, and he would return to it immediately. . . .

Just as he reached the third floor, the door opened and Madge appeared.

"Hullo! you're come back then."

"Yes, I've come back. So you're going out?"

"Not for long. Geoffrey Fern turned up with Clarence just after you left. You remember I told you about him. He lives with his aunt on the first floor. I think he'll amuse you."

"Is there anyone else?"

"No, just the two of them."

D

Julian entered the hall, then paused – a gramophone was playing in the sitting-room. Presumably Geoffrey Fern had brought it. Julian listened intently – then decided that Geoffrey Fern must take the gramophone with him when he left.

As he opened the door, Harlowe got up from the couch and said angrily to Fern:

"Now you'll have to stop that damned thing!"

Fern stretched out an arm gracefully and the music ceased.

Harlowe looked from one to the other, then laughed abruptly.

"Just given Fern a description of you, Grant. Quite inadequate, of course. But then we don't know very much about you, do we? Never mind. Take a good look at Master Geoffrey Fern. Then I'll tell you about *him*."

He spoke in a staccato manner, moving his shoulders up and down, as if the action helped to jerk out the words.

Julian examined Fern with some interest, while the latter submitted to this scrutiny with the complacency of one who has nothing to fear.

He was about twenty-two, tall, sleek, debonair. His features had almost a babyish softness of contour, but the impression they created was short-lived, for the eyes were penetrating and cold. His thick fair hair evidently gave him the greatest satisfaction, as he caressed it frequently with his right hand. Also, he kept glancing appreciatively at his clothes, which were prophetic of the fashion about to be. Attitude, expression, everything denoted superb self-assurance.

"*That* is Master Geoffrey Fern," Harlowe announced, "a member of the most advertised, the most self-satisfied, and the most impotent generation in history. See what you can make of him."

He picked up his book and returned to the couch.

"I wanted to meet you, Grant," Fern said familiarly. "Madge told me about you just before I went away. Clarence and I don't agree, because I'm a realist and he's romantic."

"A realist!"

Harlowe threw the words at him, as if they were a bomb, then buried himself more deeply in the cushions.

"Sit here and let's talk," Fern went on with a gracious gesture. He made quick decisions, and had already decided that Julian was worth while. He was good-looking and he wore excellent clothes. "But, first of all, tell me this: aren't you dying to meet Gracie?"

"I admit I should like to see Gracie," Julian replied.

"Those photographs of her in the hall are definitely fascinating. She must be huge fun. I adore triumphant vulgarity, don't you? Of course George must have been hatter-mad to have married her. I'm *so* glad his name's George."

"Yes, it is satisfactory. I'm surprised you've not seen them – as you live in the building."

"I'll explain. We only came here a few months ago. I live with my aunt, did you know? Well, the poor creature believes there's a National Crisis, and that she must economize. She even believes there's a National Government. She reads these myths in her newspaper and believes them. She's a sentimental virgin, but well intentioned. We get on quite well."

He paused, touched Julian's knee, and indicated Harlowe with a slight nod of the head.

Fern's expectations were realized, for Harlowe raised himself and exclaimed angrily:

"All of which means that his aunt brought him up, as his parents died when he was a child, stinted herself to give him a decent education, and so on. You see the result – and her reward."

"Clarence is in a state of high nervous tension to-day," Fern explained to Julian, as if they were alone. "It's inevitable, because he's in permanent rebellion against facts."

"Whereas you are a realist," Julian interposed quite seriously.

"Yes, I'm a realist," Fern replied, passing his hand affectionately over his hair.

"In what sense, exactly, do you use that celebrated word?"

"I'll explain. I accept my environment – that's realism. I've no wish to alter things, so long as they suit me."

"And do they suit you?"

"Perfectly!"

"How very satisfactory! I congratulate you."

"I'll explain. I'm twenty-three. There's nothing whatever for me to do – even if I wanted to do anything. There are millions of unemployed, and they are going to remain a permanent feature of the economic landscape. The Mechanical Age is here. We've made our choice. We've hitched our wagon to a car."

Harlowe gave a shout.

"I warn you, Grant, he never uses a phrase of his own. He reads a lot, and he's a super-parrot."

"There's nothing for the young to do," Fern went on airily. "That's a fact, and you accept it – if you're a realist. If I'd no money, I'd be a Communist. Or I'd fight the old to get one of their jobs. All this irritates Clarence——"

"Never mind about Harlowe," Julian interrupted. "Let's stick to you. I take it you have some money?"

"I'll explain. I haven't a sixpence, but I've prospects. My aunt has enough to keep me. Also, she has two rich and crumbling relatives. One lives at Bath: the other at Cheltenham. That tells you everything. I cultivate them for all I'm worth. That's my profession."

"Well, it's a programme," Julian admitted.

"It isn't a programme – it's a *profession*. And it's the only one open to aspiring youth. I have to work devilish hard, I can tell you. The competition is razor-keen. It's necessary to be a first-rate psychologist, and a pretty good actor."

"I don't doubt it, but it would interest me to know why."

Fern stretched, with the minimum of exertion, then corrected the angle of his tie.

"I'll explain. It's essential that those old ladies in Bath and Cheltenham should believe that dear Geoffrey is what they imagine him to be. So he has to seem enthusiastic, desperately keen to get a job, immensely patriotic, and all the rest of it. When dear Geoffrey stays with them, he says all the things that are expected. Sometimes the poor dears take pen in hand and write to retired and yellowing colonels, asking if they can't get a *most deserving* young man a position of some kind. Of course they can't – thank God! But when dear Geoffrey stays with them he answers advertisements feverishly. Whenever the postman's knock is heard, he rushes to the letter-box. No reply is ever received, of course, because dear Geoffrey's letter of application amounts to this: – 'I went to a public school. I know nothing. I can do nothing. Will you give me a job?' So, perhaps you now understand why it is necessary to be a first-rate psychologist and a tolerable actor."

Fern paused, studied his nails critically, then added:

"Sometimes, when I'm very hard up, I give Bath and Cheltenham a good jolt, however."

"Successfully, I hope?"

"Oh yes! I say to them, with just a dash of drama: 'I can't *stand* doing nothing any longer! I'm going to get a job as a professional dancer.' That usually does it. Chequebooks are fumbled for, trembling hands guide a squeaky pen, and the bank is instructed to pay Geoffrey Fern, esquire, or order, a decent round sum, so that he may remain a British gentleman – and do nothing."

"I understand the level on which you're a realist. You've made it very clear."

But Fern was not listening to Julian.

"Last Christmas," he went on reminiscently, "I delivered a heavier jolt. Bath was staying with Cheltenham, and my aunt and I were also there for the festive season. After dinner one night, unemployment was discussed – very gingerly, you understand. A kind of mental snapdragon. Still, it was discussed. It was even admitted that all was not quite as it should be. I took advantage of this revolutionary uprush, and said rather snappily: '*I'm* surprised there aren't *more* Communists.' Panic! Dear Geoffrey might become a Communist! Dear Geoffrey got a cheque."

"I understand your methods perfectly," Julian said respectfully. "I have one criticism, however. Aren't you a little indiscreet?"

"You mean: Clarence might tell my aunt? She wouldn't believe a word of it. Neither would Bath nor Cheltenham. They're certain that I'm Young England. A little wayward at times – boys will be boys! – but Young England, nevertheless."

Harlowe flung down his book, rose, and crossed to Fern. He stood surveying him for nearly a minute, as if he were a repellent specimen in a medical museum, then said jerkily:

"There's only one chance for you – and those like you. And that is that you'll get cancer. Then you'll discover that there is such a thing as suffering in the world."

"Very melodramatic, Clarence. Surely, in the good old days, snowflakes used to descend after such a speech. But you don't impress me. Your environment has broken you, and you're jealous of me because I dominate mine. You'd be all right if you had a good part in a good play – and you know it."

It was the first time, in Julian's experience, that a direct reference had been made to Harlowe's predicament. Julian looked up quickly to see its effect.

Harlowe winced, as if he had been struck, then turned and went slowly out of the room.

"Do you know what he'll do now?" Fern asked directly the door had closed. "He'll wait outside for Madge and come back with her. We always have a row when we haven't met for some time. But I know how to deal with him."

"Apparently you deal with him very effectively."

"Quite! I understand relics – and he's one. And I have quite enough to put up with from relics, I can tell you. Professionally, of course, I have to put up with them. He needn't dither about cancer. Loneliness is his cancer, and it's destroying him. Still, he's an amazingly honest relic. Once, in the middle of a row, I asked him whether he'd rather be with me than be alone. It nearly killed him to admit that he'd rather be with me, but he *did* admit it."

Further conversation was rendered impossible at this point by a major disturbance in the flat above. The clamour increased till, finally, a heavy piece of furniture fell with a crash, and a door banged violently.

Julian looked inquiringly at Fern.

"You know what that is, of course?"

"I've no idea," Julian replied.

"I'll explain. It's a Grand Guignol drama. The man in the flat above was a clerk for thirty years – sober, steady, and all the rest of it. Then, some months ago, he won a big sweepstake prize.

Immediately he gave up work, began to drink a bottle of whisky a day, and started to bet heavily. His wife, his son and daughter are in a state of panic because they're afraid he'll live long enough to do in all the money. So they encourage him to drink for all they're worth. My God! *What* a theme for a Sunday editor!"

"And those are facts?"

"Ask Madge. They confide in her – so does the drunkard, when he can speak, which isn't often. Madge won't talk about it because it depresses her. This block is worth study, Grant. That is, if you're interested in a collapsing social system. Incidentally, keep one eye open for the Mad Major."

"I know the Mad Major by sight," Julian replied. "Madge pointed him out. You mean the man who waves his arms about and has an odd walk?"

"That's the Major. Always unearthing Communist plots. He's on half-pay, he's also half-baked, and half-cracked. In fact, he does everything by halves. He ought to be psycho-analysed immediately. I've a theory that he'll run off with Gracie – if one *could* run with Gracie – and murder her shortly afterwards."

For the first time there was a silence, during which Julian decided that Fern was an acquisition. Recently Julian had spent many hours alone with Harlowe, and the experience had not been stimulating. He was aware of an antagonism between them, and one which was deeper and subtler than that existing between Harlowe and Fern. In fact, it was so obscure that, until to-day, Julian had not been certain that Harlowe was conscious of it.

Fern's presence would solve the problem of conversation – that was certain. It would only be necessary to introduce a theme occasionally, and Fern would juggle with it so long as he had an audience. This knowledge was a relief, for, recently even when Madge had been present, silent periods had become more and more numerous and of longer and longer duration.

"Do you come here often?" Julian asked casually.

"For hours, every day, when I'm in town. I have to escape from my aunt, as you can imagine. I come up here and read, or goad Clarence, or put on the gramophone. My taste in music is bad – definitely. On the other hand, my literary standards are rather elevated. I——"

"Have you known Madge long?"

"Only since she came here. Don't know what I shall do when she goes in October. I shall either have an affair with Gracie, or join a club. I've lots of friends, of course, but I usually see them at night."

The door opened and Madge appeared with Harlowe.

"You've come back then," Fern said to the latter. "I thought you would."

"I come here to see Madge," Harlowe muttered, not looking at him. "None of us would meet if it weren't for her. Grant knows that just as well as I do. Better, perhaps."

"All of which reminds me that I ran into Purdle yesterday," Fern announced lightly. He turned to Julian. "Purdle is one of Madge's most dynamic discoveries. He's grand fun. He's coming to-morrow night. Don't miss him."

"I shall make a point of meeting Mr. Purdle," Julian replied.

E

Julian dined early the next night and reached the flat soon after eight o'clock. Somewhat to his surprise he found Madge alone.

"What's happened to Fern and Harlowe?"

"They're dining together."

"That's amusing. So Harlowe's willing to dine with him?"

Madge hesitated, but Julian was insistent.

"Well?"

"Clarence gets drunk whenever he gets the chance," she said, unwillingly.

"So that's the explanation. I wonder you didn't tell me before."

Madge did not reply. She was sitting on the edge of the couch, leaning forward. Something in her attitude made Julian say:

"You're depressed to-night. What's the matter?"

"I don't know."

"You do know. What is it?"

"Oh, several things, I suppose – Clarence among them. It's madness for him to drink. He's ill for days afterwards." Then, after a long pause, "I wish to God I'd never come to this flat!"

"Why?"

"You hear too much, and see too much. All the tenants tell me their troubles. I don't know what's going to happen if things go on like this much longer. Most of them haven't a job, and those with jobs are terrified of losing them. So they all do nothing but quarrel."

"Why do you stay?"

"You know why – because I'm rent-free here."

"And – after October?"

"Oh, that's months off! But we won't talk about me. There's something I want to ask you. Have you any friends in London?"

"Why doesn't Harlowe ask his own questions?"

"But – but——"

"You know perfectly well that it's Harlowe who wants to know, not you. Well, you can tell Harlowe, if you like, that I haven't one friend in London. Also, you can tell him, if you like, that he's nothing to fear – yet."

"I don't understand you."

"Possibly not, but perhaps he will. That's enough about him. I've a damned good mind to take you out to-night and leave the others to amuse Purdle."

"I couldn't do that, Julian."

"You'd come if I said you were coming."

She did not reply. Her silence irritated him to frenzy. He took her roughly by the arms and drew her up to him.

"You'd come – and you know it. You've no will – none! You'd do anything you were ordered to do – anything! You didn't want to live with Duncan, but you did. He didn't ask you to – he told you that you were going to. And you obeyed."

"But – you – how do you know?"

"I discovered, a week or two ago, that Harlowe gets drunk whenever he has the chance. Also, I discovered that, when he's drunk, he becomes very communicative – and not only about his own affairs."

"Let me go, Julian. You're hurting my arms terribly!"

"You'd come out to-night if I told you to."

"Yes, I suppose I should. Please let me go."

He released her and she sank on to the couch.

A few minutes later, Harlowe and Fern arrived.

Fern was festive, for two reasons: the spectacle of Harlowe, the moralist, half drunk always amused him; and he anticipated additional amusement from Purdle's visit.

He bowed low to Madge, greeted Julian, then held up a bottle of whisky for their inspection.

"Must have a drink for old Tobias. But wait a minute! – Grant hasn't met Purdle. Come on, let's get settled, then I'll give an impression of Mr. Tobias Purdle. Tobias! Isn't that a grand and glorious name? But what's wrong with you, Madge? You look exhausted."

"I am exhausted, Geoffrey."

"You're being vamped by someone. This age is overrun with vultures and vampires. I belong to the former denomination. Nevertheless, I know a lot about vampires. My aunt is one – although she looks like the Parish Magazine. So are Bath and Cheltenham. They vamp babies in their prams. And——"

"Oh, do *stop,* Geoffrey! And I do wish you wouldn't let Clarence drink when you take him out."

"I'm all right, I tell you," Harlowe announced unsteadily. "I'm all right, Madge. I'm abso-lutely all right."

He tottered to an uncomfortable chair, seated himself in a very upright position, then stared at the others with blazing eyes.

"I can tell you this about vampires——"

"We'd better have your impression of Purdle," Julian interrupted. "He'll probably be here soon."

"Right! Mr. Tobias Purdle. Listen attentively. Tobias is a slave who spent forty years on a treadmill, then – without warning – it stopped. If it hadn't stopped, Tobias would be of no interest, and would never have met Madge."

Fern paused.

"Rather a good opening, don't you think? Just a hint of the symbolic, and yet definitely realistic. I think it's good."

"I think it's excellent."

"In other, and more prosaic, words – Tobias is sixty-four and is a builder. He started with nothing, saved like a maniac, and has a passion for his work. For forty years he and his wife lived literally like misers. In fact, they have such long, bleak memories in common that they hate each other. Tobias made her pay half the cost of the wedding-ring – and, as a result, she still has doubts as to the legality of the marriage."

"That's a lie, Geoffrey."

"I admit it, Madge, but it's the only one."

He turned to Julian and continued:

"Doubtless the marriage was duly consummated in the approved manner, but it was not blessed till Tobias was forty. Then a son was born. Tobias regarded the red and wriggling infant, and privately decided – to his immense gratification – that in due course his son would carry on the business. At this point I pause, for two reasons: one, for dramatic effect; and, two, I want a cigarette."

Fern rose, lit a cigarette with a histrionic flourish, studied his audience narrowly, then continued:

"Over twenty years pass. The treadmill revolves. Tobias toils titanically. Rises at five – retires at midnight. The business grows, but – recently – it began to reel under the onslaught of the economic blizzard – so justly celebrated and still raging. But Tobias has his dream. The youthful Purdle has now been in the business for some years. He will save it. He will carry it on after Tobias is carried out. I pause again, leaving Tobias bloody but unbowed."

Fern caressed his hair, adjusted his tie, then flicked the ash from his cigarette.

"*But*, the youthful Purdle rebelled. Ah, these young moderns! Yes, he rebelled. He didn't want a life like Tobias's. Clearly, therefore, the youthful Purdle had been contaminated by Soviet propaganda. Anyway, he rebelled. He had a passion for jazz. He practised in the coal-cellar. He became expert. He got a job in a jazz band – where there was wailing and gnashing of teeth. I pause again, leaving the youthful Purdle, living in din."

The pause was a brief one.

"The shadows deepen. National Crisis approaches. Politicians supply the jazz. The youthful Purdle gets the sack. But does he go to Tobias and say: 'I have dinned against heaven and before thee'? Does he return to the business? He does *not*. He marries a widow, twenty years older than himself, with four hundred a year, and a house in Tooting. Ah! these young moderns! Tobias sees his dream in ruins. The business is dwindling. It will die with him. Suddenly – the treadmill stops. He realizes what his life has been. He decides to have a look at the world he's ignored. He meets Madge. He begins to talk. He tries to think. He starts to read. Such is Tobias to-day. Favourite poem: *After me cometh a builder, tell him I, too, have known.*"

Fern made a profound bow to each of his listeners in turn, then seated himself elegantly, and looked round expectantly.

"If anyone would care to ask a question," he said at last, as the silence continued, "I'm sure I should be only too happy to illuminate any obscurities."

Harlowe rose with surprising agility and went to the table.

"Fern, old boy, got to be fair – that was devilish good. Tell you a story myself later. Now I'm going to have a drink – just a tiny little drink."

"Oh, don't drink any more, Clarence!"

"It's all right, Madge, don't you worry about me. Just a tiny little drink."

Julian turned to Fern.

"You exaggerated a bit, I take it."

"Not in the least. You can cross-examine Tobias. He does practically nothing nowadays. He goes to his workshop – or pretends to – but that's only to get away from home. He's sacked all his men, except about six, and——"

A ring at the bell pealed through the flat.

"The Ancient Mariner! You talk to him, Grant – get him well started. I'll go and let the nineteenth century in."

Fern glided out of the room. A moment later they heard him exclaim:

"Tobias! My old friend! How are you?"

"I'm very well, and I hope you are," a rugged voice replied.

"Come on in. A brilliant and distinguished company awaits you."

Purdle was a small wiry man, with a prominent nose and deep-set serious eyes. The face was seared with lines and the half-clenched powerful hands testified to a lifetime of labour. He wore heavy, square-toed shoes and old-fashioned clothes; nevertheless there was a certain dignity in his appearance – possibly conferred by the knowledge that he was a master workman in every branch of his trade.

He greeted Madge with great respect, asked her a number of

questions, and listened attentively to every word of her replies. Then he shook hands with Harlowe. After which Fern claimed him.

"Tobias! Meet an old friend of mine – Mr. Julian Grant – Mr. Tobias Purdle."

"I'm sure I'm very pleased to meet you, Mr. Grant."

"I'm delighted. Do sit down; then, perhaps Fern will get us some drinks."

Possibly as the result of being welcomed so uproariously in the hall, Purdle had brought his bowler into the sitting-room. Consequently, having sat down, he put it carefully under his chair – to the secret and unalloyed delight of Fern.

Julian glanced at Madge and Harlowe: the former seemed half asleep, and the latter was evidently determined to remain within reach of the whisky. Julian realized that he would have to entertain Purdle.

"I was sorry to hear," he began, "that business was not too good with you, Mr. Purdle."

"There's no business, sir. Leastways, what's going is no good to me."

"That's interesting."

"I'm doing very little nowadays, so I see what's going on. Care to know how I spent my time last week?"

"I should indeed."

"Watching 'em build four houses in North London. Fifteen hundred each, they're asking for 'em. I wouldn't give fifteen hundred for the lot!"

He stared at Julian with gloomy intensity.

"So the work's as bad as that?"

"What can be scamped *is* scamped – foundations, woodwork, painting, or anything that can be hidden. People don't think about foundations. All they care about is appearance. Man came to me some months ago – desperate he was. He'd bought a house that looked all right, but whenever there was a storm the ground floor was filled with thousands and thousands of flies. For why? Built on a rubbish-heap – that's why. The house had to come down and they had to lay a thick foundation of concrete."

Fern came over and handed them drinks.

"Tobias! You're thrilling! Go on with the decline and fall."

Purdle continued in a manner which suggested that he had forgotten his audience and was thinking aloud.

"When building becomes rotten, you can be certain that everything's rotten. Take a man's money when you know you mean to swindle him! Put in such workmanship that you know that doors will sink, windows won't fit, walls will crack and become damp! I can't do it – and I won't do it! These flung-up houses will be ruins in a few years, unless a fortune is spent on 'em in repairs."

He turned to Julian and held his hands out for his inspection.

"Believe me or not, sir, many a job I've done with these hands which, when it was finished, I've known it was good for a century. And once you get away from that, you're done for – and I don't care what your trade is. Mr. Fern's laughing, but he's not in business and——"

"Not in business!" Fern interrupted indignantly. "I'll have you know, Tobias, that I most certainly am in business! My head office is in London, and I've branches in Bath and Cheltenham."

"I understand how you feel, Purdle," Julian cut in. "All the same, isn't anything good enough for most people to live in?"

"And, Tobias, anything that is built to last a few years will probably outlive civilization. So up with the dud houses, and let the writing appear on the jerry-built walls!"

Purdle looked from one to the other in great perplexity.

"Well, it all seems wrong to me. You're educated men, so I expect you understand. But I know one thing – my day's over. I see that plain enough. I worked, starved, and saved to get a business of my own – so I could do things *my* way. Well, I got it. And now I watch it crumble under my eyes, because I won't do rotten work. So I live on my savings, and that's blood-money, believe me."

Harlowe got up noisily and reeled over to them, glass in hand.

"Purdle, old boy, you're a fool! D'you know that? You're a fool – like me. Nobody wants us. See? Understand? We're just meaningless – that's what we are, old boy, *meaningless*. M-E-A-N-I——"

He returned to his chair, gesticulating wildly.

Fern glanced at the whisky.

"My God! Old Clarence has done himself pretty well! And I

believe Madge is asleep. Well, call it a party! Better have a drink, Tobias, while there is one. What about you, Grant?"

They both refused and a long silence ensued.

"I'd like to ask you a question, sir."

Julian started. He was staring at Harlowe and had forgotten Purdle.

"It's this," Purdle went on. "Looking at you, I should say that you were a man who had thought a lot and read a lot. That's why I want to ask you what you think of things as they are to-day. Because I can't see for the life of me how they can go on much longer like this."

"They can't. We've reached the final stage of an order of consciousness. Our civilization has entered its Babel phase. No man understands the words of another. What is Order to one man is Chaos to the next. So theories multiply like flies round a corpse. Still, there are two programmes, Purdle. One is to underpin Babel. The other is that *our* Babel can be made to reach the skies because we have machinery to help us – and the old builders hadn't. That's, roughly, how I see the situation."

"But what I mean, sir, is the state of trade and——"

"Economic conditions? Well, if you're not hypnotized by a pseudo-technical jargon, you'll discover that our famous economic problems are created by one fact. The age of expansion is ended, and so there's no longer any loot. That's the point – just that – there's no *loot*. We're gangsters without victims."

"Then, sir, you don't see——"

"Let's leave it at that, Purdle."

Julian rose to get a cigarette. He was intensely irritated by the discovery that Harlowe was staring at him as if he were an apparition.

But Fern was delighted – the evening had bettered his expectations. Only the fear of anti-climax disconcerted him. Then he remembered a subject which never failed to rouse Purdle.

"How's your son getting on with his widow in Tooting?"

"Don't talk to me about him! He's a waster and a sponger!"

Harlowe, who was now very drunk, staggered to his feet and shouted:

"Sponger! Who's a sponger? Tell me that – blast you!"

"I wasn't speaking about you. I——"

"I know! I know! You think I'm a sponger because I let that little rat Fern make me drunk. Well, I'm not! See? Prove it to you."

He lurched toward Purdle, then stood swaying from side to side.

"I've a half-brother. D'you know that? Rich – rolling – and a swine! Everyone 'fraid of him. 'Cept me. No one stand up to him. Now – you listen. . . . What was I saying? M-E-A-N-I – That's not it. Wait a minute."

He looked round wildly, then went on:

"Two years ago – met him in the street. I was looking like this. See? Up he comes – looks me over. Interested – curious. Understand? Asked me to lunch next day. Little restaurant where he took his mistresses. Wretched little underpaid typists. See? Understand? Well – cut the story short – I knew why he'd asked me. Wanted to gloat. Sat and looked at me, wondering what it was like to be *like* me. See? Know the type? Well, after lunch – just to see if I was wrong – asked him lend me a fiver. Wouldn't! Right! I'd ten shillings in my hand – separate. A week's food. Understand? Well, I crashed the lot on the table in front of him and yelled: 'There's the price of your bloody lunch!'——"

He began to laugh hysterically. Madge ran to him and put her arms round him.

"Clarence! . . . *Clarence!*"

He stared at her, then his mouth began to tremble and tears welled into his eyes.

"Can't help it, Madge, I can't help it! I can't bear it, I tell you!"

She turned to the others.

"Go! For God's sake, go! He'll stay here to-night."

F

Julian turned a page of the book he was pretending to read, glancing at the clock as he did so. It was nearly midnight.

Harlowe, huddled in an arm-chair the other side of the fireplace, was aware of the action, but did not raise his eyes from the newspaper which served him as a screen.

For the last hour they had been alone. Madge had left them

to visit a woman who was ill in the flat opposite, and since her departure they had not spoken. Each had pretended to read, hoping that the other would go.

They had not been alone together for some months. Ever since the night of Purdle's visit Fern had come to the flat almost daily and – as Julian had anticipated – his presence had removed a number of difficulties. But now Fern was abroad, and it was probable that he would remain out of England for a considerable time.

As a result of skilful manœuvres and masterly acting on his part, Bath had become convinced that he was in imminent danger of a breakdown, and so had provided him with the means for an extended holiday.

His absence revealed the extent to which Madge, Julian, and Harlowe – in their different ways – had become dependent on him. Consequently the situation now confronting them was more complex than the one existing before Fern's arrival. It was more complex – and they were more isolated.

During the last few months visitors had become the exception rather than the rule. Purdle was one example. It was true that he continued to meet Madge, but not at the flat. She believed that Fern was responsible for the lack of visitors, whereas Harlowe was convinced that the responsibility was wholly Julian's. Logic favoured Harlowe, for, after all, Julian was the newcomer – not Fern. But, whatever the cause, the result was a fact – and one which was not fully appreciated till some days after Fern's departure.

The antagonism between Julian and Harlowe had developed during the months which had elapsed since Purdle's visit. It was now so established that each took elaborate precautions to hide it from Madge. Her ignorance was essential. Otherwise she might end a conflict, of which she was the cause, by banishing one of the combatants. Consequently, as neither Julian nor Harlowe was certain that he would be the survivor, they masked their enmity in Madge's presence. She remained unaware, therefore, of the subtle conflict between them. It continued, nevertheless – each employing that caution which a man instinctively adopts when his adversary's weapons are wholly different from his own. . . .

Julian glanced again at the clock. It was a quarter past twelve. For the last three nights there had been a contest of wills as to who should be the first to go. Recently the competition to be alone with Madge had become acute. But, to-night, the clock had beaten Harlowe, for, if he remained, he would have to walk home – and it was raining heavily. His address remained a mystery, but it was known that he lived a considerable distance from Fulham. On occasions, such as the present, he had reason to regret the fact.

He rose, folded the newspaper carefully, and put it on the table. Then – without a glance or a word – he went slowly out of the room. A moment later the front door banged.

Julian threw his book aside. The manner of Harlowe's departure was not merely an insult, it was also a declaration of policy. In future, he would make no attempt to conceal his hostility in Madge's absence. No other interpretation was possible, but as Julian had anticipated some such crisis, and had made his plans, it only amused him.

Ten minutes later he heard Madge enter the flat and go to the bedroom. He rose quickly and went into the hall.

"Is that you, Clarence?"

"Harlowe has gone."

"Is it as late as that?"

"It's half-past twelve."

He was standing in the doorway, looking round the room. Its dreariness fascinated him. He glanced in turn at the colourless strips of carpet on either side of the large brass bedstead, the enlarged photograph of Gracie over the mantelpiece, the hideous wardrobe, the child's cot in the corner.

"Was he all right?"

"Who?"

"Why, Clarence, of course!"

"Perfectly. Why shouldn't he be?"

"Oh, I don't know! I've thought he's been more wretched than ever lately."

Julian did not reply. Madge was sitting on the bed, in the attitude of one unable to decide what was the next thing to be done.

"Have you bought those clothes yet?" he asked after a long silence.

"Yes. As you made me take the money for them, I thought I'd better get them."

"Show them to me."

She opened the wardrobe and took out one dress after another for his inspection.

"You'd better put one on and we'll go out somewhere."

"Oh, not to-night, Julian, really! I'd much rather go to bed."

"Very well – go to bed, and I'll stay for half an hour. There are one or two things I want to say."

He sat down and lit a cigarette. Madge glanced at him, then began to undress.

"Why do I always do what you tell me?"

"You'd obey anyone. You're that type."

Several minutes passed. Julian did not look once in her direction. He remained motionless, staring in front of him, apparently forgetful of her presence.

He almost started when she said:

"You might give me a cigarette."

He rose, discovered that she was in bed, then laughed abruptly.

"You're ludicrously out of place in Gracie's bedroom."

"Not nearly as much as you are. Why do you come here, Julian? Why do you want to see me?"

"So you're getting curious – at last?"

"Well, yes, I am – a little. It's natural enough, don't you think? You don't want anything from me. You just want to be with me. Why? I can't talk about any of the things that interest you."

"And supposing that – just for the time being – nothing interests me very much?"

"You're a mystery to me, and God knows I've met enough queer people!"

"Here's your cigarette – and here's an ash-tray."

"Thanks. You'd better sit on the edge of the bed. What is it you want to tell me?"

"There's going to be a change of programme. That's why I made you buy those clothes. We're not going to meet here in future. It's not been a success since Fern left. So I'm going to take you out to shows and restaurants. Also, I'm hiring a car so that you can get some air. You're always tired lately. This flat's no good to you – it's too damned depressing."

"You talk as if I shall never be in it."

"You won't – often."

"But – that's impossible, Julian!"

"Why?"

"What about Clarence?"

"Don't see what Harlowe could do for you if you were ill. You'll need to be well when October comes, and it's only a few months off."

Madge moved uneasily.

"I do wish you wouldn't talk about October."

"Why?"

"I don't know, but I wish you wouldn't."

"It's because George and Gracie return then, and you'll have to leave, and you don't know what you will do. For the first time in your life, you're a little worried about the future."

"Well, are you surprised? Everyone tells me every day how impossible it is to find a job of any kind. There's only one chance for me, Julian, but it won't come my way."

"And what's that?"

"To marry someone as hopeless as myself, who had just enough to keep us. Very little would do. The kind of man you'd despise probably – but there's no good talking about it."

She settled herself more comfortably against the pillows, then added:

"Anyway, October isn't here yet. You never know. Perhaps George and Gracie will give me the job of running the flat for them."

"George might – but I don't think Gracie would."

"No, I'm not too sure about Gracie."

They did not speak for some minutes. It was still raining heavily, and every now and again great drops pattered against the window-pane.

"Not surprised Clarence didn't want to walk home to-night," Madge said at last. "What time did he go?"

"A few minutes before you came in."

"What did you talk about?"

"We didn't talk. We read."

"I'm sorry I didn't see him. I wanted to ask him something. But it doesn't matter. He'll be here to-morrow."

"We're going out in a car to-morrow – and we're leaving early."

"But, Julian, I *can't* desert Clarence! He needs me much more than you do. For one thing, you've money – and he hasn't."

"You won't desert him. You'll see less of him – that's all. Anyway, that's the programme till October."

Something in the tone of his voice made her ask, a little apprehensively:

"Are you going away in October?"

"Probably."

"You mean, you'll go abroad?"

"Yes, very likely."

"What – for some time?"

"It's possible. Why?"

"I only wondered."

"Still – as you always say – October isn't here yet. I'd better go now and you'd better sleep. We'll have a long day in the country to-morrow."

"You're good to me, Julian, in your queer way."

"It's a queer way, certainly. In fact, it's so queer that I shouldn't try to convince Harlowe that it exists, if I were you."

"I wish you got on better with him."

"We've seen too much of each other lately. We shan't in future. Good night."

"Good night."

G

Julian entered the club and asked for his letters. He was trying to recognize the handwriting of the topmost envelope when he heard a man say:

"Hullo, Grant! Haven't seen you for ages!"

A round, middle-aged man with watery eyes was regarding him with all the curiosity of which he was capable. He was rather jauntily dressed, wore a button-hole, and his general manner denoted considerable satisfaction with the standard of preservation he had managed to maintain. He held *La Vie Parisienne* in one hand and a sporting newspaper in the other.

"Not for ages," he repeated emphatically, having realized the truth of his own statement.

"That's because I've ceased to move in the great world," Julian replied.

"Nonsense, nonsense!" the round man exclaimed, with a little wriggle of pleasure. "Glad to see you, anyway. You've not altered much. What about me?"

"I'm afraid you're much the same."

"Aha! Devilish good! You always were one too many for me."

Then, after a pause, he added:

"I say, though, it really is the devil's own time since I saw you. Why, it must be years! What on earth have you been doing with yourself? Seen anyone we know?"

"Not very lately. I've been abroad a lot."

"Any news of Jim Farquharson? He's for it, if you ask me. Just crumpled up. Too damned bad! I told him ages ago he was overdoing it. By the way, do you remember Carruthers? Well, his wife and young Tony Walters——"

A long richly-detailed scandal followed, rendered more tiresome by the fact that the narrator regarded sex as the highest altitude of humour. However, having punctuated his story with guffaws, and having at last reached the climax, he ended by saying:

"That's what she said – and Carruthers believed her. Merciful thing that pretty women always marry fools. Otherwise, you and I might have had a lot more trouble. Aha! That was worthy of you, wasn't it? Now, tell me – what do you think of things? Couldn't be much worse, could they? Everything would soon be settled if those damned fools would really have tariffs instead of nibbling at 'em. Not a man amongst them! Well, I must go and telephone my bookmaker. Look me up some time. Same address."

Julian watched him disappear in the direction of the bar. He was amused that it was taken for granted that he would remember the address, as he had entirely forgotten the man's name.

He flicked his letters over indifferently, till a familiar handwriting made him pause. It was Stella's.

Stella! Since her departure he had had only a card from her, giving her address. He had ignored it, and had interpreted her subsequent silence as resignation and acceptance. Why, then, this letter? He looked at the date of the postmark. It was nearly a year since she had left London. She was returning – that was why she had written.

He tore open the envelope. A letter from Stella – whatever its contents – seemed so irrelevant to his present plans that it irritated him even to glance at it. Nevertheless, he forced himself to read it with some attention. After all, it was possible that her return might affect his programme. It was unlikely, but it was possible.

The letter was short. With the exception of its closing sentences, it contained only statements of fact.

Farquharson was no worse; if anything, he was somewhat better. The specialist believed that he would remain paralysed in the arms, but that the menace of total paralysis no longer existed. Their expenses had been greater than they had anticipated. They would have to move to a cheaper flat.

We arrive in London on the 14th of next month. I beg of you to see me, Julian. If you ever cared for me – if only for an hour – scribble me a line when you get this.

Stella.

He looked at the head of the letter. It was dated the twenty-third of September. Evidently it had arrived some days ago, but, recently, his visits to the club had been very irregular.

When did she return? He glanced at the last paragraph. The fourteenth – Friday week. Yes, that was right. He tore the letter into fragments and threw them into a waste-paper-basket. Then he thrust the other letters, unopened, into his pocket, went upstairs, and entered the library. It was nearly empty. He chose an arm-chair by the window and settled himself for a final review of his plans. . . .

He had decided to live with Madge. This decision, which had been reached many weeks ago, had prompted a course of action calculated to leave her no alternative. The conversation he had had with her in the bedroom, on the night of Harlowe's unceremonious departure, had convinced him that she was afraid of the future. Her unwillingness to discuss what she would do after the return of George and Gracie had made that very evident.

During the weeks which had elapsed since then, he had

accustomed her to luxuries hitherto unknown. They had dined frequently in expensive restaurants, visited theatres and night clubs regularly, and every other day a car had taken them to the country as a means of escape from a London sweltering in a permanent heat-wave. His demands had been imperative, and Madge lacked the will to resist them. She was tired, physically and mentally. Luxury was not only a novelty, it was also a drug which soothed and stimulated her simultaneously. Gradually she ascribed the depression she had experienced during the last year to the atmosphere of the flat. Its heavy semi-respectable squalor had reduced her to its own level. It was glorious to escape – to watch life, to be amused, to surrender.

She was surprised to discover, however, that – as the weeks passed – Julian referred more and more frequently to the problem which would confront her on the return of George and Gracie. As she imagined that his motive in entertaining her was to banish depression, these continual references to the subject most likely to cause it were inexplicable. She, like Cinderella, knew that midnight would strike eventually, but to be constantly reminded of the fact was to be robbed of half the joys of freedom.

Another, and a deeper, cause of perturbation was the knowledge that she was deserting Harlowe. Again and again she urged his claims to Julian, but the latter invariably dismissed them with the statement that she would be able to see Harlowe often enough when October came, as he – Julian – would probably leave England then. As a result, Madge realized the extent of her dependence on him. To be penniless, with only Harlowe for a companion, was a grim contrast to her present luxurious existence. Imperceptibly, therefore, Harlowe became associated in her mind with that squalor from which Julian's generosity had delivered her.

But possibly the chief reason why, eventually, she ceased to be Harlowe's advocate was the discovery that continued reference to him irritated Julian to frenzy. Soon, she dared not provoke him. His intensity paralysed her will, hypnotized her whole being, till she was capable only of instant and abject obedience.

This, in essentials, was the situation Julian was now reviewing in the library of his club. Finally, he decided that Harlowe could be disregarded. They had met seldom during the last few months, and only when Madge had been present, but the dejection apparent in Harlowe's bearing convinced Julian that he had recognized and accepted defeat. He stared at Madge in her smart evening clothes as if he had difficulty in recognizing her and, more than once, he had asked Julian – with a note of entreaty in his voice – to let Madge spend a few hours with him.

There was no reason to delay any longer. He would tell Madge that she was going to live with him, and they would leave England almost immediately – certainly before the date of Stella's return.

And yet, perhaps it would be wise to wait a day or two. Last night, when he had taken Madge home at about midnight, Harlowe had been waiting for her in a state of extraordinary excitement. Julian had left them together, knowing that Madge was tired, and believing that Harlowe's hysteria would bore her unendurably.

Perhaps it would be policy to continue the process – to let her spend two or three days in the flat with only Harlowe for company. This might serve to impress her with the kind of existence she would have if it were not for him. Also, October had arrived. It might be as well to let her realize the fact, and its implications, before telling her his decision. George and Gracie returned in three weeks. Yes, he would let her spend a few days with Harlowe alone, then he would turn up and tell her that she was going abroad with him. The announcement would gain colour on a drab background.

He knew that the decision to live with Madge was merely a device to outwit loneliness. His need for her was psychic, not physical. When he was with her, things had substance: when he was alone, they were spectral. She enabled him to live by proxy.

Julian rose and stood looking out of the window, realizing that he would be free for the next two or three days. To his surprise, and somewhat to his amusement, he found the prospect inviting rather than the reverse. For weeks he had lived in a state of perpetual motion. He would go home now and rest, then – to-morrow – he must make the necessary arrangements for leaving England.

He left the club and walked to Piccadilly Circus, then took a taxi and drove home.

On arrival, he stood for a moment looking up at the house. Somehow it seemed ridiculous that it still belonged to him. He had lived in it only for short periods, separated by long intervals, experiencing always the sensations of a lodger. Looking up at it now, he discovered that he hated it. It was the only remaining link with his old life. He would sell it! If it had not been for Lady Sarah he would never have bought the place!

He let himself in, told the servant that he would be dining at home, then went upstairs to the study on the first floor.

He glanced at the book-shelves lining the walls with a view to finding something to read, but was unable to concentrate. To disturb one memory is to wake another. He had just recalled that it was owing to Lady Sarah that he had bought the house, and – now – he found that he was thinking of Clytie Lessing.

He remembered the night of her first visit. She had come at nine-thirty. He had stood by the window, listening for the sound of her taxi. He seemed to see her with extraordinary clarity. He even——

He'd put the damned house on the agents' books to-morrow! And he'd leave London and never return! He'd——

The door opened and a servant appeared.

"There's a gentleman to see you, sir."

"What?"

"A gentleman is asking for you, sir."

"And why the devil did you tell him I was at home?"

"I didn't, sir. He saw you come in. He seems very excited. He – he didn't know you lived here."

"Would it be possible, do you think, to make yourself plain?"

"He thought you were calling here. He said it's important. Then he asked whose house this was."

"What's his name?"

"Mr. Harlowe, sir."

Nearly a minute passed.

"Show him up."

Directly Harlowe entered the room, Julian knew that something exceptional had happened. He was well dressed, shaved, and radiated a happiness which even astonishment was unable to obscure. For Harlowe was unmistakably in a state of considerable astonishment. He looked round the room, glanced out of the window, then stared at Julian with an intensity which irritated the latter almost beyond endurance.

"You – *live* here? This is *your* house?"

"It's my house, but I don't live here. I let it furnished. At the moment, I can't get a tenant. There's no mystery about it – except, perhaps, your discovery of it."

"I had to see you, Grant! I saw you get into a taxi in Piccadilly Circus, so I jumped into another and told the driver to follow you. Something marvellous has happened! I can't believe it. I must tell someone else about it to make it seem true."

He laughed joyfully. It is probable that if Fern had entered the room at this moment, he would not have recognized him. Happiness had transformed Harlowe.

"You'd better sit down and tell me."

"I couldn't sit. I feel more like dancing. But I'll tell you everything. I *must* tell you. Then I'll have to rush off. I've got to go to Manchester for a few days."

"It certainly sounds very thrilling."

"Listen – listen! You remember I had a half-brother. I told you how I quarrelled with him in a restaurant. Well, he's dead. I heard from his lawyer yesterday. I'm to have an annuity of three pounds a week. It's in his will. It says I'm to have it 'to keep me out of the gutter.' Pretty grim, that, but I don't care."

"I congratulate you, Harlowe."

"Oh, that's all nothing! You probably saw that I was excited when you brought Madge home! last night. I was – terribly excited! Directly you'd gone, I told her. Then – then – I asked her if she'd marry me. And – and she said she would. My God! can you imagine what that means to me? It's – it's like being raised from the dead."

"How long will you be in Manchester?"

"What? Manchester? I can't think – wait a minute! Ten days – I come back on Friday week. We stayed up all night talking. We've arranged everything. We're getting out of London. We're going to a cottage in Cornwall – I used to go to it years ago. But I can't *believe* it, Grant. I know that directly I get to Manchester I shall think it's all a dream."

"When are you going?"

"Now – this afternoon. I shall go to the station directly I leave here. God! I'm glad I saw you get into that taxi. I want to say this, too."

He hesitated, then went on:

"I hated you – you knew that, of course – but it was only because I was utterly wretched. I was afraid of you. I can't explain, but I was afraid of you."

"The past is never interesting, Harlowe. Well, it doesn't look as if we shall meet again. You return on Friday week – and, as it happens, I'm leaving England on that day."

"I shall be in Cornwall when you get back."

"Yes, you'll be in Cornwall. Everything seems extremely satisfactory, doesn't it?"

"Satisfactory? Miraculous! I *must* go, my dear fellow."

He held out his hand.

"There's no ill-feeling – is there, Grant?"

"The past doesn't exist. I've forgotten it. I'm only interested in the present."

"Yes, the present – and the future."

"The future, of course. I'll come down with you."

"There's no need. Don't trouble. Good-bye. Do hope I didn't disturb you."

"Not in the least."

He did not move till he heard the front door close, then he groped to an arm-chair and sat down. Minute after minute passed, but he remained motionless – increasingly aware of a total inability to think. He waited, convinced that at any moment some plan would dart into his mind, but an hour crept by and he still remained stunned.

At five o'clock tea was brought to him, but he ignored it. Shadows began to invade the room. It grew darker and darker, but he did not move. Then, after an eternity had passed, the lights were switched on and he heard a muffled exclamation.

"I didn't know you were here, sir. I thought you were dressing."

"Dressing?"

"It's nearly a quarter to eight, sir."

He rose and passed through the folding doors into the bedroom.

Yes, of course! The servant was perfectly right – he was dining at home. And – what happened to-morrow? And the day after?

And the day after that? . . . Time seemed a tangible menace – a serpent slowly enfolding him in its toils.

After dinner he returned to the study. Somehow it seemed that he was waiting for something. It was inconceivable that he would remain here, hour after hour, all through the night. He must be patient and wait. . . .

He started violently and looked round. Then he listened intently. The only sound was the muttering of the wind. He glanced at the clock. Midnight.

He rose and went downstairs noiselessly, put on the first overcoat that came to hand, then went out into the night.

He walked slowly, aware that it was colder and that his overcoat was a light one. He forced himself to think of these trivialities in order to evade the knowledge that his actions were uncontrolled by his will. He was like a man just conscious that he was walking in his sleep – who could neither stop nor wake.

In a few minutes an empty taxi overtook him. He stopped it and gave the driver the address of the Fulham flat.

He leaned back and watched gleams from the passing lights flash in and out of the taxi. He had no plans, no anticipations. He had surrendered to a power which dictated his actions one by one – and he watched himself obey.

He dismissed the taxi and began to climb the steep stone stairs. Why was he certain that she would be alone? . . . "Indecision is the natural accomplice of violence." Where had he read that sentence – and why had he just remembered it?

He had reached the third floor. He paused outside the flat. It was in darkness. He waited for some moments, then rang the bell.

He could hear her footsteps in the passage.

She did not switch on the light, and only opened the door a few inches.

"Who is it?"

"Julian."

She seized his hands.

"Oh, my dear, I've been expecting you for hours. I gave you up at last and went to bed. I'm dreadfully tired. I didn't have any sleep last night. I've marvellous news! Let me go, then I'll switch on the light, and tell you everything."

"I know everything."

The tone of his voice frightened her. It imposed a silence which continued till she became hysterical.

"Julian!"

"Go into the bedroom."

To obey had become automatic, but when she reached the door of the bedroom she turned and faced him.

"What are you——"

He pushed her into the room, followed her, and slammed the door.

"*Julian!*"

"I thought even you had the intelligence to know that you belonged to me. I was wrong. So I'm going to prove it in a way you'll understand."

"But you don't know – you *can't* know – Clarence and I——"

"I haven't come to talk."

His intensity hypnotized her. She stood, staring at him, trembling.

"We'll *talk* – later."

H

He left the flat at two o'clock.

It was very cold, and the wind had strengthened, nevertheless he decided to walk home.

He paused on the pavement for a moment, and looked up at the building, then crossed the street slowly, his open overcoat fluttering in the wind. . . .

He should have made Madge his mistress weeks ago. Then, it would have seemed commonplace enough. There would have been nothing sensational about it. Harlowe would have been hysterically angry for a day or two, but his indignation would have lacked a moral background. Madge had had several lovers – he could not have condemned her for taking another. But to have made her his mistress now, when she was engaged to Harlowe, created a number of melodramatic possibilities.

Probably Madge had not understood anything he had said to her, just before leaving the flat. She had been lying across the bed, trembling convulsively, her face hidden in her hands. It was unbelievable that anyone could suffer like that! He envied her! To be capable of such emotion – to surrender to it from the depths of one's being! To be able to feel with tragic intensity! Only those with a mighty capacity for happiness could experience despair. Yes, he envied her, and he envied Harlowe – who would soon be stretched on the rack that was torturing Madge.

Of course, eventually, he would exert his influence over her in such a way that to-night would lose its horror. That would not be difficult. She believed that he had been seriously ill – just before their first meeting. He would let her think that the illness had been mental. Once she was with him, alone, out of England, he would be able to make her believe anything. She had no will, no memory – and so neither future nor past was real to her. This frenzied remorse would soon consume itself, and then she would realize that she had only to break with Harlowe, and go abroad with him, for to-night to be reduced to the level of the commonplace.

Julian paused and looked round. The streets were silent: the dark houses seemed to be dreaming. He remained motionless for some minutes, feeling like a statue in a deserted city, then he walked on slowly.

It was some time before he could pick up the trail of his thoughts.

Possibly she would refuse to break with Harlowe. The prospect of marrying that drunkard, and living with him in a cottage on three pounds a week, had made her radiantly happy. Also, she had told him, some months ago, that her only chance was to marry someone as hopeless as herself, who had just enough to keep them. She might cling to this romanticism – although she had become his mistress within twenty-four hours of her engagement to Harlowe. When her hysteria had burned itself out, she might decide to say nothing to Harlowe, and marry him directly he returned to London. But, in order to believe this to be a possibility, she would have to ignore what he had said to her just before leaving the flat.

He had told her that he would let her spend the next few days alone in order that she could realize the obvious facts of the situation. He had reminded her that Harlowe returned to London on Friday week, and had explained that – on that day –

he would come to the flat soon after dawn to take her abroad. If she refused, he would stay with her till Harlowe arrived, and tell him what had happened.

Again Julian stopped. He stood, looking at the pavement, thinking intently.

What courses were open to her? She might join Harlowe in Manchester immediately, tell him nothing, and marry him as soon as possible. But she would hardly dare to do that, without attempting to secure *his* collaboration. On the other hand, she might go to Manchester and confess. If so, that would be the end of it. That was certain. Harlowe's hatred of him was very real and very deep. If she told Harlowe that she was his mistress, that hatred would be transferred to her. What else could she do? Commit suicide? She hadn't the will. No, in the end, she would realize that there was one thing to be done, and one only – to break with Harlowe, and go abroad with him.

Julian walked on slowly.

Probably, in a day or two, she would write to him, agreeing to everything. But, if not, he would go to the flat soon after dawn on Friday week.

Friday week? Of course! That was the day on which Stella arrived in London. It was an odd coincidence that she and Harlowe returned on the same day. Well, *he* would leave London on that day, and Madge would go with him.

To live with her was essential. Her presence delivered him from that spectral loneliness which had haunted him more and more persistently of recent years. He dare not let her escape. His sanity depended on her. Perhaps it was this knowledge which had made him ruthless to-night. Once she was with him permanently, all his former interests would revive. He would leave England with her, and never return. A new life was beginning.

He looked round and discovered that he had walked some distance past his house – also that he was extremely cold. He buttoned his overcoat and retraced his steps.

He would think no more of Madge during the next few days. But, whatever happened, he *must* remember to go to her flat soon after dawn on Friday week . . . .
. . . .

VII

He felt he was standing on the verge of an abyss, from the vapoury depths of which multitudinous voices were calling: behind him, was a chaos of roaring waters, lashed by screaming winds.

Then, in an instant, silence and darkness. He remained motionless, feeling that the debris of a universe surrounded him. All sense of time was obliterated. Then, by imperceptible degrees, a sense of the familiar invaded his consciousness. Suddenly he heard a man's voice.

"Well, what do you think of that cigarette?"

Julian opened his eyes.

He was in the Metropolitan Café. . . .

He looked round slowly. The place was nearly deserted. Two men at a neighbouring table were talking loudly: a man near the entrance was crouched over a newspaper: near him, an old man and a young woman were talking excitedly. Several waiters were standing about, staring disconsolately at the avenues of empty tables.

Julian decided that it was all very dull and boring, then began to wonder why he had come here instead of going to his club. Anyway, here he was, with a cocktail in front of him, which he might as well drink.

He was about to pick up the glass when he remembered the artist he had encountered at the entrance to the café. That strange emaciated fellow with eccentric clothes and remarkable eyes! He had shown him a large drawing – a kind of satire of the Metropolitan. He remembered it perfectly. He could see it.

The treatment was dominated by a love and knowledge of perversity which extended to every detail. The artist had not only created a café of decadent splendour in mockery of the Metropolitan, he had transformed its patrons, for the men and women revealed at the various tables bore little resemblance to everyday humanity. They were studies in mental and emotional corruption, delineated so subtly that the degree of recognition would vary with each observer.

But – hadn't he had an argument with the artist about something? Of course! The idiot had denied the existence of that infernal brood, flitting above the tables, like materializations of the thoughts and desires of the men and women below them. He had even denied the existence of that spectre, just below the ceiling, controlling the phantoms, and – through them – the men and women at the tables. He had said that the spectre was the chandelier!

Still, it was unfortunate they had had that argument. It had deprived him of the artist's company, and the man had interested him. Now, he was alone in the Metropolitan, half dazed with boredom, but unable to think of an alternative. Why had he come to the damned place!

He looked round, as if in search of an explanation. The swing doors opened and a man entered with a dog on a lead. He hesitated, then chose a table near the entrance. The dog jumped on a chair, and stood wagging his tail – evidently highly delighted with his master's procedure.

Indistinctly Julian seemed to remember that a number of unusual incidents had occurred prior to his meeting with the artist. Also, hadn't he been vaguely aware that he had left the house, soon after dawn, in order to keep some appointment? What, exactly——?

Dorothy!

Yes, now he remembered! A scene from the past had risen to claim him! He had had a vision of that miniature bay in Cornwall. It had emerged from the darkness with perfect clarity. Then two figures had appeared on the beach. He had hurried towards them, only to discover that the woman was Dorothy and the man was himself. They were standing looking out to sea, just as they had done on their last evening together – twenty-five years ago. He had stared at them, terror-stricken, till at last he had turned and fled. Almost immediately he had heard someone shouting quite near him – the sunshine had flashed out like a limelight – and he had found himself on the threshold of Piccadilly Circus.

Julian began to tremble violently.

But – but – while he had been in this café, a *number* of scenes from the past had claimed him! Scene after scene had presented itself and faded! He had re-lived each in turn! The Hermitage, Mandell's office, his flat, Upper Brook Street——

A flame of faces seemed to surround him. He saw his father, Mandell, Rawlings, Stella, Frank Derwent, Farquharson, Clytie Lessing, Lady Sarah, Minchin, Madge, Harlowe——

Julian leapt to his feet.

He must be mad to be sitting here dreaming! *To-day was Friday.* Harlowe returned to London to-day! *That* was why he had left the house at dawn! He should have gone to Madge's flat. *That* was the appointment he had been unable to remember! What, in God's name, was he doing in a café in Piccadilly Circus?

Why, he had *seen* Harlowe on his way to the Metropolitan! He had——

Julian rapped the table to attract the attention of the waiter, but, as his summons was ignored, he flung down a coin, then rushed from the café.

No one seemed to take any notice of this hurried exit, but the dog began to bark excitedly.

PART III

ADVENTURE BEYOND PICCADILLY

A

The swing doors of the Metropolitan closed behind him. . . .

The sky was faintly lit by a citron-coloured afterglow. Everything was extraordinarily still. But, although he remembered that the sun had been shining when he entered the café, the necessity for reaching Madge's flat with the minimum of delay was so imperative that he began to run in the direction of Piccadilly. He must find a taxi immediately. He would think later. Now, he must act.

He continued to run for some minutes, then slackened to a rapid walk, but, to his astonishment, it seemed that each step covered an enormous distance. Soon, he became certain that he had lost his way in the darkness, and was now hastening with giant strides in the wrong direction.

Eventually, he turned and began to run in the direction of Piccadilly Circus, but instantly he seemed to be travelling at such speed that he dared not continue.

He came to a standstill and looked round.

The citron-coloured afterglow had faded. The silence was that of an endless plain. His mind began to fumble for facts like a man seeking familiar objects in a dark room. Slowly, and with difficulty, he tried to define his situation. He was in, or near, Piccadilly: it was night: he wanted to go to Madge's flat. But – what had happened to the traffic? He listened intently. Nothing! It was ridiculous, monstrous! However late it might be, there was always traffic – and stray pedestrians – in Piccadilly!

Julian stamped with irritation.

Immediately he began to tremble. He had stamped – but the action had created no sound. He stamped again and again. Silence.

All this must be a dream, an adventure in unreality. Yes, he was dreaming. Soon he would wake and everything would become clear again.

But there had been nothing fantastic about those scenes from the past which had risen before him in the Metropolitan Café. What mysterious power could have reproduced them, one after another, with a fidelity different in kind from that of memory? Memory! These had been no shadowy evocations – they were actual scenes from his life. He had not summoned them: he had returned to them. In one sense, they had been *more* real than at the time of their actual occurrence, for he had penetrated to the mental and emotional states of those surrounding him. Even the secrets of their solitude had been revealed.

Farquharson was an example. How had he known the nature of Farquharson's suffering when Stella had deserted him to sleep at the flat? *At the time,* he had been wholly indifferent to Farquharson's feelings, yet – when scenes of those early days with Stella had risen before him in the Metropolitan Café – he had known the anguish Farquharson had endured as intimately as if he had experienced it.

But, apart from such subtleties, why had those particular scenes emerged from the past? Many of them had no significance. They were isolated incidents, which he had forgotten the day after their occurrence. All those scenes, even taken in their totality, were a travesty of the life he had lived. It would be perfectly easy to imagine a different retrospect in which scarcely one of them would appear. Why had so many irrelevancies been included – so many essentials omitted? Why had whole years been ignored – and the events of certain days revealed with an absolute fidelity? What principle had determined the selection of——

How long had he been in that café?

The question so dominated him that his present predicament was forgotten.

He recalled his conversation with the artist at the entrance to the Metropolitan. They had parted and he had entered the café alone. It had been nearly empty. So empty, in fact, that he had particularly observed those present. There had been a man, near the swing doors, crouched over a crossword puzzle. A few tables away, an old man and a young woman had been having an intricate argument as to the precise time at which they had arranged to meet. Yes, he remembered perfectly! Later, two men had entered, talking loudly, and had sat at a table near his own. One had offered the other a cigarette and asked him to tell him what he thought of——

But these people had been there when he *emerged* from his retrospect! Why, he had heard one of the men near him say:

"Well, what do you think of that cigarette?"

Did that mean – could it mean – that he had spent only a few *minutes* in the Metropolitan?

No, he was dreaming – he must be dreaming!

Then he remembered that, when he had left the house, soon after dawn, several unusual incidents had occurred. In the first place, he had felt that he had just parted from two strangers. Later, he had entered the Park and sat near the Daisy Walk. When he left, he had had the curious impression that he had been there for hours. Then he had seen that beggar in the gutter near the Ritz. Soon after, he had had a vision of that bay in Cornwall.

Had all these incidents – and several others – actually occurred, or were they, too, part of his dream? Possibly, for some hours, he had been drifting in and out of a dream. . . .

He looked round – darkness and silence. It seemed to be getting colder every moment. Also, he had the unpleasant sensation that he was surrounded by invisible beings, each of whom was aware of his presence.

His thoughts became chaotic. A number of ideas invaded his mind simultaneously. When, at last, one theme became dominant, he discovered that he was thinking of a book he had read some years ago. Why he should have remembered it now was inexplicable. It could hardly have any relevance to his present desperate situation, for it had been concerned with the lives and practices of magicians in Tibet. One theory in particular had interested him, and – to his surprise – he found that he remembered it in detail.

Apparently the Tibetans, like the Egyptians, believed in an "ethereal double." They held that – in a normal state – this "double" is closely united with the material body. In an abnormal state, however, it can leave the material body – which remains inert till its return. The Tibetans claimed that those who had trained themselves could effect this separation at will, but that it could also happen involuntarily. The case of a woman was cited who had remained inanimate for a week. She said she had been astonished by the lightness and agility of her new body and by the extraordinary rapidity of its movements.

Was it *possible* that this separation had happened involuntarily to him and——

"Well, that's as good an explanation as any. In fact, I'm not sure that it's not the best of the lot."

Julian started violently. The artist was by his side.

B

"How could you possibly know what I was thinking?" Julian asked apprehensively.

"What's really worrying you is the fact that you are not more surprised. But we'd better arrange certain preliminaries. So do you mind telling me just where you think you are?"

"Are questions necessary?" Julian asked ironically. "You knew what I was thinking without being told."

"Questions are not necessary, my dear fellow. I'm merely trying to make you feel at home."

"Well, I'm somewhere near Piccadilly. It suddenly got dark and I lost my way. I take it the same has happened to you."

"Not a bit of it! But we'll let that pass. Let us agree on an environment mutually agreeable. How would you like to be sitting at a table, under a tree in a garden? Might have a river at the garden's end. What do you say?"

"For God's sake talk sense!"

"Sense? Oh yes, of course! I remember! But, seriously, what about that table under a tree?"

"Of course I'd rather be there than here, you fool! Do you imagine——"

The sound of a great rushing overwhelmed him. When he dared to open his eyes, he found he was sitting opposite the artist at a table under a large tree. Birds darted hither and thither in the sun-dappled foliage and, at the garden's end, a stream flowed lazily by.

"Cigarette?" asked the artist, offering one in the palm of his hand.

"Thanks," Julian replied. "Perhaps you'll now explain."

"Well, wait a minute! I want to look round to see if the setting is all right. If you'd care for the Alps in the distance, just let me know. It's no trouble."

While the artist studied the scene, Julian watched him intently. His appearance had not altered since their meeting outside the Metropolitan Café. His coat seemed to belong to a short stout man, his waistcoat to a tall thin one, and his trousers to a giant. His emaciation was so extreme that he might have been the ghost of a scarecrow.

Julian burst out laughing.

His companion turned to him slowly. Julian had forgotten the vitality of his eyes and therefore experienced a shock on encountering their direct glance.

"Glad to find you're still amused, Mr. Grant. I'll only say this: the appearance I present to you may be no more real than this garden. Also, it may be no more amusing than the appearance you present to me. A mind as subtle as yours will appreciate the implications of those simple statements."

"And what sort of appearance do I present to you?"

"My dear fellow, I know what you *think* you look like – and I accept it. That is, I respect your illusion. And I think you might respect mine. The etiquette here is very strict. Tell me: does the scenery seem solid to you?"

"Perfectly!"

"Good! Fortunately, you have a powerful imagination. We may be able to talk for a bit, but spare a thought for your surroundings now and again – I beg of you – or they'll vanish. It's such a damned bore creating new ones. Also, it's exhausting."

"Now, look here," Julian began angrily. "I'm sick of riddles and pantomime tricks! Where the hell are we – and what's happening?"

"I looked you up on purpose to communicate my discoveries. You ought to be grateful. I'm not an altruist any more than you are. Anyhow, I'll tell you my theory, and then you can say what you think of it. Naturally, it's only based on my own experience, so it probably isn't worth much."

"Let's have it! Why all this talk?"

"Right! But just to give you a pleasant shock – and so make certain of your attention – I may tell you that I witnessed the whole of that retrospect which rose before you in the Metropolitan Café."

"You're a damned liar!"

"It began with The Hermitage, passed to Mandell's office, then to Stella, Clytie Lessing, and so on, and it ended with your somewhat abrupt courtship of Madge. Ah! you're a little frightened now and therefore a trifle more humble. Also, I know all that rubbish you were thinking in Knightsbridge about some synthesis you had created; and that you were a man wholly concerned with the everyday world."

"My God! this is madness! I must be mad!"

"That, too, is a theory, Mr. Grant, but it's not my chief one. Listen! It's very simple, really."

The artist threw his cigarette away, lit another, then glanced swiftly at Julian.

"Take a pull on yourself. You're not looking too good. Anyway, this is my theory."

He paused, then continued in the same off-hand manner:

"Every night millions of people dream – as they call it. That is, they enter the dream-world for a few moments. Odd things happen, some of which they remember when they wake, and some they don't. My theory is that you and I have become *fully conscious in that dream-world*. Do you get that? Our bodies are sleeping somewhere and, at any moment, we may wake up in them again."

"I wish to God we could!"

"Quite! So do I. Perhaps we shall soon, and then all this – if we remember it – will seem only a very vivid dream. Possibly we've had this dream – and, therefore, this conversation – a dozen times, and forgotten all about it when we woke up in the usual way."

"I'm beginning to think that anything is possible."

"My dear fellow, believe me, it is! Still, I'd better tell you my discoveries in this dream-world. Sounds like a sentimental play, doesn't it? Well, don't you worry, because it isn't in the least sentimental here, as you'll discover."

The artist broke off and looked round apprehensively.

"Where's that blasted river?" he demanded.

"There, of course! Are you blind?"

"Good! Keep an eye on it, will you? Surely you know how quickly scenery changes in dreams. Well, you're in a dream now. You've wakened up in a dream, so to speak. For the love of God, get *that* into your head, once for all, and stop thinking how you can get to Madge's flat. You can't get to it. And that's all there is to it."

"And why the hell not?" Julian demanded. "If we can create our surroundings here, as if we are gods, why can't I get to Fulham?"

The artist exploded with laughter.

"That's about as intelligent as a fish asking why it can't go where it wants to go on land, when it can go whichever way it likes in the sea. You're in the *dream-world*, I tell you! But thanks all the same for mentioning Fulham. Years ago, one of my models lived there, and I have the pleasantest memories of that convenient suburb."

"I'd really rather hear about those famous discoveries of yours, if you don't mind."

"Good! I'd cut out irritability, if I were you, Mr. Grant, but that's by the way. Listen! Of course you've noticed, when you've been dreaming, how often your environment changes. Also, you've no sense of time, and very little of space. First you're here, then there. Well, follow this. I know you're as arrogant as Satan, but don't dismiss what I'm going to say just because it's simple."

"I assure you I'm giving you the whole of my attention. Incidentally, there doesn't seem to be an alternative."

"Follow this closely. In the everyday world, your conception of time is conditioned by your interior state. Your mood, if you like. That's obvious, isn't it? If you're happy, time flies: if you're anxious, it crawls. The same is true of your conception of space. If you're in a desperate hurry, a yard seems a mile. Well, here, in the dreamworld, everything is *created* by your state. Get that! Everything is *created* by your state. Scenery, distances, everything! If you're happy, you find yourself in delightful surroundings – which are the projection of that particular state of

happiness. And they are real *only for you*. As your state changes
– say, you get the hump suddenly – so your environment alters.
Perhaps you become lustful – then you find yourself in a brothel.
Or you become elevated – then you find yourself in a temple.
Each environment in turn is merely a projection of your interior
state. And it is real only for you."

"There's nothing particularly new about any of that, is there?"
Julian asked, with simulated indifference.

"There's nothing particularly new about the bottom of the
ocean, Mr. Grant, but it might seem a trifle unusual if you suddenly found yourself there. We're not *speculating* as to the nature
of the dream-world. We're in it – up to the neck."

"Your ingenious theory does not explain how we were able to
create our environment at will – as we have just done."

"That's not difficult, my dear fellow. As you and I are somewhat alike, we are able to create – and share – the same illusion.
This garden, for example, with its birds and sunlight, and its river
– if it's still there!"

Julian did not reply. He was perplexed by the discovery that
he was experiencing two violently conflicting emotions simultaneously. Thus, at the present moment, he felt immensely stimulated and, at the same time, unendurably depressed. At last he
forced himself to say:

"Suppose I agree that we're in the dream-world and——"

"There are other explanations," the artist interrupted.

"Such as?"

"Your own most magical one about the ethereal double. But
there are others. For instance, we may be under an anæsthetic.
Perhaps, really, we're both sitting in a couple of dentists' chairs.
I'm in Paris and you're in London. On the other hand, we may
be mad – temporally – of course."

"That's nonsense!"

"Why? Why shouldn't we be mad? We're remarkable men –
living in an age which drives everyone mad except Robots. After
all, it was the fear of madness which turned you into a vampire that fastened on Madge. And, between ourselves, my dear
fellow, your last visit to the lady was just a little like insanity, don't
you think? I mean, surely it was the action of that mad Julian
Grant, to whom you referred so movingly in that eloquent letter

you wrote to Stella – and then destroyed – ever so many years ago."

Julian leapt to his feet.

"I can't stand this another second! I can't stand it, I tell you!"

The artist rose, took Julian by the shoulders, and looked him in the eyes.

"Don't be such a damned fool! You can't let yourself get into a state like that! Haven't you understood one word I've said to you? Why, you idiot, if you get into a paroxysm of fear, that state will materialize, and so will become your environment. You can't play tricks here: control is essential. Now, have a drink – a stiff whisky-and-soda?"

"Yes, and as quick as you can."

"Well, you must help. You must want one, desire one like hell – then, your craving will materialize. Ah! that's better!"

"What do you mean?"

"You've got a drink in your hand. So have I – thank heaven! Now sit down, and cut out the hysterics. All the best!"

The artist emptied half his glass, then looked over at Julian.

"That's more like it, Mr. Grant. You've a strong will, don't forget that. And will seems to be capital here. You'll probably boss the show once you begin to feel at home."

After a long silence, Julian said:

"I can't stand the knowledge that you can see my thoughts – that you can read my memories like a book. It's damnable! I can't see your thoughts, or penetrate to your memories."

"That's only because you're such a damned egotist. You will – when you get sick of yourself. And one does get very sick of oneself in this dream-world, where everything is only a projection of oneself. . . . My God! that confounded river's gone! Quick! Concentrate! or the damned lot will go! *That's* better. I say, you really have a first-class imagination. You owe that to The Hermitage upbringing."

"Tell me this," Julian exclaimed desperately. "Have you seen a retrospect of your past – something like I had in the Metropolitan Café?"

"I should think I have! And a wretched, futile, fiddling affair it was! I'm an artist – the last real artist the Western world is going to get. The bastards only want scientists nowadays, and they'll get 'em, and be blown sky-high by 'em – and a damned good job too. Well, in my retrospect, there was nothing relating to my development as an artist. Nothing! Lot of silly incidents with women, and one or two little escapades that weren't too pretty perhaps, but normal enough for a genius. And that was all! I tell you I was furious!"

"What's your name?"

The artist crashed his fist on the table.

"Would you believe it – I've forgotten it! That's what this damned dream-world has done for me! It's the ultimate insult. I *am* my name. It *is* I. I made it famous. It's the monument I raised to myself in the desert. And now I can't remember it!"

"Don't be so dramatic about it. I wonder you dare get into such a state. Do be scientific. Our job is to wake up. You agree, I take it?"

"I should think it is! To wake up in that solid well-planned world, which has an objective reality. Instead of floating about in this fluid world, where all is subjective. Still, I'm tempted to tell you my latest and most depressing discovery. Let's have some more cigarettes. Make it a dozen, if you can."

Julian exerted his will and a little shower of cigarettes fell on the table.

"My God, you're like a factory! Good for you! All the same, you've forgotten the matches——"

"There's a box in your hand," Julian replied loftily.

They lit their cigarettes, then Julian asked:

"Would women appear if we wanted them?"

"Good Lord, yes! So don't want them! It's easier to get women here than it is to get rid of them. The dreamworld is very like the waking one in that respect. Here am I, exerting my will for all I'm worth to prevent women appearing, and you glibly suggest producing a beauty chorus! If you knew how I struggled to escape from women to get to you, you wouldn't be so amused."

"Sorry! You often find yourself with them, then?"

"Of course! Directly my will weakens, and my imagination can no longer project decent surroundings for me, I find myself in indecent ones. You'll find your own particular horror soon. In fact, you're going to make a number of interesting discoveries."

"All that only reminds me that you were going to tell me your latest and most depressing one."

The artist threw his cigarette away and stretched luxuriously.

"What a bit of luck!" he exclaimed. "I'm tired. I'm going to have a sleep."

"Surely you don't *sleep* in the dream-world?"

"Don't you! That proves how little you know. Why, it's your chance. You may wake up in the normal way. I'm going to sleep now – but you must keep awake."

"Why?"

"To maintain the scenery, of course! If you go to sleep as well – God knows what we shall find when we awake. You've got to promise."

"Oh, all right! Sleep if you want to. I've enough to think about."

The artist threw himself on the grass. It seemed to Julian that he fell asleep almost immediately.

C

It was very still in the garden. The birds had ceased to sing, but every now and again their shadows flitted over the lawn as they darted from tree to tree. Sometimes a jewelled butterfly hovered on a swaying flower. Sometimes a leaf spun idly down. The river sighed in its sleep.

Julian gazed at the high walls enclosing the garden, lazily wondering what lay beyond them. Then he looked over his shoulder, expecting to see a house, only to discover that a few yards behind him was thick impenetrable white mist.

He rose and walked slowly to the river. He could just see the opposite bank. He glanced to the right, to the left, then at the sky – thick impenetrable white mist everywhere. Yet shafts of sunlight still quivered through the shifting leaves. The shadows made an intricate pattern on the velvet lawn. It was pleasant in the garden.

He began to walk towards the table, but had taken only a few steps when a bird fell dead at his feet. Simultaneously, he heard voices.

He looked up quickly. A man and a woman emerged from

the mist, which rose like a cliff a few yards behind the table. They moved slowly, hand-in-hand, gazing rapturously into the distance. When they were level with Julian, they stopped, and the woman said:

"If you knew how I've longed for this – just for this! The sea – stars – silence. Tell me that all this isn't a dream."

"It's not a dream."

"You're certain?"

"Certain! Let's go and stand by the waves. We've waited long enough for this."

"Yes, long enough."

They passed on and vanished in the mist beyond the river.

Julian returned to the table and sat down. It was peace to be unable to think – to drift like a leaf on a stream. All sense of urgency had vanished. Indistinctly he remembered that, recently, he had been obsessed by the necessity for getting somewhere, but now all action seemed sterile and a little ridiculous. Shadows thronged through his mind. The garden lulled him: it was so still. The breeze stirring the tree-tops only deepened the silence. The flowers were dreaming. The river was asleep.

He found he was staring at the artist. What a ridiculous figure he looked lying there in his absurd clothes, his head resting on his arm! What was it he had said? Something about being the last artist the Western world was going to get? What a mountebank! And all that hysteria because he had forgotten his name! Surely he could find more interesting companions than this mono-maniac! There must be——

But at this point the artist stirred restlessly, stretched, then opened his eyes.

His glance met Julian's.

"Oh hell! No luck! Damn it, how sick I am of it all!"

He rose wearily, then looked round.

"It's getting darker!" he exclaimed. "Don't like the look of it. Anything happened?"

"A man and a woman walked through the garden. They seemed to imagine they were alone near the sea."

"How monotonous! I'm sick of dreams and dreamers. Any-thing else?"

"A bird fell dead at my feet."

"Ah! This isn't for long then. Chuck me one of those cigarettes."

He looked narrowly at Julian, then added:

"Still, you've ceased to think about Fulham. That's something, anyway."

"Fulham?"

"Aha! Mr. Grant's forgotten! But he's still a little worried because nothing surprises him. Why the hell should it? One's not surprised at anything that happens in a dream. Throw us a match."

They lit their cigarettes. A long silence ensued, which Julian ended at last by asking irritably:

"When are you going to tell me that depressing discovery of yours?"

"What? Oh yes, of course! How infernally consecutive you are! Still, it won't last. I've discovered, my dear fellow, that this confounded dream-world isn't so very different from the waking one."

"That's rubbish! Here, we can see each other's thoughts, create——"

"Yes, I know, I know! For God's sake don't repeat what I've just told you. Of course you can *see* people's ideas here, when they've got any. And, in the world, you soon found out that they hadn't an idea in their heads. So where's the difference?"

"Anyhow, we can create our environment here. We couldn't there."

"Are you so certain? Not so dramatically, of course. Still, I think we created our surroundings in the waking world. Also – here – we accept appearance as reality, and we did just the same there. Here, we live in our particular illusion – and so we did there. There's damn little in it."

"Then perhaps you'll explain why you were so anxious to find yourself in the waking world again."

"Because, Mr. Grant, in the waking world things *resist* you, and here they don't. There are no walls to knock your head against here. There are no obstacles – that's the devil of it! Money is one example. In the waking world, if you haven't money, there are no end of things you just can't do. Whereas, here, you've only to want something – and there it is. Or you think it's there, which is precisely the same thing."

"How long have you been here?"

"How *long!*" the artist exclaimed. "I don't know what you're talking about."

"Can't make it much plainer! At times you're almost an idiot. How *long* have you been here?"

"Oh Lord, must we go on talking in terms of time? It puts a terrific strain on me. I think only in terms of *state.* That is, I ask: 'Am I at peace? Am I amused? Am I bored?' And so on. I tell you that as your state – or your mood, if you like – creates everything here, you think only in its terms."

Julian looked round quickly.

"It's getting devilish dark! I can't see the end of the garden!"

"Why, you blasted fool, I warned you! Imagine the garden! Imagine it, do you hear? Quick! For all you're worth!"

"I can't! The mist is closing in."

"Lord! Now we're for it! Think! Quick! A garden, a table under a tree, a river—— It's no good! Too late! It's just vanishing. I can't see you."

The sound of a great rushing, then darkness absolute.

"Are you still there?"

Julian's voice was a whisper.

"Yes, I'm *here* – if the word has any meaning for you."

"Wait! I can see a light. Look! Over there! It's coming towards us."

A vague circle of light approached them, growing more defined as it came nearer. Suddenly a woman emerged. She passed within a yard of them, with arms outstretched, as if she were seeking someone. Her hair shone like a halo: the lips were parted expectantly: luminous eyes scanned a distant horizon. She seemed to glide by on invisible wings.

"God! who's that?"

"Oh, I'm always seeing her," the artist replied. "She haunts me. She's a prostitute, who evidently always has the same dream. She's always looking for her first lover. Always looking for him! I'm sick of seeing her. She never seems to see me, though. Well, *that's* what she looks like in the dream-world, Mr. Grant. Actually, of course, she's probably in bed with a drunk in a squalid room near Paddington."

A long silence, then Julian said:

"I can't see anything . . . Where are you? . . . Where *are* you?. . . ."

D

A great highway winding through a valley. On one side, precipitous hills: on the other, a broken chain of rocky eminences, like vast abandoned altars. From the far distance, the boom of an imprisoned sea.

No moon was visible, but the scene was illuminated by a white spectral light, which created an effect of fantastic noonday. And, crowding down the highway, an endless multitude.

Julian stood on a mound, in the shadow of a great rock, watching the passing throng.

At first glance, it seemed that the denizens of a world were hastening to a fancy-dress ball, but a closer scrutiny demanded a deeper explanation.

Some strutted majestically in rags, others – regally robed – slunk by with down-bended heads. Men on horseback whined for alms, stretching out hands filled with golden coins. Tatterdemalions – evidently believing they were officers, resplendent in glittering uniforms – marched, stiff as ramrods, pausing at intervals to yell words of command at their companions. Athletes went on crutches, while cripples kept falling to the ground as a result of frenzied efforts to dance. Some sang ribald songs, some shouted, some moaned, some wept. Disputes, brawls, fights flamed up and flickered out on all sides. Some ran hither and thither, seeking someone. Others kept touching transparent masks – which they imagined concealed them – in order to assure themselves they were hidden. Some stood at the side of the highway, gesticulating wildly. Some argued; some prayed; some sang softly to themselves. Here, one parted with a magnificent cloak in exchange for a tiny mirror. There, one trafficked his sword for the image of a woman fashioned in mud. Many believed they were entirely alone. Many were certain they were away for their holidays. Many were convinced they had just won a prize in a sweepstake. All, eventually, moved on down the great highway, mimicked by their shadows.

Julian stood motionless, watching them. . . .

Were these the dreams of those who lay sleeping in their beds? That was the artist's theory. These were their dreams made visible. He – Julian – was in the world of fantasy, watching the dream-visitants pass by. What separated him from them was that *he* was conscious on this dream plane, and they were not. They were visitors, he was a resident. Yes, that was the artist's theory.

God! to wake, to *wake* – now! Suddenly to hear the roar of the Piccadilly traffic! To feel the solid resisting earth under his feet! To touch things, to know that they existed – that they were independent of him.

Nevertheless, he continued to gaze at the passing multitude, and soon he became aware of activities hitherto unnoticed.

Stationary among the moving crowd, and facing it, were solitary figures scanning the passers-by, as if seeking those who bore a sign. They stood like luminous statues, and it was not possible to gaze long at them. Their beauty synthesized that of man and that of woman. They stood like beings of another race, watching and waiting.

Not one of the thousands passing endlessly by them seemed aware of their presence, but, very rarely, one of the figures touched a dreamer and – instantly – both vanished.

Julian was speculating on this mystery, when he noticed that there were other figures, who also stood stationary, scanning the passing multitude. But these were male cadaverous figures whose eyes burned fiercely in masklike faces. Also, some in the moving throng recognized them. Now and again, a dreamer stopped and accosted one of them. Instantly, both vanished.

The desire for adventure stirred in Julian. A flame of curiosity consumed him. He would mingle with these phantoms, penetrate to their secrets, and discover if there were any who were conscious that this was the dream-world, and that they were only dreaming.

He leaped down from the mound and joined them, but before he had taken a dozen steps he noticed a man by the highway who was waving his arms about as if delivering an oration. Julian stopped and joined him, interested that no sound proceeded from the moving lips.

Suddenly, he found he could enter the man's illusion. What was real to him became real to Julian.

The scene vanished.

Julian discovered that he was standing by an orator on a large platform, decked with flags. Facing them, was an audience consisting of eminent representatives of the different nations, each of whom listened spellbound to a series of platitudes delivered by the speaker in a dignified and impressive manner. When, at last, he was silent, the distinguished audience rose in a transport of enthusiasm. Cries of "Saviour!" rose on all sides. It was then unanimously decided that the orator should become Dictator of the universe.

At this point, however, Julian ceased to share the man's illusion. The highway reappeared, and Julian found himself watching a small dumb man who was waving his arms about without attracting the smallest attention.

"Some politician's dream, I suppose," Julian muttered to himself, then rejoined the moving multitude.

Almost immediately he saw a figure, like a luminous statue, a few yards ahead of him. He tried to approach, but instantly was unable to breathe. Nevertheless, he struggled nearer and nearer till, finally, he fell to the ground.

Someone was helping him to rise. He resisted angrily, but unavailingly, and soon found himself on his feet, confronted by a cadaverous figure, who was watching him through half-closed eyes.

"Well, Julian Grant?"

"How do you know my name?"

"You'll forget it soon, and be given a more appropriate one. Now, what can I do for you?"

"Get me away from this damned place."

"Where do you want to be?"

"I was in Piccadilly. I lost my way."

"How do you know you're not in Piccadilly now? Wait a minute! Supposing you stood in Piccadilly and saw – not men and women – but their hopes, their fears, their desires, their dreams. Mightn't it look a bit like this crowd?"

"Talk sense – or get out!"

"You'll do! I never make a mistake. You're very curious, aren't you? Well, I'll show you one or two side-shows. You'll find your own particular side-show – later. Meanwhile, what do you think of this?"

Instantly the highway disappeared. They were in a dark building, the immensity of which could be felt. A polar silence enveloped them.

"I'll switch on the lights," he heard his companion say.

"The lights!"

"Why not? Everything is up-to-date. Here we go!"

Julian gave a cry.

They were standing in a circular building, half the size of the world. Tiers of bunks rose one above another in never-ending ascension, extending far out of sight. There were millions of them. In each bunk lay a sleeper, motionless.

"Who are these?" Julian whispered.

"These are they who have not the vitality to dream. You need not whisper. They won't wake. They are waiting."

"Waiting! For what?"

His companion laughed, and switched off the lights.

"Come on," he said. "Here's another side-show for you. Look! What do you think of this one?"

Julian discovered that he was looking down on a magnificent cricket-ground. It was surrounded by one huge pavilion, full of men smoking, drinking and chatting. A game was in progress.

Every now and again a spectator shouted:

"Oh, well hit, sir! Well *hit!*"

A brilliant sun shone in a cloudless sky.

"What in God's name is this?" Julian demanded irritably.

"This? This is the Englishman's Paradise. This is the dream of all right-minded Englishmen – and here you see their dream come true. The game never stops. The cigarettes, and the beer, are free. Here they loll, watch the game, cheer, and tell each other about every other match they've ever seen."

"But why does the pavilion extend round the whole of the ground?"

"Surely you know that the dream of every right-minded Englishman is to watch cricket from the *pavilion!* So – here – they are *all* in the pavilion. But, of course, the professional players go on to the field from one entrance and the amateurs from another. Also, the latter have 'Mr.' before their names in the newspapers. Quite near here is the Golfers' Paradise. It's a huge bar where everyone tells everyone else how he once did the ninth hole in par – and no one ever gets bored . . . What! tired of it already?"

Julian seized him and shook him violently.

"I want to *wake!* I must wake – I tell you – or I shall go mad!"

Only a laugh answered him.

The next moment he was alone, and in darkness.

E

He welcomed solitude, and even darkness. It was essential to think – to dominate these thronging visions which threatened to rob him of reason. He would isolate himself from these hallucinations, deny them, refuse them harbourage in his memory. Disassociation might lead to deliverance.

He would review all that had happened to him in terms of time. He would not allow his time-sense to be obliterated. He would cling – mentally – to the successive; and not be overwhelmed by the confusions of this chaotic realm, where everything seemed to exist simultaneously.

How long, then, was it since he had left his house in Knightsbridge, soon after dawn, intending to keep an appointment which – temporarily – he had been unable to remember?

Perhaps it would be simpler if he divided his experiences into three epochs. The first consisted of that series of events which had ended with the disappearance of the Metropolitan Café, and the beginning of his retrospect. This epoch had been more or less normal. It had belonged to the waking world, although intermittently, it had been disturbed by hallucinations. The second epoch was the retrospect. But the third epoch, which had begun with his hurried exit from the Metropolitan Café, had belonged wholly to the abnormal realm. He had experienced a different level of consciousness. He had entered a new dimension of thought and emotion.

Well, and how long was it since he had left his house in Knightsbridge, soon after dawn? An hour? A day? A week? Where was he now – actually? Had he fallen asleep on that seat near the Daisy Walk? He remembered feeling drowsy. Or was he, in reality, sleeping in his bed? But what was the psychic mechanism which enabled him to ask these questions? How could he – the dreamer – speculate concerning the sleeper? The end of dreams is awakening. Yet, here he was – awake – in the labyrinth of a dream.

Well, and how long was it since——

Perhaps the mystery had a simple explanation. Possibly it was something like this.

In the *physical* organism, only a certain number of thoughts and impressions can be received by the intelligence. Say, one hundred – in one minute. But when we go to sleep and dream, we enter a *psychic* state. We dream – and, within one minute of physical time, the intelligence may experience thoughts and impressions at the rate of four or five thousand. We may live through years in a dream-consciousness, and every event may be there. We may know the vicissitudes of a lifetime. Yet, when we wake, we discover that all this occupied only a minute or two of physical time, and probably only a few seconds. This new dimension of consciousness can only be attained in the psychic state of a dream, for, then, the intelligence is functioning in a finer medium.

Yes, he seemed to remember reading that somewhere, ages ago. Probably it was true. If so, it was possible that only an hour – or even a few minutes – had elapsed since he had left his house in Knightsbridge, soon after dawn. . . .

He had closed his eyes, in order to think more clearly, but – although they were still shut – he was aware that it was getting lighter. A new quality pervaded the silence. The air was heavy, inert, lifeless.

Julian opened his eyes.

He was standing on a plain which extended endlessly in every direction. Not a blade of grass was visible; nothing moved on the vast monotony; no bird hovered above it. It was a brown arid immensity – cold, menacing, deathly still. A low-lying leaden sky brooded above it like a doom.

Terror numbed him till he felt like a statue of ice. There was nothing to appal, but it was this very nothingness which was more fearful than a host of visible terrors.

He could not endure this a second longer – not for one second!

He closed his eyes and, by a supreme effort, tried to *imagine* other surroundings. Anything! A field, bounded by a wall! Anything! He visualized it – a field bounded by a wall. Unconsciously, he adopted the method – taught him by the artist – by which a new environment could be created.

When he opened his eyes, he was standing by a wall in a field. . . .

It was dusk. He stood motionless, listening. Although he could hear nothing, the certainty entered him that he was on the threshold of the familiar. It was quite near him. He was separated from it by a stride. He was certain – certain! Excitement, terrible in its intensity, pulsed through him.

He knelt by the wall, pressed his ear to it, and listened. A vague murmur reached him – a faint echo of movement, a hint of things known, and now desperately dear.

He began to tear at the wall with his hands. It was made of a soft yielding substance like cotton-wool. He tore at it more frantically, making a deeper and deeper cavity. Suddenly, a gleam of light——

Sunshine! Traffic! People!

He was awake! *Awake!*

F

He stood, swaying from side to side, dazzled by the sunshine.

Two men stopped near him. One struck a match and held it for the other to light his cigarette.

"Thanks, old boy. I tell you, Dick, if I could only get the capital, I'd make a packet. The thing's dead right – and dead easy."

"Yes, but how will you get the capital with things as they are?"

"Search me!"

They walked on, talking animatedly.

English! He looked round. This was The Mall. He was in The Mall! Admiralty Arch – cars – taxis – Buckingham Palace! This was no dream. He was awake at last.

Absurd, chaotic ideas trooped through his mind. He wanted to stop a passer-by and tell him his story. He wanted to fling his arms round a tree and so convince himself of its identity. He wanted to take a taxi to the Metropolitan Café. He wanted to go into a shop and buy something. And he felt that he could do all these things *simultaneously*.

To do one thing at a time suddenly seemed supremely ludicrous. The waking world was very jolly, but people really were the most stupendous fools. They did one thing at a time!

Julian began to laugh and continued to laugh helplessly. Some minutes elapsed before he regained control.

Well, here he was – awake, sane, and in The Mall. Now what should he do? What was it he used to do? It was odd, but he couldn't remember.

It was at this point that he saw an arm-chair. Now, this annoyed him, for arm-chairs in The Mall were an innovation, and recent experiences had made him intolerant of change. Still, the arm-chair was an excellent one, and it was unoccupied. It was in the corner of a room, and there was a picture above it. He had seen the picture before somewhere.

But all this was ridiculous in The Mall! Also, a fog had appeared. Perhaps that wasn't very unusual in October, but it was extraordinarily thick. He couldn't see Admiralty Arch. The traffic had stopped——

He was in a room. In a corner was an arm-chair with a picture above it. A man was seated, motionless, in a wheeled-chair by the fire. Opposite him, sitting on the end of a couch, with her head buried in her hands, was a woman. The man's eyes never moved from her.

"You know now – at last."

She raised her head wearily.

It was Stella.

Why had she suddenly grown old? And why did he see, standing by her side, the Stella he had met in that bookshop? Was it the contrast between them which made the actual Stella seem old? And yet, perhaps, it was chiefly the expression of the eyes which had altered. Yes, that was it. Once, the eyes had looked courageously out on the world, and now they gazed at it blankly, seeing nothing.

He glanced at the man in the wheeled-chair. Could that be Farquharson? That withered, sensitive-looking creature with white hair and frail hands? The Farquharson he remembered had been solid as a block of marble. How had he dwindled to this wraith-like being?

"You know now – at last."

She repeated the words in the same dull passionless tone.

"Don't distress yourself, I – I beg of you. And don't reproach yourself. You never lied to me, Stella. Any happiness I've known is due to you."

"Happiness!"

She rose and went nearer him.

"What happiness have you ever known? Your love for me destroyed you – just as my love for him destroyed me. Oh, my dear, we haven't lived together – we've died together!"

"Stella!"

She sank on to a cushion near him, clasped her knees with her hands, and gazed into the fire. When she spoke, her voice was a whisper.

"I couldn't help loving him. He was so young, so eager, so – innocent. When he altered, when he became the opposite of everything he had once been, I couldn't believe it. I waited for him to come back to me."

She turned and looked up at Farquharson.

"I had no pity for you – then. I knew that you loved me, that you were suffering, but it meant nothing to me. How wretched we all must be, for we all leap at happiness with the fury of a beast. But you soon had your revenge. He soon tired of me."

"Tired of *you!*"

"In a few – a very few – months. So I shared him with others. Then the war came and I did not see him for years. You thought he had gone out of my life. Later – much later – I used to go and sit in his flat alone, going over my memories, like a miser counting his coins. Why do I tell you all this? What does all this matter – now?"

"I want you to talk. I want you to tell me everything."

"*You've* always had to be silent."

"It doesn't matter about me. You don't understand – and I can't explain. I thank God that I married you. You're – you're wrong in thinking that I suffered. I can't explain – but you're wrong."

"I've ruined you. That's the truth. Your career, your health – everything! But I was suffering so much that I did not think of you."

"Was he unkind to you, Stella?"

She began to laugh hysterically.

Farquharson tried to touch her with his hand, but could only move his arm a few inches.

"Unkind! You'll never know how funny that is! He killed everything in himself and everything in me. The last time I saw him – just before we went to Germany – he destroyed even my memories."

"But what happened to him, Stella? I don't understand."

"I don't understand either. Directly he possessed anything, he destroyed it. Everything died in him. He was utterly alone, like a man in a wilderness."

"But you still love him?"

"I don't know. I'm too numb to know. Somehow – now – it's like a dream. But I'm glad I've told you."

She turned and put her hands on his.

"Our lives are over. I want you to forgive me."

He looked away and she went on quickly:

"I've thought of something since – since we came back. It's odd, isn't it? that we returned some days earlier than we intended. We expected to get back to-day. But what I want to say is this: couldn't we leave London and – hide somewhere?"

"You'd be terribly bored alone with me."

"We've only got each other, my dear. Life's over and done with. Let's look back on it together."

"You're crying, Stella."

"Yes – thank God! – at last."

"My darling . . . my darling. . . ."

Julian had listened, unable to move. But, now they were silent, and seeing Stella at Farquharson's feet, her head leaning against his knee, he became furiously angry. They had dared to pretend they were alone! To discuss him——

He went nearer to them, then stopped. His anger flickered out and he began to tremble.

Stella . . . Stella!

He waited, but she did not move.

It is I, Julian! I need you. I need you terribly.

A mist was rising in front of him. He could no longer see two figures – only a dark shapeless mass.

Stella!

The room faded. There was the sound of a great rushing, then he heard the artist's voice.

"Well, did you have a good sleep?"

G

He raised himself and looked round slowly. He was lying on the floor of a small room and the artist was bending over him.

"Get up! What the devil do you want to lie there for, now you're awake? Come on, I'll give you a hand."

Julian pushed him aside roughly, then rose and stared at the room.

It was unbelievably squalid: the walls were mud-coloured, the ceiling low-pitched, the floor bare. It was lit only by the flickering light of a candle on the mantelpiece. Near the empty fireplace was a deal table with a chair on either side of it.

"What are we doing in this hole? There isn't even a window."

"Best I could do, my dear fellow. Sorry, and all that. But, if you remember, our attempt at more sylvan surroundings was a failure. You've not forgotten the garden, the river, and so on? We couldn't keep it up, so – this time – I thought we'd be more modest in our demands. Have a window, with a pleasant outlook, if you like, but it's an additional strain and——"

"Do I have to listen to you?"

"Well, I'm damned! There's no more gratitude in the dream-world than there is in the waking one. As I said before, they're very alike. But it really is a bit too thick! I find you, frozen, on a vast plain, and——"

"You're lying. I *know* you're lying."

"And I take the trouble to transfer you here – no easy task, by the way – and get cursed for my pains. However, just to make things even, I assure you that I loathe you quite as much as you loathe me."

A furious anger flamed up in Julian. He seized the artist and shook him violently.

"I was awake, do you hear? Awake! And you dragged me back to this mad-house."

The artist freed himself, with the minimum of exertion, then laughed.

"Awake! You were asleep. If you sleep here, you often dream of the waking world. Don't be a fool. Have a cigarette and listen to me. I've a number of discoveries for you."

"If you had the remotest idea how you bore me——"

"Oh, do stop being elementary! Of course I bore you! And you bore me. We only meet because we're alike. So, naturally, we're mutually bored. I tell you again that one gets awfully sick of oneself here. And – in a way – everyone here *is* oneself."

Julian flung himself into a chair and lit a cigarette. A sense of frustration and impotence numbed him.

"The first discovery, Mr. Grant, which I lead modestly to the bar of your imperial and impartial intellect, is this: – some dreamers do very well here. Recently, I visited certain uplands, and found some charming residences. Their occupants were radiantly happy. Also, their surroundings – unlike ours – do not keep disappearing. They vary, of course, but the changes are only minor. If the people living there become happier, their homes become lovelier. That's just an example. Now, why is it – do you imagine – that you and I reel from one environment to another, like a couple of astral drunkards?"

"I'm not in the least interested."

"No? Sorry! Mr. Julian Grant is not interested. Next, please! Ah! This, I think, may intrigue you. It relates to that retrospect of yours in the Metropolitan Café."

"Well, and what about it?"

"Mr. Julian Grant *is* interested. Good! You regarded that retrospect in two ways. You admitted that each scene was valid, but you denied that all the scenes – taken in their totality – were representative of your past. One moment, Mr. Grant – as learned counsel so often says. You believed you could have witnessed a different retrospect – in which scarcely one of those scenes would have appeared – that *would* have been representative. Isn't that so?"

"Of course it is!"

"Well, you're wrong."

"That's easily said."

"It's also easily proved."

"Nonsense!"

"Better listen, anyway. I shall convince you."

"You won't, but you can go on."

"It's most kind of you."

The artist rose, looked round the room critically, took a cigarette, then sat down again and put his feet upon the table.

"I'll mention your objections first – otherwise you'll chuck them at me like brickbats. That retrospect omitted so much: skipped whole years: featured the trivial: left out your spiritual development. And, above all, it did not reveal your sufferings. Too bad! That's about the list, isn't it?"

Julian did not reply, and after a pause the artist continued:

"Well, I suggest this to you: that retrospect revealed your emotional life. It showed your emotional Rise, Decline, and Fall. Each scene was a spiritual turning-point – to quote one of your favourite phrases. That retrospect was the history of a man who committed emotional suicide."

"Very ingenious!"

"You're impressed all the same. And you didn't like my knowing one of your favourite phrases. Well – just to prove that it wasn't a lucky shot – I'll repeat one of your favourite quotations. One you've thought about a lot. It's this: 'I can find no words for what I feel. My consciousness is withdrawn into itself. I hear my heart beating, and my life passing. It seems to me that I have become a statue on the banks of the river of time.' . . . Ah! *That's* shaken you! I thought it would."

"Do I have to listen to you?"

"The alternative is the plain – and you didn't seem to care about that much. Think over my theory about the retrospect."

Julian turned to him fiercely.

"You've some hidden motive in all this. You pretend you're helping me, but – actually – you're torturing me. Do you think I don't know it? You want to make me as big a madman as you are."

"My dear fellow, I keep telling you that we may both have gone mad – temporally, of course. Anyway, I want to explain this. In the waking world, a man has two lives – that of his will: and that of his understanding. Mentally, he may be brilliant: and, emotionally, he may be debased. Well – here – in the dream-world – he has only one life. It is created by that which he loves best."

"And how does a man know what he loves best?" Julian demanded irritably.

"He loves that best for which he would sacrifice most. And it is that ruling love which creates his environment here. All thoughts not organically related to it vanish like smoke. And *that* is why, Mr. Grant, the retrospect you had in the Metropolitan Café was significant and representative."

Julian said nothing. After a long silence, the artist added:

"And if a man had committed emotional suicide, it might be that – *here* – his state would materialize as an endless arid plain."

Julian leapt to his feet.

"By God! I'll stand no more from you! You're just a rat, and I'll kill you like one!"

"You can't put a hand on me. You can't even move an inch. You see? Motionless as a post. Don't you try your Madge tricks on me. They won't work. Bit frightened now, aren't you? Well, sit down – and don't make a fool of yourself again."

Julian collapsed into his chair, flung his arms across the table, and buried his head in them.

The artist yawned, stretched, whistled half the chorus of a popular song, then said nonchalantly:

"Oh, by the way, I *do* think you might recognize me when we meet in this delightful dream-world. Recently – as you would say – I had the privilege of taking you round certain side-shows. I showed you the sleepers in their circular building. I showed you the Englishman's Paradise. Not only did you fail to recognize me, you omitted to tip me. Too bad! Then, you disappeared. Then, having indulged in some abstract calculations concerning the dream-consciousness and physical time, you found yourself alone on that plain."

"For God's sake, let me go!"

"Where? – as you would say."

"Anywhere!"

"To the plain?"

Julian did not reply.

"Do answer! Not that it's necessary, but it is polite."

A long silence.

"Well, well, my dear fellow, you really are very dull. Still, some of the cleverest and most renowned of men, in the waking world, are no better than village idiots – here. And some of the simplest, in the waking world, are geniuses – here. I've explained to you why that is so. *Here,* you are what you love. And, *there,* you are what you seem. . . . I say! Do brisk up and have a cigarette."

Julian remained silent.

"It's no good thinking about Stella, my dear fellow. She's had a great shock and is thinking a lot about you. That's why you were able to see her. Too bad she didn't see you! You were a vulture with her, and a vampire with Madge. Well, most vultures become vampires when they reach middle age. Hullo! What's happened?"

Julian was staring at him with intense concentration. Suddenly he burst out laughing.

"You're not altogether a liar," he said slowly. "It *is* true that we can see each other's thoughts here. *I can see yours.*"

"Only some of them, I venture to think," the artist replied carelessly.

"I can see this, at any rate. That woman who appeared in the garden – you remember? You said she was a prostitute, dreaming of her first lover. Well, *you* were her first lover."

"Perfectly correct, Mr. Grant."

"Also, you've given up being an artist here because you can only draw a scene in a café. Men and women at the tables and, above their heads, an infernal——"

"Perfectly correct, Mr. Grant."

"I'm afraid of you no longer. We meet on equal terms now."

"Not quite. For instance, you haven't witnessed *my* retrospect. That is, you haven't penetrated to my interior memory."

"Oh, to hell with you! And to hell with this room, too! A thought created it – and a thought destroys it!"

Instantly the room vanished. Julian was alone.

H

He was standing on a plain which extended endlessly in every direction. It was a brown, arid immensity – cold, menacing, deathly still. A low-lying sky brooded above it like a doom. . . .

But, now, Julian realized that he had long been familiar with the psychic solitude of which this plain was the physical representative. To escape was impossible. It was his shadow, and so it would accompany him.

It was true that – by exerting will and imagination – he could conjure up a new environment which would seem real for an hour. He could produce an illusion by resorting to psychic drugs, but, in the end, he would be confronted by the plain.

He closed his eyes. After all, he was free mentally. At least, he was free if he rejected the artist's theory that – here, in this dream-world – all thoughts not organically related to his ruling love would vanish like smoke. But, of course, the artist was not serious. Also, on reconsideration, it was fantastic to believe that this plain represented his interior state. Yet, for years, he had been conscious of an immense inner isolation, related in some mysterious manner to that Will which on many occasions had possessed him and made him its instrument. There were innumerable examples of his sudden and complete subservience to it, but the most notable, perhaps, was the night on which he had gone to Madge's flat for the last time.

He remembered all the events preceding that visit with extraordinary precision. He had returned home in the afternoon and, almost immediately, Harlowe had appeared. He had been very excited, and had explained the change in his circumstances. Then he had told him that he and Madge were going to be married.

When Harlowe had gone, he remembered how he had groped to an arm-chair and remained motionless, hour after hour, till the servant had told him it was time to dress. After dinner he had returned to the study, then – gradually – it had seemed that he was waiting for something. The hours passed and, at midnight, he had gone out into the night.

Julian interrupted his reminiscences at this point to ask himself this question: When he left the house, had he had any definite plan which he had decided to execute? He was certain that he had *not* – completely certain! Neither then, nor later. Why, he remembered that, in the taxi driving to Madge's flat, he felt he had surrendered to a power which dictated his actions one by one – and he had watched himself obey.

Even when he rang the bell at her flat – even when he heard her footsteps in the passage – he had had no idea what his next action would be. None! He was certain of it!

Then, what *was* that Will which had so dominated him

that he had become the spectator of his own deeds? What was its origin? Surely not in such trifles as his desire to take Stella straight from Farquharson's house to the flat! Or in that perversity which had prompted him to humiliate Clytie Lessing! But, if not in trifles such as these, then in what had that Will originated? It had grown in the darkness and emerged only when its sovereignty was absolute. And although for long periods it would make no demands, invariably, in the end, it had made him its automaton and compelled him to serve its ends.

Finally, it had destroyed him. He had become incapable of feeling. He had died emotionally, and it was the recognition of this emotional death – this spectral psychic solitude – which had driven him to Madge.

But, was it *possible* that this perverse Will had become his life; that, soon, every thought unrelated to it would vanish like smoke?

To believe that would be madness. It would be worse than madness. . . .

Julian opened his eyes.

He was standing in the bedroom of Madge's flat.

I

He was standing at the foot of the bed, facing the fire.

It was night. Everything was very still. He glanced at the enlarged photograph of Gracie over the mantelpiece, the hideous wardrobe, the child's cot in the corner. Then he heard a movement behind him and turned round.

Madge was in bed, propped up by pillows, and Harlowe was sitting in a chair near her. She did not look at him, she was staring at the foot of the bed. Harlowe watched her in evident perplexity. At last he said:

"But why didn't you say you were ill when you wrote? I half thought something was wrong because your letters were so short and – odd! What is the matter with you, Madge?"

"I shall be all right soon."

"Have you been ill ever since I left?"

"Yes – no – I can't remember."

"Haven't you had a doctor?"

"No."

"You haven't been alone all the time?"

She did not reply and he repeated the question.

"What? Yes, I've been alone. It's nothing. I'm all right."

"Something's happened. You're – different. Tell me what it is."

"I – I don't want to marry you."

"Good God! Why not?"

"I don't know. I've always lived with men. Why shouldn't we live together?"

"But I want to marry you. Why have you changed?"

"I don't know. I've had time to think – lying here. I know nothing about myself, so what's the use of marrying?"

"There's something queer about all this. When I left London you were radiant, and now——"

"Now?"

"You're like someone who's been stunned."

Harlowe rose and began to pace slowly up and down the room.

"You've scarcely looked at me since I came in," he said at last.

She did not reply. He glanced at her, then went quickly to her side.

"Look here, Madge, there's something devilish wrong! You frighten me. Either you're seriously ill, or something's happened. Which is it?"

"I must be ill – seriously ill."

"But you said just now it was nothing! And, if you're ill, why haven't you had a doctor? What was the idea of lying there alone day after day? Do you mean to say that no one's been to see you?"

"No – no one."

"What's happened to Grant, then? . . . What? I didn't hear. Surely he came?"

"No."

"That's very odd – Why, you're trembling all over! What, in God's name, is wrong with you?"

"Oh, leave me alone! I can't bear this another minute!"

"But – but——"

"All right! All right! Then I'll tell you!"

She shouted the words. He stepped back involuntarily, then stood staring at her.

"Grant came the night you left. Here! Here! You understand? here – in this room! We're lovers! We became lovers that night——"

"You're – *lying!*"

"Here – in this room! . . . If – if you could only see how funny you look!"

She began to laugh hysterically.

"You're delirious. You don't know what you're saying."

"Yes, I'm delirious! That's it. All the rest's nonsense. Grant hasn't been here. I haven't seen him. I've been ill. I've had terrible dreams——"

She broke off and they stared at each other.

"You're not delirious. What you said was true. You are his lover. You've been his lover for months——"

"No! I——"

"For months! Why did he take you out, buy you clothes? Grant wasn't a philanthropist. You did everything he told you. You obeyed him like a dog afraid of the whip. You *thought* you wanted to marry me, but – that night – Grant came and soon showed you what a much better time you'd have as his mistress than you'd get in a cottage with me – a failure and a drunkard."

"It's not true!"

"Isn't it? My God, if *your* story were true – but that's nonsense. Why make up such a bad lie when it's unnecessary?"

A long silence.

"Well, why?"

"I don't know."

"Where is he? When was he last here? I want to see him."

"I don't know where he is."

"Are you sane, Madge? You mean to tell me you don't know where he is?"

"No, I haven't seen him, or heard from him, since that night."

"*Which* night?"

"I tell you he came here the night you went away."

"Why do you keep harping on that night? What on earth's it got to do with anything? You'd been lovers for months. He persuaded you – that night – to remain his mistress. I understand that perfectly, but it's not very important *when* he persuaded you. Why hasn't he been here since – that's what I want to know? Or, when is he coming? I suppose you know that?"

"He said . . ."

"Well?"

"He said he'd come to-day, soon after dawn, and——"

"Well – what?"

"He wanted me to go abroad with him. He knew you were coming back to-day. He thought you'd be here early——"

"And I had to come by a later train, as it happened. Well, go on! Why was he so interested in my movements?"

"He said that, if I refused to break with you, he'd tell you the truth – and then you wouldn't want me."

"Why not? I know you've had lovers. I'd marry you to-morrow – although you've been Grant's mistress for months."

"But if – if since you went away——"

"Why didn't you write and tell me that Grant had persuaded you to change your mind? Why on earth didn't you write? Anyway, I know where he lives – and I'm going to see him. And I'm going to-morrow, perhaps to-night."

"He'll tell you what I've told you, Clarence. We became lovers the night you went away."

"Is that true?"

"Yes. Listen, listen, Clarence! For God's sake, don't go! Listen for a minute – only a minute!"

"Well?"

"I was afraid of him. I had no will when I was with him. He – hypnotized me. I can't explain, but believe me – do believe——"

"You're telling me that you became Grant's mistress within twenty-four hours of promising to marry me. Is that it?"

"Yes, but——"

"There's no need to go on. We don't speak the same language."

He stood irresolute, looking round the room as if he doubted its existence.

"All right, Clarence, you go. And, later, much later, when you're alone and thinking things over, you might remember this: I didn't lie to you."

"*He'd* have made you tell the truth."

"If I'd said we'd been lovers for months, you'd have taken my word against his. Wouldn't you? . . . Wouldn't you?"

"Yes, I'd have taken your word against his."

"So I could have lied to you. You might remember this, too: *you* were afraid of him."

After a long silence, she added:

"You're all I've got, Clarence – and all I want."

"Would you write to him, tell him you've told me the truth, and that you will never see him again?"

"Yes, I'd write, but whatever happens now makes no difference. He's destroyed us. Whenever you look at me, you'll see him. And I shall see him always – everywhere."

Harlowe sank into a chair and buried his head in his hands. Madge lay motionless, staring at the foot of the bed.

The ticking of the clock filled the room.

J

"My *dear* fellow! Awfully sorry and all that, but I simply had to appear at this somewhat dramatic moment. This sort of thing won't do – really it won't. Just think how many visits you could make like this! One or two in Paris, and a notable one in Berlin. Still, sit down and have a cigarette."

Julian started like a sleep-walker suddenly awakened. He was in a studio with the artist.

"Also, Mr. Grant, I can guarantee the surroundings. Yes, absolutely! As you see, the studio is small, draughty, and we've only candles. But what's that, among friends? My model has just gone. She has a nasty habit of turning into a goat occasionally, but, otherwise, she's entirely normal. *Such* a comfort, in one's old age! There's a chair for you – and a nice bright fire."

As Julian was extremely cold, he drew the chair nearer to the fire, sat down, then stared into the flames. His whole attitude suggested that he was unaware of the artist's presence.

"Odd, don't you think? that on this occasion it never occurred to you that you were awake. Too bad! You were thrilled, you remember, at finding yourself in The Mall recently."

Julian remained silent. The artist pulled a dismal couch to the fire, then stretched himself full length upon it.

"I admire your courage in remaining silent, Mr. Grant. I'd admire it more if I did not know that it's born of ignorance. It was dangerous to be silent in the waking world. It's positively foolhardy here. I mean, in your present state, of course."

Julian turned to him in a frenzy of irritability.

"Now, understand this, once for all——"

"I'd cut out the irritability, if I were you. I can *see* it."

"Really! How interesting! And what's it look like?"

"It looks like an enormous cactus. Now, no more childishness. This is our last conversation, bar one, and——"

"You encourage me to get to the end of it as quickly as possible."

"Good! You're nearly yourself again."

"And now, doubtless, I shall be compelled to listen to your discoveries. That's usually the programme, I believe."

"My dear fellow, what astounds me is that *you* don't make more. No, our present conversation will interest you. It will deal wholly with Mr. Julian Grant. I thought you might care to have a last glance at one or two of your ideas, before you bid them a long and fond farewell."

Julian moved uneasily. There was a change in the artist's manner and a new note in his voice, both of which disconcerted him.

"First, Mr. Grant, you remember the scene in your retrospect in which Purdle appeared. Nice man, Purdle – a builder. Well, do you remember telling him that all the economic troubles of the Western world were created by the fact that there was no longer any *loot?*"

"Of course I remember!" Julian exclaimed angrily. "It was the only intelligent remark that was made during the whole of the evening."

"Quite! And, like most remarks, it illuminated the speaker more than the subject. *There was no more loot for you.* That's the whole point. You had exploited yourself to exhaustion. You had reached a final frontier on every level of your being. You had nothing left but an impotent hatred of everyone and everything. And the joy of it is that you were the apotheosis of everything you despised."

"Do, please, go on," Julian exclaimed, as the artist paused. "I like you better as a psychologist. You're more amusing."

"Good! Now you're quite yourself again. Yes, my dear fellow, how you hated! You had a genius for hatred. You judged everything and everyone, except yourself, by the standards of a saint. Hermitage upbringing, no doubt! And how you loathed the age! Its love of sensationalism, and all the rest of it. You didn't seem to realize that you were a sensationalist – on much subtler and more interior levels, of course – but a sensationalist, none the less. In fact, all the more."

"Why stop? You're interesting me in this stranger."

"Not up to form, my dear fellow. You're degenerating mentally – I told you you would. But let's get back to your sensationalism. You remember your periods of fierce intellectual activity? Mental sensationalism! And your sudden raids on the mystics in that solitary cottage of yours in Kent? Spiritual sensationalism! Yes, by God, you were a sensationalist all right! You probed deeper and deeper into yourself. You analysed every thought, every emotion, every act. You raped your whole being with your insatiable curiosity, seeking subtler and subtler sensations, till you were capable of none. Perhaps you are a symbol of the Western world. I know that's a favourite theory of yours. Well, if so, the Western world has only one more job – and that is to choose its grave. But, anyway, for you – the superman of sensationalism – to judge and condemn the poor little brutes who tried to get a kick out of sex, or the pictures, or the pub, or the dirt-track really was a bit too thick."

"You're just a clown, turning mental somersaults. You know that, I suppose?"

"I didn't expect Mr. Grant would like seeing himself in perspective. You always hugged your ideas to yourself, didn't you? Always wore a mask with others. There are no masks here, my dear fellow. Which proves that there is not always a supply when there's a demand. Well, I'm going to show you one or two of your ideas. You won't have any soon."

"Why can't you say straight out that you have the power to torture me, and that it amuses you to do it?"

"Soon, my dear fellow, you will be in a position to torture me – and I'm not expecting much mercy. I'm acting under orders – orders which I dare not disobey. My job is to carry out a preliminary investigation of Mr. Julian Grant. And I've got to do it."

"I was wrong just now. You're not a clown – you're a madman."

The artist leaned forward, gave the fire a poke, then settled himself more comfortably on the couch.

"One of your chief theories, my dear Mr. Grant, was that all really exceptional men and women make a mess of life, and they fail because they are immeasurably greater than the average man. You called these exceptional men and women Psychic Geniuses. They were Nature's rough attempt at a synthesis of the masculine and the feminine. They were her first fumbling efforts towards the creation of a new race of beings."

"I can just recognize the theory."

"Good! These exceptional people could not adapt themselves to life as it's lived. In each was the stuff of half a dozen ordinary mortals. In fact, in many cases, the very richness of their endowment rendered them impotent. But, even if they were artists, nevertheless – in life – they were lonely, desperate beings, haunted by the awful necessity of achieving a synthesis – a unification of their different selves. Your father, Nathan Grant, was one of them."

"You find it necessary, I suppose, to discuss him?"

"Certainly! He solved his problem by living like a monk. He rejected the world. You would have been like him, but you detected his weakness. You were always devilish good at detecting people's weaknesses. You saw that he was afraid of the world. That decided you – you went into it. You were sensitive, imaginative. You'd not been brought up in The Hermitage for nothing. Curiosity consumed you. You made tremendous demands. You were going to find out everything about the world of which your father was so afraid. You were going to achieve a mighty synthesis."

"I hate to interrupt you, but I really must point out that I've already endured one retrospect in the Metropolitan Café. Do I have to assist at another?"

"I'm filling in one or two of the many gaps in the first one."

"Oh, I see! It's most kind of you."

"Not at all. . . . And the astounding thing is, Mr. Grant, that you got your chance. And your chance was Dorothy. You destroyed her. You had money. Your will was free. You plunged headlong into Experience. You, who belonged to Imagination. I use the word, Imagination, in the sense in which Blake used it."

"I'm quite sure you do."

"Thanks so much. You had a profound contempt for life as it's lived, and yet, again and again, you hurled yourself into it, determined to make it yield you something. When you were in it, you loathed it. It was barren, futile, unreal. But, directly you left it, and went into solitude, your imagination suggested another exploit in the world of experience – something *new*. You swung like a pendulum between the actual and the abstract. But, and this is the point——"

"Oh, there is a point, is there?"

"There are several, this is one of them. Each time your perversity prompted another experiment a new Will slowly formed itself in you. A dark obscure Will, of whose existence you were ignorant. You were still immensely elevated – mentally. You still had ecstatic experiences – spiritually. You still believed you were free; a Psychic Genius; a superman in the making; and all the rest of it. You still thought you would achieve a unification of those twelve gentlemen – it was twelve, wasn't it? – each of whom called himself Julian Grant. And, all the time, imperceptibly, that Will was growing in obscurity – and it did not care one damn for all the fine theories of all the twelve Julian Grants rolled together."

"Well, go on! There's an answer to all this."

"Good! And now I must remind you of that letter you wrote to Stella – the destruction of which I shall never cease to lament. In it, you stated that the incident with Clytie Lessing was not an isolated one. You added that there had been many since – each more degrading, more stupid, more meaningless than the last. And, incidentally, that letter contained an excellent analysis of perversity. Very penetrating, my dear fellow, very penetrating. I congratulate you."

He produced a crumpled cigarette from his pocket, tapped it into shape on the back of his hand, then lit it hopefully.

"You'd be quite interesting," Julian said after a long pause, "if you could discriminate between facts and fiction. But you can't."

"No? Too bad! Doubtless you'll deal with that more fully in your answer. I only mentioned that letter to Stella because it contained one or two traces of genuine feeling. Soon after writing it, you became incapable of any. In a very real sense, that affair in Paris was the end of all the Julian Grants. You remember it – and the famous trial? Still, others will discuss the details of that affair with you. I don't want to, although it was a masterpiece in its way. But, as I say, I leave it to others."

"What *are* you talking about?"

"I've told you, my dear fellow, that this is the preliminary investigation of Mr. Julian Grant. I shan't be present at the second – thank God!"

"I can only repeat that you are a madman."

"And I can only repeat that it is quite possible that both of us are mad – temporally, of course."

A long silence ensued. Although the artist had spoken at length, and often with emphasis, nevertheless there was something off-hand in his manner which alarmed Julian. It made him feel that his adversary used his weapons contemptuously, knowing that – if they failed him – he had others in reserve which were invincible.

"Not very talkative, Mr. Grant. Possibly it's the effect of seeing Madge again. She must remind you of a number of things. Incidentally, it was ironical that the great Julian Grant – who had dreamed of creating a God-like synthesis – ended by being abjectly dependent upon an instinctive creature like Madge. Just *one* minute, please! So dependent that, for a whole year, she was your world. So dependent that you dared not face existence without her. In fact, so dependent that you committed a crime in the hope of handcuffing her to you. That's how the great synthesis ended."

Julian rose and stood towering above him, trembling with anger.

"Well, and what of it? It was better – *better*, do you understand? – to attempt what I attempted, and to fail as I failed, than to lounge through the world, or drug myself with work, in a crowd of wretched little frightened nonentities! At any rate, I had the courage to explore myself, to learn what I was, to experiment, to look into those abysses that are hidden in each one of us. It was better – I tell you! What could God Himself do with the average man?"

"Why ask me, my dear fellow? I'm not in the least likely to know."

"I had money. I was twenty-two. I had the vitality and the curiosity of ten men. Was it likely I should marry Dorothy? A sentimental affair between two children who knew nothing! Was it probable I should marry her, having met Stella? Then – soon – when half a dozen worlds were open to me, wasn't it inevitable that I should fling myself into them? I, who had been brought up in a monastery, and who had ten times the imagination of a wretched drivelling little artist like you!"

"I *did* want to keep this impersonal," the artist said sadly, throwing his cigarette away.

"What sort of a life was yours? When you weren't working, you just hung about with a weedy little set of petty egotists, all chattering endlessly about each other, in a stuffy little cul-de-sac which you called Art. You were ten times as narrow as those you despised. Your only distinction was your absurd vanity. *You* attempted no synthesis. You were as self-satisfied as a prosperous publican with a fat wife. You spent your time trying to convince yourself that you were original. I can see your life now as clearly as you can see mine – and I know all about your tuppenny-ha'penny perversities of which you were so proud. You were, then, what you are now – a caricature of other people's ideas."

"Well, upon my soul, this reminds me of Christmas – old friends together round the blazing log."

"I went into a wilderness – do you understand? – the wilderness hidden in each one of us. I went out into it alone, and I perished. But I'm greater than those who never even dared to recognize its existence. You're so intent on my failure, aren't you? If you had the insight of a bat, you would see in that failure the shadow of my potential triumph. It's better to go to hell than to saunter through life on the pavement with your hands in your pockets. You're nearer God."

"It relieves me so much to hear you say that."

"And now I'm going. I've finished with you."

"Au revoir, my dear fellow – and thanks for the swansong."

K

A sinister twilight enveloped the plain: each moment it grew darker. A baying wind hunted its immense solitudes.

He felt that Fear was making him its monolith; that here he would stand for ever, a thing of stone in a wilderness.

Then – out of the thickening shadows surrounding him – one by one, figure after figure emerged in slow succession. Every man, every woman, he had known stood before him. But, as he gazed at each in turn, each faded into his own likeness.

Then the last appeared. It was Dorothy.

She stood before him, as if she had come from that sunset-hooded bay in Cornwall. But, as he gazed at her, she did not fade into his own likeness. To her, and to her only, he had once surrendered himself.

Then she vanished, and darkness confronted him.

And he knew that she, and she only, could deliver him from this spectral solitude. He would invoke her, summon her to his aid – not as the woman he remembered – but as the being she now was.

He raised his head. She stood before him, a luminous statue – and, by her side, was the Julian Grant of twenty-five years ago.

And, as he gazed, a mist enveloped them, hiding them from sight, till from it emerged a figure of transcendent beauty – who was neither, being both.

A frenzy of jealousy possessed him: an insensate desire to destroy.

He raised his hand to strike.

"*Really,* my dear fellow! Haven't you any limits? I simply cannot allow you to commit celestial suicide."

L

"I told you that I'd finished with you – and I have. You can talk, if you like, but I shan't answer."

The artist stretched and yawned simultaneously.

"You don't really mean to say that you haven't guessed yet?"

"Guessed?"

"Yes – guessed!" the artist repeated, with tremendous emphasis. "How much more evidence do you want? God! It's unbelievable! Surely there's only one explanation of all that's happened to you. Anyone overhearing our conversations would have guessed long ago."

"I don't know what you're——"

"You're dead. I'm dead. *Now,* do you understand?"

"*Dead?*"

"Oh, good Lord, yes! We call it being born over here. *You're in the next world.* And I do hope you're not going to be so surprised – and kick up such a fuss – as most people do. I tell you it's no joke trying to convince them that there's a life after death, especially those who've believed in it firmly for fifty years – every Sunday, for two hours. And when we do get it into their thick heads that they're in the next world, you should see the way they carry on. They're certain that they deserve heaven – and they're equally certain that heaven consists of twanging harps in front of a throne and shouting Hosanna – so, inevitably, they find themselves on the steps of a throne, and immediately begin twanging and shouting, till they get so bored that they hurl the harps at each other and start swearing like stokers. After which they discover the nature of their real desires. . . . You understand, of course, that I'm talking just to distract you while you get over the shock."

The artist paused, then, having glanced at Julian, said emphatically:

"Looks to me as if I'd better go on talking for a bit. . . . Yes, most people cut up pretty rough on finding that they're in the next world. Children are the best – they tumble to it in no time. Women are next – but sailors run them pretty close. Don't know what to say about clergymen. It's difficult to be fair. Most of 'em, at any rate, *try* not to look surprised. Civil servants are a nuisance – they keep asking how they stand in regard to their pensions. Authors are very tiresome, particularly if, by some fluke, there's money due to them from their agents. Fortunately, it's nearly always the other way round. . . . I say! Aren't you all right yet? Oh, very well! I'll go on for a bit."

He paused, stretched hugely, then continued:

"Mind you, I'm not the first to greet new arrivals. Two very different spirits meet every newcomer. Perhaps you haven't forgotten those two strangers from whom you parted when you thought you were in Knightsbridge. Also, I only meet those who come from the world – and only the English at that. Most of 'em curse a bit, and then trot off quite happily to astral cricket or football grounds, or golf-links, or some nonsense or other. I showed you the Englishman's Paradise, you remember? But some are immensely dignified and demand to see God. Newspaper proprietors, mayors, and butlers always demand to see Him. It's a great bore, of course. They are told that they can enter His presence whenever they desire That presence more than anything else: which is pretty seldom, I can tell you. Also – if they'll listen, which is very rare – it is explained to them that heaven is a state of being, not a place. *A state of being.* But they won't listen, my dear fellow. You're not listening. I didn't listen. Everyone rushes off to seek the illusion he loved best on earth. And, inevitably, he finds it. He has only to desire it – and it creates itself. And he stays in it, until – at long last – he gets fed up with it. Then he moves on. It was just the same on earth. There's very little difference, believe me. There are some, however, but that comes later. . . . Surely you're all right now, aren't you? I mean, confound it all! you've studied the mystics in your day – you ought to be an easy case. Oh, very well! I'll go on for a bit. But I shall put in for overtime. And I must have a puff or two at a cigarette. I'm not through even that illusion yet. And I've been dead for five years."

He lit a cigarette, inhaled the smoke deeply several times, then threw it away reluctantly.

"There's an example of illusion, Mr. Grant. I desired a cigarette. Instantly that desire became objectified *as* a cigarette. It materialized because, at that moment, I wanted a cigarette more than anything else in all the worlds. A grim thought, but there it is. . . . Do take a pull on yourself. All this isn't really new to you. I'll quote from one of your favourite authors to prove it. He wrote: 'We make for ourselves our own spiritual world, our own monsters, chimeras, angels – we make objective what ferments in us. The bad man creates around him a pandemonium, the artist an Olympus, the elect soul a paradise, which each of them sees for himself alone.' There you are! And it's all in that. I say – really! Well, have to go on, I suppose."

The artist yawned several times, then continued.

"I'd better tell you some more about newcomers here. The trouble is that most of the poor nit-wits imagine that the act of dying must wholly transform them. Why? What's easier than dying? It's one of the few things that people can do for themselves. Yet the poor dears seem to regard death as a spring-board from which they will leap to celestial bliss. They'd soon be very sorry for themselves if they did. How many people, do you imagine, would find the company of saints enjoyable? Good Lord, they'd be wanting to see Greta Garbo before they'd been with them half an hour. And I don't blame them, mind you, because I think the Garbo's just grand. And now, all joking apart, you feel all right, don't you? You've known hundreds of worlds – everyone has. This is only another. We put up at a lot of inns on the road to Reality."

"I – I want you to – to tell me – when? – how?——"

"That's very simple. You remember that, when you left Madge's flat that night, you walked home; and perhaps you also remember it was extremely cold. You had only a light overcoat which you did not trouble to button up. Also, you stopped frequently. Well, you caught pneumonia that night. You had had it badly once before, you remember, after you had been wounded in France. They warned you then that if you had it again you'd stand very little chance."

"I caught pneumonia that night!"

"Yes – and you died a week later. Now, don't ask me what happens the first three days after death. It is known only to few, and to none that we are likely to meet. But, when you became conscious in *this* world, your whole mind was so imbued with the necessity for getting to Madge's flat, soon after dawn, on that Friday – do you remember? – that it *seemed* to you that you were on your way there. Actually, at that precise moment, your body was being buried – but that's only a detail. I know that it also seemed to you that you went to Piccadilly Circus instead of Fulham, but, naturally, errors of that kind are inevitable. Then you had that retrospect, when you were haunting the Metropolitan Café. That, also, was inevitable. Everyone arriving here has a retrospect – scenes from their lives rise before them. And, believe me, whatever the appearance may seem, there is a deep organic reality underlying those retrospects. I know I pretended that mine was a dud, but that was only to buck you up."

"But – how long? – I can't think! Wait a minute."

Julian broke off, then added after a long pause:

"How long is it since it seemed to me that I was in Knightsbridge?"

"A few hours. The retrospect took only a few minutes. But, when you thought you were in the Daisy Walk, some hours passed."

"But I saw *you*!" Julian exclaimed. "I saw you outside the Metropolitan Café."

"Oh yes – and you saw that beggar in the gutter near the Ritz. He and I belonged to this world, of course. You see, now and again, you caught glimpses of happenings here – although you thought you were in Piccadilly. That's about all, I think. Now, if you're all right, there are one or two things that must be discussed. Are you all right?"

"Yes, I'm all right."

The artist glanced at him, then said:

"All the same, I think you'd better rest for a bit. Then, afterwards, I'll explain. This is our last conversation."

M

"First of all," the artist began, "I want you to understand that the famous phrase about being 'gathered to his people' does *not* mean that you rejoin your relatives in the next world. Most people derive enormous satisfaction from that statement. Here, you only meet your affinities."

"Do you mean that you only mix with those whose state is the same as yours?"

"That's it. For instance, you could have been greeted here only by me. For years, you wished you had been an artist. That desire attracted me to you. We couldn't have missed. And I may as well say this: if I've been most unpleasant, it's just as well you should know that I had to be exactly what I was, or you would have had no use for me."

"That's all very well, but why did you make out that you wanted to get back to the waking world? In that garden, you pretended to sleep in the hope——"

"Of course!" the artist interrupted. "I had to create the idea of a possible return in *your* mind. It was essential for you to revisit the world twice. I'm not allowed to explain why, but it was essential."

"I still believe I'm only dreaming," Julian said deliberately. "I still believe I shall wake and find myself in the world."

"Well, the world's only a dream, anyway. In the world – as here – each man dreams his own dream, and has the nerve to call it Reality."

"I still believe I shall wake," Julian said slowly.

"Well, before I go, I'd better tell you one or two differences between this show and our old friend the earth. I've already explained that – here – everything is created by one's state. Your mood, if you like, but state is the better word. Anyhow, the chief difference is this: in the world, you can be a divided being, and here you can't. You can't will one thing and think another – here. It can't be done. And you can't deceive your companions here, because they can see your thoughts. Another difference is this. If you think of anyone, here, he appears instantly. We have very subtle bodies – as you'll discover. Those you love are always present with you. But they are not, necessarily, those you *thought* you loved when you were in the world. Here, you are linked to whoever – or whatever – you really love best. In fact, you *are* what you love."

"What I want to know is——" Julian began, but the artist interrupted.

"Wait! When a man is in the world, he is – spiritually – in company with beings here. Those beings have the same ruling love as he has. When the man dies, he finds himself with them. You are about to join those to whom you belong."

"But, listen to me! You must——"

"It's useless for you to speak. You belong to certain spirits here because you have loved and served what they love and serve. You have no will in the matter. Your will is in their keeping. It has long been in their keeping. You will go to them now, and they will remove from you everything not organically related to your ruling love. That's essential, because – then – you will discover the precise nature of what you have loved and served."

"Yes – but——"

"It is useless! Already we are moving towards them."

N

It seemed to Julian that they were at a great height, floating slowly through white mist. Sometimes sounds rose from the vapoury abyss below: sometimes the veils of the mist parted, revealing scenes which were scarcely glimpsed before they faded. Finally, in the distance, a city appeared.

"There are cities here, then?"

"Listen, my dear fellow. Do understand this, once for all. *Everything* here is created by the spiritual state of the inhabitants. If *you* see a city, it is proof positive that your state is akin to that of those who dwell in it."

"Then don't you see a city?"

"Yes – unfortunately. A saint wouldn't. It's very much the same – I keep telling you – as it was in the world. You see what is real *to you* – and you call what you see Reality."

The city seemed to rise towards them. Each moment its buildings, monuments, and streets became clearer.

A few minutes later, they stood in one of the chief thoroughfares. It was thronged with people. A babel of sound rose on every hand.

"This is better than the plain, at any rate," Julian announced decisively.

"This is another aspect of the plain," the artist replied. "And this is where we part."

"Why?"

"I will tell you. Once I belonged wholly to those to whom you are now on your way. I have known the depths of servitude to them. Gradually, very gradually, I am leaving them, but they still have power over me."

"But how shall I find them without you?"

The artist laughed.

"If only you had the remotest conception of how impossible it is for you *not* to find them! Now, these are the last words we shall speak. If we meet again, speech would be fantastically unnecessary. Listen! If you are afraid, when you look on those who await you, you may as well know that the men are one aspect of yourself, and the women are another."

"Of myself!"

"Yes. The appearance of these men and women will reveal yourself to you. Finally, and I beg this of you, endure all that they can inflict on you. Then, having endured it, and so having entered into a seeming power, do not exercise that power. Then, soon, you will leave them. Otherwise——"

"Otherwise?"

"You will remain. You will become great among them. And, incidentally, you will be able to have your revenge on me. I'm afraid all these sound dark mysteries, but you'll soon penetrate to their meaning. In the end, you – and all of us – will discover that evil is only a projection of our own unreality."

Julian turned to him impatiently. But the artist had vanished.

O

After a few moments' indecision, he began to walk slowly along the crowded thoroughfare. At first, he noticed nothing. Soon, however, the stir and animation of the city captured him. A feeling of exhilaration possessed him and, simultaneously, he discovered that he was glad to be alone.

Suddenly he burst out laughing. Of course the artist had no real existence! He was only a phantom in a dream! For he, Julian, was dreaming – there was not the slightest doubt about that. Often, when one is lost in the labyrinth of a dream, one knows perfectly well that it is only a dream. This was his present predicament, but to believe one word the artist had said was madness. Why, the fool had told him that he was dead! Dead! And that this was the next world! That, of course, was utter nonsense. He was dreaming – a strange, tumultuous, bewildering dream. But that was all. Sooner or later, he would wake to find himself in London.

He stopped and looked round. Buildings towered to the brooding sky: a network of crowded streets surrounded him: in the near distance, a great bridge spanned a sluggish, muddy river. The size of the city was unbelievable – it seemed to extend endlessly in every direction. But he must decide what to do, for it was growing darker, and a few drops of icy rain were beginning to fall.

He walked on quickly, crossed the bridge, and found himself confronted by more streets and more gigantic buildings in which dim lights were beginning to appear.

Suddenly, a fierce desire for companionship flamed up in him. He must find someone – anyone – who could initiate him into the intricacies of this mysterious city. A sense of infinite possibilities thrilled him. He began to watch the passers-by with intense curiosity. Everyone seemed grimly intent on his own affairs, though many slunk along as if they were afraid. Oddly enough, there were no children.

Then he noticed a woman a few yards ahead of him. Instantly, a number of chaotic and fantastic projects thronged through his mind. Eventually, however, the determination to speak to her dominated him. He quickened his pace and put his hand on her shoulder.

She turned, uttered a cry, then ran away – disappearing almost immediately in the crowd.

Several onlookers laughed, but in a manner which suggested that the incident was common enough, then they hurried on more quickly than ever, as if even a second's delay must be instantly retrieved.

"You picked wrong that time, guv'nor!"

The voice came from behind him. Julian turned to find a seedy cadaverous individual whose piercing eyes blazed out of a mask-like face. The man's attitude expressed contempt and amusement.

"She's not *your* sort!" he added emphatically. "You'd better come along with me."

"I haven't the least desire to come along with you," Julian replied, with immense dignity.

"No? Well, what do you know about that? Guess again, Mr. Julian Grant."

"Who are you? And how do you know my name?"

"Ah, that's telling. But I *do* know it. Listen!"

He put his head close to Julian's and began to whisper:

"Well, what do you say? It's a fact. Here! Wait a minute!"

Again he leaned over and whispered:

"It's a fact. Come on!"

Julian found he was walking by the man's side.

They traversed several streets in silence, till at last they reached a maze of noisome alleys in a dark quarter near the river.

A figure emerged from the obscurity, slunk up to Julian's companion, and muttered some request. He flung him roughly aside with an oath, then strode on more quickly.

"Who was that?" Julian asked.

"A fat lot you care."

"How much further is it?"

The man laughed.

"Getting impatient? They'll wait till you come. They're expecting you. The men will want to have a good look at you. The women can't – because they're blind."

"*Blind!*"

"Of course! You're a bit of a fool in some ways, aren't you?"

"It's devilish dark here. I can't see anything."

"You'll see all you want to – soon. Perhaps more. There's a lot of tricks you don't know."

They walked on in silence. Each moment the darkness thickened. They strode on as well as they could through deep sticky mud.

"I'm getting out of this!"

"That so? Well – try. It'll soon seem quite familiar. I'd no idea you'd be such a fool. Anyway, here we are."

He stopped in front of a railing on which hung a lantern. By its flickering yellow light a spiral iron stairway, leading to a basement, was dimly discernible.

"Well, what are you waiting for? Down you go!"

Julian descended slowly. When he reached the bottom, he found himself in a dimly-lit damp hall, the size of a small room. Facing him, was a dingy curtain which quivered in the draught.

"Through there! Have you gone to sleep?"

Julian parted the curtain.

He was standing at the top of a short flight of stairs. Below him was a café, containing about twenty tables at which men and women were sitting.

He recognized it instantly. It was the café depicted in the artist's drawing.

He knew that everyone was aware of his presence, that everyone was waiting for him. Also, he knew that some activity had ceased at his approach.

Then, as if in response to a pre-arranged but hidden signal, each man turned and stared at him. Their faces were like masks, but the eyes blazed with devouring curiosity. The women craned their heads in his direction, as if they were listening intently.

Terror possessed him; nevertheless he watched himself descend the stairs and walk to the centre of the room.

Everyone rose, picked up a glass, and held it towards him.

"Welcome, Mr. Julian Grant!"

THE END

RECENT AND FORTHCOMING TITLES FROM VALANCOURT BOOKS

Michael Arlen	Hell! said the Duchess
R. C. Ashby	He Arrived at Dusk
Frank Baker	The Birds
H. E. Bates	Fair Stood the Wind for France
Walter Baxter	Look Down in Mercy
Charles Beaumont	The Hunger and Other Stories
David Benedictus	The Fourth of June
Charles Birkin	The Smell of Evil
John Blackburn	A Scent of New-Mown Hay
	Children of the Night
	Our Lady of Pain
John Braine	Room at the Top
Michael Campbell	Lord Dismiss Us
David Case	Fengriffen
R. Chetwynd-Hayes	The Monster Club
Isabel Colegate	The Blackmailer
Basil Copper	The Great White Space
Hunter Davies	Body Charge
Jennifer Dawson	The Ha-Ha
Lord Dunsany	The Curse of the Wise Woman
A. E. Ellis	The Rack
Barry England	Figures in a Landscape
Ronald Fraser	Flower Phantoms
Michael Frayn	The Tin Men
	Towards the End of the Morning
	Sweet Dreams
Gillian Freeman	The Leather Boys
Rodney Garland	The Heart in Exile
Stephen Gilbert	The Landslide
	The Burnaby Experiments
	Ratman's Notebooks
Martyn Goff	The Plaster Fabric
F. L. Green	Odd Man Out
Stephen Gregory	The Cormorant
Alex Hamilton	Beam of Malice
Thomas Hinde	The Day the Call Came
Claude Houghton	Neighbours
	I Am Jonathan Scrivener
	This Was Ivor Trent

Fred Hoyle	The Black Cloud
James Kennaway	The Mind Benders
Cyril Kersh	The Aggravations of Minnie Ashe
Gerald Kersh	Fowlers End
	Nightshade and Damnations
Francis King	To the Dark Tower
C.H.B. Kitchin	Ten Pollitt Place
Hilda Lewis	The Witch and the Priest
John Lodwick	Brother Death
Gabriel Marlowe	I Am Your Brother
Kenneth Martin	Aubade
Robin Maugham	Behind the Mirror
Michael McDowell	The Elementals
John Metcalfe	The Feasting Dead
Michael Nelson	A Room in Chelsea Square
Beverley Nichols	Crazy Pavements
Oliver Onions	The Hand of Kornelius Voyt
Dennis Parry	The Survivor
Christopher Priest	The Affirmation
J.B. Priestley	Benighted
	The Other Place
	The Magicians
Forrest Reid	Uncle Stephen
	Young Tom
	Denis Bracknel
Nevil Shute	Landfall
	An Old Captivity
Andrew Sinclair	The Raker
	The Facts in the Case of E. A. Poe
David Storey	Radcliffe
	Saville
Bernard Taylor	The Godsend
	Sweetheart, Sweetheart
Russell Thorndike	The Slype
	The Master of the Macabre
John Wain	Hurry on Down
	A Winter in the Hills
Hugh Walpole	The Killer and the Slain
Keith Waterhouse	There is a Happy Land
	Billy Liar
Robert Westall	Antique Dust
Colin Wilson	Ritual in the Dark
	The Philosopher's Stone

Lightning Source UK Ltd.
Milton Keynes UK
UKHW04f0620170818
327343UK00001B/267/P